THE BLOOMING SHADOWS

Hector L. Bones

Debbie N. Bones

The Bones Family

Library of Congress Control Number: TX0009577319

Book Cover by Hector L. Bones

Illustrations by Hector L. Bones

1st edition 2024

DEDICATION

I dedicate this book to my beautiful wife **Debbie N. Bones**, who has been a great support and source of inspiration. She is the most brilliant person I know to which I can count to bounce off ideas and helping me through but also helps me keep on track and complete our projects in life.

Without you **Debbie** my love I would never have got the courage to get this book out.

I also dedicate this book to my children who inspired me to put my ideas on paper and bring them to life. Thanks **Aerith Nyomi, Alisher Krystal and Aiden Kalel**, for being great kids and an infinite source of inspiration.

INTRODUCTION

Welcome to "The Blooming Shadows", a story born from the mysteries that lie within small towns, the power of tradition, and the haunting beauty of the supernatural. This tale takes us to Lowridge, a town steeped in legend and bound by an ancient pact with the land—a bond forged through fear, sacrifice, and a hunger that is never quite sated. At the heart of this story is a group of young friends caught in a web spun by generations before them, faced with a challenge that will test their courage, resilience, and loyalty to each other.

The inspiration for "The Blooming Shadows" comes from the strange, sometimes unsettling history of places that feel almost alive, where the land itself seems to hold secrets and memories of times long past. The forest of Lowridge and its hunger for balance represent the weight of inherited expectations and the struggle we all face between honoring the past and shaping our own future. Mark, Alyssa, Pecos, and Tommy are each in their own way bound by loyalty, guilt, and a shared sense of responsibility. Their journey mirrors that of so many who must confront the shadows in their lives—the mistakes, regrets, and legacies that linger, demanding reckoning.

As you step into the world of Lowridge, I invite you to walk with these characters through the fog-filled forests, to hear the whispers of the past, and to witness their fight against forces they can't fully understand. This story is about more than just facing the supernatural; it's about confronting the inner demons that hold us back, about the courage it takes to break cycles, and about the power of unity in the face of darkness.

Thank you for joining me on this journey. I hope "The Blooming Shadows" will draw you into its world, and that, like the characters in this story, you'll find light within even the deepest shadows.

With anticipation,

Hector L. Bones

CONTENTS

PROLOGUE: THE LAST ROUTE

The flowers were part of Lowridge the way humidity was part of summer—present enough that no one bothered to explain them.

They showed up on signs and letterheads. Painted on the side of the booster club trailer. Printed on glossy programs the announcer called keepsakes, like paper could preserve anything worth keeping. Purple petals curled around the Lowridge Lions logo, a decorative flourish that made the whole thing feel older than it was—as if football had always been here and always would be.

Up close, the flowers were stranger.

Too vivid for the dirt they grew from. Too stubborn about where they chose to bloom.

Tonight, they glowed.

It was not dramatic—nothing like a spotlight or a flare. More like the soft shine of a watch face in moonlight, a private light you noticed only when you turned your head at the right angle. A low purple gleam clung to the cemetery beyond the far fence, gathering around the stones like a secret.

Eli Carter had seen those rows of headstones his whole life. He drove past them twice a day, every day, on the way to school and back. He'd heard older kids joke about Lowridge's violets. He'd watched tourists slow down with their windows cracked and their phones out, trying to capture small-town charm without paying attention to what it cost.

He had never once thought the flowers were beautiful.

Not like this.

In the locker room, the air was thick with heat and deodorant and the sharp bite of athletic tape. Shoulder pads thumped into place. Cleats scraped concrete. Someone laughed too loud. Someone else sat too still with his head bowed, fingers locked around a mouthguard like it was a prayer bead.

Eli rolled his neck and felt the familiar ache between his shoulder blades —the one that had lived there since sophomore year. The crowd was already awake outside, even through cinderblock and steel doors. A rising, falling roar that made your ribs hum.

That sound was a kind of weather in Lowridge. People said the town came alive on Friday nights.

Eli had always suspected the town came alive because it was hungry.

Coach Whitman leaned in the doorway, jaw working like he was chewing on something bitter. He didn't have to shout. He never did. His disappointment had its own volume.

"Carter."

Eli looked up. "Yeah."

Coach's eyes flicked over him: taped wrists, captain patch, the scrape on his forearm that refused to fully heal. "You ready?"

Eli wanted to say the truth.

He wanted to say, I'm ready to leave.

He wanted to say, I can't breathe in this place.

He wanted to say, I don't want to be a symbol anymore.

But truth had never been Lowridge's favorite language. Truth was what people whispered in kitchens and swallowed before stepping onto the porch.

So Eli gave the town what it liked.

"Yes, sir."

Coach nodded once, like that was all that mattered, and stepped aside.

Eli turned back to his locker. Something small and dry shifted against his palm. He frowned, opened his hand.

A petal.

Purple. Paper-thin. Caught in the seam of his glove like it had been placed there on purpose.

For a second he stared at it, stupidly, as if the petal could explain itself. The cheer squad handed out purple paper flowers every home game, cheap and crinkled, tucked behind ears and pinned to jackets.

But this was not paper.

This was real—velvet-soft, cool as damp soil.

Eli should have thrown it away.

Instead he rubbed it between thumb and finger. It left no pollen, no stain. Just a faint slickness, like oil, on his skin.

A teammate slapped his shoulder as he passed. "Man, you see the fog?"

Eli looked toward the open door at the end of the hall. The night outside was thick with it—mist rolling low over the field. Stadium lights chopped it into layers and made it seem almost solid.

"Yeah," Eli said.

"Feels like Hollow's Eve," the kid added, half joking. "Like the dead are gonna walk out there."

Eli didn't laugh. In Lowridge, people joked about the dead the way they joked about storms—because fear was easier to carry when you pretended it was entertainment.

They ran out together in a surge of noise and light.

The stadium was a bowl of faces. Parents in jackets with breath fogging the air. Kids painted purple and gold. Old men in worn caps, Lions logos faded by decades. The band blared like it could drown out anything.

At the far end, beyond the fence, the cemetery lay quiet and watchful—rows of headstones arranged like an audience that had been here longer than anyone alive.

Eli's gaze snagged on the flowers.

They were brighter now that he was closer. Not bright enough to make people point. Bright enough to make you feel, for no logical reason, that you were being observed.

The announcer boomed, "LOWRIDGE LIONS!"

The crowd answered like one body. The sound hit Eli in the chest. He'd always called it pride.

Tonight it felt like a current.

Warmups blurred into muscle memory: stretches, sprints, quick throws, the ball snapping into his hands and leaving again. He moved the way he always moved—clean, practiced, efficient.

And underneath it, something began to build.

Not pain. Not nausea.

Pressure.

Like the air had thickened and started pressing behind his eyes from the inside.

Eli blinked hard. For a fraction of a second, the stadium lights smeared —white streaks dragged across his vision as if someone had shaken a camera mid-shot. He steadied himself and looked down at the turf.

The grass was damp. Dark. Glittering with condensation.

And near the sideline, threaded through it like a quiet infection, were tiny purple buds.

They were not supposed to be there.

Eli crouched without thinking. He touched one with the tip of his glove.

The bud trembled—subtle, deliberate—like it had responded to him specifically.

A cheer rose. A whistle cut the air. Someone shouted his name.

Eli stood and wiped his glove on his pants like he'd gotten dirt on it. His heartbeat was steady. His mouth tasted faintly metallic.

It's nothing, he told himself.

Everything in Lowridge came with a story, and most of those stories were decorations hung over rot. He'd learned to ignore them.

The game started.

For a while, the world behaved.

The opposing team was fast but sloppy, the kind Coach liked to call outsiders. Eli ran his routes. He took hits. He got up. The crowd roared and the band played and the fog refused to lift.

Then, late in the second quarter, Eli took a hard tackle near the sideline.

His shoulder slammed into the ground. Something sharp bit into the skin of his forearm where tape didn't cover. Pain flared.

He rolled, sucking in air, and looked down.

Blood.

Not much. A shallow scrape. Bright against his skin.

As he pushed himself up, the petal caught in his glove shifted again.

He didn't know how he still had it.

He didn't remember deciding to keep it.

The petal brushed the fresh blood.

For an instant, nothing changed. The crowd still roared. The band still played. The lights still burned.

Then the pressure behind Eli's eyes snapped into focus—like a lens clicking into a new depth.

The fog thickened.

Not enough for anyone to notice. Enough to make the world feel wrong, like a dream you hadn't realized was a dream yet.

A low hum rose under everything—under the crowd, under the band, under the announcer's voice. It was not sound exactly. It was vibration, as if the ground itself had found a rhythm and wanted Eli's body to match it.

One-two. One-two.

Like cleats in a tunnel.

Like the count that starts a play and ends a prayer.

Eli looked toward the cemetery.

The flowers along the grave rows pulsed—slow brightening, slow fading—as if they were breathing. The headstones weren't just stones anymore. They were markers in a pattern.

And for a heartbeat, Eli understood that the field and the cemetery were not separate places.

They were connected.

Coach shouted from the sideline. Eli saw his mouth move. He could not hear the words. The sound felt like it had to cross water to reach him.

Eli blinked.

For a fraction of a second, someone stood near the far goalpost.

A player.

Old uniform. Helmet with a crack down one side. Purple petals clinging to the facemask like dried memory.

Eli's stomach dropped.

He blinked again and the player was gone. The goalpost stood alone—bone pale against fog.

A hand grabbed Eli's shoulder pad. "You good?" the trainer asked.

Eli opened his mouth.

Nothing came out.

The trainer's face blurred at the edges. Behind him, in the fog, movement shifted that did not match the living crowd—shapes standing too still, heads turning in unison.

"Carter!" Coach snapped. "You're in!"

Eli jogged onto the field.

He ran the play.

Except he didn't.

His legs moved, but the decision wasn't his. He cut left when the call was right. He adjusted his route without thinking—perfect footwork, perfect timing—as if some invisible coach had learned his body better than he had.

Panic tore through him, hot and sharp.

Then it slid away, smothered by the hum.

He could feel the pattern.

He could feel where he needed to be.

He turned his head mid-stride and saw his own teammates staring at him with confusion. The quarterback's face twisted as he shouted, but Eli could not understand why.

The spacing was correct. The defense collapsed exactly the way it was supposed to.

He was running the best route of his life.

And he was trapped inside it.

The ball came toward him through fog.

Eli lifted his hands and caught it without effort.

For the space of one heartbeat, it was not a football.

It was a clump of purple petals—damp, heavy—pressed into his palms.

His fingers closed.

The petals compressed like something alive.

Something cold threaded between his knuckles.

Eli stumbled. His knees nearly buckled.

Stop, he tried to think. Stop.

His body did not stop.

It angled downfield, straight toward the far fence.

The crowd screamed—delighted at first, because it looked like a breakaway, because they wanted a miracle. The sound rose like a wave and shoved Eli forward.

The fog swallowed the sideline. The numbers on the field vanished. The lights above seemed farther away.

Eli ran.

The headstones grew larger. The purple glow deepened. Eli's breath burned. His chest tightened—not from exertion, but from something closing around his lungs like roots.

He reached the fence.

His hands grabbed the metal.

It should have been cold.

It should have been solid.

Instead it felt like wet bone.

His fingers slipped through.

Eli jerked back, breath catching.

The fence shimmered like it had never been there. Like it had been a suggestion.

The hum deepened.

A presence pressed against the inside of his skull—not words, not quite, but hunger given shape. The pressure behind his eyes sharpened until he saw the cemetery as more than a place.

Marked stones.

Unmarked stones.

Space waiting to be filled.

Eli's feet moved again.

He stepped off the field and onto cemetery ground.

The soil was softer than it should have been. It gave under his cleats like it had been freshly turned. Purple buds pushed up around his ankles, brushing his skin.

His stomach lurched. He tried to shout, but his throat locked.

In the fog between the stones, figures stood watching.

Not solid.

Not fully human.

The outlines of players—helmets and shoulder pads and numbers half-lost to time—threaded with faint purple light.

Eli recognized a jersey number.

He did not want to.

His eyes watered. The air carried something sweet and metallic at once. It clung to the back of his throat.

He moved deeper, pulled along the aisle between graves like it was a hallway and he was late for class.

A stone rose ahead, older than the rest, half sunken. Its inscription worn down by years and rain. At its base, purple flowers bloomed in a thick ring, petals trembling in moonlight.

Eli stopped.

For the first time since the tackle, his body hesitated.

In that pause, his own voice surfaced—a thin thread of himself in the dark.

He saw his mother in the stands, hands clasped. He saw Coach's hard face. He saw the scholarship letter folded in his desk drawer. He saw the highway out of town, the one that ran toward bright buildings and clean neighborhoods with names that promised a future.

And he saw, with sudden brutal clarity, that Lowridge did not celebrate champions.

It kept them.

Eli's lips parted.

He could confess.

He could say what he'd never said out loud—that he wanted out, that he was done being a symbol, that he was tired of carrying the town's hunger like it was his own.

The pressure surged.

The ring of flowers brightened as if listening.

Eli tried to force the words past his throat.

Nothing.

The hum steadied.

One-two. One-two.

His body stepped forward into the ring like it belonged there.

Pain flashed in his scraped forearm as petals brushed the wound. The sting was immediate—sharp and intimate, like a needle under skin. His breath hitched.

Inside his chest, something shifted—not heart, not lungs.

Something else.

Something that had been waiting a long time.

Eli was still aware. Still watching. Still trapped behind his own eyes.

But the driver had changed.

He turned his head toward the field.

Through fog and distance, the stadium looked like a bright rectangle behind glass. He could hear faint shouting now, his name carried on wind like an afterthought.

He lifted one hand and pressed it against his facemask.

His fingers trembled.

Then he smiled—slow and empty—as if the expression had been practiced by someone who only understood humans from a distance.

He pivoted.

He walked into the fog between the stones.

The purple glow followed, pulsing like a heartbeat.

Behind him, the crowd continued to roar, unaware that their captain had crossed a line no one was supposed to notice.

By morning, there would be a story.

A tragic accident.

A medical episode.

A young man under too much pressure.

Something small enough to fit inside the town's denial.

And at the edge of the cemetery, where the soil stayed damp no matter the weather, a new cluster of purple flowers would bloom—bright and mesmerizing—marking the place Lowridge had taken another name and turned it into a symbol.

The town would add a ribbon to a sign. Print another program. Post another photo.

And the flowers would wait for the next game night, the next fog, the next drop of blood—

for the next boy to run the last route Lowridge had already drawn.

CHAPTER 1: THE WEIGHT OF LEGACY

In Lowridge, Friday nights weren't an event. They were a verdict.

Even on a Wednesday afternoon, the town moved like it was already listening for the whistle. Trucks with Lions decals rolled past the high school like pilgrims. The diner on Main Street had a hand-written sign in the window—HOMEcoming Week Specials—purple marker bleeding into the paper. The hardware store had painted a lion on its plywood display, mane flared, claws out, as if the town needed to remind itself what it was.

And always—on signs, in corners, in flourishes no one questioned—there were flowers.

Purple petals curled around the Lowridge Lions logo on the field house door. Purple vines traced the edges of booster club letters and fundraising flyers. The flowers showed up the way humidity showed up in summer: present enough that no one bothered to explain them.

Mark Rivers told himself that was all it was.

Just a town motif. A tradition. Something somebody's grandma had once liked, and now it was on everything from the marching band banner to the napkins at the pizza place.

He could repeat that story in his head and almost believe it.

Almost.

The practice field sat behind the school, a rectangle of stubborn green bordered by chain-link fence and pine trees. Beyond the far end zone, past the fence, the cemetery rose in a gentle slope—rows of headstones like teeth in the ground, pale and patient under a sky that couldn't decide if it wanted to be bright or heavy.

If you stood on the fifty-yard line and looked up, you could see the stones between the uprights, framed perfectly like a target.

The flowers were there too, scattered among the older graves in tight clusters. Not blooming. Not glowing. Just… there. Dark stems. Closed buds. Purple hints tucked into dirt that looked too thin to support anything, let alone something that refused to die back when the season changed.

Mark had been staring at them long enough that Coach Whitman's voice cracked through his helmet like a slap.

"Rivers!"

Mark snapped his attention forward. "Yes, sir."

Coach Whitman didn't yell. He didn't need to. He carried a kind of disappointment that traveled on its own, a silent pressure you felt behind your eyes.

"You with us today?" Coach asked.

Mark nodded like he'd been caught daydreaming in class. "Yeah. I'm with you."

Coach's gaze flicked past him, toward the cemetery. His mouth tightened for half a second—so quick Mark wasn't sure he'd imagined it.

"Good," Coach said. "Because Homecoming's in two days and this town doesn't do second-best."

He turned and walked away, whistle bouncing against his chest.

Mark exhaled, slow, and forced his focus back to the drill. The air smelled like cut grass and sun-warmed rubber from the track. Under it was something else—faint, sweet, like violets left too long in water. Like a perfume that had learned to hide.

"Eyes on me, quarterback," Tommy Bell said as he jogged up beside him, grinning under his facemask.

Tommy played running back, built like speed and attitude. He had a laugh that made teachers roll their eyes and a mouth that could turn anything into a joke—especially the things that scared him.

"I'm looking," Mark said, and shoved him lightly with his shoulder pad.

Tommy bumped him back. "You were looking at the graveyard again."

Mark shrugged. "It's literally in the end zone."

"That's your excuse for everything," Tommy said. "You stare too long, you're gonna end up seeing somebody wave."

Pecos Alvarez, lined up at linebacker across from them, snorted. Pecos didn't joke the way Tommy did. He didn't talk much at all unless it mattered. When he did speak, his voice always sounded like it had been thinking first.

"Don't say that," Pecos muttered.

Tommy's grin widened. "Why? You scared of old bones?"

Pecos's eyes flicked toward the cemetery and away again, fast. "I'm not scared. I just don't like inviting things."

Mark didn't comment, because he'd learned Pecos wasn't superstitious in the way people in Lowridge were—crossing themselves before kickoff, touching the Lion statue by the gym for luck. Pecos didn't do that. Pecos listened. When the wind shifted, he noticed. When the ground felt different after rain, he said something about it.

He'd once told Mark, very calmly, that the woods behind the school felt "wrong" after dark.

Mark had laughed it off at the time.

He hadn't laughed last night, driving home past the cemetery, when he'd seen fog pooled around the fence like it was waiting.

"Set!" Coach barked.

Mark stepped under center. The line settled. Jason Rivers crouched wide to the right, hands on his thighs, chin lifted. Jason was two years older, same dark hair, same broad shoulders, same Rivers jawline that their mother swore came from their grandfather. But where Mark moved with careful control, Jason moved like the world had promised him something and he meant to collect.

Jason met Mark's eyes across the line and flashed a grin.

There it was—Jason's grin.

It had been on every team photo since Mark was old enough to understand what football meant in this town. It had been in the stands when Jason scored his first varsity touchdown as a freshman. It had been there the night they won state, bright under stadium lights, as if nothing in Lowridge could touch them.

Mark grinned back automatically, because that was what brothers did, what captains did. They kept the team steady. They kept the town steady.

"Blue eighty—blue eighty—hut!"

The play started clean. Mark took the snap, dropped back, eyes scanning routes like a habit carved into his bones. Tommy cut through the line, taking a fake handoff and pulling defenders. Pecos crashed into a guard with controlled violence. Jason broke into his route, sharp and fast, cleats chewing up turf.

Mark's eyes tracked him—one-two, one-two—the count that started a play and ended a prayer.

Then something tugged at the edge of his vision.

Not movement on the field. Not a defender slipping coverage. Something behind the end zone.

For a split second, he saw purple.

A bud in the cemetery, closed tight, seemed to tilt toward him.

Mark blinked, and the moment vanished. He threw to the left instead, a safe pass, and the ball hit the receiver's hands with a thud.

Coach's whistle blew. "Reset!"

Mark stood there, pulse steady, trying to convince himself he hadn't seen anything.

"Nice," Jason said as he jogged past, but his voice had an edge to it, too intense for a practice rep.

Mark watched him go. Under Jason's facemask, his eyes looked… bright. Not happy. Not fired-up. Just bright, like he hadn't slept and was running on something sharper than adrenaline.

Across the field, Alyssa Hargrove sat in the lowest row of the bleachers with a notebook balanced on her knees. She wasn't on the team—obviously —but she was around the team like she had a reason to be. Student paper, yearbook, debate club, whatever program needed a kid who actually took notes, Alyssa was there.

Her grandfather had been the town historian, the kind of man who got quoted in the Lowridge Gazette and invited to speak at Rotary breakfasts about "legacy." Alyssa had inherited his sharp focus and his habit of looking at Lowridge like it was a puzzle with missing pieces.

She lifted her pen as Mark glanced up, like she'd been watching him specifically.

Mark frowned and looked away.

"Rivers!" Coach called again. "Quit sightseeing."

Mark jogged back into position, but the cemetery stayed in his periphery like a weight.

Practice carried them through the usual routine—routes, scrimmage reps, conditioning. The sun slid lower. Shadows lengthened across the turf.

The stadium lights weren't on yet, but the field already felt dimmer, as if the day was being swallowed faster here than anywhere else.

By the time Coach blew the final whistle, Mark's jersey was soaked and his throat tasted like metal and dust. The team gathered around Coach as he paced in front of them.

"You boys want to win Friday?" Coach asked.

"Yes, sir," the team answered, automatic.

Coach's eyes moved across helmets, across faces hidden by bars. "You want this town to remember you?"

"Yes, sir."

Coach nodded once, satisfied. "Then you act like it. You eat right. You sleep right. You stay out of trouble. I don't care if it's Homecoming, I don't care if your girlfriend's got a dress, I don't care if your uncle's cousin's brother has a party. You keep your head in the game."

He paused, and his gaze snagged—again—on the cemetery behind them.

"This town," Coach said, quieter, "takes care of its champions."

The phrase landed like a compliment. The team murmured approval. Someone slapped a shoulder pad. Tommy muttered, "Damn right."

Mark felt his stomach tighten.

Because Coach's voice had made it sound like something else too.

A promise.

Or a warning.

They broke the huddle and headed for the locker room. The walk across the field took them past the end zone fence. Up close, the cemetery looked less like a backdrop and more like a presence. The chain-link was old, metal pitted by weather. Someone had tied purple ribbon to it for Homecoming week, the bows fluttering in the breeze like tiny flags.

Mark's eyes went to the ground near the fence. Dry dirt. Weeds. One closed bud, purple so dark it was almost black, tucked against a stone that faced the field like it was watching practice.

He kept walking.

Inside the locker room, the heat hit hard—steam from showers, the sour tang of sweat, cheap deodorant trying and failing to cover it. Boys shouted, laughed, argued about the upcoming game like it was a life-or-death debate.

Mark stripped off pads and sat at his locker, rubbing a sore spot on his wrist where tape had dug in. Across from him, Jason peeled off his helmet and ran a hand through sweat-dark hair.

"You're gonna light them up Friday," Tommy said to Mark, throwing a towel over his shoulder like a cape.

"Yeah," Mark said, distracted.

Tommy leaned in. "Seriously, dude. You're gonna look good in front of all the scouts. Everybody's coming to Homecoming. Whole town. Probably the dead too."

Pecos's head snapped up from tying his shoes.

Tommy held up both hands. "Kidding. I'm kidding."

Pecos didn't laugh.

Jason laughed—too loud, too quick. "Let him talk, man."

Mark looked at Jason again. Something about the laugh didn't match his eyes.

Jason's hands were shaking slightly as he unwrapped tape from his fingers.

"Hey," Mark said, low. "You good?"

Jason didn't look up. "Yeah."

"You're sure?"

Jason's jaw flexed. "I'm fine."

Mark waited. Jason finally met his gaze, and for a second, Mark saw something there that didn't belong.

Not fear. Not sadness.

Hunger.

Jason blinked, and whatever it was vanished behind that familiar grin. "Don't do the worried mom thing," he said. "We're good. You're good. We're gonna stomp Friday."

Mark forced a smile. "Yeah."

Jason stood fast, too fast, and slammed his locker shut. The sound echoed off tile.

Alyssa appeared in the doorway a minute later, holding a stack of papers and looking mildly offended by the locker room's existence.

"Coach said I could grab quotes," she announced, like she was stepping into a battlefield.

Several boys booed. Someone tossed a sock at her. Alyssa dodged without flinching and shot them a look that could have peeled paint.

Mark's phone buzzed in his locker. A text from his mom: Dinner at 7. Don't be late. Love you.

Jason's phone buzzed too. He looked at it and went still.

"What?" Tommy asked.

Jason shoved the phone in his pocket without answering. "Nothing."

Mark stood. "I'll walk with you."

Jason hesitated like he wanted to refuse, then shrugged. "Sure."

They left the locker room together, the noise fading behind them. Outside, the evening had cooled, but the air felt thick anyway, heavy with the promise of rain or something else. The parking lot was half-empty. A few parents waited near cars. The marching band practiced in the distance, the drumline tapping out a cadence that made Mark's teeth vibrate.

Jason walked with his hands in his pockets. His shoulders were tense.

"You've been weird all day," Mark said.

"Stop," Jason muttered.

"I'm serious."

Jason stopped walking. Mark stopped too. The field was behind them. The cemetery was visible over the fence, headstones pale in the deepening dusk.

Jason looked at it like he didn't mean to.

"You ever feel like…" Jason started, then cut himself off.

Mark's stomach tightened. "Like what?"

Jason swallowed. His throat bobbed. "Like the town's watching."

Mark's skin prickled. "People watch. You're a captain. That's normal."

Jason shook his head, sharper. "Not people."

A breeze slid through the trees. Somewhere in the cemetery, a ribbon tied to the fence fluttered and snapped softly against the wire.

Mark forced a laugh that came out wrong. "You're messing with me."

Jason didn't smile.

He reached into his pocket and pulled out his mouthguard—black with the Lions logo printed on it. He held it out in his palm like evidence.

Mark frowned. "Why are you holding that?"

"Because," Jason said, and his voice dropped so low Mark had to lean in, "it tastes like flowers."

Mark stared. "What?"

Jason turned the mouthguard over. Along the edge where teeth had bitten down, there was a faint purple stain—barely there, like ink that had bled into plastic.

Mark's throat went dry.

"That's paint," Mark said automatically. "From the logo. Or... I don't know. Something."

Jason's eyes were fixed on Mark's face, searching. "You didn't see it today?"

"See what?"

Jason's gaze flicked toward the cemetery again. "Nothing. Forget it."

He shoved the mouthguard back into his pocket and started walking.

Mark hurried after him. "Jay—"

Jason didn't slow. "Don't, okay? Don't do this."

Mark's pulse thudded. One-two, one-two.

They reached Jason's truck. Jason yanked the door open and climbed in. Mark stood by the driver's side, hand on the frame, not ready to let the moment go.

"Homecoming's just a game," Mark said, like saying it out loud could make it true. "We'll win. We'll celebrate. Then it's over."

Jason stared straight ahead through the windshield. The sky beyond the field had turned a bruised blue. The stadium lights clicked on one by one, bright white squares cutting into the dusk. From this angle, Mark could see the end zone fence and the cemetery beyond it, the stones lined up like an audience.

"It's never over," Jason said softly.

Mark opened his mouth, but no words came.

Jason finally glanced at him, and for a heartbeat, his eyes looked too bright again—reflecting the stadium lights in a way that didn't feel right.

Then he blinked, and he was just Jason again.

He smiled. "See you at home."

The engine started. Jason backed out and drove away, taillights disappearing down the road that led past the cemetery, past the woods, toward town.

Mark stood there alone in the cooling air, listening to the band's cadence and the distant shouts of teammates. Behind him, the field lights hummed. Ahead of him, the cemetery sat quiet.

He told himself he was being stupid.

He told himself the flowers were just a logo.

He told himself his brother was just stressed.

And then, as he turned to go, he caught a movement at the edge of the cemetery fence—so small he almost missed it.

A closed purple bud, tucked against a stone, shifted.

Not blooming. Not opening.

Just… turning slightly, as if it was following him with no eyes at all.

Mark's mouth went dry.

He walked faster, refusing to look back.

He didn't stop until he was halfway home, breath shallow like he'd run sprints instead of a walk to the parking lot.

In his room, the noise of the day fell away. A camera sat on his desk beside a cracked paint palette and a half-finished sketch of the stadium at dusk—light towers, bleachers, the end zone framed clean and empty. Mark liked catching Lowridge when nobody was performing.

He opened his laptop and pulled up a photo he'd taken last week: the field at twilight, fence line sharp, the cemetery beyond it blurred into pale stone.

It was supposed to be black-and-white.

But when he zoomed in, there—right where the fence met the first row of graves—was a faint wash of color, a bruise of purple that didn't belong in the image at all.

His stomach tightened. He snapped the laptop shut.

"Mark?" his mother called from downstairs. "Dinner."

"Coming," he answered.

He washed his hands anyway, scrubbing hard. When he turned the faucet off, a thin purple streak clung to the pad of his thumb like dye.

He rubbed at it. It didn't move.

Behind him, the end zone stayed framed by headstones, and Lowridge kept its breath held—one-two, one-two—waiting for Friday night to pass judgment.

CHAPTER 2: WHEN THE FLOWERS WATCH

Homecoming in Lowridge wasn't a weekend. It was a season that pretended to fit inside three days.

By late afternoon, Main Street had been dressed like a bride—purple-and-gold streamers braided around lampposts, Lions banners hung between brick storefronts, chalk paw prints stamped across the sidewalks like a trail you were supposed to follow. The new coffee place—glass-front, minimalist, the kind of spot that would've fit better up the highway near the tech park—had a chalkboard sign out front:

WELCOME BACK, CHAMPIONS.

A cluster of purple flowers had been sketched beneath it in looping marker, petals curling around the word champions like a flourish.

Mark stood at the curb across from the window and stared at that drawing longer than he meant to.

Everyone used the flowers. On signs. On letterheads. On the booster club trailer, airbrushed so bright they looked wet. The symbol had always been treated like local flavor, like the Lions were the only thing Lowridge ever invented that the rest of the world cared about.

But Mark couldn't stop thinking about Eli Carter.

Last year, on a night with fog thick enough to chew, Eli had run a route and never come back. That's how people said it, even now—never came back—like a boy could misplace himself the way you misplace keys.

There'd been a hundred explanations offered by people who needed the world to make sense. Heat exhaustion. Panic attack. A bad decision after the game. An accident down by the fence.

Anything except the one thing Mark's mind kept circling: the way the cemetery sat beyond the far end zone, quiet as an audience that never left, and the way the air on game nights sometimes smelled sweet—too sweet—and made your throat feel like it wanted to close.

A pickup rolled past, horn blaring, the driver waving an enormous foam paw out the window. Mark gave a small nod back, automatic. Thoughtful. Restrained.

That was his problem. He was good at the automatic things.

His phone buzzed.

JASON: where you at

Mark typed back with his thumb.

MARK: walking. heading to stadium.

A second later:

JASON: hurry. pep rally got Coach all fired up. he's smiling. that's how you know it's serious.

Mark's mouth twitched once, almost a smile, but it didn't stay.

Jason could make anything sound normal. He could take pressure and wear it like a jacket that fit. Mark didn't know if that was talent or survival.

He started walking again, camera strap cutting across his chest under his hoodie. He'd told himself he brought it for pictures—homecoming, lights, crowd, that kind of thing. Something to remember.

The truth was simpler. When Mark looked through a lens, the town made sense in frames. Boundaries. Edges. Focus.

Without the camera, Lowridge bled into everything.

The closer he got to the stadium, the more the air changed. The scent of grilled meat and kettle corn and popcorn oil thickened. The crowd noise rose and fell like surf. Somewhere a marching band practiced the same six measures on a loop, bright brass struggling against damp evening air.

And underneath it all—quiet enough that he might've imagined it if he didn't already know to listen—was that other smell.

Earthy. Sweet. Floral in a way that didn't belong to asphalt and metal bleachers.

Violet, salted faintly with iron.

Mark shifted the strap on his shoulder and kept going.

At the stadium gates, volunteers in booster club jackets waved people through with smiling urgency. There were tables lined with purple paper flowers and ribbons. Kids jammed the cheap petals into their hair. Parents pinned them to lapels. Someone had draped a huge floral garland around the Lions statue by the ticket booth.

The garland looked like the symbol made real.

Mark passed it and felt his skin tighten, the way it did before a hit.

Tommy Blake was leaning against the brick wall by the team entrance, helmet dangling from one hand. He had a paper flower tucked behind his ear like he'd been dared.

"Look at you," Tommy said when he saw Mark. "You're late to your own legend."

Mark glanced at the flower. "That's new."

Tommy tapped his ring against the wall, metal clicking in a rhythm he pretended was nothing. "Booster club lady said it's tradition. I told her my tradition is surviving."

"You're wearing it."

"Because she's eighty and she stared at me like she could ground me."

Mark's gaze slid past Tommy to the end of the fence line. Past the far goalpost. Past the field where the turf lights made the yard markers look painted on.

The cemetery sat out there, tucked behind the chain-link fence, headstones barely visible between the trees.

From here, it looked quiet.

Tommy followed Mark's eyes and lowered his voice as if the fence could hear him.

"You thinking about Eli again?"

Mark didn't answer right away.

Tommy kept going, softer now, friendly troll turning careful. "People are saying the county's gonna build a new fence this offseason. Taller. Like that's… supposed to fix whatever happened."

Mark adjusted his camera strap again. "Fences don't fix things."

Tommy blinked at him. "Was that… philosophical? Are you okay?"

"I'm fine."

Tommy opened his mouth to make a joke and stopped when Alyssa Dawson appeared, cutting through the crowd with a determined kind of speed. She had her backpack on even though it was homecoming and everyone else was dressed like the world was ending in a parade.

Her hair was pulled back. Her expression said she'd already been annoyed three separate times today and was collecting a fourth.

"You two are blocking the door like paid security," she said.

Tommy lifted his hands. "We are the door. Behold our greatness."

Alyssa's eyes flicked to his paper flower. "You look like a mascot."

"It's fashion," Tommy said. "Small-town couture."

Alyssa ignored him and looked at Mark. "Did you bring it?"

Mark touched the camera strap. "Yeah."

"Good." Her voice dropped. "I want pictures tonight. Not the game. The edge."

Mark's stomach tightened. "Alyssa—"

"Just say yes," she said, quick and sharp, like she was cutting the argument off before it started. "Say you'll do it."

Tommy leaned in, grinning. "Are we starting a secret club? Because I've always wanted a secret club."

Alyssa shot him a look. "You would last five minutes in a secret club."

"Wrong," Tommy said. "I would last forever because nobody would tell me anything important."

Mark held Alyssa's gaze. There was tension there, a controlled urgency she kept tucked behind sarcasm.

"What did you find?" he asked.

Alyssa's hand tightened on her backpack strap. "Not here."

Tommy's grin faltered a little. "If you say 'after the game,' I'm going to pretend I didn't hear you."

"After the game," Alyssa said anyway.

Tommy groaned. "Of course."

Then Jason's voice came from inside the tunnel, loud and familiar.

"Mark!"

Jason Rivers jogged out, already in his shoulder pads, jersey stretched tight across his chest. He looked like what Lowridge loved: strong, smiling, made for Friday nights. His face was open, confident.

But Mark saw the small things. The way Jason's eyes were a little too bright. The way he kept flexing his fingers like he was waking them up. The way he glanced once—quick as a reflex—toward the cemetery fence and then away again.

Jason clapped Mark's shoulder. "You ready?"

Mark nodded once. "You?"

Jason's grin flashed, too sharp. "Born ready."

Tommy stepped in, elbowing Jason lightly. "Born dramatic."

Jason laughed, but it didn't reach his eyes. "Save the jokes for the third quarter."

Alyssa watched Jason for a beat longer than the others, her expression shifting from sarcasm to something clinical. Something measuring.

Jason noticed. His grin thinned. "What?"

Alyssa lifted her hands. "Nothing. It's just—"

"Just what?" Jason pressed, still smiling, like this was a game too.

Mark felt the moment start to tilt.

Alyssa chose her words with care. "Just... don't play like you're trying to prove something tonight."

Jason's smile twitched. "That's what homecoming is."

And then Coach Whitman barked from inside the tunnel, and Jason's attention snapped away, expression resetting like a mask sliding back into place.

"Come on," Jason said. "We've got a town to feed."

He said it like a joke.

Mark didn't laugh.

The locker room was heat and noise and sharp tape smell. The team moved in practiced patterns—pads tightened, helmets clicked, names shouted across benches.

Mark taped his wrist in silence, fingers steady. He could feel the crowd through the walls like pressure changes before a storm.

Jason sat a few lockers down, lacing his cleats with too much force. He kept tugging the laces until the knots looked like they might snap. Every so often, he lifted his head and stared at nothing, eyes unfocused, like he was listening to something the rest of them couldn't hear.

Pecos Morales sat across from Mark, calm in a way that made the rest of the room seem louder. He adjusted his gloves slowly, methodical, like ritual.

Tommy flopped down between them and leaned back, stretching his arms across the bench. "Okay. Everybody breathe. We're going to win. We're going to go home. We're going to eat something that's terrible for us."

Pecos glanced at him. "That is a lot of certainty."

Tommy tapped his ring against the bench. "I am a man of routine."

Pecos's gaze slid past Tommy, toward the lockers by the door. Toward Jason.

"It feels different," Pecos said.

Tommy made a face. "You always say that."

Pecos didn't react to the joke. "The air. The ground. Like it's waiting."

Mark's tape paused halfway around his wrist. "Waiting for what?"

Pecos looked at him, expression steady. "For a moment."

Tommy opened his mouth and closed it again, as if he couldn't find a joke big enough to cover the unease.

Coach Whitman's voice cut through the room. "Listen up!"

The team quieted. Coach walked the aisle like he owned it, hands clasped behind his back. His eyes moved over them, assessing, weighing.

"This town takes care of its champions," Coach said, voice low enough that it pulled everyone in. "You give everything, and you get everything."

Mark felt the words settle in his chest like a stone.

Coach's eyes landed on Jason. "You hear me, Rivers?"

Jason's head snapped up. "Yes, sir."

Coach nodded once. "Good."

Mark didn't miss the way Jason's jaw clenched, the way his smile didn't show.

Then Coach turned to Mark. "And you, quarterback—keep your head. Keep your rhythm. You're the one who decides where this goes."

Mark swallowed. "Yes, sir."

Coach's gaze lingered a half-second too long, as if he wanted to say something else. Then he clapped his hands once, sharp.

"Let's go feed the lights."

They surged toward the tunnel.

The field hit Mark like a wave: cold air, damp turf, stadium lights burning down through fog that refused to lift.

The crowd roared as the Lions ran out, one body of sound. Mark jogged to the sideline, helmet on, chin strap tight, mind settling into the familiar track of plays and reads.

He could do this.

He had done this.

And still—tonight felt wrong.

Not in the obvious ways. Not like a storm warning, not like the lights flickering out. The wrongness was quiet. Layered. In the pauses between noise.

Mark looked across the field at the visiting team lined up for warm-ups. They were bigger than their record suggested, fast on tape. Outsiders, Coach called them.

But they moved like they didn't want to touch the turf.

One of their linemen kept rubbing his forearms, glancing toward the far fence like he expected something to come through it. Their quarterback stared at the cemetery longer than made sense, lips moving like he was counting.

Mark lifted his camera for a second, just to do something with his hands, and snapped a photo of the fog under the lights. The image on the display looked almost normal.

Almost.

The fog had a seam in it—an odd straight line near the far end zone, as if something in the air had been cut and stitched back together.

Mark lowered the camera, pulse steady.

The band played. The announcer boomed. Homecoming court waved, smiling too hard.

Purple ribbons fluttered from the cheerleaders' wrists.

And out by the cemetery fence—

Mark's eyes snagged there again.

The flowers.

They weren't supposed to be blooming.

Everyone knew that. Even if people didn't say it out loud, even if they pretended the flowers were just flowers, everyone knew they were stubborn about season and place.

Tonight, in the thin strip of ground between headstones, they were open.

Small at first. Easy to ignore if you didn't look.

Then, as the sun finished sliding away and the moon rose pale behind the clouds, Mark watched a ring of purple brighten like someone had turned a dial.

Not a spotlight. Not a flare.

A watch face in moonlight.

Private light.

He felt the hair lift on his arms.

Tommy jogged past and slapped Mark's shoulder pad. "Hey! Eyes on the living, photographer."

Mark blinked and forced his focus back to the field.

"Yeah," he said. "I'm here."

Tommy's grin returned like a shield. "Good. Because if you start staring at flowers mid-play, I'm going to have to tackle you myself."

Pecos was nearby, hands on hips, scanning the field. When Mark caught his eye, Pecos gave a small shake of his head.

Different, Pecos mouthed.

Mark didn't respond. He didn't know how.

The first whistle blew.

The game started.

For most of the first quarter, Lowridge looked like itself.

The offense clicked. Mark's arm was clean and controlled, timing sharp. The crowd responded to every completion like it was proof of something bigger than talent. The Lions defense hit hard, fast, disciplined.

And Jason—Jason played like he was trying to outrun a shadow.

He launched into tackles with an edge Mark hadn't seen since they were kids, playing backyard football with their dad watching like the world depended on their form. On offense, when Jason lined up as a receiver, he ran routes like they were a last chance to say something without words.

Mark threw him a slant on third and medium. Jason caught it, turned upfield, and stiff-armed a defender so hard the kid went down like his legs had been unplugged.

The crowd screamed. Mark should've felt the rush.

Instead, he felt a tightening in his chest.

Jason jogged back to the huddle, face bright with sweat, eyes a little glassy. He stared straight through Mark for half a second before his focus snapped back.

"You good?" Mark asked quietly.

Jason blinked, smile flashing. "I'm great."

But Mark saw Jason's fingers twitch, as if something in his hands wanted to move without his permission.

By the second quarter, the fog thickened.

It rolled in low over the field, layered under the lights. The yard numbers blurred at the edges. Players moved through it like they were swimming, their legs cutting pale wake in the air.

The opposing team started making mistakes that didn't match their training. False starts. Missed assignments. A punt that wobbled like the ball had forgotten what spin meant.

Their quarterback looked toward the cemetery after every play.

Mark's mouth tasted faintly metallic. He couldn't tell if it was adrenaline or something else.

During a timeout, Mark jogged to the sideline for water. Alyssa was there, tucked behind the bench with her backpack, watching the game with the expression of someone watching a lab experiment.

Tommy leaned toward her as he gulped water. "Are you enjoying your Friday night entertainment?"

Alyssa's eyes flicked to him. "I love watching people get concussions for community bonding."

Tommy choked a little. "Okay. Point taken."

Alyssa shifted her gaze to Mark. "You see it?"

Mark didn't ask what she meant. "Yes."

"They're open," Alyssa said, voice tight. "They shouldn't be open."

"I know."

Alyssa pulled something from her backpack—an old folded photocopy, edges worn. She shoved it toward Mark.

On the page was a grainy newspaper image from decades ago: a team photo, boys in old uniforms, smiles bright. Behind them, barely visible, the faint outline of the cemetery fence.

And at the corner of the image, like an ink blot, a dark cluster of flowers.

Alyssa tapped the caption with her finger. "This is from the year Lowridge won its first state title."

Mark stared at the photo. "That's—"

"Old," Alyssa finished. "And it's not an accident. Every championship year I've found? There are flowers somewhere in the picture. Always in the background. Always watching."

Mark's stomach clenched.

Tommy leaned in, squinting. "That could be… anything. It could be somebody's mom's purse."

Alyssa didn't look at him. "Your denial is impressive."

Tommy lifted his hands. "I am an optimist."

Alyssa finally met his eyes. "No. You're a deflector."

Tommy's grin flickered, just for a second, something tighter beneath it, and then it was gone. "Fine. Maybe I'm both."

Mark kept staring at the photo. He thought of Coach saying the town took care of its champions.

He thought of Eli Carter. The way the story had been folded into the town like it belonged there.

Alyssa's voice dropped. "Old-timers used to say champions 'gave everything.' I thought it was just… dramatic language. But in my grandfather's notes—"

Her mouth tightened. "He wrote that the town's success is a kind of exchange."

Mark didn't speak. Silence was his defense. Always had been.

Alyssa pressed harder. "Mark, your family—"

Mark's head snapped up.

Alyssa held his gaze, not cruel, just relentless. "I'm not accusing you. I'm saying your family name shows up in the town's early records. A lot. It's not random."

Mark swallowed. The guilt that lived under his ribs shifted, awake.

Before he could answer, the whistle blew again. Coach shouted. Players surged back onto the field.

Mark folded the photocopy and shoved it into his hoodie pocket like it burned.

As he jogged back to the huddle, he glanced toward the cemetery again.

The purple ring of flowers was brighter now.

Not enough for the crowd to notice.

Enough for Mark to feel it behind his eyes like pressure.

Late in the fourth quarter, the Lions were up by six.

The game should've felt locked. The opposing team was rattled. The crowd was already tasting victory.

But the air had a thickness to it now, and the fog had turned the stadium into a bowl of light floating on a sea of dark. Mark could see the cemetery fence like a black line across the world.

And beyond it, the flowers glowed steady.

No pulsing now.

Just watching.

Mark called the next play. His voice was even. His hands steady under center.

Jason lined up wide, shoulders squared, staring at the defender across from him like he wanted to snap him in half.

Mark met Jason's eyes. For a heartbeat, Jason looked like himself.

Then Jason's gaze flickered past Mark—toward the fence—toward the dark strip of cemetery ground—and something in his expression tightened, like he'd heard a sound no one else could.

The ball snapped.

Mark dropped back. The pocket held.

He saw Jason break off the line hard, route crisp, perfect—too perfect, like it wasn't coming from thought but from something deeper in muscle. He threw the ball.

Jason caught it clean and turned upfield.

And for a second, as Jason ran, Mark saw something impossible.

Jason's eyes flashed, quick as a camera shutter, a bright violet gleam that made Mark's stomach drop.

Jason kept running. He cut between defenders like the space had been made for him. His stride lengthened. His body moved like it belonged to a different rhythm.

The crowd roared—delighted, hungry.

Jason broke free and sprinted toward the end zone.

He scored.

Touchdown.

The stadium exploded.

And Jason, standing in the end zone with arms lifted, looked like a statue for a moment—still, smiling, face turned slightly toward the cemetery as if acknowledging someone in the dark.

Mark jogged downfield, heart hammering, not from the play.

From dread.

When Mark reached Jason, Jason turned, grin wide, and clapped Mark's helmet hard enough to rattle his teeth.

"We did it," Jason said.

Mark's voice came out low. "Yeah."

Jason's smile didn't change. "Feels good, doesn't it?"

Mark stared at his brother's eyes. They looked normal now.

But Mark couldn't forget that flash.

The extra point went through. The lead widened. The game ended with the Lions kneeling out the clock.

Fans poured onto the field, a tradition as old as the town's certainty that the Lions belonged on top.

Mark moved through the chaos, helmet off now, sweat cooling on his neck. The air smelled like damp turf and sugar and something floral that didn't belong.

Jason was laughing with teammates, shoulders loose, as if the intensity had been wrung out of him and left behind.

Then Jason stopped laughing.

It was abrupt—like a switch thrown.

His hand went to his chest. His face tightened. His eyes went unfocused.

Mark saw it and started moving before his brain caught up.

"Jason?"

Jason swayed.

A cheerleader brushed past, purple pom-poms flashing. Someone shoved a homecoming banner up in the air. A booster yelled about pictures.

Jason took one step, as if he meant to walk, and then his knees buckled.

He hit the turf hard.

The crowd noise shifted—confusion rising like a wave.

Mark dropped beside him. "Jason. Hey. Look at me."

Jason's eyes fluttered open, and Mark saw the fear there, sudden and raw, like Jason had surfaced from underwater.

His mouth moved, but no sound came at first.

Then, hoarse and strained, Jason whispered, "Get it out."

Mark leaned closer. "Get what out?"

Jason's eyes jerked toward the cemetery. Toward the fence. Toward the watching purple line.

His lips moved again. "Mouth."

Mark's hands went cold.

He reached for Jason's facemask, fingers shaking just enough to make him angry at himself, and unhooked the mouthguard strap. The guard was tucked inside, still warm.

Mark pulled it free.

Jason gagged once, shallow and dry, and his eyes squeezed shut.

A trainer shoved through the crowd, hands already out. Coach Whitman's voice cracked sharp orders behind him. Tommy appeared at Mark's shoulder, his usual grin gone.

"What's happening?" Tommy asked, voice too loud, too fast.

"I don't know," Mark said.

Alyssa was there too, pushing in, eyes wide but focused, as if she'd been waiting for this moment and hated that she was right.

Pecos stood back half a step, face pale, gaze fixed on Jason's chest like he could hear something inside it.

"Mark," Alyssa said, tight. "The mouthguard."

Mark looked down.

The inside of the mouthguard was wet. A smear of saliva. A faint metallic tang that hit Mark's nose like a memory of bitten lips.

And tucked against the rubber, pressed into the groove where the teeth fit—

A petal.

Purple. Velvet-soft. Real.

Mark's stomach lurched.

Alyssa inhaled sharply, as if she'd been punched. Tommy's hand flew to his own mouth like he was trying to keep something in.

Pecos whispered, almost to himself, "Blood and petals."

Mark's voice came out low, controlled, because if he let it go higher it might break. "How did this get here?"

Jason convulsed once—small, not violent—and then went still, breathing shallow.

The trainer grabbed Jason's shoulders and started barking for space. Someone called for an ambulance. The crowd shifted, people stepping back, phones coming out, faces hungry for a story.

Coach Whitman arrived, eyes hard, jaw clenched.

"What happened?" Coach demanded.

Mark held up the mouthguard. "This was in it."

Coach's gaze flicked to the petal and away so fast Mark almost missed it. Coach's expression didn't change, but something in his eyes did.

A calculation.

A denial forming at speed.

Coach's voice dropped. "Put that away."

Mark didn't move.

Coach leaned closer, voice low enough that only Mark could hear. "Now."

Mark stared at him.

Coach's eyes held his, steady, unblinking. "This town takes care of its champions," Coach said softly, as if reminding Mark of something sacred. "Don't make it harder than it has to be."

Mark's grip tightened around the mouthguard until it squeaked.

For a moment, the world narrowed to the petal, to Coach's calm command, to the sound of Jason's shallow breathing.

Mark's silence rose in him like a wall.

And then—beneath it—something else.

A truth he'd swallowed for years because swallowing was easier than saying.

He turned his head toward Jason, who lay on the turf like a broken statue, eyes half-open, fear trapped behind them.

Mark's voice came out rough. Honest. "I'm sorry."

Coach stiffened as if Mark had cursed, but Mark kept going, the words scraping out of him like they'd been lodged in his throat for too long.

"I'm sorry I didn't tell you," Mark said, not sure who he meant it for—Jason, himself, the air. "I'm sorry I kept pretending everything here is normal."

Jason's eyes focused for a fraction of a second, locking on Mark's face.

In that instant, the violet pressure behind Mark's eyes eased—just a hair—like something loosened its grip.

Jason's lips moved. A whisper, barely there.

"Don't..." Jason breathed. "Let..."

Then the moment snapped.

Jason's eyes rolled, not dramatically, just slipping away like a light fading. His body went slack.

The crowd noise rose and fell, distant, muffled. The ambulance siren wailed somewhere outside the stadium, getting closer.

Mark stared at his brother's face, and the petal in his hand felt heavier than it should have been—like it carried weight that didn't belong in the human world.

Alyssa's voice cut in, tight and shaking. "Mark. That's not just a flower."

Mark looked toward the cemetery fence.

The purple line beyond it glowed steady, quiet, patient.

Watching.

Waiting.

And Mark understood—cold and certain—that whatever lived in the roots beneath Lowridge had found a door.

It had used the game. The blood. The crowd's hunger.

And now it had its hands on Jason.

Mark closed his fingers around the mouthguard, petal trapped inside like a secret.

The ambulance lights flashed red-blue against the fog.

And the flowers beyond the fence did not move.

They didn't have to.

CHAPTER 3: THE CLAIMING

The ER doors hissed open and shut like the building was breathing—letting people in, letting them out, pretending it had any control over what came with them.

Mark stood in the harsh fluorescent light with his helmet still in one hand, his shoulder pads half-unclipped, his jersey damp against his spine. His fingers wouldn't stop tapping the helmet's facemask—thumb, knuckle, thumb—like the start of a cadence that never reached the snap.

Across the hall, Jason lay on a gurney in a curtain bay that didn't feel wide enough for him. Not because Jason was big—though he was—but because his presence had always been too loud for tight spaces. Jason was the kind of person who made rooms rearrange around him. Even when he was quiet, he pulled attention like gravity.

Now he didn't pull anything at all.

He lay flat, eyes half-lidded, breathing shallow, with a nurse adjusting an oxygen mask that looked wrong on his face—wrong on any Rivers, really. Mark's father stood beside the bed, one hand on the rail like he could hold Jason to the world by gripping metal.

Coach Whitman paced at the end of the hall, phone pressed to his ear, voice pitched low. Booster dads hovered near the vending machines. Someone's mother cried softly into her hoodie. The town had followed Jason here the same way it followed Friday night lights: instinctively, without asking whether it should.

Tommy leaned against the wall near Mark, still in his game pants, still restless. He kept pulling his ring off, rolling it over his knuckles, sliding it back on, repeating the cycle like it was a drill.

Alyssa stood on Mark's other side with her arms folded tight. She didn't look scared the way most people did—wide eyes, open mouth, shaking hands. She looked focused. That was scarier, sometimes.

"You're still holding your helmet," she said.

Mark looked down like he'd just noticed it. "Yeah."

"That's… very you," Tommy muttered. Then, louder, trying to make it a joke: "If you put it on, do you think you'll get a better signal in here? Like a satellite dish?"

Alyssa's gaze flicked to him. "If you're going to cope, cope quieter."

Tommy's mouth twitched. "Noted."

Mark didn't say anything. His throat felt packed with cotton. Every time he tried to think, his mind slid sideways back to the field—Jason collapsing near the sideline, the fog low and stubborn, the way Jason's hands had curled like he was grabbing for something invisible.

And the mouthguard.

Mark hadn't told anyone about the petal yet. He could still feel it in his pocket like a piece of heat, like something alive that didn't have a right to be alive.

A nurse stepped out of Jason's bay and approached them. She had the practiced expression of someone who'd delivered a thousand small disasters and learned not to carry any of them home.

"Family?" she asked.

Mark's father straightened. "I'm his father."

The nurse nodded, gentle. "Doctor's on the way. He's stable right now. But we need to run some tests."

"What happened?" Mark's father asked. He asked it like a demand, like the right words would force reality to behave.

The nurse hesitated—just a fraction, just long enough for Mark to feel it. "We're not sure yet. He collapsed, and his oxygen levels dropped fast. Could be an allergic reaction, could be… a lot of things."

"An allergic reaction," Tommy repeated, eyebrows lifting. "To what? Winning?"

Alyssa elbowed him without looking.

The nurse glanced at Mark, then away. "Did he get hit hard? Any injury?"

Mark pictured Jason's last play. Not a hard hit. Not the kind that rang your bones. Just… a stumble. A hand on his chest. His eyes unfocusing.

"No," Mark said. His voice came out quieter than he meant. "Nothing unusual."

Alyssa added, "He didn't take a headshot. I was watching."

The nurse nodded like she'd file that away with everything else in a drawer labeled Things That Don't Matter Until They Do. Then she stepped back into the bay.

Mark's father exhaled hard, a sound close to a growl. "This town," he said under his breath, not meaning to say it out loud. "This pressure. This —"

He stopped himself. Swallowed whatever came next.

Truth was not Lowridge's favorite language.

Mark stared at the curtain, at the shape of his brother behind it. His own hands had started tapping again without permission. One-two. One-two.

He could almost hear the crowd still. Not in his ears—under his skin. A vibration that hadn't faded when the stadium emptied.

Alyssa shifted closer to him. "Mark."

He didn't look at her.

"You saw something on the field," she said. Not a question. A clean statement, like she'd solved an equation.

Mark finally turned his head. Alyssa's eyes were sharp, almost bright under the hospital lights. Tommy watched them both, ring caught between his fingers.

"I saw Jason go down," Mark said.

"Before that." Alyssa's voice stayed flat, but her fingers tightened on her own sleeve. "You were staring at the cemetery."

Tommy let out a short, humorless breath. "Everyone was staring at the cemetery. The fog made it look like it was... I don't know. Breathing."

Alyssa didn't take her eyes off Mark. "Did you see the flowers bloom?"

Mark's silence was an answer.

Tommy's grin tried to show up and couldn't quite make it. "Okay," he said, too loud. "So we're officially doing this. We're officially saying out loud that the cemetery did something."

Alyssa's tone cut clean through him. "We are officially saying out loud that something is happening that nobody wants to say out loud."

Mark's pocket felt heavier. The petal pressed against fabric like it was listening.

Before he could decide whether to speak, the doctor arrived—tall, tired, hair flattened from a long night that had already started before theirs. He pulled the curtain closed behind him as if that thin strip of cloth could keep everything contained.

Mark's father, Mark, and Jason's mother were allowed into the bay first. Tommy and Alyssa stayed out, but Mark could feel them there, like anchors.

Jason looked smaller than he should have. Not physically—his shoulders still filled the bed—but in a way that made Mark's stomach turn. Like someone had turned down his brightness.

His eyes fluttered open when Mark stepped close.

"Hey," Mark said.

Jason tried to smile. It barely lifted one side of his mouth. "You look… terrible."

Mark huffed once—a laugh that didn't know how to be a laugh. "I had plans to shower."

"Don't," Jason whispered. "You'll wash off the luck."

Mark's father made a sound like he wanted to snap at him for joking and couldn't bring himself to. Jason's mother stroked Jason's hair back from his forehead.

The doctor cleared his throat. "We're seeing inflammation in his lungs," he said. "And something unusual in his airway."

"What kind of unusual?" Mark's father asked.

The doctor hesitated again—another fraction, another seam of reality splitting. "We suctioned out some material."

He nodded to the nurse, and she handed him a small sealed specimen cup.

Inside, under the harsh lights, were purple flecks.

Not a lot. Not enough to scream. Just enough to steal all the air out of Mark's lungs.

Mark's father stared at it like it was a trick. "What is that?"

The doctor's expression tightened. "We don't know. It isn't behaving like typical pollen. It's… clumping."

Jason's mother put a hand to her mouth.

Mark's mind flashed to the cemetery. The low glow. The fog thick as milk. The way the flowers seemed brighter during the game—wrong-season color under wrong-season moon.

"Pollen?" Mark's father said, voice flat, disbelieving. "In his lungs?"

"We're treating it like an irritant," the doctor said carefully. "But his vitals are… inconsistent. His oxygen saturation drops and rises without pattern. It's like—"

He stopped himself, then chose different words. "It's like something is interfering with his breathing in a way we can't fully map yet."

Mark leaned closer to Jason, like proximity could stitch him back together. "Jay. Did you breathe something in? On the field?"

Jason's eyes shifted. For a second they focused on Mark's face, clear and familiar.

Then his gaze slid past him, toward the corner of the ceiling where nothing hung.

And his pupils flickered—not with light, not like a reflection—but with color.

A thin, unmistakable purple flash.

Mark's skin went cold.

Jason's lips moved. No sound.

Mark leaned closer, heart hammering. "What?"

Jason's mouth worked again. His throat bobbed like he was swallowing something that wasn't there.

"Don't…" he rasped.

His mother's hand tightened around his.

"Don't let them…" Jason's eyes fluttered, and the purple flicker returned —stronger now. His voice dropped to a whisper, the words scraped raw.

"Don't let them bloom."

Mark's chest tightened like a fist had closed around his ribs. "Who? Who is 'them'?"

Jason's eyes rolled up for a second. His jaw clenched. A low sound came out of him—half breath, half something else.

Mark's father leaned in. "Jason."

Jason's face tightened as if he was fighting for space inside his own body. His gaze snapped back to Mark—Mark, not the corner of nothing.

"Listen," he whispered. "You can't—"

The monitor beside the bed chirped once, sharp.

Jason's chest hitched.

The doctor moved fast. Nurses stepped in, adjusting lines, checking pressure, calling numbers.

Mark was guided backward with a firm hand on his shoulder. "Let us work," someone said.

Mark stumbled out into the hall before he realized he'd moved. His palms were damp. His mouth tasted faintly metallic, like old blood.

Alyssa and Tommy rushed toward him.

"What did he say?" Alyssa asked immediately.

Mark opened his mouth and nothing came out.

Tommy's voice filled the silence, loud and frantic. "Is he okay? Are we doing okay? On a scale of one to 'this is fine,' where are we?"

Mark swallowed. "He said… 'Don't let them bloom.'"

Alyssa's face went still. "He said that?"

Mark nodded once.

Tommy's ring slipped, almost hit the floor, and he caught it at the last second. "That's… not a normal sentence to say while you're—" He stopped himself. "While you're in a hospital."

Alyssa's eyes darted toward the far windows at the end of the hall. It was darker now. Later. The world outside the hospital had shifted into that late-night quiet that made every parking lot light feel too bright and every shadow too patient.

"I need air," Mark said suddenly, because if he stayed under the fluorescent hum another second, he might come apart in front of them.

He walked before anyone could stop him.

Outside, the night hit him like a wall—cold, damp, heavy. The hospital sat on a low rise above town, and from the parking lot you could see parts of Lowridge laid out like a brochure: Main Street lights, the water tower, the dark smear of trees.

And beyond that—faint, but unmistakable—the cemetery.

It wasn't close enough to see headstones. It was close enough to see color.

A low purple glow gathered over the ground like spilled ink. Not bright like neon. Not obvious enough to make the town call the news.

But bright enough that Mark felt it in his teeth.

Bright enough that it felt like being watched.

He stared, breath fogging in front of him.

One-two. One-two.

The cadence didn't come from his head. It came from the earth. A slow pulse traveling up through asphalt and bone.

Behind him, the door opened. Alyssa stepped out beside him, arms folded.

"You see it," she said.

Mark didn't answer.

Alyssa's voice sharpened, the way it did when she was trying not to feel something. "That glow wasn't there last week. I've driven past it every day. It's changing."

Mark's hand slid into his pocket before he could stop it. His fingers touched the petal.

Alyssa's gaze dropped immediately. "What's that?"

Mark hesitated. Then he pulled it out.

Under the parking lot light, the petal looked impossibly vivid—deep purple, velvet-soft. It didn't wilt. It didn't dry. It sat in Mark's palm like it belonged there.

Alyssa's breath caught. "Where did you get that?"

"In Jason's mouthguard," Mark said quietly. "After he collapsed."

Alyssa stared at the petal like it was proof made physical. "The flower isn't just… around them," she murmured. "It gets into them."

Mark's fingers curled around it without thinking. A faint slickness touched his skin—like oil, like sap.

Alyssa's eyes snapped up. "Don't."

Mark froze.

"Blood and petals," Alyssa said, voice low. "That's what my grandfather wrote. I didn't want it to be literal."

Mark's throat tightened. "What does that mean?"

"It means the flowers are conduits," Alyssa said. Her tone went flat, clinical, like she was reading a report. "A way in. A way through. The land doesn't need… claws. It doesn't need teeth. It needs access."

Mark stared out at the cemetery glow. "Then Jason—"

Then the door opened again, and Tommy stepped out with Pecos behind him.

Pecos looked worse than he had on the field. Not injured—just drained, like the night had taken a bite out of him. He stood with his hands shoved into his jacket pockets and his shoulders slightly hunched, as if bracing against something no one else could feel.

Tommy pointed at the horizon. "Okay. So. That's not normal."

Pecos didn't look at the glow. He looked at Mark. "It's active," he said calmly.

Mark's eyes narrowed. "What?"

Pecos nodded toward the petal in Mark's hand. "The land is awake. That's what this is. That's what Jason is caught in."

Tommy's voice cracked into the space between them. "Cool. Awesome. Love that for us."

Alyssa's sarcasm flashed sharp. "Tommy, if you make one more joke, I'm going to staple your mouth shut."

He held up both hands. "Noted. No jokes. Only screaming internally."

A nurse opened the door and called Mark's father's name. Mark went back inside with them. Back under lights that made everyone's faces look a little sick.

Hours blurred. Tests. Waiting. The thin hospital clock ticking too loud.

Mark sat in the chair beside Jason's bed, shoulders folded in, hands clasped so tight his knuckles hurt. Jason's breathing rose and fell in shallow waves. Every so often, his eyes fluttered open, unfocused.

Once, near midnight, Jason's gaze fixed on Mark's face. Clear.

"Hey," Mark whispered.

Jason's lips moved. "You… okay?"

Mark swallowed. He wanted to say yes. He wanted to lie the way Lowridge taught everyone to lie—smooth, comforting, denial shaped into words.

But the purple glow outside the window existed. The petal existed. The specimen cup existed.

Jason was fading right in front of him.

Mark's voice came out rough. "No," he admitted. "No. I'm not."

Jason's eyes stayed on him, and for a second Mark saw his brother—really saw him—like the fog lifted for one breath.

"You gotta…" Jason whispered. His throat worked. "You gotta get out."

Mark's chest tightened. "Out of what?"

Jason's gaze drifted toward the window, toward the night. "Out of… this."

Mark felt his throat burn. "I can't leave you."

Jason's eyes flickered purple again—fast, like a glitch. His jaw clenched.

Mark leaned closer. "Jay. Listen to me. I'm here. I'm not going anywhere."

Jason's breath hitched. His fingers twitched against the sheet.

Mark's mind flashed—confession and honesty breaks the conduit. Alyssa had said it. Pecos had felt it. Mark hadn't believed in rules like that.

But he believed in his brother.

"I'm sorry," Mark whispered, the words coming out before he could stop them. "For what Dad did. For what Grandpa did. For… the way we keep pretending it's just football."

Jason's eyes widened slightly. The purple flicker faltered, like a signal interrupted.

For one heartbeat, Jason looked fully himself.

And in that tiny stolen space, his fingers tightened around Mark's hand.

"Don't… let…" Jason rasped. His voice was thin, fraying. "Don't let them—"

The monitor spiked.

Jason's chest stuttered.

Nurses moved in. The doctor followed. Mark was pulled back again.

This time the curtain closed fully, and Mark stood outside listening to muffled commands and the sharp, repeating chirp of machines.

One-two. One-two.

The cadence beat through Mark's ribs.

At 3:07 a.m., the curtain opened.

The doctor stepped out with his face carefully arranged into something that wouldn't break a family apart any more than it already was.

Mark already knew.

His mother made a sound like the air had been punched out of her. Mark's father went very still, as if he'd been braced for impact his entire life and it finally arrived.

Mark didn't move. His body refused. He watched his father's hand grip the wall, watched his mother fold into a chair.

Alyssa arrived sometime after—hair messy, eyes wide, jacket thrown over pajamas like she'd sprinted out of her house. Pecos and Tommy were there too, silent in the hallway like shadows.

Mark walked into the bay.

Jason lay on the bed the same way he had all night. Only now the room felt emptier, like something had been removed that wasn't flesh.

On the sheet near Jason's collar, a dusting of purple had settled—fine as flour, visible only under the angle of the overhead light.

Pollen.

Mark's stomach rolled.

The doctor's voice came quietly behind him. "We didn't... we couldn't find a cause that explains the speed of it." He paused, and then, like he couldn't help himself: "It's like something drained him."

Mark stared at his brother's face. Jason's expression was neutral, but Mark couldn't shake the feeling that the body was only pretending to be done.

Mark stepped closer, careful. He touched Jason's hand.

Cold.

Real.

His own fingers trembled.

Behind him, Pecos moved in without speaking. Pecos's face was calm, but there were shadows under his eyes like bruises.

Pecos reached out and placed two fingers against Jason's wrist.

The moment he made contact, Pecos flinched hard—like he'd grabbed a live wire.

He jerked his hand back, breath sharp.

Tommy surged forward. "What? What happened?"

Pecos shook his hand out, staring at his own fingertips. "It... bit," he said quietly.

Alyssa's voice came out tight. "Like electricity?"

Pecos nodded once. "Like the land doesn't want him let go."

Mark's throat tightened. "What does that mean?"

Pecos's gaze lifted to Mark's. "It means he's not just dead," he said, calm as a weather report. "He's claimed."

Mark's mouth went dry. He turned toward the window.

Outside, far across town, the cemetery glow had intensified.

It looked closer now, as if the night had leaned in.

When the sun rose, Lowridge did what it always did with things it couldn't explain.

It made a story small enough to swallow.

Jason Rivers, beloved Lion. A sudden medical event. A tragedy. A reminder that life is fragile. A call to support the family. A moment of silence planned for Friday's Hollow's Eve Festival kickoff because Lowridge never wasted a chance to turn grief into ritual.

Coach Whitman made a statement. The mayor posted a photo. The booster club printed a ribbon.

People cried. People prayed. People said, "He gave everything," like it was a compliment instead of a warning.

Mark went home sometime after dawn with his jersey still on. The house felt wrong without Jason's noise in it. The hallway outside Jason's room looked too clean, too empty, like it had already started erasing him.

Mark stood in his own room, hands shaking as he dumped his pockets onto his desk.

Keys. Phone. Helmet strap.

And the purple petal.

It lay there like a piece of the cemetery brought inside.

Mark stared at it until his eyes burned.

Outside his window, fog gathered in the low places of the yard even though the morning was clear. The kind of fog that didn't belong to weather.

Mark didn't sleep.

That night, when the town finally went quiet, Mark drove without thinking.

He parked near the cemetery fence and walked up to the gate.

The air smelled sweet and metallic.

Inside, the flowers had multiplied.

Where there had been clusters before, now there were carpets—purple blossoms pressed thick around headstones, glowing faintly under moonlight, their petals lifting and lowering like slow breathing.

Mark's chest tightened.

He stepped closer, hands clenched at his sides. The gate creaked as if it recognized him.

Somewhere deeper among the stones, a figure stood.

Tall. Still.

Mark's throat went tight. "Jason?"

The figure shifted slightly.

And in the thin wash of moonlight, Mark saw the outline of a football jersey.

He took one step forward—and the flowers closest to him brightened, as if responding.

One-two.

One-two.

The cadence rose under his feet.

The figure turned its head.

For a second, Mark thought he saw his brother's face.

Then the eyes flashed purple.

And Mark understood—cold, clear, absolute—that whatever had taken Jason wasn't finished.

Not with the town.

Not with the team.

Not with him.

CHAPTER 4: THE FIRST HAUNTING

Jason Rivers was buried on a clear morning that felt like it belonged to somebody else.

Lowridge showed up in uniforms—black coats, clean boots, Lions hoodies pulled over bowed heads. The town had learned how to do tragedy the same way it did Friday nights: together, on schedule, and with just enough polish that grief could pass as pride.

Mark stood between his parents at the cemetery gate, hands jammed into his jacket pockets. His mother clutched a wad of tissues like it was the only thing keeping her upright. His father stared straight ahead, jaw locked, as if he could will the day into behaving.

Beyond the gate, headstones lined up in neat rows that always reminded Mark of bleachers—quiet, waiting, permanent. Lions plaques flashed in the sun—brass lion heads with a purple flower worked into the border. Mark had walked past those plaques his whole life without noticing the detail that now snagged his attention hard:

One eye on every plaque was polished brighter than the rest.

Not an accident. Not random. A deliberate shine, as if the lion's stare was meant to catch you.

He swallowed and forced his gaze away.

The pastor spoke. Coach Whitman spoke. Mayor Halvorsen spoke. Words stacked on words: legacy, pride, brotherhood, community. Mark heard them as if from underwater. The sound that mattered came from the shovel when the first dirt hit the lid—dull and final.

Then a different sound threaded through it.

A soft crack.

Mark's eyes snapped down.

A purple shoot broke through fresh soil, fast enough to steal his breath. It unfurled a petal. Then another. A second bud rose beside it. A third.

Impossible. The grave had been filled minutes ago.

No one else reacted. People stared where they were supposed to stare. A flower blooming out of place was a detail you could ignore if you needed the world to stay ordinary. Lowridge had always been good at that—talking straight through the wrongness until the wrongness learned to sit still.

Alyssa's fingers hooked Mark's sleeve. Her voice was barely air. "You see that."

Mark didn't trust his voice. He nodded once.

Pecos stood a step behind them, face calm but eyes unfocused, like he was listening to something under the ground. "It's awake," he said quietly. "And it knows the name it just got."

Tommy hurried up from the crowd, face pale beneath the flush of cold. His ring—always on his finger, always something to fidget—was rolling between his thumb and forefinger so fast it looked like it might blur.

"That's… that's not normal, right?" Tommy tried to joke, but the words came out thin. "That's not seasonal."

Alyssa flipped the funeral program in her hand and tapped the lion-and-flower emblem. In the center of the purple bloom was a tiny red mark—a dot you'd miss unless you stared too long.

"That's the same symbol in the old archives," she said. "They call it the Scarlet Eye."

Mark's stomach tightened. "It's just a logo."

"It wasn't a logo first," Alyssa replied, and for once her sarcasm didn't soften the fear in her eyes. "Meet me at the library after school. I'm not saying this in front of half the town."

The mayor's speech rolled on. Mark watched him shift position—subtle, practiced—until his body blocked the view of the new purple buds pushing higher from Jason's grave.

That single movement told Mark more than any speech could.

The town saw. The town knew. The town covered.

Mark looked down at his knuckles—scraped from practice, still healing. He thought of the prologue story Alyssa had forced into his mind: blood plus petals = access. A conduit. A door.

He shoved his hands deeper into his pockets, as if hiding skin could hide consequence.

When the final "amen" was spoken and the crowd began to drift away in solemn clusters, the purple flowers at Jason's grave continued their quiet work—blooming as if they'd been waiting for permission.

And Mark couldn't shake the certainty that the ground had been waiting a long time.

***

That night, Tommy went to the stadium.

He told himself it was for Jason—one more set of routes, one more lap, one more proof that the world still followed rules. The kind of logic that sounded solid in your head but crumbled the moment you stepped into the dark.

Fog sat low over the field, thin as breath. The scoreboard was black. The only light came from a single service lamp above the home tunnel, throwing the turf into a narrow strip of gray.

Tommy jogged the sideline, trying to work up sweat, trying to work down fear. His shoes hissed over damp grass. His lungs burned the clean, familiar way that usually meant safe. Usually meant real.

He was halfway through a shallow out when the air shifted.

Sweet.

Violets.

He stopped so suddenly his muscles protested. The scent wasn't coming from the concession stand or some kid's cologne. It was earthy, wrong, and threaded with a faint metallic edge that made his tongue taste like pennies.

Tommy turned toward the far fence.

Something moved across the field.

At first, his brain did the easiest thing and tried to name it normal—a player. Someone sneaking in to practice. A coach. A security guy.

Then the figure ran.

Not randomly. Not wandering.

A crisp route through empty space—three hard steps, a cut that snapped sharp as a knife, hips turning with perfect discipline. It was the kind of movement coaches replayed in film sessions because it was correct.

And that correctness was what made it wrong.

The figure reached the sideline and stopped—exactly on the mark—as if waiting for a pass that would never come.

Tommy's throat tightened. "Hey," he called, hating how small his voice sounded in that huge, open bowl of dark. "Field's closed."

The figure didn't react.

Tommy took a step closer.

The figure turned.

Old helmet. Chipped paint. Facemask too narrow—something out of a trophy-case photograph. And caught in the bars like dried weeds, purple petals clung and trembled in the fog.

Behind the facemask, two faint lights pulsed—purple with a pinprick of red at the center.

The Scarlet Eye.

The figure lifted one hand and flicked its wrist down.

Come here.

Tommy's lungs forgot how to work.

Then instinct—older than courage—kicked in.

He turned and ran.

He hit the gate hard enough to rattle the chain and tore into the street. When he finally dared to look back, the field was empty again.

Only the cemetery beyond the fence held that slow, breathing glow.

Tommy didn't go home.

He went straight to Mark's.

***

Mark was awake when Tommy knocked.

Not a polite knock. A frantic, keep-it-quiet knock—knuckles against siding, breathy whisper through the screen.

Mark slipped out the front door and met Tommy on the porch.

Tommy looked like he'd run through a nightmare and brought pieces of it back with him. "I saw one," he said. "On the field. A player. Not—" He swallowed. "Not alive."

Mark's stomach dropped. "Was it Jason?"

Tommy shook his head too fast. "Older. Like a trophy photo. And the petals—" His hand twitched toward his ring like he needed to touch something familiar. "It wanted me to go to it."

Mark stared past Tommy into the street. Fog lay low between the houses like a spill. The night felt too quiet, like the world had leaned in to listen.

"Go home," Mark said. "Lock your door. If it calls you—don't answer."

Tommy started to argue, then stopped. Something in Mark's face shut him down. He nodded once and backed off the porch.

The moment Tommy vanished into the dark, Mark felt it.

Pressure behind his eyes.

A low hum under the quiet, as if the ground itself had started to vibrate.

A cold wind slid down the street. Fog pooled at the curb as if it had been waiting.

The air smelled of violets.

Mark's chest tightened. He looked down the empty road toward the streetlight at the corner.

A figure stood beneath it.

Jason.

Not solid. Not right. A thin outline of his brother wearing the shape of him like a costume. The edges of him wavered, as if the night couldn't decide what to do with a dead boy who refused to stay dead.

Mark stepped off the porch before he knew he was moving.

"Jason," he said.

The figure smiled. It was Jason's smile and it was empty.

"Come on," the figure said. The voice was close—too close—like it was inside Mark's skull. "You don't have to be alone. The field is waiting. The stones are waiting. I can show you."

Mark took one involuntary step and felt the ground answer—hum rising, pressure tightening. A pull toward the cemetery, toward the grid of headstones that suddenly existed in his mind like coordinates. Open spaces waiting to be filled.

He forced his shoes to stop moving.

"No," Mark said.

The figure's eyes pulsed purple. The pinprick of red at the center flashed.

"Lowridge needs you," it whispered.

The easiest lie in the world rose up—Yes. Okay. I'll do it. The kind of surrender a town trained into you without ever calling it training.

Mark swallowed it.

He said the truth instead.

"I wanted out," Mark said, voice shaking. "I wanted to leave this town and never hear a crowd chant my name again. I was scared to say it because I didn't want to disappoint everybody. And I'm not trading my brother for a trophy."

The smile cracked.

For a heartbeat, the figure flickered—Jason's real face beneath the wrong light, eyes wide with fear instead of glow.

"Run," Jason breathed.

Then the hum surged again, hungry.

"Champions belong to the roots," the thing in Jason's mouth said.

Mark felt the pull return—stronger, impatient. His body leaned without permission.

A door opened behind him.

His mother's voice carried into the night, small and broken. "Mark?"

The sound cut through the pressure like a blade.

Mark jerked back.

The figure beneath the streetlight shuddered. Petals lifted around it, then fell like damp confetti.

Jason's outline thinned.

"Run," a voice that sounded like his brother whispered again.

And then the streetlight flickered, and he was gone.

A single purple petal lay on the sidewalk, damp as fresh soil.

Mark stared at it until his eyes burned—then picked it up with two fingers and carried it inside like it was both proof and poison.

***

The next day, Mark went to the hospital to collect Jason's belongings.

The building smelled the same as it had the night Jason died—bleach and stale coffee and too much recycled air. The receptionist's sympathy was automatic, polished by small-town repetition.

A nurse returned with a clear plastic bag: Jason's wallet, his phone, the bracelet Mark's mother had made him wear "for luck," and a crumpled mouthguard wrapped in gauze.

"His room's open," the nurse said softly. "If you need a minute."

Mark nodded because words were still unreliable.

The room looked smaller in daylight. The bed was stripped. The monitors were gone. Only the indentation on the pillow hinted someone had rested a head there.

Mark set the bag on the chair and stood beside the bed.

He didn't know what he expected to feel—closure, anger, nothing.

Instead, his gaze caught on the bed rail.

Someone had carved into the plastic: an oval shape with a slash through it, like an eye half-blinded. At the center was a puncture mark—dark, stained, embedded.

Scarlet.

Mark ran his thumb over the groove. The edges were rough, cut by something sharp. The scarlet dot didn't smear. Didn't lift. It looked like it had been pressed in hard enough to become part of the rail.

His phone buzzed.

ALYSSA: Did you go back yet?

Mark stared at the message, then at the carved eye. He raised the phone and snapped a photo.

On-screen, the symbol looked unnervingly crisp—oval, slash, red center. A signature.

A faint hum threaded through the air, almost too soft to notice, and Mark's gaze drifted to the bed's edge.

At the seam where the mattress met the frame, a tiny purple bud had pushed through—pinhead small, impossibly vivid.

Mark backed away.

He didn't look back until he was outside.

Alyssa was waiting in the lot like she'd been there for an hour—arms folded, hoodie pulled tight, eyes sharp despite the sun.

"You look like you didn't sleep," she said.

"I didn't," Mark answered.

He showed her the photo.

Alyssa leaned in, and for the first time since the funeral, fear broke through her controlled expression. "That's it," she whispered. "That's the seal."

Mark's voice came out rough. "The Scarlet Eye."

Alyssa nodded once. "My grandfather wrote about it, but I found older mentions too. Early newspapers. Booster minutes. Founding records." She glanced past Mark toward the line of trees beyond the highway, toward where the cemetery sat behind the stadium. "The first time the Scarlet Eye shows up is late 1800s—before the Lions were a team. Before football mattered."

Mark's stomach dropped.

"So this isn't about the game," he said.

"It's about the land," Alyssa replied. "And it's been collecting people longer than anyone's willing to admit."

Mark looked back at the hospital doors, thinking of the purple bud in the bed seam, the scarlet eye carved into plastic, the way Jason's grave had bloomed like it had been waiting.

And for the first time, the thought landed with cold certainty:

Jason hadn't been the beginning.

He'd been the next piece.

CHAPTER 5: THE PATTERN REVEALS

Mark didn't sleep.

He lay on top of his blankets, fully dressed, phone face-down on his chest like it might vibrate with an answer he'd missed. Outside his window, Lowridge held its breath the way it always did on the nights it pretended were normal. A truck passed on Main, tires hissing on damp pavement. Somewhere a dog barked once, then thought better of it.

When Mark closed his eyes, he saw the cemetery grid again—stones like coordinates, purple rings like lit matches. He saw Eli Carter's empty smile as he disappeared between headstones. He saw his brother's face in fog, and then he didn't. His mind kept trying to pull Jason into the shape of a solution, and every time it did, something in him recoiled.

At 4:17 a.m., he got up and went into the kitchen.

His mom was already there.

She stood in a pool of refrigerator light, robe tied tight, hair pinned back the way she wore it on game days. A coffee mug sat untouched on the counter. She wasn't drinking; she was holding it, knuckles white, like warmth was the only thing keeping her tethered.

"You're up early," she said.

Mark stopped. In the half-dark, her eyes looked older than they should have.

"Couldn't sleep," he replied. It came out careful. Thoughtful. Restrained. The way he spoke when the truth was too large to fit between words.

She studied him for a long moment. "Homecoming week does that."

He nodded, because nodding was safer than speaking.

She shifted the mug from one hand to the other. "You were at the field late."

It wasn't a question.

Mark's throat tightened. "Coach ran us long."

Her gaze flicked to his forearm, to the faint scratches he hadn't bothered to cover. Then back to his face. She didn't ask about the scratches. She didn't ask about the cemetery. In Lowridge, people had an instinct for what topics were live wires.

"Eat something," she said, and opened the cabinet like this was just another Thursday.

Mark watched her for a second and felt something cold settle behind his ribs. Not fear. Not exactly. Something like recognition.

Lowridge didn't just love football. It used football as an excuse to practice denial.

At school, the halls were already dressed for Homecoming—purple streamers, gold balloons, posters taped crookedly to lockers with slogans that were equal parts cheer and command.

GLORY WEEK.
DEFEND THE PRIDE.
BRING IT HOME.

Someone had drawn a purple flower around the lion logo on every sign, the petals exaggerated into little tongues.

Mark moved through it like he was underwater.

Tommy found him at his locker, already talking before he fully arrived, like the words were what kept him upright.

"Okay, hear me out," Tommy said, tapping his ring against his teeth once, twice, then sliding it off and spinning it on his finger. "If we survive Homecoming, we should demand hazard pay. Like, actual money. Or at least free pizza for life. I'm thinking a contract."

Mark stared at him.

Tommy's grin faltered. "I'm kidding," he added quickly. "Mostly."

Mark didn't answer. He could feel the weight of his own silence, the way it made Tommy fill the space harder.

"You're doing that thing," Tommy said. "The staring. Like you're about to tell me my dog died."

"I don't have a dog," Mark said.

"Exactly. That's how bad it is."

Tommy's laugh came out too loud. He tapped his ring again, faster. The motion wasn't a habit anymore. It was a metronome for panic.

Alyssa slid up on Mark's other side with a stack of folders under her arm and the kind of calm that always looked like sarcasm from a distance.

"Congratulations," she said. "You two are officially the least subtle people I know."

Tommy's eyes narrowed. "Good morning to you too, sunshine."

Alyssa's mouth twitched. "I only save sunshine for people who believe me before the dead start walking."

Mark's stomach dropped at the word dead, even though she said it like a joke. Alyssa didn't scare easily. When she joked, it was usually because she'd already decided how serious things were.

Pecos approached from down the hall, backpack slung over one shoulder, expression neutral. He walked like he was trying not to wake the floor.

"You feel it," Mark said before he could stop himself.

Pecos's eyes flicked to him. "Yeah."

Tommy's ring stopped spinning. "Feel what?"

"The air," Pecos said, calm as a weather report. "It's… heavier. Like it's waiting."

Alyssa's gaze sharpened. "It's Homecoming week. The town's basically vibrating."

"No," Pecos said softly. "Not like that."

Alyssa adjusted the folders under her arm. "Library after school. Same table. I pulled obituaries and game programs going back to the twenties. Mark, bring whatever you can find on Eli Carter. Tommy—try not to get possessed during second period."

Tommy held up his hands. "I will do my best to remain unclaimed by demonic flora. No promises."

Mark's throat tightened. He could taste that earthy sweetness again, faint, as if someone had opened a jar of violets somewhere out of sight.

By lunch, the whole school had heard what happened at last night's game.

Not the real story. The version that fit inside the town's denial.

Eli Carter had "collapsed" during the second quarter. Heat exhaustion, someone said, even though it was fifty degrees. A seizure, someone else whispered. The ambulance had taken him, the game had stalled, and then—somehow—the Lions had rallied anyway. The announcer had called it resilience. The booster club had posted a photo with a caption about community strength.

Eli's name floated through the halls alongside purple ribbons already pinned to backpacks—pre-printed grief.

A story was forming before anyone asked questions.

After the final bell, the four of them walked to the library together.

Lowridge Public Library sat on the edge of downtown like a polite old woman who'd watched too much and learned to keep quiet. Ivy crawled up its stone walls. The steps creaked in a way that felt like judgment. Inside, the air was cool and smelled of paper, dust, and the lemony cleaner someone used to pretend history wasn't rotting.

Alyssa had already claimed a back table. Newspapers were spread out like evidence. Old yearbooks lay open beside them, faces frozen in sepia and early color. She'd brought a legal pad and a handful of colored pens, because if she could categorize it, she could control it.

Mark sat down. Tommy dropped into the chair opposite and immediately started flipping through a yearbook like it was a menu.

Pecos didn't sit. He hovered at the end of the table with his hands in his pockets, eyes unfocused, like he was listening to a frequency only he could hear.

Alyssa slid a clipping across to Mark. "Read that."

It was an obituary from 1936. A senior halfback named Calvin Dorsey. "Sudden illness." Beloved son. Promising future. Lions captain.

Another from 1959. A linebacker, "tragic hunting accident."

Another from 1978. A quarterback, "car crash on County Road 12." No skid marks.

Mark's jaw tightened.

Alyssa tapped her pen on the paper. "Now look at the dates."

Mark scanned. November. October. Late October. Early November. Always near playoffs. Always near the weeks the town cared most.

Tommy frowned, finally quiet. "That's… a lot."

"Keep going," Alyssa said.

She handed them a program from 1999, glossy and patriotic, the kind of thing boosters framed. On the back, there was a list of "Fallen Lions"—names of players who had died young, honored before kickoff. Purple flowers printed in the corners.

The list ended abruptly at 2003.

"Why does it stop?" Mark asked.

Alyssa's eyes flashed. "Because it got too long. Or because someone told them to stop printing it."

Tommy flipped the program over and stared at the purple flower logo. "We put this on everything."

"That's the point," Alyssa said. "It's a symbol. You make it decorative, nobody asks what it means."

She pulled a folder closer and opened it, revealing photocopies of death certificates. "I requested these last year for a school project. My teacher thought it was 'morbid.'"

Tommy snorted. "Lowridge loves morbid. They just don't like honest."

Alyssa's mouth twitched. "Exactly."

She pointed to a column she'd highlighted. "Cause of death is always vague. Accident. Illness. 'Undetermined.' But look at the notes section."

Mark leaned in.

Several had the same phrase, written in different hands, across different decades:

NO FOUL PLAY SUSPECTED.
CASE CLOSED PER COUNCIL RECOMMENDATION.

Mark's skin went cold. "Council."

Pecos spoke without looking up. "My grandmother used to say the council didn't run the town. It ran what the town refused to see."

Tommy blinked. "There's a council? Like—what, the PTA?"

Alyssa gave him a look. "Not that council."

Mark's eyes dropped back to the papers. He found his brother's name in a stack Alyssa hadn't highlighted yet.

JASON RIVERS.
Car accident.
No skid marks.

Under "notes," the same phrase.

Per council recommendation.

Mark's throat closed. His silence wasn't a choice anymore. It was the only thing keeping him from shattering in public.

Alyssa's voice softened, just barely. "I'm sorry."

Mark nodded once. He didn't trust his voice.

Tommy reached across the table and—awkwardly, like he didn't know where to put his hands—patted Mark's wrist. His ring clicked against Mark's skin.

"Okay," Tommy said, trying for light, failing. "So. We've got a creepy secret committee that signs off on mystery deaths, and we've got dead players that… what? Turn into flowers?"

"Not the players," Alyssa said. "The land. The flowers are… conduits."

Pecos finally sat, slow and careful, like the chair might hurt him. "Network," he said.

Alyssa looked at him. "What?"

Pecos stared at the table like he was seeing through it. "Last night, when we were at the cemetery… it felt like lines. Like something connecting everything. Cemetery to field. Field to town. Like veins."

Mark swallowed. The image snapped into place with the way he'd seen the headstones as a grid.

Alyssa leaned forward, pen poised. "Tell me what you felt."

Pecos inhaled. When he spoke, it wasn't dramatic. It was worse because it sounded like something simple and inevitable.

"I didn't see with my eyes," he said. "I felt it. Like… the flowers aren't just on graves. They're nodes. And the roots under them run out like wires."

Tommy's mouth opened, then closed. He spun his ring again, slower. "Wires. Great. We're living on a haunted extension cord."

Alyssa didn't smile. "If it's a network, then there's a purpose."

Mark stared at the list of names again—champions, captains, stars. The best. The ones the town lifted up.

"What if it's feeding," Mark said quietly.

Alyssa's eyes met his. "That's what I think."

Pecos nodded once. "It feeds on… energy. Emotion. Want. Fear."

Alyssa pushed another document across. "Look at this."

It was a hand-written ledger, copied from an old church record. Under "donations," the same family names appeared over and over. Rivers. Dawson. Reed. Shaw. Turner. The founders. And beside several entries, in small script:

FOR THE FIELD.
FOR THE SOIL.

Mark's stomach turned. He remembered his dad making him kneel on the fifty-yard line when he was eight, placing a hand on the grass like it was sacred.

Respect the field, his dad had said. It gives you everything.

Mark had believed him.

Alyssa drew a line down her legal pad. "Pattern: deaths spike when the team is winning. The council covers it. The same families keep donating. And the flowers show up where the dead are buried."

Tommy leaned back, staring at the ceiling like it might offer an exit. "So what do we do? Call the police? 'Hi, yes, I'd like to report botanical possession and a conspiracy.'"

Alyssa's smile was sharp. "We gather proof. We figure out the rule. And we stop being predictable."

Mark thought of Eli, walking into fog between stones like someone had turned his muscles into a puppet.

"We need to know where else the flowers are," Mark said.

Alyssa nodded. "Cemetery. And…"

"The field," Pecos said.

Tommy's eyes widened. "Wait. You're saying they're on the field? Like… where we practice?"

Mark remembered the tiny buds he'd seen threaded through turf in the stadium lights.

"Yes," he said. "Near the sideline. Like they're… migrating."

Alyssa's pen scratched across paper. "Then we go there. Tonight."

They left the library just before dusk.

Downtown Lowridge looked like a brochure—string lights over the coffee shop patio, banners about the "Innovation Corridor," a billboard down the highway promising a new satellite tech park and housing developments with names meant to sound like nature: Fox Hollow Estates. Cedar Ridge Commons.

Growth, the mayor called it. Progress.

Old rot, Mark thought, watching a purple flower decal on a campaign sign flap in the wind.

They cut behind the school to avoid Main. The football complex loomed ahead, stadium lights already warming up for practice. Fog clung low over the practice field like a thing that didn't trust the sun.

As they approached, Mark's skin prickled. Not with cold.

With recognition.

Pecos slowed, eyes unfocused again. Alyssa's grip tightened on her flashlight. Tommy spun his ring so hard it slipped, then caught it with a cough.

"Okay," Tommy said, forcing cheer. "If the grass starts humming, I'm transferring."

"It already is," Pecos said.

Mark heard it then — a faint vibration under the normal sounds of distant whistles and the thud of a ball. Not a sound exactly. A pressure. Like standing too close to a subwoofer.

They skirted the chain-link fence and slipped through an unlocked maintenance gate. The practice field was empty, but the stadium beyond it glowed, lights spilling through fog in wide, pale beams.

Mark walked out onto the grass.

The turf felt damp. Softer than it should have.

Alyssa crouched by the sideline, sweeping her flashlight low.

"There," she said.

Tiny purple buds, threaded through the grass like stitches. Not many. Not enough for anyone to notice unless they were looking. But they were there — stubborn and wrong — pushing up through soil that should have been too compact for anything delicate.

Mark crouched beside her. The buds shivered when his shadow passed over them, as if reacting to him specifically.

He didn't touch them.

"Blood and petals," Alyssa murmured. "That's what my grandfather warned about. That's what the journal kept circling like it didn't want to say it straight."

She glanced at Pecos. Pecos's face had gone pale.

Pecos stepped closer, then stopped like he'd hit an invisible line. "It's stronger here."

Tommy stood back on the track, arms crossed tight. "Stronger how?"

Pecos didn't answer right away. His breathing had changed—shallower, careful, like he was trying not to inhale too deep.

"Like standing near a hornet's nest," he said finally. "You don't see them until you move wrong."

Mark looked up, eyes scanning the stadium through fog.

That's when he saw them.

At first, he thought it was a trick of the light—shapes in the bleachers, shadows between rows. But then one of the shapes moved, slow and deliberate, and Mark's heartbeat stuttered.

A player stood in the middle section of the stands.

Not a living player. Not a kid in a hoodie. This figure wore an old uniform, shoulder pads bulkier, facemask bars thicker. Purple petals clung to the helmet, caught in the edges like dried seaweed. The figure's posture was too still, too patient.

Mark blinked.

Another figure stood near the end zone, close to the uprights. Taller. Thinner. Jersey number faint under grime. The outline shimmered in the fog like heat haze.

A third shape lingered near the far sideline, half-hidden behind the equipment shed—only the glint of a facemask visible, and the faint pulse of purple where eyes should be.

Alyssa sucked in a breath. "Tell me you see that."

Mark didn't trust his voice, so he nodded.

Tommy's laugh came out brittle. "Cool. Great. Fantastic. We have a fan club."

Pecos didn't joke. He stared at the field like he was seeing the roots under it.

"They're not here for us," Pecos said.

Alyssa's eyebrows lifted. "Then who?"

Pecos's eyes flicked to Tommy. Then to Mark. Then back to the buds in the grass.

"They're here for champions," he said quietly. "For the ones the town feeds."

Mark's stomach dropped.

The figure in the stands moved.

It didn't walk down the steps. It simply… appeared closer, as if the fog had folded space. One second it was halfway up the bleachers. The next it was at the bottom row, hands on the railing, head tilted.

Tommy took an involuntary step back. His ring slipped from his fingers and clinked onto the track.

"Dang it—"

He bent to grab it.

His knuckle scraped against something sharp along the track edge—an old staple, a torn metal strip, Mark didn't know. Tommy hissed, then froze.

A bead of blood swelled bright on his skin.

The air snapped cold.

Alyssa's flashlight beam flickered.

Tommy stared at his knuckle like it wasn't his.

Mark's body recognized the shift before his brain did. The pressure behind his eyes sharpened. The hum under the turf deepened.

Tommy lifted his head slowly.

His eyes were wrong.

Not glowing. Not rolled back. Just… unfocused. Like he was looking at something a foot behind Mark's shoulder and listening to instructions through it.

"Tommy," Mark said.

Tommy didn't respond.

Alyssa stood up fast. "Tommy, look at me."

Tommy's mouth moved. No sound came out.

The figure from the bleachers was on the field now, standing just beyond the painted sideline.

It lifted one hand.

It wasn't threatening. It was inviting.

Tommy stepped onto the grass.

The buds near his cleat brightened, a soft purple pulse like an inhale.

Alyssa grabbed Tommy's arm.

Tommy didn't react. He simply turned his head toward the stadium, toward the fog, toward the cemetery beyond the far fence.

He took another step, pulling Alyssa with him like she weighed nothing.

Mark moved. Instinct. He stepped in front of Tommy and blocked his path.

Tommy walked into him.

Mark felt the impact—solid shoulder, familiar strength—and then something colder slid through the contact, like a draft under a door.

Tommy's lips parted.

"Run," he whispered.

It wasn't Tommy's voice.

It was too flat, too patient—like someone mimicking speech from memory.

Alyssa's face went pale. "Tommy—"

Tommy's eyes flicked to hers, and for a fraction of a second, Mark saw him inside himself, trapped, aware. Panic flashed. Then it smothered under that steady hum.

Tommy's hand lifted—moving toward Mark's forearm, toward the thin scratches, toward the places skin wasn't sealed.

Mark jerked back.

The figure in the fog took a step closer. The air filled with that sweet violet tang rimmed with metal.

Pecos moved.

He stepped in and placed both hands on Tommy's shoulders.

"Tommy," Pecos said softly. "This isn't you."

Tommy's body stiffened.

Pecos pressed his forehead to Tommy's helmet, eyes shut tight like a prayer.

Alyssa's voice shook. "What are you doing?"

"Listening," Pecos murmured.

The hum under the turf surged.

Mark's vision smeared for a fraction of a second. The white yard lines dragged like wet paint. In the smear, he saw roots under the grass, black and slick, threaded with purple light like veins. He saw the buds flaring, responding to Tommy's heartbeat, to the bead of blood on his knuckle.

The figure in the fog lifted its hand again.

Tommy's body leaned forward, pulled.

Pecos tightened his grip, knuckles white. His face contorted like he'd been punched from the inside.

"Tommy," Pecos said, voice strained but steady. "Tell the truth."

Alyssa blinked. "What?"

Pecos's eyes snapped open, fixed on Tommy's unfocused stare. "Tell it. Out loud."

Tommy's chest heaved. "I—" he choked.

The figure in the fog jerked, as if tugged by a line.

Tommy's eyes widened. For a second, the fog in them cleared enough for Mark to see his friend.

"I saw it," Tommy gasped.

Alyssa tightened her grip. "Saw what?"

Tommy's voice cracked, raw. "When I was little. Three, maybe four. Homecoming night. I woke up and my window was fogged and—" He swallowed hard, shaking. "—and there was a player in our yard. In full gear. Walking backward. Like he was rewinding. And he stopped and looked at me and… his face was flowers."

The words hit the air like a thrown rock.

The stadium lights flickered. Just once.

The figure in the fog recoiled—not fear. Irritation. Like a hand slapped away.

Tommy sucked in a breath, eyes watering. "I told my dad. He got mad. He said I was dreaming. He said… never say it again."

Alyssa's face tightened. "Tommy…"

Tommy's mouth twisted. "I tried to forget. I did forget. But my body didn't. It's been… there. Every year. I just joked because—because if I took it seriously, I'd never leave my house again."

As he spoke, the hum under the turf changed pitch—less command, more static.

Pecos shuddered. "Keep going," he whispered.

Tommy's hands clenched. "I don't want it," he said, louder. "Whatever this is, I don't want it. I'm not yours."

The buds in the grass dimmed, like a breath released.

Tommy's knees buckled.

Mark caught him and lowered him to the track. Tommy trembled like he'd run a hundred sprints.

The figure in the fog didn't vanish.

It leaned in, head tilted. Another figure stepped closer near the end zone. Another near the shed. They were patient. They were not leaving.

Pecos staggered back.

He held his hands up in front of him, staring like he didn't recognize them.

Alyssa's voice went tight. "Pecos?"

Pecos's breathing was shallow. "I… I pulled too hard."

Mark's stomach dropped. "What does that mean?"

Pecos turned his hands palm-up.

A bead of blood surfaced at the center of one palm.

Then another.

The beads didn't run. They sat there, round and bright.

And in the blood, something purple unfolded.

Tiny petals—no larger than pinheads—pushed up through Pecos's skin like a slow, obscene bloom.

Pecos's face went blank for a second, and then he dropped—hard—to his knees.

"It's in me," he said softly, like he was reading the sentence off his own skin.

Alyssa moved fast, snapping out of freeze. She yanked a small first-aid kit from her backpack and tore it open with shaking hands.

"Hold still," she said. "Don't touch anything. Don't—Pecos, don't close your hands."

Tommy coughed on the track, sucking in air. "Did I—" he began. "Did I just—"

"Not now," Alyssa snapped, then softened a fraction. "Later. You're here."

Tommy blinked, eyes clear now, panic arriving late. "I'm here? Pecos has flowers coming out of his hands."

"Stop talking," Alyssa said. "You'll make it worse."

Tommy clutched his ring like a talisman, knuckle still bleeding.

Mark looked up at the field.

The ghosts were closer.

Not in a way that obeyed distance. In a way that obeyed attention. The more Mark looked at them, the more solid they felt. Like witnessing was feeding them too.

One of them stood at the painted sideline with its hand extended, palm up, as if offering something.

The buds in the grass pulsed again, more insistent.

"Move," Pecos said, voice strained. "We need to move. The field is… open."

Mark helped Tommy up. Alyssa grabbed Pecos's elbow, guiding him to his feet without letting his bandaged hands brush anything.

They backed away from the grass toward the equipment shed.

As they crossed the track, Mark's gaze snagged on the far fence.

Beyond it, the cemetery lay under fog, purple glow faint but visible. The flowers there pulsed in time with the buds on the field. A network. A circuit.

Cemetery to field.

Field to town.

And them, standing in the middle like pieces someone had finally decided to move.

They made it to the equipment shed and slammed the door behind them. The interior smelled of rubber, sweat, and old mud. Alyssa braced the door with her shoulder.

Something scraped outside.

Metal dragged slow across chain-link.

"We need a plan," Alyssa said, voice tight.

Tommy laughed once, short. "My plan is to become a chess club guy."

Alyssa shot him a look. "You don't get to deflect right now."

Tommy's grin flickered and died. "I'm sorry," he said, quieter. "It's just... that thing in my head. It wasn't like voices. It was like... a playbook. Like I knew where to go and my body said yes."

Mark swallowed. "Like a route."

Tommy nodded, eyes haunted. "Like the best route I've ever run."

Pecos sagged against a shelf, face slick with sweat. The gauze around his hands was damp, purple staining through in small spots.

"I felt it," he whispered. "When I stopped Tommy, it... noticed me."

Alyssa's jaw clenched. "Because you interrupted."

Pecos nodded once. "Because I listened back."

Mark looked down at his own forearm, at the thin scratches.

"We can't bleed," he said, voice flat.

Tommy stared at him. "That's your takeaway?"

Mark didn't look away. "On the field. In the cemetery. If blood meets petals... it opens something."

Alyssa's eyes narrowed. "And the field soil—"

"—makes it easier," Pecos finished. "The field is... prepared. Like an altar you mow."

Outside, the scraping stopped.

Silence pressed in, thick and listening.

A knock came at the shed door.

Three slow taps.

Alyssa's beam shook. "Who is that?"

Another knock. Same rhythm.

Mark stepped forward and pressed his face close to the small window in the door.

An old man stood outside.

He held a flashlight that pointed down, not at the door. His face was lined in a way that didn't come from age alone.

Mark cracked the door open an inch, chain still latched. "What are you doing here?"

The old man's gaze lifted and pinned him with a tired, sharp look.

"Keeping you alive," the man said.

Alyssa stepped up beside Mark. "Who are you?"

"Harold," he said. "You don't know me because you weren't supposed to. But you're starting to see things you can't unsee."

Tommy swallowed. "Cool. Great. A random old guy knows we're haunted."

Harold didn't react. His eyes stayed on Mark. "This isn't the first time kids went digging. It's the first time they lasted past the first scare."

Alyssa's voice sharpened. "You knew."

"Everybody knew something," Harold said. "That's how Lowridge works. You keep your eyes on the lights and you don't ask why the fog comes in on schedule."

Mark's stomach twisted. "Eli Carter. Where is he?"

Harold's gaze flicked, just a fraction. "Gone where they take them."

Alyssa leaned forward until the chain stopped her. "Who is 'they'?"

"The ones wearing the dead like uniforms," Harold said. "The ones using the flowers like wires."

Pecos, barely above a whisper: "Network."

Harold nodded once. "Yeah."

Tommy's voice came out thin. "We'd like the version that helps us live."

Harold's eyes sharpened. "Then you need the book."

Alyssa froze. "What book?"

"Your grandfather knew," Harold said. "He didn't finish. He didn't want you in it. But you're in it anyway."

Alyssa's fingers tightened. "The journal?"

"Not the journal," Harold said. "The grimoire."

"Where?" Alyssa demanded.

Harold glanced toward the field, as if expecting the fog to decide it was done waiting.

"Not here," he said. "Not out loud. You've got ears under the grass."

Harold's voice went colder. "Find the grimoire before Homecoming. Before the festival. Before the fog decides it wants a parade."

Alyssa's voice shook with anger. "You're telling us this now? After people have died?"

"People have been dying for a hundred years," Harold said.

He leaned in, close enough for Mark to smell peppermint and cigarette smoke. "And one more thing," he said, quiet.

Mark didn't blink.

"If the flowers start blooming in you," Harold said, eyes flicking to Pecos's bandages, "the land will speak through you. It'll try to make you its mouth. Don't let it."

Pecos swallowed. "How?"

"By holding on to what's true," Harold said.

Alyssa's eyes narrowed. "Confession."

Harold nodded once. "Truth burns it. Not forever. But long enough."

He stepped back and walked away into the fog.

Mark watched him go until his jacket dissolved into white.

When Harold vanished, the pressure in the shed eased, just a fraction.

Tommy let out a shaky breath. "Okay," he said. "So we're doing this."

Alyssa stared at the door. Her voice came out thin. "The grimoire."

Mark looked at Pecos, at the purple stains bleeding through gauze, at the tiny bulges under skin.

Pecos met his eyes—calm and terrified at once.

"It's starting," Pecos said.

Outside, the stadium lights flickered again, just once, like something blinking awake.

And somewhere beyond the fence, the cemetery flowers pulsed in the dark—patient, mesmerizing, hungry—waiting for the next drop of blood to open the line.

CHAPTER 6:
FRACTURED GROUND

Pecos's hands wouldn't stop shaking.

Mark kept both palms on the steering wheel, driving too fast for the empty road and not fast enough to outrun the cemetery in his rearview mirror. Fog still pooled in the low places behind them. A faint purple glow hung beyond the fence line like a secret the town had decided was normal.

Alyssa sat in the passenger seat with Pecos's wrists wrapped in her hoodie, hiding them from the dashboard light. Tommy was in the back, knee bouncing, his class ring off his finger and rolling between thumb and forefinger in the anxious loop he pretended was a habit.

"Tell me it's sap," Tommy said, trying for humor and landing on brittle. "Tell me you stuck your hands in a tree."

Pecos kept his voice calm, like he was reporting the weather. "It's not sap."

In Alyssa's flashlight beam, violet lines branched across his palms—too precise to be veins, too deliberate to be a rash. At the center of each palm, the skin looked slightly raised, as if something underneath was testing the surface.

Alyssa swallowed. "Does it hurt?"

Pecos's mouth twitched. "Like a nail being turned."

Mark's phone buzzed against the console—home, curfew, where are you —messages he couldn't answer without lying. Silence was his oldest defense. Tonight, it felt like surrender.

He turned onto River Road and the first view of Lowridge's new "growth corridor" rose ahead: neat LED streetlamps, fresh pavement, the clean angles of buildings that had appeared in the last five years. Data center. Drone parts. Offices with polished names. Progress with perfect lighting.

And still, fog.

"Harold wants to meet tomorrow," Alyssa said quietly. "After school. He told me at the gate."

Tommy's laugh caught. "The boiled-peanut guy? The church-steps guy? That Harold?"

"The same," Alyssa said.

Pecos leaned his head against the window, eyes shut. "It's not done," he murmured. "It heard us."

Mark didn't ask what that meant. Part of him already knew.

The next day, Lowridge behaved like Lowridge.

Hallways gleamed. Trophy cases shone. Eli Carter's name floated around school in the careful language of denial—medical episode, family privacy, don't make it into a thing. Mark kept moving, past Jason's framed jersey, past the photos that made grief look like heritage.

By afternoon, the field smelled like cut grass and rubber.

Practice started ordinary—routes, cadence, muscle memory—until the field answered back.

A dry crack split the turf near the numbers. It wasn't loud. It was wrong in a way Mark felt in his teeth.

The seam widened a fraction, and beneath the grass, darkness opened like a mouth. Threaded through it ran slick purple roots—veinlike, living, pressed against the underside of the earth as if the field had a second skin.

Routes, Mark thought, stomach dropping. A network under their feet.

Tommy jogged up beside him, breathing hard. His ring was back on, but he kept rubbing it like it could ground him. "Please tell me you see that."

Mark kept his voice low. "Don't point."

Pecos crossed the field before Mark could stop him. He halted at the crack, shoulders tight, eyes fixed on what was underneath.

The roots shifted.

A faint violet sweetness drifted up—floral and metallic, like beauty with teeth.

Pecos flinched. "Cemetery to field," he whispered. "Field to town."

Coach Whitman's whistle screamed. "Move it! Drill on the far end!"

A manager hurried in with a bucket of sand and a look that begged for a simple explanation.

Coach's jaw tightened. "No one says sinkhole," he snapped.

Mark stared at him. Coach didn't look away, but something in his expression felt practiced—like a man choosing a story the town could live with.

Coach stepped close, voice pitched for only Mark. "Rivers. Focus on the game. Let adults handle town business."

"Eli's missing," Mark said.

Coach's eyes didn't change. "Eli's family asked for privacy."

"That's not an answer."

"It's the one you're getting."

He turned and shouted the next drill, cutting the conversation like it had never happened.

Alyssa appeared at the gate as if she'd been summoned by Mark's anger. Her hair was wind-tangled, her eyes bright with that sharp, controlled energy she got when she'd found a thread worth pulling.

"Mark," she called, and he jogged over.

She handed him a folded printout—an old scanned list on town letterhead, filed under something bland like maintenance. Names. Dates. Football positions. Beside certain entries: a small circle with a dot at its center.

A scarlet eye.

Mark's stomach turned when he found Jason's name.

"This was in the historical society catalog," Alyssa said. "Someone's been cleaning records, but they missed this. Deaths cluster around championship seasons. Not every year. Not random."

Tommy leaned in, squinting. "That's… messed up."

"Pattern," Alyssa said, and the word sounded like a verdict.

At the edge of the field, a figure waited by the fence.

Harold Baines stood there in his faded jacket, hands in his pockets, looking less like an old man and more like a warning that had learned how to walk.

When the last players cleared out, Harold gestured once with his chin. "Walk."

They followed him off the lot toward the church hill. The banner out front advertised the Hollow's Eve Festival, purple flowers printed along the corners like cheerful lies.

Harold tapped the flower graphic with one knuckle. "Proud leash," he said.

Alyssa didn't waste time. "You said the flower is a door."

Harold's gaze flicked to Mark's hands, to any sign of injury. "Blood and petals," he said. "That's the lock. You bleed on soil that's been fed and it hears you. Finds a way in."

"Fed," Mark echoed.

"The founders started with crops," Harold said. "Then factories. Then they wanted the town to be something bigger—progress, legacy, a place people moved to. But the land didn't give for free. So they listened when a man came offering a shortcut."

"The man in the red cloak," Alyssa said.

Harold's head snapped toward her. "You've read the right pages."

"It's in my grandfather's journal," she said. "And in old notes hidden in 'civic' files."

Harold's mouth tightened. "It wasn't civic. It was survival. And it became habit."

Tommy's voice came out rough. "So the pact is real."

Harold met his gaze, steady. "Real enough to keep this town shining while it rots."

Pecos shifted, breath shallow. "It's in me," he murmured.

Harold's eyes softened by a fraction, then hardened again. "Your family used to keep certain duties. Before the council got comfortable." He nodded toward town below. "They meet when the ground starts talking too loud."

Alyssa leaned in. "They're meeting tonight."

Harold didn't deny it. "They'll decide what lie to feed everyone. Meanwhile, the book that explains the bargain sits in a case they call 'preservation.'"

Mark's pulse thudded. "The grimoire."

Harold nodded once. "Historical society basement. Locked. Restricted. Sanitized." He looked at Mark as if measuring him against something older than football. "And you don't have time to ask permission."

"Why me?" Mark asked, hating how small the question sounded.

Harold's answer came flat. "Because you're what this town loves most. A Rivers boy in a Lions jersey. Easy story. Easy offering."

Pecos flinched hard, like a cable had snapped inside him. He tugged his sleeves back before anyone could stop him.

His palms were worse. The violet branching had darkened, and at the center of each palm, a tiny closed bud had formed—tight as a fist.

Alyssa sucked in a breath. "Pecos—"

Harold's voice sharpened. "Don't cut it. Don't pick at it. You'll open the door wider."

Pecos's eyes found Mark's. "It's talking," he whispered. "And it says it's owed a champion."

The air felt heavier. The church banner fluttered once, a bright advertisement against a sky that suddenly looked too pale.

Alyssa's voice went hard. "Tell it no."

"It doesn't hear no like we mean it," Pecos said. His calm cracked for a heartbeat. "It hears what we hide. It hears your guilt."

Mark's first instinct was silence. Then he thought of Eli—aware, trapped —and he felt something inside him refuse.

"My family knew something," Mark said, the words scraping out. "Not the whole thing. But enough. And I kept pretending it was just grief, just tradition."

Pecos exhaled like he'd been holding his breath underwater. "That helps," he whispered. "Truth pushes back. For a second."

Harold nodded, grim approval. "Honesty breaks the conduit. Temporarily."

Alyssa lifted her chin. "Then we don't wait. Tonight we go down there."

Tommy's ring flashed as he shoved it back onto his finger like armor. "Great," he said, trying for brave. "Illegal research in a haunted basement."

Harold leaned in, voice low. "No bare skin. No blood. And if the air tastes sweet—don't breathe deep."

Mark looked toward town, toward the stadium beyond it, toward the cemetery behind that fence where purple light waited like a heartbeat.

Homecoming tomorrow. Hollow's Eve right after. The town lining up its celebration like it wasn't also setting a table.

Mark nodded once. "Tonight."

And in that single word, he felt the smallest thing he'd felt in years—choice—push back against Lowridge's hunger.

They didn't go home right away.

Alyssa insisted they watch the town do what it always did when the ground whispered too loud: gather the right people in a room, speak in careful half-sentences, and call it leadership.

Town hall sat on Main Street between a boutique coffee place and a bank that still had the old marble columns from when Lowridge pretended it was grand. New banners hung from the streetlamps—HOLLOW'S EVE FESTIVAL—each one framed with the same purple flower graphic, bright and harmless.

The parking lot was already filling when Mark pulled in and killed the headlights two streets over. He and Alyssa watched from behind the dark shape of the hardware store sign. Tommy hovered with his hands shoved in his jacket pockets, trying not to look like he belonged to the story he was afraid of. Pecos sat on the curb, hood up, breathing through his nose like he could filter the air.

Through the glass doors of town hall, Mark saw familiar faces: Mayor Harlan in a pressed suit, the booster club president with his perfect hair, Coach Whitman in a windbreaker, the church deacon, a man from the new tech park with a badge clipped to his belt. Different titles, same posture. Authority arranged like a formation.

Alyssa's voice was flat. "They don't even hide it."

Tommy managed a shaky grin. "Maybe they're just planning the parade."

Mark didn't answer. His eyes stayed on Coach.

The doors opened and closed in short bursts as more people entered. A piece of conversation slipped out on warm air—thin, casual, like nothing important.

"…structural issue…"

"…keep it quiet…"

"…homecoming cannot be disrupted…"

A second later, a man with a clipboard stepped out to take a call. Mark recognized him: Mr. Lasky, the city engineer, the one who always spoke at council meetings about "infrastructure resilience" like it was prayer.

He didn't look like a man thinking about road repairs. He looked like a man calculating casualties.

"Sinkhole?" the man on the phone said, voice sharp.

Lasky's answer came quick. "No. We are not using that word."

Mark's stomach tightened.

The door shut again.

"See?" Alyssa whispered. "Same phrasing as Coach."

Tommy's laughter came out too small. "So they have a script."

A woman in a neat blazer stepped into view behind the glass—someone Mark had seen at school board meetings. She held a folder with the Lions logo stamped on the corner, as if football paperwork belonged in town government. She said something to the mayor, and the mayor nodded with the steady confidence of a man used to being believed.

Pecos spoke without looking up. "They're feeding it."

Mark turned. "What?"

Pecos's eyes were distant, unfocused. "The meeting. The lies. The calm. It likes… obedience. It likes when people agree the story is true. It makes the door easier to open."

A cold itch crawled up Mark's spine. "And Eli?"

Pecos swallowed. "They're… shaping what people remember."

Mark looked back at the doors. For a heartbeat he imagined Eli's mother sitting inside, hands clenched, being told which version of her son she was allowed to mourn.

The doors cracked open again, and this time Mark caught a slice of a voice he knew too well—Coach Whitman, low and urgent.

"…Carter family understands the narrative…"

Mark's jaw locked.

Alyssa's fingers tightened around the strap of her backpack. "They already decided what happened to him," she whispered. "Before anyone even asked."

Tommy's ring flashed as he twisted it. "Isn't that… illegal?"

Alyssa's glance cut to him. "Everything about this is illegal. It's just been legalized by tradition."

The doors shut. The room swallowed its own truth.

Mark exhaled slow, trying to keep his hands from shaking. He wanted to march in there. He wanted to grab the microphone they used for public comments and say the words no one in this town ever said: You're lying.

But Harold's warning burned in his mind—don't do this in daylight, don't do it where the town can see you pushing back, don't give the hunger a clean excuse.

Alyssa leaned closer, voice a blade. "They can't keep the book buried forever. Not if we take it."

Tommy swallowed. "Tonight."

Pecos's head tilted as if listening to a distant rhythm. "It's counting," he murmured. "Like a cadence. Like it's lining up."

Mark didn't want to ask, but he did anyway. "For what?"

Pecos's gaze lifted, and for a second Mark saw fear beneath the calm. "Tomorrow night. Homecoming. The fog. The lights. It thinks it's… time."

Mark's mouth went dry. He pictured the crack in the turf, the roots under the field like wires. He pictured Eli's body moving without permission. He pictured the town roaring, delighted, as if applause could drown out a scream.

"Then we don't wait for tomorrow," Alyssa said.

Mark looked at the glass doors of town hall one last time. Coach's silhouette moved behind them, a dark shape framed by fluorescent light.

The adults were handling town business.

They were handling it the way Lowridge always handled rot—by painting it purple and calling it heritage.

Mark turned away.

"Tonight," he said again, quieter now. "We go to the historical society. We get the truth before they decide it for us."

Later, in his room, Mark stared at the open drawer where Jason's old gear still lived—an extra pair of receiver gloves, a mouthguard still in its plastic case, a folded playbook with notes in the margins. His mother called up once, asking if he'd eaten. He lied and said yes because lying was easier than explaining the taste of violet metal still stuck in his throat.

He pulled on the gloves and flexed his fingers. Not for football. For protection.

On his desk, his phone lit with another text from Alyssa—MEET 11:30. BACK DOOR. BRING FLASHLIGHT.

Tommy followed with a single line that made Mark's chest tighten in spite of everything.

I'M IN. NO ONE RUNS ALONE.

Mark set the phone face down and listened to the house settle, to the quiet that always felt like Lowridge holding its breath. Outside, the night air smelled clean—winter coming, woodsmoke from a neighbor's chimney—until, faint and impossible, a sweet violet note threaded through it.

Somewhere beyond town, the cemetery waited.

Mark closed his eyes and pictured the crack in the field, the roots beneath the turf like veins in a hand. He pictured the council smiling behind glass.

Then he opened his eyes, stood, and started packing what he could carry —flashlight, gloves, a small first-aid kit—like preparation could buy them a little time.

It wasn't courage. Not yet.

It was refusal.

CHAPTER 7: THE LAND'S VOICE

The Lowridge Historical Society sat one block off Main Street, brick and white trim, the kind of building people pointed to when they said the town had "roots." A purple flower was etched into the corner of the plaque by the back door—heritage turned into branding.

At 11:27 p.m., the fog made it look less like history and more like a warning.

It slid along the sidewalk in thin sheets, pooling beneath the streetlamps where the light turned it the color of old milk. Mark parked two streets over, killed the engine, and kept his gloves on. No bare skin. No fresh cuts. Harold's rules had lodged in his bones.

Across town, beyond the tidy storefronts, Lowridge's "growth corridor" glowed with new money—fresh asphalt, glass-front offices, and a row of brand-new streetlights that made the night look staged. People drove in for jobs, for subdivisions with hopeful names, for the promise that this place was becoming something bigger. Mark used to photograph those buildings for art class—clean lines, bright angles, the kind of images that looked like a future.

Tonight, all he could see was how the new lights didn't push back the fog. They just gave it more places to hide.

Alyssa checked her phone. "Two minutes."

Tommy leaned forward from the back seat. "If we get arrested, I am putting this on a college application."

Alyssa didn't blink. "If we get arrested, the town will call it an 'unfortunate incident' and nobody will remember your name."

Pecos sat hunched beside Tommy, hood up, breathing shallow. His sleeves were down, hiding his palms. Quiet didn't mean calm. It meant pressure—like he was holding something back with both hands.

They moved along storefront shadows. Mark kept counting his steps without meaning to—one-two, one-two—the same rhythm he used under center. Muscle memory from football, except tonight it felt like the town had trained his body a prayer.

Homecoming decorations hung everywhere—purple ribbons, Lions logos wrapped in petals—like Lowridge had stapled a smile over rot. Mark kept his eyes off the stadium lights glowing faintly beyond rooftops. Tonight wasn't about football.

The back door was where Alyssa promised. Painted steel. Old deadbolt. A camera above it.

Mark looked up at the lens and felt a bitter twist. He saw the world through lenses because he loved it. In Lowridge, even a camera felt like a way of counting who belonged.

Tommy stared at the camera. "That's new."

"It's been there," Alyssa said. "You just look at scoreboards."

She crouched and slid a pick into the lock.

Pecos whispered, "The air tastes sweet."

Mark's stomach tightened. "How sweet?"

"Flowers," Pecos said. "And metal."

The scent wasn't strong enough to make you gag. It was worse: subtle, confident—like it expected you to accept it as normal. Mark had smelled it at funerals, on hoodies, near the cemetery fence. He'd believed his mother when she said it was "just flowers," because believing her had been easier than fighting the town's denial.

Alyssa's fingers paused. "Pecos, stay with me."

He lifted his head. Under the hood, his eyes reflected the streetlamp wrong—too much shine, too much depth.

"It followed," he said, calm as a weather report.

Then the buds in his palms pulsed.

Violet light bled through the seams of his sleeves.

Tommy took a hard step back. "Nope."

Pecos raised his hands as if something else was lifting them. His sleeves slid up.

The buds opened—tight knots unfurling into living petals, deep purple, edges faintly luminous. Thin threadlike lines—almost like veins—ghosted beneath Pecos's skin around each bloom, faintly violet, branching toward his wrist as if searching for routes.

Pecos's breath hitched. Sweat beaded at his temple despite the cold. He tried to clench his hands into fists, but the flowers kept them open.

"It hurts," he said softly. "It wants to talk."

Alyssa's flashlight trembled. "Pecos, look at me. Your name is Pecos Morales. You're here."

For a heartbeat, Mark saw Pecos the way he usually was—quiet, observant, the kid people ignored until they needed him in the trenches. Pecos had told Mark once that being "local lore" didn't feel special. It felt like being watched.

Pecos's gaze slid past Alyssa, fixed on the fog.

His pupils widened until brown nearly vanished. Violet threaded the whites.

When he spoke, his voice layered—Pecos underneath, and something older over it, slightly out of tune.

"Lowridge."

The name sounded like possession.

Alyssa lifted her chin. "Who are you?"

"Your hunger," the layered voice said. "Your blessing. Your debt."

Tommy's fingers found his ring, yanking it on and off like a nervous habit turned into a lifeline. "We didn't ask for—whatever this is."

"You wore the colors," the voice replied. "You ran the routes. You fed the field with wanting."

Mark swallowed. "It's a game."

"Games are rituals," the voice said. "Crowds are choirs. Victory is fuel."

The layered voice wasn't angry. It sounded indifferent, like a disease describing how it spread. Under it, Mark could hear Pecos's own breathing, strained and fast—his body paying the price for being used as a mouth.

Alyssa's tone sharpened. "Tell us the rule. Tell us the cost."

Pecos's head tilted, listening to something beneath the brick, beneath the street. "Blood opens the door," the voice said. "Petals carry the signal. Soil holds the circuit."

Mark felt the words click into place with sick logic: Eli's scrape. The petal. The fog.

"The founders were starving," the voice continued. "They offered blood. I gave harvest. Then industry. Then progress. And always—glory."

The flowers on Pecos's wrists brightened at the word.

"And they build," the voice added, softer. "Each champion is a stitch. Each season is a tightening. I am learning your shape."

Mark's skin prickled. It wasn't only feeding. It was assembling—using devotion, using bodies, using the town's obsession like raw material.

"The payment stayed the same," the voice said. "Champions."

Mark's chest tightened. Jason's smile in a framed photograph. The way the town said his name like a hymn.

Alyssa's voice went tight. "What happens after they die."

"They root," the voice said. "They bloom. They ride."

"Ride?" Mark repeated.

"A body is a vehicle," the voice said. "A will is a gate. The flower is the conduit."

The fog shifted, and Mark's vision stuttered—like a lens snapping into focus. For a blink, he saw Lowridge from above: streets like lines on paper, the stadium a bright oval, the new tech buildings like clean white squares.

Around it all, a ring.

Purple points dotted the boundary—old graves outside the official cemetery, forgotten stones in overgrown lots, roadside markers swallowed by weeds. Each one a faint node of violet light. Roads that seemed to lead out of town bent subtly and returned, like a loop disguised as an exit. Cell towers stood inside the ring and beyond it there was only dark—no signal, no clean line out.

Mark sucked in air and tasted iron. "We can't leave."

"No," the voice said, almost kindly. "You are inside what you built."

Alyssa's eyes flashed. "The council knows."

"They have always known," the voice said. "They call it stewardship. They keep the story clean. They keep the sacrifices regular."

Pecos's shoulders jerked as if the word stewardship tasted bad. For an instant, Pecos's own tone threaded through, strained and brief: "It used to be… rules. Limits." Then the layered voice swallowed him again.

Mark felt heat rise behind his eyes. "Coach."

"Mayor," the voice answered. "Families. Boosters."

Tommy's voice cracked. "What do you want now."

Pecos's flowers opened wider, petals catching the streetlamp like wet velvet. "The champion who carries devotion," the voice said, and Pecos's head turned toward Mark with slow certainty. "The next Rivers."

Mark's pulse hammered. "I don't belong to you."

"Your blood repeats the ink," the voice said. "Your name is a promise."

Movement stirred in the fog at the mouth of the alley.

Silhouettes—helmets, shoulder pads—old uniforms that didn't match the current Lions set. One broke from the group and ran across the street.

A perfect route. Crisp cut. Hands up at the exact right moment for a pass no one threw.

Mark's stomach turned because it wasn't clumsy like a haunting. It was beautiful—athletic, efficient, exactly what every coach in Lowridge worshiped. The horror was in the perfection. In the fact that the runner didn't look like he was choosing any of it.

The runner stopped at an invisible boundary, turned, and ran it again. Empty eyes behind the facemask, faintly violet.

"They recruit," Alyssa whispered, the word landing like ice. "Ghost-riders."

"Proof," the voice said. "A reminder."

Mark's throat tightened when the runner's helmet shadow lifted for half a second and he saw a pale face beneath it.

Eli Carter. Washed-out. Distant. Like a photo left too long in sun.

Then the violet surged and the face went blank again.

Mark's hands clenched. "He didn't choose."

"He chose to play," the voice replied, indifferent. "Your town taught him to want what I offer."

Mark forced his gaze back to Pecos—back to the thing wearing his friend's mouth.

"My brother," Mark said.

The fog thinned, and a figure stepped into the streetlamp's reach.

Jason Rivers.

Translucent. Edges shimmering. His old jersey number faint as if it were printed on smoke. At first his face looked wrong—too smooth, too calm—like the curse was wearing him.

Mark's heart slammed. "Jason."

Jason had been Mark's first hero and his first warning. After the crash, people had told Mark the usual things: time heals, he's in a better place, make him proud. None of those phrases had ever fit. Seeing Jason now, trapped in fog and violet light, proved what Mark had feared in his quietest moments—Lowridge didn't let go.

Jason's eyes held violet light—until they didn't.

A stutter. A crack.

His jaw clenched hard. The violet faltered as if someone inside him shoved against glass. His lips moved.

No sound.

But Mark read it anyway.

Fight it.

Jason's hand lifted, trembling, fingers flexing like he was trying to pry free.

Then the fog surged. Violet swallowed him. The mask snapped back. Jason's expression emptied.

"He is mine," the voice hissed through Pecos.

Jason blurred backward, pulled by something unseen. For a fraction of a second the real Jason looked out—fear and apology in one glance—then he was gone.

Mark stood frozen, grief and anger braided tight.

Alyssa's voice was rough. "They're still aware."

Pecos bent forward, coughing hard, as if the spores had teeth. The flowers on his palms trembled.

The layered voice returned, low and intimate. "Choose."

The word hit Mark like cadence—ready, set, obey.

Mark felt his own muscles answer it—tiny shifts in stance, the readiness he'd trained into himself. For a second he understood the trap with brutal clarity: the town had made him easy to command. That was what discipline looked like from the wrong angle.

The ghost runner resumed his route, perfect and empty, over and over.

The voice softened, coaxing. "Accept what is written. Carry the town. Carry your guilt. I will make it quiet."

Quiet sounded like peace. Quiet sounded like surrender.

Alyssa touched Mark's arm—glove to glove. "Talk to us," she said. "Don't let it make you alone."

So Mark did the one thing Lowridge never did.

He told the truth out loud.

"My family knew," Mark said, steady because he refused to shake. "They stayed anyway. They called it tradition."

The fog thinned a fraction, like the night had blinked. Confession and honesty—Harold's rule—wasn't poetry. It was mechanics. The conduit did not like words that named the rot.

"I hated being the next Rivers," Mark said. "And when Jason died, I pretended it was an accident because admitting anything else meant admitting my name helped sharpen the knife."

His throat tightened. He pushed through.

"I feel guilty," he said. "Every day. And I'm done paying you with people."

The flowers on Pecos's wrists flickered. Violet dimmed a fraction.

The voice sharpened. "Then the town breaks."

"Then we fix it," Mark said.

Pecos shuddered. For a heartbeat, Pecos's own eyes surfaced—brown, desperate, human.

"It doesn't like truth," Pecos gasped.

Alyssa snapped back into motion. She rammed her pick into the lock and twisted.

The deadbolt clicked open.

Pecos's head jerked up. The layered voice surged again, angry but strained. "You cannot outrun the roots."

"We're not running," Mark said, and his voice sounded like the start of a fight instead of the start of a play. "We're cutting them."

For one second, Pecos was himself. He grabbed Mark's sleeve, grip strong despite the tremor.

"Find the grimoire," Pecos rasped. "Before I'm gone completely."

Then his hand slipped away and the violet returned—weaker, like a signal losing strength.

Alyssa yanked the door open. Dry, stale air spilled out—paper and dust, ordinary and safe.

Mark stepped inside and held the door for the others.

Tommy went next, whispering fast as if words could keep the dark back. Alyssa's flashlight cut a hard line through the hallway. Pecos stumbled last, and as he crossed the threshold, the glow on his skin dimmed as if the walls interfered with whatever was riding him.

Mark shut the door.

Outside, fog pressed to the windows, searching.

Inside, the building was quiet enough that Mark could hear his own breathing without the town's roar under it.

They moved toward the stairs that led down.

Mark pulled his phone out and snapped a picture of Pecos's hands—not for proof to convince the town, but for proof to convince himself later, when denial tried to creep back in. The screen caught a smear of violet across Pecos's skin and, in the glass of a front display case, a faint blur behind them.

A helmet. A facemask. Empty eyes.

Mark locked the phone and kept moving.

Toward the book the town had hidden.

Toward the truth that could cut the roots—or wake something worse.

CHAPTER 8: THE BOOK OF ROOTS

The Historical Society's basement smelled like paper and damp stone—old things sealed away and pretending they were harmless.

Alyssa moved first, flashlight low, beam kept off the windows. The building above them creaked the way all old buildings did, settling into itself. The sound felt normal until Mark remembered what Pecos had said outside: It followed.

"Please tell me you're not about to pull a cursed book off a cursed shelf," Tommy whispered.

Alyssa didn't look back. "Please tell me you didn't vote for Homecoming King by writing your own name in."

"I was manifesting," Tommy said, quiet but indignant.

Pecos didn't join in. He moved like every step cost something, shoulders tight, jaw set. The flowers had dimmed when they came inside, but Mark could still see a faint violet wash beneath Pecos's sleeves, like light leaking through cloth.

Mark kept his gloves on. He kept his hands away from his face. He kept breathing through his mouth to avoid the sweetness in the air.

It didn't help. The smell was still there—violet and metal—thin as a lie, persistent as humidity.

Alyssa stopped in front of a row of rolling shelves. She pointed her flashlight at a small brass placard: LOWRIDGE FOUNDERS / EARLY

RECORDS.

The flower symbol was etched into the corner of the plate, so small you could miss it unless you were already looking for it. Mark hated how much of the town was like that.

Alyssa's fingers skimmed labels. "Harrow. Reed. Shaw. Turner." She said the names like she was tasting something bitter. "Founders. Council. Ritual. Denial."

Tommy's voice went flat. "You're enjoying this."

Alyssa flashed him a look. "I'm terrified. I'm multitasking."

She pulled a binder free. Dust lifted in a lazy cloud. In the flashlight beam, the particles looked like a swarm for half a second, and Mark's pulse jumped.

He blinked hard. Dust. Just dust.

They spread materials on a scarred oak table: brittle minutes from town meetings, newspaper clippings, handwritten ledgers with water-stained edges. Ordinary history. Until it wasn't.

Alyssa flipped a page and froze.

Mark saw it too: a pressed purple petal wedged between lines of ink, old as the paper itself. The petal held color the way bruises did—deep, stubborn, refusing to fade.

Pecos exhaled through his teeth. "That's not... normal."

Tommy leaned in and then recoiled like the petal had moved. "Okay, I don't like that."

Alyssa's voice went quieter—more careful. "It's a bookmark."

Mark's throat tightened. "From when?"

Alyssa traced the date with her light. "1890."

The petal looked fresh.

They followed the petal like it was a trail. Binder after binder. Ledger after ledger. And the farther they went into the records, the more often they found them—pressed into margins, tucked beneath signatures, glued into corners like a private seal.

Mark started noticing patterns that made his stomach twist:

The same names signing different documents decades apart, as if the ink had learned to repeat itself.

Pages that should have been blank but weren't—faint violet stains in the fibers, like something had bled into the paper and stayed there.

A series of maps of Lowridge that looked normal until Alyssa laid them one over the other and pointed.

"Look," she whispered.

The oldest map showed farmland and woods and a creek line. The next added roads. The next added the first school. The next, the stadium.

But each map shared the same faint marking in the same place: a circle, drawn lightly and then corrected and then redrawn, like someone couldn't decide whether to admit it.

The circle centered on the cemetery.

Pecos swayed, hand braced on the table. "It's the heart."

Alyssa's flashlight beam trembled as she angled it closer. Around the cemetery circle, the maps had tiny dots drawn in violet ink, so faint the human eye might dismiss them.

Graves. Mark understood, and the understanding landed like cold water. Old stones outside the official cemetery. Forgotten markers. Places where the town had buried its cost.

"Nodes," Alyssa said.

Tommy shook his head, whispering too loud. "You're telling me the town's haunted Wi-Fi is—"

Alyssa shot him a look.

Tommy lowered his voice. "Sorry. Haunted… network."

Mark stared at the map until his vision threatened to stutter again. He felt the familiar rhythm trying to start in his muscles—one-two, one-two—like his body wanted to align with the diagram the same way it aligned with a play call.

He forced his shoulders loose.

Not mine, he told himself.

Alyssa pushed back from the table. "This isn't it."

"How do you know?" Mark asked.

"Because my grandfather wrote about a book," she said, voice tight with memory. "Not minutes. Not maps. A source."

She moved to the far wall where the basement turned darker—less shelves, more storage. The flashlight beam caught a filing cabinet with a lock, old and ugly. On the cabinet's top drawer, someone had carved a small symbol: a circle with a slit down the middle.

An eye.

Mark felt his skin prickle. "That wasn't there before."

Alyssa's mouth was grim. "It was always there. People just… don't see what they're not allowed to see."

Tommy's laugh came out thin. "That is not a comforting sentence."

Alyssa knelt and worked the lock.

Metal clicked.

The drawer slid open, slow as a confession.

Inside was a box—wooden, dark, the lid carved with the Lowridge Lions logo…and wrapped in a border of flowers. Not painted flowers. Not printed.

Pressed, preserved petals inset into the wood like inlaid stone.

The purple was too deep. The shape too perfect.

Alyssa didn't touch it. She looked at Mark. "Gloves."

Mark nodded. He stepped forward and lifted the box with careful hands, like it might bite.

It wasn't heavy. It was wrong-light, the way a dead thing can feel too easy to carry until you remember what it used to be.

He set it on the table.

No one spoke for a moment. The basement seemed to hold its breath with them.

Then Pecos whispered, almost reverent. "It's alive."

Tommy whispered back, "Please stop saying things like that."

Alyssa opened the lid.

Inside lay a book.

It was bound in something that looked like leather until the flashlight hit it and Mark saw the truth: a surface made of layered petals—pressed, fused, stitched together. Purple flowers flattened into a skin.

The binding smelled sweet and metallic at the same time, like violets left too long in a closed room.

Alyssa's voice went raw. "My grandfather called it the Book of Roots."

Mark stared at the cover. In the center, a symbol had been burned in: an eye, ringed by tiny lines like roots.

"The Scarlet Eye," Pecos murmured.

Alyssa swallowed. "That's in his journal, too."

Tommy leaned back, hands up like surrender. "We are in trouble."

Mark didn't answer. His gaze had snagged on one detail: the book's edges were uneven, as if the pages weren't paper at all.

Alyssa turned the cover carefully.

The pages were thin and pale and fibrous. Not parchment.

Petal-paper.

The text wasn't printed. It was etched—dark lines pressed into the surface, the letters slightly raised, like something had written by carving rather than ink.

Alyssa exhaled once. "It's a cipher."

Mark watched her face change—the fear still there, but layered under it was something else: focus. Purpose. The part of Alyssa that wanted to understand and prove, even when the truth could break her.

She pointed to a section at the beginning: a diagram.

A circle.

A network.

Lines branching outward from the cemetery like veins.

And along the lines: small glyphs that looked uncomfortably like football routes.

Mark's stomach turned.

Tommy leaned in despite himself. "That's a playbook."

Alyssa didn't look up. "It's worse."

She traced the lines with the flashlight tip. "It's showing signal strength."

"Signal," Mark repeated, and hated how the word fit.

Pecos's hand found the edge of the table, knuckles white. "Distance matters."

Alyssa nodded. "Bloom density matters. Moonlight matters. Fog matters." She glanced at Mark, eyes sharp. "Blood matters."

Mark's jaw tightened. "Blood plus petals equals access."

Alyssa's head snapped up—surprised. Then her mouth pulled tight, like the confirmation hurt. "Yes."

Tommy swallowed. "So Eli—"

"We're not saying his name like it's a statistic," Mark cut in.

Tommy's eyes flicked away. "Sorry."

Alyssa kept translating, voice low, steady. "It says the flower is a conduit. The conduit can… carry."

Mark felt his chest go tight. "Carry what."

Alyssa's eyes tracked across the lines. "Will. Hunger. Command."

Pecos whispered, "Ride."

Alyssa nodded once, rigid. "Yes. It uses hosts. It rides them."

A chill moved through Mark—not the cold, not the basement damp. The chill of understanding that what happened to Eli wasn't random. It was procedural. Mechanically repeatable.

Alyssa turned the next page.

A name appeared in the text, carved deeper than the rest. The letters looked older, darker.

E O R A Z I E L

Alyssa's voice went thin. "Eoraziel."

Pecos flinched like he'd been struck.

Tommy whispered, "That's not a town founder."

Alyssa shook her head. "No. That's the thing the founders bargained with." She read the line beneath it, translating as she went. "The Scarlet Eye who watches through petals. Who drinks devotion. Who learns the shape of men."

Mark's stomach rolled.

Alyssa turned another page and stopped.

There was a passage underlined in violet ink—fresh-looking, like it had been marked yesterday instead of a century ago.

Alyssa read it out loud, voice shaking but stubborn.

"The network can be severed."

Silence.

That one line hit the room like a match in a dark house.

Tommy let out a breath he didn't know he was holding. "So we can cut it."

Alyssa's gaze stayed on the book. "Maybe."

Mark's pulse picked up. "How."

Alyssa's finger slid down the carved lines. "It says the cemetery is the anchor. The heart." She tapped the diagram. "If the heart is severed—"

Pecos's voice was strained. "It will fight."

Alyssa nodded. "Yes."

Mark leaned closer. "Where's the altar."

Alyssa flipped pages, hands careful. "It's under—"

The basement lights flickered once.

Not the flashlight. The actual overhead fluorescents—ancient bulbs that had no business responding to anything.

They dimmed.

Brightened.

Dimmed again.

Tommy's voice went small. "Did you do that."

Alyssa didn't answer.

Because Pecos was already bending forward like something had yanked a hook in his spine. His breath hitched. His hands rose slightly from his sides, sleeves sliding back.

The flowers in his palms opened.

Brighter than before.

Violet light spilled across the table, across the book, across Alyssa's face.

Mark felt the pressure behind his eyes return, sharper this time—like a lens turning itself.

Alyssa backed up a step, voice tight. "Pecos."

Pecos looked at her.

His eyes were wrong again—violet threaded through them like roots.

When he spoke, it wasn't one voice.

It was many.

Men and boys layered together—different ages, different tones—speaking at once in a chorus that made Mark's skin crawl because he recognized the texture of it.

It sounded like a crowd.

It sounded like a stadium.

It sounded like every player Lowridge ever applauded.

"You opened it," the chorus said.

Alyssa's chin lifted, sarcasm gone now, replaced by steel. "Eoraziel."

The name fell like a brick.

The basement air thickened.

The fog outside pressed harder against the windows, as if it wanted in.

Pecos's mouth twitched—not a smile, not a frown—an expression someone had practiced by watching humans from far away.

"You learned my name," the chorus said. "You learned my routes."

Mark stepped closer without meaning to, body reacting to the cadence in the voices. He stopped himself. Clenched his fists inside his gloves.

"You're not him," Mark said, staring at Pecos. "You're using him."

The chorus laughed softly—dozens of laughs misaligned, a sound like breath through petals.

"A body is a vehicle," it said. "A town is a field. A season is a harvest."

Alyssa's voice stayed steady, even as her hands trembled. "What do you want."

The chorus turned Pecos's head slowly toward Mark.

"I want what you already are," it said. "A promise. A legacy. A gate."

Mark felt his name press against him like a hand. Rivers.

Then the chorus spoke the sentence like it had been waiting to say it for a century.

"You will serve," it said, "willing or broken."

The book on the table shuddered.

The pages fluttered without wind.

And from the binding, something moved—thin, pale tendrils like roots soaked in moonlight, unfurling from between pressed petals. They slid across the wood, reaching.

Alyssa's breath caught. "Move."

Tommy didn't need to be told twice. He grabbed the nearest chair and swung it instinctively—not at Pecos, not at the book, but at the roots crawling across the floor.

Wood cracked. Roots recoiled—then surged again, faster.

The flowers wanted the room.

Mark backed Alyssa toward the stairs. "Go."

Alyssa stared at Pecos, voice fierce. "Fight it. Pecos, look at me. Your name is Pecos Morales."

Pecos's body trembled like a man holding back a current. His jaw clenched.

For a heartbeat, Pecos's real voice surfaced—ragged, desperate.

"It's in my head," he gasped. "It's—every voice—"

Then the chorus snapped back over him.

The roots slammed against the table leg and climbed.

Petals shook loose from nowhere and drifted through the air like slow snow.

Mark felt them brush his sleeve. His skin prickled beneath the fabric as if the petals were looking for warmth, for blood, for access.

Alyssa grabbed the Book of Roots.

Mark caught her wrist. "Gloves."

"I'm not leaving it," she snapped, and yanked her sleeves down over her hands—fabric barrier, thin but better than bare skin. She scooped the book up like it was a bomb and held it against her chest.

Tommy swung again, loud and frantic. "This is not worth extra credit!"

A root snapped toward his ankle.

It didn't wrap. It stabbed—not sharp, but invasive, pushing under the cuff of his pant leg like a needle searching for a vein.

Tommy screamed—not words, just sound—and kicked hard.

The root slid away, leaving behind a faint violet smear on his sock, like a bruise blooming too fast.

Pecos stepped forward.

Not walking.

Pulled.

His feet dragged as if the floor was trying to reclaim him.

Mark's heart slammed. "Pecos!"

The chorus answered through Pecos, calm as gravity. "He is already bound."

Alyssa's voice turned sharp, desperate. "Truth breaks you," she said—half statement, half test. "You don't like confession."

The chorus paused.

Mark felt it—like a hitch in signal.

Alyssa took the opening and spoke the truth like a weapon.

"This town is complicit," she said, voice shaking but loud. "Your deal was never prosperity. It was theft. You take boys and call it tradition."

The roots faltered.

The overhead lights steadied.

For a second, the violet glow dimmed.

Pecos gasped like he'd been allowed air.

Mark stepped in close, voice low, aimed at Pecos—not the chorus. "Pecos. I'm here. Stay here."

Pecos's eyes flicked—brown trying to surface. "I can't—" he whispered.

Then the chorus surged again, furious now, and the basement temperature dropped so fast Mark's breath fogged.

The roots exploded upward—not from the book this time, but from the cracks between tiles, from the drains, from the seams where the building met earth. It wasn't attacking from one source. It was the building's foundation turning hostile.

"Go," Pecos rasped suddenly—his own voice, a burst of himself. "Now!"

Alyssa grabbed Mark's sleeve. "Stairs!"

They ran.

The roots snapped after them like whips, scattering petals that clung to walls like damp confetti. The air tasted sweet and metallic. Mark kept his mouth shut and swallowed the panic instead.

Halfway up the stairs, Mark glanced back.

The basement had become a garden.

Not pretty. Not natural.

Purple flowers erupted along the floor tiles, blooming too fast, petals wet-looking in the flashlight beam. Vines coiled around table legs. Spores thickened the air into a haze.

And in the center of it, Pecos stood with his hands out—trying to hold something back.

Roots climbed his calves.

Wrapped his knees.

Pulled tight.

Pecos's face contorted with pain, sweat pouring down his temples. He tried to step.

His feet didn't move.

The floor had him.

Tommy stumbled on the stairs, coughing. "We can't leave him!"

Pecos's voice tore through the haze, raw and human.

"Yes you can," he shouted. "You have to!"

The chorus rose behind him—voices stacking, swelling, a stadium roar without joy.

Pecos's jaw clenched. His eyes squeezed shut.

He forced words out anyway, like he was shoving them through thorns.

"Find... the altar," he gasped. "Sever... the heart."

Then his head snapped up, and Mark saw something else in the fog behind Pecos.

A figure.

Translucent. Edges shimmering.

Jason.

He was not fully himself—violet threaded through him like veins of light—but his expression was strained, furious, fighting.

Jason's gaze locked onto Mark.

And for the briefest second, the violet in his eyes cracked the way ice cracks under pressure.

He lifted his hand and pointed—not at Mark.

At a side door.

An exit Mark hadn't noticed. An old service door, half hidden behind display cases on the ground floor. A way out that wasn't the main stairwell.

Jason mouthed words without sound.

Now.

Mark's throat tightened. He nodded once.

Alyssa saw it too—saw Jason's direction, saw the shift in Mark's eyes.

"Service exit," she breathed.

They hit the ground floor at a run.

Behind them, the basement noise rose—roots tearing tile, wood splintering, something heavy shifting like the building itself wanted to kneel.

Tommy shoved open a hallway door—

—and froze.

The hallway was filled with fog.

Not the thin street fog they'd walked through. This was thicker. Pressing. Indoor fog, wrong fog, the kind that shouldn't exist in a sealed building.

In the fog, shapes moved.

Helmets.

Shoulder pads.

Old uniforms.

They stood in the corridor like an opposing line, unmoving, watching.

The chorus spoke from everywhere at once, not only Pecos now.

"You cannot take what is mine."

Alyssa clutched the book tighter, voice fierce. "He is not yours."

The figures didn't advance.

They didn't need to.

The air itself pushed forward. Spores thickened, turning breath into effort.

Mark felt the pressure behind his eyes sharpen until his vision threatened to split. The hallway became a map again—lines, routes, nodes. A play unfolding with no whistle to stop it.

Then Jason stepped between them and the fog-line.

The ghost version of his brother lifted both hands as if he were bracing against a wall.

His face contorted with strain.

And Mark saw it—Jason's awareness, trapped inside the curse, forcing his body to do something it wasn't meant to do.

The fog shuddered.

The ghost-player shapes flickered.

Jason's mouth opened soundlessly, and Mark heard it anyway—in his chest, in his bones.

Run.

Alyssa grabbed Mark's sleeve and yanked.

They sprinted for the service door.

The door was old. Rusted.

It should've stuck.

It didn't.

It swung open like it had been waiting.

Cold night air hit them, sharp as relief.

They spilled out into the alley behind the Historical Society, coughing, gasping, the fog following like breath from a mouth that didn't want to close.

Mark turned back.

Through the doorway, he could still see down the hallway.

Jason stood braced in the fog, shaking. His edges blurred as violet surged against him.

Then the fog swallowed him.

The door slammed shut on its own.

Not with a gentle click, but with force—like a final decision.

Alyssa grabbed Mark's arm. "Don't."

Mark's chest felt like it was caving in. "Pecos—"

From inside the building came a scream.

Pecos's scream.

A sound so human and raw Mark's vision went white for a moment.

Then the scream broke—fractured into many voices.

The chorus rose again.

Only now one of the voices had Pecos's tone woven into it, unmistakable beneath the layered crowd.

Tommy stumbled back, shaking his head. "No. No, no, no."

Alyssa's face went pale in the streetlamp light. She pressed the book against her chest like it could anchor her.

Mark stood rigid, staring at the closed door.

He could hear the chorus through the brick now—faint, distant, like a stadium roar carried on wind.

And inside it: Pecos.

Not speaking.

Not warning.

Joined.

The fog thickened in the alley.

Purple light pulsed faintly beneath the doorframe, slow and steady, like a heartbeat.

Mark forced himself to inhale.

Forced himself to stay standing.

He looked at Alyssa. "We sever the heart."

Alyssa nodded, eyes bright with terror and resolve. "We sever the heart."

Tommy wiped his face with his sleeve, loud now, trying to outrun panic with sound. "Okay. Okay. We're doing this. We're doing this for him."

Mark's voice stayed low, restrained, but it carried steel. "And for everyone it's taken."

The fog rolled past them toward the main street, toward the stadium lights, toward the places Lowridge pretended were safe.

Mark stared after it, and the vow formed in his chest like a new kind of cadence.

Not a play call.

A promise.

CHAPTER 9: BOUND BY THE NETWORK

By morning, the fog had lifted, but the sweetness hadn't. Violet-damp and faintly metallic, like cut lips in October. Mark kept catching it on his hoodie and wishing he could scrub last night out of his skin.

They met at Pecos's house because it sat back from the road behind pecan trees, easy to miss if you weren't looking. Pecos's mother let them in without questions, only a tired, intent look that said she knew more than she wanted to.

"Kitchen," she murmured. "Light's better."

When she left them, she paused at the doorway. "If the ground starts talking," she said, "don't answer."

The door shut.

Alyssa set the Book of Roots on the table like it might bite. In daylight, it looked worse—pressed petals fused into the cover, an eye scarred into the leather, routes carved into the pages like play calls meant for a different kind of field.

Tommy hovered, ring half off his finger. "This is the part where the book opens itself and we regret being curious."

"It already did," Alyssa said, and opened to the diagram they'd seen in the basement: a cemetery circle, a stadium circle, and branching lines that matched football routes too perfectly to be coincidence.

Pecos sat across from the book, shoulders tight. He was here, he was breathing, he was himself—yet every time he flexed his hands, Mark caught a bruised purple tint along Pecos's cuticles.

"It tried to root me," Pecos said quietly. "Like stepping into wet cement."

Alyssa's eyes sharpened. "And you got out how?"

Pecos hesitated. "I lied. Told it I was alone. Nobody would come."

Mark felt his stomach drop. A door-opening bargain, even if it was spoken to survive.

"It doesn't let go for free," Pecos added.

Alyssa flipped to a section marked with a torn strip of notebook paper. Her voice changed—less sarcasm, more precision—like she was reading a set of rules she needed to obey.

"Each season, the bloom begins with the first home game," she said.

Tommy's smile flickered. "Friday."

"It builds through homecoming," Alyssa continued, "then spikes near Hollow's Eve. Fog nights help. Spores spread. People breathe it in without knowing."

Mark pictured the stadium lights cutting fog into layers and shivered.

Alyssa turned a page. "The conduit rule is simple: blood plus petals equals access."

"Doors," Mark said.

Alyssa nodded. "And it starts small—signal interference. Memory gaps. Exhaustion. Dreams. Then it moves to physical markers." She swallowed. "Purple under fingernails. Drowsiness. Aggression."

Tommy's hand stopped moving on his ring.

Mark looked down at Tommy's nails.

At the edges, beneath the pale crescents, a faint violet seeped like ink that refused to wash off.

"It's paint," Tommy said too fast. "Homecoming banners."

Alyssa's eyes didn't blink. "Wash them."

"I did."

"Then it isn't paint."

Silence thickened the kitchen. The refrigerator hum sounded too loud.

Pecos exhaled through his nose, steadying himself. "It's targeting the team."

"Not just the team," Alyssa corrected. "Us. We opened the book. We pulled on the circuit."

She grabbed butcher paper and spread it on the table. Pecos took a marker and, without asking where to start, drew a circle.

Another circle.

A thick line between them.

Then lines branching outward—streets, creeks, the old church, the industrial park at the edge of town where new glass buildings sat like imported teeth.

Tommy leaned in despite himself. "That's the growth corridor."

Pecos nodded, face pinched with pain. "New roots."

Alyssa tapped the cemetery circle. "Anchor."

She tapped the stadium circle. "Amplifier."

Pecos drew small dots around the stadium—homes, neighborhoods, the school. Lowridge's expansion made visible as a web.

Alyssa checked her calendar, fingers fast. "Homecoming is next week. Hollow's Eve is two weeks after."

Mark's shoulders went tight, as if pads had settled there again.

Alyssa flipped to a carved table—numbers and symbols laid out like an equation. "The grimoire says the circuit strengthens when the team becomes champion."

Tommy's voice went small. "We're undefeated."

"Exactly," Alyssa said. "If the champion falls at peak—homecoming, Hollow's Eve, playoffs—the anchor can't hold the signal. It pushes outward. New nodes. New blooms."

Mark pictured purple flowers blooming on highway shoulders, in medians, outside towns that had never heard of Lowridge.

"County," Tommy whispered.

Pecos's gaze went distant, listening to something under the floorboards. "It wants reach," he murmured. "It wants to take a physical form."

Alyssa snapped her eyes to him. "That's in the book?"

Pecos flinched. "No."

Mark's pulse thudded. "Then how do you know?"

Pecos didn't look up. "Because it keeps practicing. Through us."

Tommy's phone buzzed. Mark's followed a beat later.

Captains. Office. Now.

They drove separately. Looking normal was a kind of camouflage in Lowridge.

On the drive in, Mark watched Lowridge slide past the passenger window in pieces: the old brick courthouse with a new coffee shop across the street; the church marquee advertising Hollow's Eve Festival — Family Friendly; the fresh-painted sign for a defense contractor's satellite office going up in the "corridor." Progress everywhere, like a coat of paint. And under it, the same purple flower on every banner, every flyer, every yard sign that said GO LIONS.

They parked behind the gym and went in through the athletic entrance. The hallway there always smelled like bleach and sweat—cleaned hard, never clean.

The locker room was half full. A few juniors were changing, laughing too loudly, making plans for the bonfire and the dance. Mark caught fragments.

"—after we crush Northgate—"

"—my dad says scouts are coming—"

"—you going to wear the flower pin or are you too tough—"

Normal.

And then not.

Cam Dorsey—starting receiver, fast hands, big grin—sat on a bench with his elbows on his knees, staring at the floor like it had something written on it. His helmet was beside him. His eyes looked dull, unfocused, as if he'd been awake all night and hadn't really come back.

"Cam," Mark said.

Cam blinked once, slow. "Huh?"

"You good?"

Cam's gaze lifted, and for a second Mark saw something wrong in the whites of his eyes—a faint violet thread at the edges, like broken capillaries tinted purple. It vanished when Cam blinked again.

"Yeah," Cam said. The word came out flat, like a line read in the wrong scene. "Just tired."

Tommy tried to slide in with his usual warmth. "That's because you've got the brain of a golden retriever and it's exhausted from thinking."

Cam didn't smile.

He stood up too quickly, shoulders tense. "Can you not."

Tommy's grin faltered. "Okay. Okay. Sorry."

Cam rubbed his hands together, hard. Mark saw the nails—purple at the edges, not paint, not bruising. More like the color had seeped up from underneath.

A junior across the room snorted and tossed a towel at Cam. "Man, you look like you got into the pep squad craft closet."

Cam's head snapped up. His eyes went sharp—too sharp—and for a moment his face looked like someone else's anger wearing Cam's features.

"Say it again," Cam said, voice low.

The junior froze. The room quieted in that instinctive way animals go quiet when they sense a predator.

Mark stepped between them before it turned into a fight. "Not today," he said, calm but firm.

Cam's gaze landed on Mark like it had been searching for him. For a heartbeat, Mark felt the pressure behind his eyes tighten—like a lens trying to focus.

Then Cam blinked, and whatever had been there slid away. His shoulders dropped, confusion replacing heat.

"What?" Cam asked, as if he'd missed his own line. He looked at the towel on the floor like he didn't remember it landing. "Never mind."

He grabbed his helmet and walked out.

Tommy exhaled. Loud. "Okay. That's not normal tired."

Alyssa stood near the lockers, quiet, watching everything with a critic's patience. "Memory gap," she said.

Tommy turned on her, voice too loud. "Do not diagnose me in the locker room."

"I wasn't talking about you," Alyssa said, and her eyes flicked to where Cam had been sitting. "But… you should let me see your hands again."

Tommy stared, offended and scared. "No."

Mark saw it anyway. Tommy's nails were darker than they'd been at Pecos's table—still subtle, but there.

Tommy shoved his hands in his hoodie pocket like hiding them could change what they were becoming.

Coach's message buzzed again, impatient.

Now.

They headed down the hallway toward the office, passing the training room. The trainer, Mrs. Harlan, stood over a sink scrubbing something with disinfectant like she was trying to erase it. She glanced up at Mark.

"Your nosebleeds still happening?" she asked.

Mark's throat tightened. "No."

Mrs. Harlan's eyes lingered on him a fraction too long. Then she looked away, like she'd asked the question out of habit and wished she hadn't.

As they walked, Mark realized Tommy had fallen behind. He turned.

Tommy stood at the water fountain, one hand braced on the wall, staring at the stream like he was trying to remember how it worked.

"Tommy," Mark called softly.

Tommy blinked. "What?"

"We're going to Coach."

Tommy frowned. "We… we are?"

Alyssa's face changed—no sarcasm, no humor, only attention. "How long were you standing there?"

Tommy looked at the fountain, then at his ring, then at Mark. His voice came out smaller than Mark had ever heard it. "I don't know."

Mark's chest tightened. The book had called it signal interference. Memory gaps. A soft beginning that still felt like a hand closing around your throat.

"Walk with us," Mark said.

Tommy did, shoulders hunched, ring clicking against his finger like a nervous metronome.

The school was already dressed for Homecoming—purple streamers, paper flowers taped to doors, banners with the flower-and-lion logo. A symbol the town wore like a varsity jacket, proud and oblivious.

Mark kept his head down as they walked past the trophy case. Jason's jersey hung behind glass, neat and permanent, like grief could be framed.

Coach Whitman's door was shut.

Mark knocked.

"Come in."

Coach sat behind his desk, hands folded. He looked at Mark and Tommy first, then at Alyssa behind them. His jaw worked once.

"Miss Dawson," he said.

Alyssa's tone was polite and sharp. "Coach."

Coach stood and closed the door. The click landed like a period.

"I know where you were last night," Coach said.

Tommy tried to laugh and couldn't. "We went for a walk."

"You broke into the Historical Society," Coach replied. "You opened the book."

Mark's stomach turned. "How do you know about the book?"

"Because I've been told to watch for it since I took this job."

Alyssa's eyes narrowed. "Told by who."

Coach's gaze flicked to the wall photo of the school board—smiling faces, the mayor centered like a seal. "The ones who keep this town running," he said quietly. "The ones who keep it winning."

Mark's throat tightened. "My brother—"

"I'm sorry about Jason," Coach said, and for a fraction of a second, something real crossed his face. Then it was gone. "But you need to understand what you're standing on."

Alyssa didn't soften. "Say it."

Coach's voice went measured, practiced. "It feeds on devotion. On attention. On the team's energy. The flowers are conduits—roots in the cemetery, spores in the fog, petals on skin. Blood makes access. Football makes volume."

Tommy's ring scraped against his finger as he fidgeted. "So you just let it happen."

"No," Coach said, and the word carried tiredness more than denial. "I try to keep it contained."

Alyssa's eyes narrowed. "Contained how."

Coach met Mark's gaze. "By paying the cost."

Mark felt something inside him go cold. "A champion."

Coach didn't correct him.

Alyssa's voice went very quiet. "Every season?"

"Every season we win big," Coach said. "Don't look for perfect patterns. Look for payments."

Tommy shook his head once, hard. "And if the champion doesn't die?"

Coach's expression didn't change, but the air did. "Then it doesn't take one," he said. "It takes many."

Mark's mouth went dry.

Coach leaned forward, palms on the desk. "If you try to break the pact without a substitute, it spreads. It blooms outside the cemetery. Outside town. It makes the county into a field."

Alyssa's grip tightened on her tote strap. "So the town feeds it to keep everyone else safe."

Coach's eyes flickered—guilt, anger, something tangled. "People here don't know," he said. "Kids. Families. They just want their lives."

"And the boys you fed it?" Alyssa asked.

Coach's voice roughened. "None of them deserved it."

Mark forced his voice past the silence he usually hid inside. "You said there's a way to redirect it."

Coach nodded once. "You can't stop the route," he said. "But you might be able to change where it ends."

He opened the door, dismissing them like this was a meeting about curfew.

In the hallway, the school was loud again—laughter, music from the gym, Homecoming flyers fluttering on bulletin boards. Normal life running on top of a buried engine.

They didn't go back to class. Nobody stopped them—another small mercy of being Lions, of being useful.

On their way out, they cut past the stadium gate. Daylight made the place look harmless: aluminum bleachers, painted lines, banners flapping lazy in the breeze. But the smell hit Mark as soon as they reached the fence —the same damp sweetness, faint as perfume on a sleeve.

Near the sideline, where the turf met the walkway, tiny purple buds had threaded up through the grass. Not many. Easy to miss unless you knew how to look. They shivered as if they recognized him.

Out on the field, Cam ran routes by himself.

No quarterback. No ball. Just Cam cutting hard angles, planting his feet with perfect timing, turning his head as if a pass were already in the air. Every move was crisp, practiced, efficient—beautiful in a way that made Mark feel sick.

Tommy gripped the fence until his knuckles went white. "He's not even —"

Cam stopped at the exact spot a slant would end. He stood there, breathing hard, staring into empty space like he was listening to a voice only he could hear.

Mark called, "Cam!"

Cam didn't react. His hands lifted, fingers spread, and for a heartbeat Mark swore Cam was holding something that wasn't there—petals, dark and damp, pressed into his palms.

Then Cam blinked and shook his head like waking from a bad dream. He means looked around, startled, and when his gaze found Mark at the fence, shame flashed across his face so fast Mark almost missed it.

Cam jogged off the field without speaking, head down.

Alyssa's voice was tight. "Practice," she whispered. "It's rehearsing through them."

Mark's throat went dry. "Then we're out of time."

Tommy slid his ring up and down his finger with shaking hands. "Redirect it," he whispered. "That means choosing."

Mark stared toward the trophy case, toward Jason's framed jersey and the purple flowers everywhere, smiling from paper and pins.

"We don't choose another kid," Mark said.

Alyssa's eyes flashed. "Then what do we choose?"

Mark swallowed, the taste of sweetness rising again like a warning. "I don't know yet," he admitted. "But we're not becoming the town's hands."

Behind them, faint as a rumor, Mark thought he heard a stadium roar—misaligned, like too many voices trying to speak through one mouth.

And for a second, the air tasted sweet.

CHAPTER 10: THE FIRST SACRIFICE

Lowridge knew how to make disappearance sound like a scheduling issue.

By second period, Principal Hart's voice came over the intercom: there had been an "incident" during Friday night's game. Senior wide receiver Eli Carter was missing. Counselors were available. Students were asked not to speculate.

Speculation filled the halls anyway—Eli ran off, Eli fainted, Eli got hurt and the adults were "handling it." Mark Rivers listened without reacting. Silence was his old defense; it kept other people's stories from climbing inside his throat.

At the trophy case, a purple ribbon had been tied to the glass. Neat. Reverent. Like it belonged there as much as the jerseys and plaques. Someone had already taped up Eli's picture beside the Homecoming flyer, the same bright smile copied into the same clean pose the town preferred. Mark's eyes slid, uninvited, to the framed jersey two slots over—Jason Rivers, #12—hung like a saint's relic.

The school smelled like floor wax and cafeteria pizza, but underneath it Mark caught that damp sweetness again, like crushed petals in wet soil. He didn't know if it was in the air or in his nerves. Either way, his body believed it.

Tommy Blake caught up beside him, breathing too fast.

"They're saying he crossed the fence," Tommy murmured. "Like he just... walked into the cemetery."

Mark studied Tommy's eyes—too glossy, like he'd slept with the lights on. "Any gaps?"

Tommy's ring clicked as he fidgeted. "Just... dumb stuff." He tried to grin. It didn't hold. "I keep ending up places without remembering the walking part."

Mark didn't ask which places. He didn't want the answer.

"Meet after school?" Tommy asked.

"Pecos's," Mark said.

Tommy nodded, then looked past Mark as if something was standing behind him.

After the last bell, Lowridge performed normalcy in bright daylight. Students poured onto sidewalks lined with new banners—WELCOME HOME, LIONS—fluttering on fresh poles paid for by booster money and "growth corridor" sponsors. A glossy brochure in the main office advertised a tech park opening just outside town, all glass and clean fonts, promising jobs and "community vitality," as if vitality could be engineered.

Alyssa Dawson waited in her car with the engine off, hands tight on the wheel. She didn't look up when Mark got in. She only said, "They already decided what story they're going to tell."

"What story?" Mark asked.

"Medical event," Alyssa said. Her voice was controlled, but anger lived in the seams. "Overexertion. Pressure. Anything that doesn't require anyone to admit the fence... didn't stop him."

Tommy climbed into the back seat and shut the door too gently. "That's better than 'the cemetery took him,' I guess."

Alyssa turned just enough to pin him with a look. "Nobody gets taken," she said. "They get used."

Tommy's ring clicked faster. "Still not comforting."

Pecos's house sat under pecan trees that threw cool shade across the yard. Pecos waited on the porch, arms folded, face pale with that specific exhaustion that wasn't from late nights.

"It's louder," he said before anyone asked.

Inside, the kitchen felt normal on purpose—clean counters, a radio turned low to a station that played soft country like it could wallpaper over anything. A bowl of salt sat near the sink, placed like a quiet boundary line. No one commented on it, which made it worse; in Lowridge, silence was how adults told the truth without saying it.

Alyssa set her bag down and unwrapped the Book of Roots.

Even closed, it tightened the room.

Tommy hovered by the doorway. "We are absolutely sure this is the right move."

Alyssa's sharp humor flashed and vanished. "No."

Mark sat with his hands flat on the table. Alyssa opened to the carved route-map: stadium, cemetery, branching lines like veins. A notched margin marked the section, as if the book had been waiting for them to catch up.

"Chapter Ten," Alyssa said softly. "It's flagged."

Tommy leaned in despite himself. "Great. The cursed book has bookmarks."

Alyssa turned the page carefully.

Nothing.

Then the air shifted—as if the kitchen had inhaled and forgotten how to exhale. The overhead light flickered once. The ticking clock stretched thin and disappeared.

Tommy reached out on instinct, either to stop the page or steady himself. His knuckle scraped the paper.

A papercut. A thin line of blood.

Mark saw the moment that blood touched the page seam where dried petal fibers were fused into the binding.

The carved routes darkened. A faint purple glow traced the grooves.

Tommy jerked his hand back. "Nope."

He tried to stand.

His legs didn't move.

"Mark?" His voice went small.

Alyssa snapped, "Stay in your own body. Do not touch him."

Mark stopped with his hand hovering uselessly in midair.

Pecos pressed his palm to the table and winced, as if the wood had turned hot. "It's pulling," he whispered.

The kitchen blurred at the edges, then dissolved in layers—sound first, then smell, then shape—until Mark felt like he'd stepped off a curb that wasn't there.

Cold replaced warmth.

Fog replaced air.

And the world reassembled under a thin, cloud-smeared moon.

They stood in a clearing ringed by bare trees. A mossy stone altar crouched at the center, carved with symbols that looked like letters until you tried to read them. A lantern burned steady in the wind.

Men gathered around it—faces tight with civic authority. A council. Old Lowridge, wearing its private rot like a uniform.

Alyssa's breath caught. "We're inside the book."

Mark couldn't answer. His throat had locked around the taste of metal.

A man stepped forward, lantern in hand. His coat was old-fashioned, his hair neatly combed, his expression controlled the way a coach's expression is controlled.

Thomas Harrow.

Behind him stood a boy—older teen, slim, athletic, a Lions letterman jacket too big at the shoulders. He shared Harrow's bones, softened by youth. His mouth moved as if he'd been trying to form the same question for hours.

Harrow's son.

Fog thickened at the clearing's edge.

A figure in a red cloak emerged from it, the hood deep enough to swallow any face. The presence made the air feel wrong—too still, as if the night leaned toward it.

The councilmen went quiet. One crossed himself like the gesture was muscle memory.

The cloaked figure spoke, voice smooth and unhurried. "You have taken and called it prosperity."

Harrow lifted his chin. "We kept our side."

"You changed the currency," the figure said. "First harvest. Then machines. Then the noise of new roads." A pause, almost amused. "Now you offer glory."

The word landed like a weight. Mark thought of the stadium roar, the way devotion hit you in the chest.

One councilman swallowed. "St. Michael's used to keep the balance."

The red cloak tilted, as if listening to a joke. "Balance is what you call hunger when it benefits you."

Harrow's jaw tightened. "The town needs stability."

"The town needs truth," the cloaked figure replied softly. "And you have starved it."

The boy shifted, eyes darting for an exit that didn't exist. "Dad... what is this?"

Harrow didn't look at him. He set his hand on the altar. In the other, a knife.

Alyssa's fingers curled. Tommy made a strangled sound.

The cloaked figure murmured, almost kindly, "Confession."

The councilmen flinched as if the word burned.

Harrow's jaw tightened. "There's no time."

The boy's voice cracked. "You said it was for luck. For the team."

Harrow's voice stayed controlled, but something brittle lived underneath it. "Do you want your mother hungry? Your sister cold? This place is all we have."

"I didn't volunteer," the boy said, louder now, panic breaking through.

Two councilmen seized him—hands on his arms, faces blank with practiced denial. The boy struggled, shoes sliding on damp leaves. His jacket tore at the shoulder seam.

Harrow cut his own palm. Blood spilled onto stone and ran into the carved grooves like water finding channels.

The wooden box on the altar—small, ornate—pulsed brighter, as if it had been waiting for the first drop.

Fog curled inward.

The knife rose again.

Mark's body jerked forward on instinct.

Alyssa hissed, "We can't."

The blade came down.

Not lingered over. Not dramatized. Just executed—an awful, clean inevitability.

The boy gasped once, a sound too small for what it meant, and sagged against the altar.

Silence fell—not emptiness, but satisfaction.

The ground trembled.

Thin black roots pushed up through soil around the altar, writhing toward the blood. Where they touched the earth, buds appeared—tiny, pale sparks in dirt—and opened with unnatural speed.

Purple flowers bloomed for the first time.

They were beautiful in the way a trap is beautiful when you don't know it's a trap. Their scent filled the clearing—sweet, damp, overwhelming— and the lantern light caught their petals like wet velvet.

Harrow staggered back, blood dripping from his palm. His face had gone gray, as if the act had unmade something inside him.

The cloaked figure touched a bloom. The flower pulsed.

A whisper rose from the wooden box—many voices misaligned, like a crowd chanting through one throat.

The cloaked figure spoke again, and the voice layered—one tone low, one tone higher, as if something rode inside it.

"Eoraziel."

The name slid into the air like oil, impossible to hold and impossible to forget.

"The Scarlet Eye opens," the voice continued. "The route begins."

For a fraction of a second, Mark saw it—an impression in the fog: a vast red eye, not physical, not fully here, but looking back.

Then the hunger behind it pressed toward them, searching.

Mark's breath hitched. A wrong voice brushed the inside of his skull, wearing a familiar sentence.

You carry it next.

Jason's words. Not Jason's voice.

Tommy's eyes glazed, drifting. "Dad?" he whispered, though no father stood here.

Alyssa gripped her own wrist hard enough to ground herself. "It's using the cut," she said, voice tight. "Blood plus petals."

Mark needed a lever. The one Pecos had hinted at. The one the red cloak had offered like a key.

Confession.

Mark forced air into his lungs and spoke into the pressure before it could climb deeper.

"I'm guilty," he said out loud.

Alyssa's head snapped toward him, startled, but Mark kept going because stopping would be another lie.

"I knew my family was tied to this," he said, voice strained. "I didn't want to know how. I let the town tell me stories. I let Jason carry it. I let everyone pretend."

The pressure wavered, like a signal losing strength.

Mark swallowed, then cut to the simplest truth. "I want out. And I'm afraid."

The hunger recoiled—interrupted, not defeated.

Tommy blinked hard. His gaze cleared, shame flooding in as if he'd just woken mid-sentence.

Alyssa exhaled, shaking. "It worked."

Pecos's voice came through pain, calm and certain. "It hates being named."

Alyssa lifted her chin and said it anyway, forcing the shape of it into the air. "Eoraziel. Scarlet Eye."

The clearing shuddered.

Fog swallowed the altar. The red impression blinked out.

And the world snapped backward.

Kitchen light. Refrigerator hum. Dish soap. The clock resumed its ticking like nothing had happened.

Tommy stumbled back from the table, breathing hard, staring at his bleeding knuckle as if it belonged to someone else.

Alyssa grabbed butcher paper and wrote in block letters, hand trembling once before it steadied:

EORAZIEL
THE SCARLET EYE

Pecos sank into a chair, palm pressed to his ribs. "It's in the routes," he whispered. "In the ground. In the way the town moves."

Mark sat very still. Confession had disrupted the grip. He didn't like that it required him to say things he'd spent years swallowing. He didn't like that it had also felt like relief.

Alyssa flipped the book open again—this time turning pages with the eraser end of a pencil, refusing skin contact. A deeper notch marked another section.

"The ancients," she read aloud.

Tommy swallowed. "Who are those."

"The ones who built this system," Alyssa said. "The families who inherited the council's role. The people Coach Whitman meant when he said 'redirect.'"

Tommy's ring clicked as he fidgeted, then he slid it off and set it on the table like an offering he didn't want to make. "And if they tell us the only way out is… another sacrifice?"

Mark looked at him. His voice stayed thoughtful and restrained, but something hard lived underneath. "Then we don't accept their route."

Pecos lifted his head slightly, listening past walls, past daylight. "Homecoming will amplify it," he warned. "Hollow's Eve will open it wider."

Mark thought of Eli Carter—missing, already being rewritten into an "incident." He thought of the boy in the clearing, currency in a letterman jacket. He thought of Jason's framed jersey, grief polished into pride.

Lowridge didn't celebrate champions. It kept them.

Mark leaned forward, careful not to touch the book, and spoke the vow like a line he would not let the town rewrite.

"We find the ancients," he said. "And we unmake this."

Alyssa's voice joined without hesitation. "We unmake it."

Tommy stared at the name on the paper, then nodded once—small, terrified agreement. "And we bring Eli home," he said quietly. "If there's anything left to bring."

Pecos closed his eyes, pain flickering across his face. "If the route still has an ending," he murmured, "we change where it lands."

The kitchen light flickered once—barely noticeable.

Just enough to remind them the circuit was live.

CHAPTER 11: THE PRICE OF GLORY

Lowridge Town Hall sat on the square like an old referee—silent, unimpressed, certain the rules belonged to it.

Streetlamps glazed the wet pavement. Fog kept low to the ground, curling around hedges and the dead fountain. In the dirt beds, purple petals lay like someone had spilled bruises and walked away. They weren't paper. They were real—velvet-soft, too vivid for October—stuck to mulch, gathered in corners, clinging to the town the way a smell clings to cloth.

Mark kept his hands in his jacket pockets so no one could see them shake.

"We're really doing this," Tommy muttered. He tried for sarcasm and landed on a whisper. "Sneaking into a council meeting like we're in some spy movie."

"We're not sneaking into the public part," Alyssa said. Her grandfather's journal was tucked under her arm, the spine cracked from being opened too many times in one week. "They do the show for the town. The real meeting starts after."

Pecos stood half a step behind, gaze fixed on the brick as if he could see through it. The purple along the veins at his wrists showed faintly under the streetlight, like bruises that refused to fade.

"It's under this building," he murmured.

Mark tried not to picture roots threaded beneath the foundations, tying government and football and graves into one knotted thing.

Alyssa held up her grandfather's brass key. "Public meeting at seven," she whispered. "Executive session after. No minutes. No recordings."

Tommy swallowed. "So we're… listening."

"We get proof," Mark said. His mouth tasted faintly metallic, like he'd bitten his lip. "We get out. If anyone asks, we were never here."

Alyssa's eyes flashed. "If anyone asks, we tell them the truth."

Mark didn't answer. Truth in Lowridge was a thing you tasted and spat out before anyone saw it on your tongue.

They waited in the shadow of the courthouse steps across the square while the council crowd arrived—business owners in fleece vests, a couple of booster-club women with matching scarves, men who looked like they'd been born holding clipboards. Coach Whitman strode up the steps like Town Hall was just another locker room, jaw set, Lions jacket zipped to his throat.

Mark watched him and felt a sick twist of recognition. Coach had stood over Jason's casket with that same expression—tight, controlled, grief pressed into something usable.

Mayor Raines arrived without ceremony, slipping out of her car and climbing the steps like she was late to something she couldn't afford to miss. Harold Reed trailed her, laughing too easily, as if the town's weight didn't touch him.

The doors shut. The windows stayed dark.

From where they waited, Mark could hear the muffled rise-and-fall of voices. Not words, but cadence—discussion that sounded, from a distance, like a huddle. The same rhythm he heard before a snap: one-two, one-two. A count that started plays and ended prayers.

Tommy's knee bounced. "You sure that key works?"

Alyssa didn't look at him. "It worked for my grandfather."

"And that ended great," Tommy muttered.

Alyssa's head turned, sharp. "He died trying to warn someone."

Tommy's mouth closed. He rubbed his thumb against the inside of his wrist, a nervous habit Mark had seen a thousand times in the huddle. Usually it meant Tommy was about to crack a joke.

Tonight it meant Tommy was trying not to throw up.

When the public session ended, laughter spilled through the doors. People walked out in small groups, congratulating themselves for surviving another week. Coach Whitman lingered on the steps with Harold Reed, talking in low voices like they were reviewing film. Mayor Raines came out last, speaking briefly with a man in a suit who nodded too much. Then she paused and looked out across the square like she was counting shadows.

Mark pulled back under the awning.

"Now?" Tommy whispered.

"Not until they're gone," Alyssa said.

Pecos didn't answer. His head had tilted, as if he'd caught the sound of something shifting under the stone.

Cars started. Tail-lights smeared red across wet pavement. The square thinned until it was only streetlamps and fog and the faint drip of water somewhere.

Finally, Alyssa moved.

She crossed to the side entrance like she belonged there, the key already in her hand. The lock turned. The click sounded loud enough to wake the whole town.

It didn't.

Inside, the hall smelled of floor polish and old paper. Warmer than it should've been, stale, as if air didn't circulate properly in places that held secrets.

Framed team photos lined the walls between portraits of founders and mayors—Lions champions under stadium lights, decade after decade, purple and gold stitched into every grin. Mark's eyes snagged on one photo from three years ago: Jason in the center, helmet under his arm, smiling like he hadn't known what was waiting.

The town didn't separate football from government. It braided them together until you couldn't tell where one ended.

They moved on soft steps toward a door marked RECORDS.

In the corners, real petals had collected—velvet-dark, too vivid for October. Mark's skin prickled. The town didn't just decorate with the flower. It carried it.

Alyssa slipped the records room open.

Shelves. Cabinets. Binders by year. Boxes stacked to the ceiling. The kind of place you hid something by burying it under other people's paperwork.

Mark yanked open a drawer and found a thick folder stamped LOWRIDGE DEVELOPMENT AUTHORITY.

Alyssa was already flipping through municipal finance. "Property values... grants...," she murmured, then went still.

Mark leaned in.

A copied sheet had a hand-drawn line graph across decades—town revenue in peaks and climbs. In the margins, someone had written names and dates.

Eli Carter — 10/21
Jason Rivers — 11/03
Owen MacReady — 10/14

Luke Benton — 9/29

Each name like a stat.

Each date followed by a spike.

Tommy made a sick sound. "They tracked it."

Mark's throat tightened around his brother's name on a finance page. He pulled his phone and started taking pictures—no flash, hands shaking.

Alyssa flipped to a ledger page labeled REMEMBRANCE INITIATIVE.

Under it: disbursements.

New turf. New lights. Scholarship fund. Weight room renovations. A grant to refurbish Main Street storefronts. A line item for "Community Beautification," which felt like a joke when the beautification was purple flowers growing from graves.

Mark scanned the next pages and found donor lists—names of families, businesses, anonymous contributions that weren't anonymous to the people who wrote them down. His eyes caught on familiar names: Torres Auto. Rivers Plumbing. Morales Landscaping.

Tommy leaned closer, face tight. "My dad's shop," he whispered.

Mark's fingers went numb. His father's name was there too, tucked among donors like a badge.

Pecos's head snapped up. "Someone's coming."

Footsteps drifted down the hall—unhurried. Not searching. Approaching like they owned the place.

Harold Reed's voice floated in first. "Not the first time kids got curious."

Mayor Raines answered, calm as an announcement. "They never understand what curiosity costs."

Mark's pulse hammered. Alyssa pulled them into the narrow gap behind stacked boxes. Tommy pressed a fist to his mouth, breathing through his nose like he was trying to keep control.

Pecos didn't squeeze in so much as fold—shoulders tight, eyes far away, one palm braced against the wall like it was keeping him upright.

The door opened. Light spilled in.

Mayor Raines stepped inside with Harold. Harold carried a clipboard, cheerful as if this was a routine inspection. Mayor Raines didn't carry anything. She didn't need to.

She flipped the finance binder closed with careful fingers. "Whitman says Rivers has been… difficult."

Mark's stomach turned.

Harold chuckled. "Grief makes people loud."

"And reckless," Mayor Raines said. "The other one—Torres?"

Tommy flinched.

"His father understands," Harold said. "He'll bring him in."

Mayor Raines's gaze moved over the shelves, the cabinets, the dark corners. Not searching—counting. "We keep the ledger balanced," she said quietly. "That's the job."

Harold's smile widened. "And we keep winning."

Mayor Raines made a small sound—almost a sigh. "No one enjoys this," she said. "But enjoyment isn't the point."

Harold laughed under his breath. "Tell that to the stadium."

Mayor Raines didn't laugh. "You know the rule," she said. "The land takes what it's owed. If we don't guide the taking, it takes blindly."

Harold's tone sharpened. "We're not having the 'guided' conversation again."

"We have it every year," Mayor Raines replied. "Because every year someone asks if we can stop."

Harold's eyes narrowed. "And every year the answer is no."

Mayor Raines turned for the door.

Mark stepped out.

Alyssa made a small, desperate sound, but he was already there, standing in fluorescent light with his anger exposed.

Mayor Raines stopped. Harold's face hardened like a snapped strap.

"Well," Harold said. "Look what the fog dragged in."

Mark's voice came out raw. "You knew."

"Yes," Mayor Raines said, like admitting the sky was up. "We know. We manage it."

"These are kids," Mark said. "My brother was a kid."

Harold shrugged. "Kids become legends. Legends keep the town alive."

Alyssa stepped beside Mark, chin lifted. "You're feeding something."

Mayor Raines's eyes stayed on Mark. "You think arresting a few people ends a pact?" she asked. "You think the land cares about your morality?"

Mark clenched his fists. "So you just… choose who dies."

"We choose the town," she said.

Tommy's voice broke. "My dad—"

Harold's smile sharpened. "Your father did his part. Don't embarrass him."

Tommy's jaw locked, eyes glossy with something he refused to let fall.

Mayor Raines took one slow step closer to Mark. There was a tiredness to her, a human edge under the steel. "People tried to fight it before you were born," she said softly. "They shut down games. They pulled boys out of town. They tried to starve the land of what it wanted."

Mark heard his own breathing in his ears. Heard the low hum under the building like distant crowd noise.

"And the land took anyway," Mayor Raines continued. "It took the wrong ones. Fathers in accidents. Babies in their sleep. It punished us until we learned the rules. It doesn't negotiate. It collects."

Harold's voice was smug. "Balance, Mark. That's the word you're looking for. The town gets prosperity. The land gets payment."

Mark's chest went hollow. "And Jason?"

Mayor Raines's gaze flickered—just once. "Your brother wasn't decided in this room," she said. "But his death was accepted. Because refusing doesn't spare anyone. It only changes who the land takes."

The lights flickered.

One dim heartbeat. Then normal.

Pecos sucked in air like it hurt. "It hears," he whispered.

Mayor Raines's voice dropped. "Go home," she told Mark. "Hold your mother. Let this go. Because if you keep pushing—"

Harold stepped toward the door, blocking it with his body, still smiling. "Glory always costs," he said. "Question is—who pays?"

Alyssa grabbed Mark's sleeve. "Not here," she hissed.

Mark forced himself to back up. One-two. One-two. The tunnel count, the prayer count.

They left with their phones full of pictures and their stomachs full of poison.

Outside, the square felt different—less like a place people lived and more like a field after the lights shut off. The fog had thickened. Mark thought he saw movement at the far edge of it—tall, thin, a shape that held still when he stared.

He blinked and it was only fog.

Tommy's voice shook. "Did you see—"

"Drive," Alyssa said.

The Rivers house smelled like lemon cleaner and something sweet in the oven—comfort staged like a set.

Mark walked in and didn't take off his jacket. His mother looked up from the counter, smile already fading. His father folded the paper like he was bracing for impact.

"We need to talk," Mark said.

His mother's fingers found the cross at her neck. "Is this about the cemetery?"

Mark's throat tightened. "You know."

Silence.

His father looked away first—toward the window, toward the dark line of trees beyond the neighborhood.

Mark's chest went cold.

"Did you know about Jason?" he asked.

His mother's face crumpled. "We tried," she whispered. "We prayed. We begged him to stop going out there."

"So you let it happen," Mark said. The words came out flatter than he meant them to.

"We were told," his father said, voice low and rough. "We were told if we fought it, it would take you both. It would take your mother. It would take… everyone."

Mark felt a laugh try to crawl out of him and die. "Who told you?"

His father's eyes flicked to the ceiling like the answer lived above them. "People who knew."

Mark thought of Mayor Raines's tired face. Of Harold's smile. Of Coach Whitman's Lions jacket in the council chamber.

"You chose," Mark whispered.

His mother shook her head, tears spilling. "We chose to save you."

Mark stared at them—at the family photos, at Jason's senior portrait still on the fridge like the house couldn't accept absence. He remembered Jason ruffling his hair after practice, saying, You'll carry it next, Mark. At the time, it had sounded like football.

Now it sounded like a sentence.

A single purple petal lay on the kitchen floor by his shoe.

His mother saw it and flinched like it had moved.

Mark swallowed the burn in his throat. "You didn't save me," he said. "You delayed me."

His father's face reddened. "Lower your voice."

"Everything this town has is because it kills kids," Mark said, and the words landed hard and final.

His mother reached for him. "Mark, please."

He stepped back. "If you knew and you didn't stop it," he said quietly, "then you're part of it."

His father's jaw flexed. "Where will you go?"

Mark looked out the window at the streetlight glow smeared by fog, at the neighborhood that felt suddenly built on top of something living and resentful.

"I don't know," he admitted. "But I can't stay here pretending."

He turned and walked out.

Behind him, his mother sobbed into her hands.

Outside, fog rolled low across the street like it was coming to meet him.

Alyssa's car waited at the curb. Tommy and Pecos were inside.

Mark got in.

Tommy held up his phone. One message from his dad.

Come home. We need to talk. Don't make this harder than it has to be.

Tommy's voice cracked. "He knows."

Alyssa's hands tightened on the wheel. "We have proof," she said again, like repetition could make it true. "We can send it. We can—"

Pecos whispered from the back seat, eyes fixed on nothing. "It's awake."

Mark's skin prickled. "How do you know?"

Pecos's answer was a swallow and a shake of his head, as if the truth was too heavy for language. "The ground," he said. "It's… leaning toward us."

Alyssa looked at Mark through the rearview mirror. "Where do we go?"

Mark thought of Town Hall's binders. Of his parents' silence. Of Harold Reed's easy certainty. Of Mayor Raines admitting guilt like it was weather.

He looked toward the edge of town—toward the cemetery fence, toward the damp ground and the purple glow that never belonged to seasons.

"There's only one place they can't pretend isn't real," he said.

Alyssa nodded, and the car rolled forward into fog that felt thicker than air.

As they drove, petals collected in gutters like the town was shedding skin.

The cemetery fence appeared ahead, black against the pale mist. Beyond it, the graves sat in rows like an audience waiting for kickoff. Purple light gathered low among the stones, breathing.

Alyssa slowed the car.

Mark stared through the windshield as the flowers brightened—just a little—as if recognizing them.

And beneath the hum of the engine, beneath the wind, beneath everything, Mark heard a deeper rhythm rising from the ground itself, keeping time with his pulse.

One-two.

One-two.

Like the land was counting them in.

CHAPTER 12: THE ENTITY SPEAKS

Mark didn't sleep.

He lay on top of his covers with his phone face down on his chest, listening to the house settle—pipes ticking, a distant refrigerator hum, the soft creak of old wood that sounded too much like footsteps when you were already wound tight.

Outside his window, Lowridge sat in its usual quiet. Porch lights. Curbs. Mailboxes. The kind of neighborhood still proud of itself. The kind that put purple flowers on welcome signs and called it tradition.

Mark stared at the ceiling until the dark turned grainy with fatigue. Every time he blinked, he saw Eli Carter's last route—fog swallowing the numbers, cleats leaving the field and stepping into cemetery soil like a line had been erased.

The town had already started shaping Eli into a story that fit. A "medical episode." A "panic reaction." A "kid under pressure."

Mark knew what it was.

Blood plus petals. Access.

His phone buzzed once, then again.

ALYSSA: Pecos says it's calling. Now.

Mark sat up. The motion made his stomach tighten, like something inside him had been braced for that message.

He pulled on a hoodie and slipped out without waking his parents. Their bedroom door was shut. The house smelled faintly of laundry detergent and the lemon cleaner his mother used when she wanted the kitchen to look like everything was fine.

In the hallway mirror, he caught his own reflection—eyes shadowed, mouth set. He looked older than seventeen for the first time in his life.

On his dresser, his camera sat half-packed in its bag. He'd promised himself he would keep shooting, keep making something that wasn't football.

Tonight, the camera felt like a joke.

Alyssa's car was waiting at the corner with the engine running, headlights off. She leaned forward over the steering wheel, hair falling in a curtain, posture tight like she'd been holding her breath for hours.

Tommy paced near the curb, tapping his ring against his knuckle. Tap. Tap. Tap. He tried to look casual and failed in every direction.

Pecos stood near the passenger door, one hand pressed against his ribs. His face was pale under the streetlight's wash. When he saw Mark, he didn't wave—just lifted his chin, a quiet acknowledgment that said: It's worse.

Mark got in the back. The seat smelled like fast food and Alyssa's vanilla air freshener, a normal scent that didn't belong with what they were doing.

Alyssa glanced at him in the mirror. "You came."

"I wasn't going to sleep anyway," Mark said.

Tommy slid into the front passenger seat like he wanted to be anywhere else. "Can we not do the whole 'we might die tonight' vibe? I have things I still want to do, like graduate."

"Relax," Alyssa said. It came out sharper than she intended. She exhaled. "Sorry. I just—" She nodded toward Pecos. "He felt a shift. Like the last time. Like before Eli."

Tommy's ring stopped tapping.

Pecos eased into the back beside Mark, moving like every breath cost him something. "It's not just calling," he said. His voice stayed calm, but his fingers trembled where they gripped the edge of the seat. "It's… making room."

"For what?" Mark asked.

Pecos looked out the window as the car started rolling. "For something to step through."

Alyssa drove without turning on her radio. The silence inside the car felt louder than any music. Streetlights strobed over their faces—bright, dark, bright—like they were being scanned.

As they crossed the last intersection before the cemetery road, Mark caught sight of a new poster taped to a pole. MISSING. Eli Carter's school photo. The Lions logo in the corner like it was part of the branding.

Below it, someone had drawn a purple flower in marker.

The town wasn't even pretending anymore.

Alyssa spoke softly, like she was reciting a lesson. "The grimoire says the pact isn't a contract. It's a circuit."

Mark's throat tightened. "Yeah."

"It says there's a center point," she continued. "A node. A place where the signal is strongest. Where the entity's voice comes through clearest."

Tommy let out a shaky laugh. "Love that for us."

"And it says blood is the key," Alyssa added. "But confession is the break. Truth disrupts the circuit."

Mark stared at the passing trees. Dark trunks. Bare branches. The road curving like it knew where it wanted them to go.

"So what," Tommy said, forcing humor over fear, "we show up and do group therapy at a graveyard?"

Alyssa's eyes stayed on the road. "We show up and we don't lie to ourselves anymore."

Pecos's hand pressed harder to his ribs. "It knows we're coming," he said.

Mark swallowed. "Then we keep our heads. We go in, we test, we get out."

Alyssa's mouth twitched. "We go in, we test, we get out," she echoed, like she didn't believe any of it.

They turned onto the cemetery lane.

Fog lay low over the field beside it, a white spill that clung to grass and swallowed fence posts. The moon above was bright and cold, sharp enough to make the world look cut-out and unreal.

The cemetery gate was open.

Mark hadn't heard of anyone leaving it open. It didn't creak. It didn't resist. It waited.

Tommy muttered, "Of course it's open."

Alyssa parked under a leaning oak and killed the engine. For a second, the car's ticking cooling metal was the only sound. Then the night pressed in.

They stepped out.

The scent hit Mark immediately—sweet violet, rimmed with something metallic, like a coin held under your tongue. His skin prickled along his arms.

The cemetery beyond the gate looked like it always did: rows of stones, some new, some so old the names had been smoothed away. But tonight, the flowers made it different. Purple clusters glowed in pockets across the grounds—around the Lions plaques, around older stones, around places that shouldn't have had anything growing at all.

Alyssa clicked on her flashlight and aimed it low. "Stay on the path," she said. "Don't touch anything."

Tommy raised both hands. "My hands are staying in my pockets. My hands are going to live a long and normal life."

Pecos didn't laugh. He stared at the ground like he could see under it.

Mark followed Alyssa past the first row. The stones seemed to turn their faces toward them as the flashlight beam moved. A low hum threaded the air—not the band, not the crowd—something beneath sound.

One-two. One-two.

Mark's feet found that cadence without choosing it.

They reached the older section where the trees grew thicker and the stones leaned at sharper angles, half-sunken like they were trying to hide. Here, the purple glow was stronger. The flowers weren't scattered. They formed a ring—dense, deliberate—around a stone taller than the rest.

The stone's face was stained dark, as if something had seeped into it long ago. Runes cut into its surface caught the flashlight beam and held it.

Alyssa's voice dropped. "This is it."

Tommy stared. "That's not a normal grave."

"It's not a grave," Alyssa said. "It's a marker."

Pecos stepped forward, one slow step at a time. He didn't touch the flowers, but his body reacted like he had—his shoulders tensing, his breath hitching.

"It's awake," he murmured.

Mark's mouth went dry. "How do you know?"

Pecos blinked, and for a moment his eyes looked unfocused, like he was staring through the stone instead of at it. "Because it's looking back."

The purple flowers around the marker brightened, then dimmed—slow, steady, like breathing.

Alyssa pulled the grimoire from her backpack. It was wrapped in a towel like something fragile and dangerous. When she unfolded it, the leather cover looked too old for a high school backpack, too worn in a way that didn't match time.

She didn't open it right away.

Mark watched her hands. Her fingers trembled, then steadied. She was afraid, but obsession had a way of making fear feel like fuel.

Alyssa glanced at them. "The book says if we want it to speak, we have to give it a path."

Tommy's voice came out rough. "No. No paths. We are pathless."

Pecos exhaled slowly. "It's already speaking," he said. "Just not in words."

Mark looked at the flowers. "What are we doing here, Alyssa?"

She met his gaze. Sarcasm tried to rise and failed. "We're doing what adults won't," she said. "We're standing where the truth starts."

Then she opened the grimoire.

The pages inside weren't blank. They were crowded with ink—tight handwriting, symbols, shapes that made Mark's eyes want to slide away. Alyssa flipped to a section marked with a pressed purple petal that had been dried between pages like a bookmark.

She read quietly at first, then louder, as if sound mattered.

"Glory feeds the roots," she said, voice steadying, "and roots drink the blood."

Tommy's shoulders jerked like someone had touched him. "Can we not read that out loud?"

Alyssa kept going. "The conduit blooms in death and opens in life. The chosen carry the town's hunger. The field is the door. The grave is the lock."

Pecos made a soft sound—pain or warning.

Mark felt the hum deepen. The air seemed to thicken, pressing against his ears. His vision sharpened, then blurred at the edges.

Alyssa stopped reading.

The night had gone too quiet, as if the trees were holding their breath.

Then the voice arrived.

It didn't come from one place. It came from the flowers, from the stones, from the soil under Mark's shoes. It came layered—old and young, male and female, like a crowd speaking at once.

"Lowridge," it whispered.

The word slid through Mark's skull, not sound but pressure. The purple ring brightened.

Tommy took a step back. "Nope."

Alyssa held her ground. "Eoraziel," she said, the name tasting strange and heavy, "we're here."

Pecos's hand flew to his ribs. He bent slightly, teeth clenched, but he didn't fall.

The voice changed—thinned, sharpened—until it sounded like a referee's whistle stretched into a syllable.

"You carry it," it said.

Mark's heart hammered.

He didn't know if it meant him or all of them.

Alyssa's voice shook but stayed firm. "We know you're not the land," she said. "We know you're in it."

The flowers pulsed. The air tasted sweeter, then bitter, then sweet again.

A laugh moved through the trees—soft, amused, almost kind.

"I am what you fed," the voice said. "What you praised. What you hid."

Mark's throat tightened. "Stop," he said, not loud, but real. "Stop talking like you're us."

The flowers around the marker leaned, petals trembling. In the flashlight beam, their edges looked wet.

The voice dropped lower, like it was leaning close to Mark's ear.

"Mark Rivers," it said.

Hearing his name from that mouth—the mouth of many mouths—made his skin crawl.

"I know your blood," it whispered. "I know your family's hands."

Mark's jaw clenched. Images flashed—his father's face when he talked about legacy, his mother's smile when she said the town needed them, Jason's jersey in a case like a relic.

Alyssa's eyes cut to Mark. "Don't listen," she mouthed.

But Mark couldn't not listen. It was inside him.

"You want him back," the voice said.

The word him didn't need a name.

Mark's breath caught. Tommy's hand grabbed his sleeve, a grounding touch.

The flowers brightened again, and fog seeped in between the stones like a slow tide.

"You want forgiveness," the voice continued, soft as a lullaby. "You want the weight lifted."

Mark heard something else under it—a distant cheer, a band drum, the steady chant of a crowd that never got tired.

"One choice," the voice said. "One route."

Alyssa snapped, "No deals."

The laugh came again—warm this time, like the sound of someone indulging a child.

"Not a deal," it purred. "A return."

The fog thickened until Mark could barely see the gate behind them. In the purple glow, shapes stood between stones—helmeted outlines, jerseys faded, numbers wrong, faces hidden by shadow and petals.

One of them took a step.

Then another.

They moved with unnatural precision, like plays rehearsed a thousand times.

Mark's stomach dropped. "Ghost players," he whispered.

Tommy's voice broke. "Those are not people."

The voice spoke over them, calm and certain.

"Give me the captain," it said, "and I give you the brother."

Mark's vision tunneled. For a second he saw Jason's face in his mind—half-smile, warm eyes, the way he used to shove Mark's shoulder and say, You've got this.

Then the memory soured, tainted by fog and purple light.

Alyssa stepped closer to the marker, flashlight shaking. "You don't have him," she said. "You wear him."

The purple ring flared.

Pecos made a strangled noise and dropped to one knee.

Mark turned to him. "Pecos."

Pecos shook his head once—tight, controlled. "Don't—" he breathed. "Don't take the bait."

The voice softened, almost gentle.

"You want to leave," it told Mark. "You want the road out. You want the bright buildings and the clean future."

Mark's hands curled into fists. His silence pressed against his teeth. He felt the old instinct—say nothing, absorb, survive.

Truth disrupts the circuit, Alyssa had said.

Mark swallowed.

He spoke anyway.

"I do," he said. His voice came out rough, but it was his. "I want out."

The hum in the ground wavered.

The purple flowers dimmed by the smallest degree, like a breath caught.

Mark kept going, pushing the words through the fear. "I don't want to be what this town needs. I don't want to be your champion. I never did."

Alyssa looked at him, startled.

Tommy's grip on his sleeve tightened. "Mark—"

Mark didn't stop. "And I'm tired of pretending my brother's death was just bad luck," he said. The words hurt. They scraped on the way out. "I'm tired of carrying it like it's my fault and like it isn't. It's both."

The air trembled.

For a heartbeat, the flowers' glow faltered, and the helmeted shapes between stones stuttered, their movements glitching like a bad signal.

Pecos sucked in a sharp breath like the pain had eased for half a second.

The voice snapped, losing its softness.

"Truth," it hissed, and the word sounded like a threat.

The flowers surged bright—purple turning almost black at the center—and the fog thickened, sweet with spores.

Alyssa shouted, "It can't stand it. Keep talking. Keep it honest."

Mark looked at the shapes between stones and felt terror rise, hot and sharp. But he also felt something else—anger.

He lifted his chin.

"My name is Mark Rivers," he said. "And I am not yours."

The voice answered, cold now.

"Then be broken."

The ground under Mark's feet shifted.

Roots punched up through soil, thin and black, lashing like whips. They snapped toward Tommy's ankles. Tommy yelped and jumped back, ring flashing as his hand shot down to steady himself.

A root caught the edge of Alyssa's shoe and tugged. She stumbled, grimoire clutched to her chest.

"Move," Mark said.

They backed away from the marker, but the cemetery seemed to change around them. Stones leaned closer. Paths angled wrong. The gate was there, then not there, swallowed by fog.

The helmeted figures advanced.

One moved with a receiver's crisp cut, hips turning, feet planting perfectly in damp soil. Another mirrored a linebacker's charge, shoulders low, speed wrong for something that looked half-dead.

Mark couldn't stop thinking of Eli Carter, running a route he didn't choose.

Alyssa swung her flashlight up and the beam cut across a face—if you could call it a face. A helmet, cracked. Purple petals pressed into the facemask like dried tissue. Behind it, something faintly human—eyes that might have once belonged to a boy who had been cheered alive.

The figure opened its mouth.

And the voice that came out was the same layered chorus, the same hunger.

"Glory," it breathed.

Tommy grabbed Alyssa's arm and pulled her back. "I am officially done with the outdoors."

A root snapped across the path like a tripwire. Mark stepped over it, then felt another brush his calf—cold and wet—before it wrapped.

He jerked his leg free with a sharp motion. The root resisted like muscle.

Pecos stumbled forward, one hand stretched toward the marker as if trying to keep something from spilling out. "Go," he said, voice tight. "Get to the gate."

Mark turned. "We're not leaving you."

Pecos's eyes met his, calm under pain. "You will if you want any chance."

Alyssa's voice cracked. "Pecos, we can pull you—"

Pecos shook his head. "It's not a rope. It's... me."

He pressed his palm to the ground.

The hum surged through the soil, and for a split second the roots around Mark loosened, as if the circuit had been rerouted through Pecos's body.

Mark staggered free.

Tommy yanked Alyssa, and the three of them ran.

Fog swallowed the stones. The purple glow followed like a tide.

Mark's lungs burned. His legs pumped with the same muscle memory that made him scramble out of sacks on Friday nights, except tonight there was no crowd, no band, no end zone—only the gate that kept sliding farther away.

Behind him, Pecos cried out.

The sound wasn't loud. It was sharp, contained, like someone refusing to give the thing what it wanted.

Then the cheer rose.

Not from the town. From the ground.

A roar that hit Mark's back like hands.

The fog parted just enough for him to see Pecos by the marker—roots wrapped around his legs, climbing his waist like veins. Pecos's face was pale, jaw clenched, eyes open.

And behind him, in the purple ring, a figure rose.

Not fully formed. Not fully human.

A silhouette stitched together by petals and shadow.

It leaned close to Pecos's ear, and Pecos's body shuddered as if something had slipped inside.

Mark's stomach turned.

"Pecos!" Alyssa screamed.

Pecos's head lifted. For a moment, his eyes were his.

"Mark," he said, and his voice was still calm, still his, even as the roots tightened. "Tell the truth. Don't let it choose your route."

Then his gaze flicked—just for a second—toward the fog beyond Mark.

Mark followed the glance.

A figure stood between two stones.

Jason.

Or something wearing him.

Tonight, the face wavered—Jason's features sliding in and out of shadow like a signal fighting interference. His eyes were wide, urgent.

His mouth moved.

No sound came, but Mark understood anyway, the way you understood a play call before you heard it.

Run.

Mark's feet kept moving.

Tommy shoved Mark forward, half dragging him when Mark's body tried to slow.

They burst through the gate like breaking water.

On the road beyond, the fog thinned. The air turned colder, cleaner. The purple scent faded to a faint ghost of itself.

They ran until the cemetery was behind the trees and their lungs felt like they might tear.

Alyssa bent over with her hands on her knees, breath coming in sharp pulls. Tommy paced in a tight circle, ring tapping again like it could keep his heart from escaping.

Mark stared back at the dark line of trees.

He expected to see purple glow pushing out, chasing them.

Instead, the cemetery sat quiet, almost ordinary.

That was worse.

Alyssa straightened, eyes wet with anger and fear. "It took him."

Mark couldn't speak. His throat felt raw, scraped by all the truth he'd forced through it.

Tommy's voice was loud, shaky. "So that's it? We just... we just leave him there?"

Mark looked down at his hands.

On his right palm, faint against his skin, a smear of purple shimmered as if something had brushed him without leaving dirt. It wasn't pollen. It wasn't paint.

It looked like a bruise deciding to become a flower.

Mark closed his fist.

"No," he said. His voice came out low and steady, the way it did in the huddle when everyone else was panicking. "That's not it."

Alyssa's sarcasm returned like armor. "Good. Because I'm not putting 'we tried' on his missing poster."

Mark swallowed, tasting metal.

Somewhere behind the trees, too far to be a sound and too close to be nothing, a cheer rose—one-two, one-two—like the town practicing for a game no one was allowed to lose.

Mark lifted his head.

"We get him back," he said. "And we end this."

The wind shifted.

For a breath, it carried a sweet violet scent, and under it, a whisper that sounded almost like a smile.

"Next play."

CHAPTER 13: THE GROWING HUNGER

A week was long enough for Lowridge to turn a horror into a story with clean edges.

Eli Carter became a "missing student" on the morning announcements and a ribbon on the booster club table. Coach Whitman said the team would honor him. The principal asked for prayers. People nodded like they understood what had happened—like understanding was the same thing as safety.

Mark watched it all with the numb calm of someone who'd already seen the other version.

The one with fog.
The one with purple light breathing around headstones.
The one where a champion crossed a line nobody wanted to admit existed.

And while the town practiced forgetting, the flowers practiced spreading.

It started where you'd expect: along the cemetery fence, in the woods behind the far practice field, in the damp strip of grass beside the stadium. Then it moved into places it had no business being. A violet bud in a crack of asphalt. A bloom tucked against a chain-link post like a secret pinned there by an unseen hand.

No one screamed. No one even stopped walking.

That was what made Mark's throat tighten.

At lunch, the marching band practiced outside, brass cutting through the autumn air. Mark sat with Tommy and Alyssa near the cafeteria windows, the table that let them see the courtyard and, if you tilted your head, the distant water tower beyond the trees.

Alyssa didn't touch her food. Her grandfather's journal lay open beneath a history textbook cover, pages crowded with faded ink and tighter notes—like the man had tried to fit a warning into the margins of a life.

Tommy talked too much, which was how Mark knew he was scared.

"They're acting like Eli wandered off," Tommy said, stabbing a fry. "Like he's a dog that slipped a leash."

"They won't say 'cemetery,'" Alyssa murmured. "They won't say 'fog.' And they'll only say 'flowers' if it's on a fundraiser poster."

Mark leaned in. "What did you translate?"

Alyssa tapped a line in the journal. "A rule."

Her voice dropped until it sounded like gossip instead of prophecy. "Blood plus petal equals access."

Mark felt the words land heavy in his chest. He saw Eli's scraped forearm on the sideline. He tasted old copper in the back of his mouth.

Alyssa kept going. "The flowers aren't decoration. They're conduits—wicks. The fog spreads the signal. It makes people... receptive. And it hides everything under something that looks natural."

Tommy tried to laugh and failed. "So we're breathing the curse now. Great."

Mark's gaze drifted past Alyssa's shoulder, out to the band. A trombone player stood a fraction apart, posture wrong—too still, too precise. When he turned his head, his eyes caught the light, and for a heartbeat the color wasn't brown.

It was bruised purple, thin as an oil slick.

The kid's mouth curved like he'd remembered how to smile from a picture.

Mark's skin went tight. "You see that?"

Tommy's voice came out rough. "Yeah."

Alyssa's fingers whitened on the page. "It's not staying in the cemetery anymore."

After school, Tommy insisted on a quick stop at Weller's Market—bread, soda, whatever his mom had texted him. Fluorescent lights. Normal errands. The kind of ordinary that made your brain unclench.

Inside, the air smelled like apples and detergent and something faintly sweet that didn't belong.

At the register, Mrs. Lyle scanned items with slow, careful motions. She was the kind of cashier who always had a story.

Today she didn't speak.

Tommy tried anyway. "Hey, Mrs. Lyle."

Her head tilted. Her eyes drifted to him like they were following a sound he couldn't hear. Something purple pooled behind her pupils—not glowing, not dramatic. Just wrong.

A petal sat tucked behind her ear like a cute accessory.

Mrs. Lyle leaned forward and whispered, soft as breath: "Keep."

Then she bagged their things without scanning half of them, hands moving with ritual precision, like the act of giving mattered more than the act of selling.

Tommy grabbed the bag and backed away. Alyssa steered Mark toward the doors.

Outside, Mark swallowed cold air like it was medicine. "It's not just players."

Alyssa's jaw tightened. "No. But football's the strongest channel. The field is primed. The town's built around it. Everyone feeds the system."

Tommy stared at his hands. "So what are we—batteries?"

Alyssa didn't answer.

Mark hated that she couldn't.

That night, Mark couldn't sleep.

He lay in the dark and listened to Lowridge breathe—wind through trees, distant traffic on the highway toward the new developments, the faint hush of a town that liked to pretend it was safe.

Then his fingers brushed something cool on his pillowcase.

He snapped his phone light on.

A purple petal lay on his bed like it belonged there.

Mark sat up slowly, pulse hammering. He scanned the room.

At first it was normal—posters, laundry, his camera bag on the chair, the corner where art supplies gathered dust because football ate his time.

Then his eyes adjusted.

A faint glow leaked along the baseboard near his closet.

Mark crossed the room in two steps and dropped to his knees. The wood felt damp beneath his fingertips. In the thin shadowed gap where wall met floor, buds pushed up in a tight cluster.

Not flowers yet.

But alive.

Pulsing faintly, like tiny hearts.

Mark backed away, throat dry. The hum he'd learned to recognize rose under his feet—quiet, steady, patient.

The flowers had found him.

There was no "away" left inside his own house.

He texted Alyssa: COME OVER. NOW.

Then Tommy: NOW. NO CUTS. BE CAREFUL.

His thumb hovered over the screen a moment after that, the ghost of another name wanting to be typed.

Jason.

Mark shoved the phone into his pocket like it could burn him.

Tommy arrived first, letting himself in like he always had. He took one look at the buds and went pale.

"No," he whispered. "That's—"

"Yeah," Mark said. "It's here."

Tommy's eyes flicked to Mark's hands. "You bleeding?"

"No."

Tommy held his own palms up like proof. "Me either. I'm not bleeding in your room, man."

They waited in tight silence until Alyssa came in, out of breath, hair pulled back, eyes already sharp with panic she refused to show.

She crouched by the baseboard and didn't touch. "That's escalation."

Mark's voice stayed flat because if he let it shake he didn't know if he could stop it. "What does it mean?"

"It means the network is expanding." Alyssa's gaze stayed fixed on the buds. "My grandfather wrote: when the blooms breach homes, classrooms, churches—when violet grows in living places—it means the keeper is awake."

Tommy swallowed. "Keeper."

Alyssa nodded once. "Hungry-awake."

Tommy forced a laugh that broke in half. "So we're doomed."

"No," Alyssa said, and the word hit hard. "There's a window. When it's reaching but not fully anchored. It's stronger, but it's also exposed."

Mark stared at the buds. "How do we stop it?"

Alyssa lifted her eyes. "We find where it's rooted."

Tommy's shoulders tightened. "We tried the cemetery. We lost Pecos."

The name dropped into the room like a weight. Mark's throat closed.

Alyssa's jaw set. "Then we get him back."

Tommy shifted, restless. His hand went to his forehead like he'd gotten dizzy.

"Tommy?" Mark asked.

"I'm fine," Tommy said too fast.

His gaze unfocused for a fraction of a second, like someone had turned the lights down inside him. Then his eyes flashed—purple, thin and sharp—and he swayed.

Mark caught his shoulder. Tommy jerked away, sudden and violent.

"Don't touch me," Tommy snapped.

The buds pulsed brighter.

The air in the room felt heavier, pressure building behind Mark's eyes like a lens tightening.

Alyssa's voice went calm. "Tommy. Tell the truth."

Tommy stared at her. "What?"

"Out loud," Alyssa said. "Something you've been swallowing."

Tommy's mouth opened and closed. His hands shook. His ring slipped from his fingers and hit the floor with a soft ping.

"I remember," Tommy whispered, and his voice cracked. "I remember it."

The hum sharpened, angry.

Tommy flinched but kept going, eyes wet and terrified and finally—present.

"When I was little, I saw something in the woods," he said. "My dad said it was a deer. My mom said it was my imagination. But I saw it. It looked like a person… wearing a person."

Alyssa went still.

Tommy swallowed hard. "I've been pretending I don't remember because if I admit it, it's real. And if it's real, it can come back."

His breath hitched. "And I'm scared, okay? I'm scared all the time. I just… act like I'm not. Because that's what we do here."

The room went strangely still—not quiet, but paused, like something listening had stopped to reassess.

The buds' glow dimmed. The pressure behind Mark's eyes eased.

Tommy blinked hard. The purple was gone.

He gripped the bedpost, breathing like he'd just run stadium stairs. "What… what was that?"

Alyssa's voice came out rough. "You fought it."

Mark stared at the quiet buds, the petal still sitting on the bed like a dare. "Honesty," he said, and the word tasted unfamiliar. "It hates honesty."

Alyssa nodded once. "It feeds on what we hide."

Tommy picked up his ring with shaking fingers. "So what now?"

Alyssa looked at Mark. "We can't wait until it takes you all the way."

Mark's throat tightened. He looked at the buds and thought of Eli's empty smile.

"Tonight," Mark said, and surprised himself with how certain it sounded. "We go to the field."

Fog clung low to the practice field after midnight. Stadium lights were off, but the moon made the turf a dark sheet of damp.

The moment Mark stepped past the maintenance gate, the hum rose through his shoes into his bones.

They swept their flashlights low, careful with their footing. Purple buds dotted the grass near the fifty-yard line like someone had scattered bruises across the field.

Alyssa stopped near the sideline where Eli had been tackled. A faint flattened line cut through the grass, as if something had been dragged.

"It's pulling routes," Alyssa whispered.

Tommy's voice went thin. "It's using the field."

They reached the far end zone. The goalpost stood bone-pale against fog.

Mark's light caught movement.

A figure in an old uniform stood near the post, helmeted, still as a statue.

Then another.

Then another.

Six, Mark counted before his brain could stop itself.

Ghost-players, spaced like a drill line, purple light threaded faintly along their limbs.

Alyssa's breath hitched. "There weren't this many."

One of them turned its head toward Mark with slow, deliberate attention.

The pressure behind Mark's eyes snapped tight.

He looked down.

A bud at his foot trembled, as if answering his heartbeat.

Then the ground pulsed.

Once.
Twice.

A heartbeat.

And beneath the hum, a presence pressed up through the soil—familiar, strained.

Mark.

Mark's breath caught. He dropped to a crouch and placed his palm on the cold grass.

Pain flashed up his arm, sharp as a live wire.

Then the voice came clearer, inside his skull.

Pecos.

Mark swallowed. "Pecos. Where are you?"

Fragments answered, like a signal through storm.

Dark. Waiting. Hurt.

Then—urgent.

Find the hybrid.

Alyssa's eyes widened. "Say it."

Mark's mouth felt numb. "He says—find the hybrid. One player escaped. Half in, half out."

Tommy's face drained. "Escaped. Like… survived."

Pecos's voice pressed again, weakening. "Knows where. Follow the old road. Under the tower."

Mark's vision blurred at the edges. "How do we find you?"

A surge of fear—not Mark's, not entirely—rippled through his palm.

"No time," the voice warned. "It's hungry."

Then, one last clear push:

"The hybrid will show you how to break."

The signal snapped away. Mark yanked his hand back, fingers numb.

When he looked up, the ghost-players were gone.

Only fog and empty turf remained.

Alyssa grabbed his wrist gently. "Mark. Are you here?"

Mark blinked. The world steadied.

"Under the tower," Tommy whispered. "Old road."

Alyssa's jaw set. "The service road behind the water tower leads to the abandoned pump station."

Mark stared across the field, across the place that had been worship and pride and now felt like a mouth.

"A player who didn't become a flower," he said.

"A ghost with a pulse," Tommy muttered, voice shaking.

Mark thought of the buds under his baseboard. Thought of the petal on his pillow like a signature.

The thing under Lowridge wasn't patient anymore.

It was growing.

And now it knew exactly where Mark slept.

"Daylight," Mark said. "We go at daylight."

They turned back toward the car, fog curling at their ankles like something fond.

Behind them, the buds near midfield trembled in subtle rhythm—keeping time for a play nobody had called yet.

CHAPTER 14: THE CYCLE

The cemetery gates didn't squeal when Mark pushed them open.

They should have.

The iron bars looked the same as always—black paint, chipped in places, a few stubborn curls of rust where rain collected—but the hinges moved like they'd been freshly oiled. Quiet. Cooperative. Like the whole place had decided to let them in.

Fog lay low across the grass. Not the normal kind that crawled in from the river on cold nights, thin and harmless. This fog clung. It pooled between headstones like breath held in a throat. Every time Mark tried to breathe deep, he tasted pennies and crushed violets.

Tommy walked with his hands shoved into his hoodie pockets, shoulders hunched against the dark. "Tell me again why we're doing this at midnight."

"Because it's when the field is quiet," Pecos said.

He didn't sound scared. He didn't sound excited, either. He sounded… tuned.

Like the way Coach Landry sounded when he watched film—eyes narrowed, mind somewhere else, listening for patterns no one else could hear.

Alyssa held her grandfather's journal close to her chest, the leather cover wrapped in a strip of cloth like it might bite. Her flashlight beam slid over names etched into marble, then jerked away as if it didn't want to linger.

Mark kept his light aimed forward. He refused to look at Jason's headstone until he had to.

They crossed rows of dead players.

Mark used to think that was just something people said—dead players— as if football made the word more poetic. Here, it was literal. The oldest stones had carved helmets. Some had a little football. Some had the Lowridge Lions logo, cracked with age. And on too many of them, purple flowers bloomed in places flowers had no right to bloom—between granite and earth, out of bare rock, out of the shadow beneath the stone.

A gust of wind moved through the cemetery, but it didn't stir the fog. It didn't touch the trees. It only made the purple blooms tremble, as if they were listening.

Pecos stopped near the eastern wall, where a line of headstones sat tighter together, older, more weathered. He crouched, pressing his palm to the ground.

Mark watched Pecos's fingers spread, and he hated how natural it looked—like Pecos was touching something alive.

"There," Pecos murmured.

Alyssa stepped closer. "That's… just dirt."

Pecos didn't look up. "It's not dirt. It's… a seam. Like a scar."

Mark swallowed. "A scar?"

Pecos lifted his hand. Something thin and pale clung to his palm—root-fiber, almost like dried skin. He stared at it, then rubbed it off on his jeans like it disgusted him.

Tommy's flashlight beam bobbed over the headstones. "Okay. Cool. So the cemetery is scar tissue. Can we please get in, get out, and never come back?"

Alyssa flipped through the journal with trembling fingers. "There's a map. He drew—he drew a mark here." She pointed to a smudged pencil sketch. A rectangle. A circle. A line that spiraled inward. "He called it the 'heart door.'"

Mark's stomach tightened. "Heart door."

Pecos stood, turning his face toward the far end of the cemetery—toward the oldest section where stones sank into earth like teeth. "It's calling," he said.

Mark hated that word more than the fog. More than the flowers. Calling meant wanting.

And whatever was down there had wanted players for a century.

They moved deeper.

The air cooled as they passed into the oldest rows. The grass here was thinner, patchy, and the headstones leaned in odd directions as if they'd been shoved from below. Mark tried not to imagine hands pressing up under the soil, searching for the surface.

Tommy stopped, staring at a stone half-buried in moss. "These are… kids."

Mark looked.

The name was worn, but the age was clear.

Sixteen.

The dates told the rest.

Alyssa's flashlight shook. "My grandfather wrote about this. 'They started young.'"

Mark felt his teeth grind together. Lowridge had always told the story like it was noble—boys giving everything for the town, legends turning into trophies. Down here, it was just hungry math. The land took what it could.

Pecos led them to a stone that looked ordinary until you were right in front of it. No helmet carving. No Lions logo. Just a smooth slab with a single word etched into it in careful, old-fashioned letters.

HARROW.

Alyssa's breath caught. "Harrow," she whispered, like she'd said it before in a different kind of fear.

Mark frowned. "You know that name?"

She nodded, slow. "Old records. Town council minutes. Donations. The Harrows are—were—everywhere." She stared at the stone. "But not on a grave."

Tommy leaned closer. "So… what? Secret family cemetery? Rich-people weirdness?"

Pecos didn't answer. He reached down and brushed his fingers along the base of the stone.

The fog moved.

It didn't drift. It peeled back, like a curtain being drawn.

A seam appeared in the ground—a thin, straight line in the soil right in front of the Harrow stone, running the width of a coffin lid.

Mark's skin prickled. "That wasn't there."

"It was," Pecos said. "We just couldn't see it."

Alyssa swallowed hard. "It's… the door."

Tommy took a step back. "Nope. No. Absolutely not. I vote we go home, set the town on fire, and start over somewhere else."

Mark ignored him. He knelt, fingers digging into the damp earth along the seam. The soil gave easier than it should have. Like it had been loosened recently.

Like something had been pushing from below.

He got his fingers under the edge and pulled.

The ground lifted.

Not earth—wood. A hatch, soaked dark with age, its surface etched with shallow grooves that reminded Mark of play diagrams. Lines. Arrows. Circles. All leading to the center.

Alyssa's voice came out in a thin whisper. "It's a play."

Mark's throat went dry. "A play to what?"

Pecos stepped over him, placing both hands on the hatch. "To feed," he said.

The hatch creaked open.

Cold air spilled out, and with it, something that sounded like a stadium in the distance—muffled cheers, old and looping, like a tape caught on a broken reel.

Mark's flashlight beam fell into darkness.

Stairs descended.

Tommy's laugh was sharp and wrong. "Of course it's stairs. It's always stairs."

Mark looked at Alyssa, then Pecos.

Alyssa tightened her grip on the journal. "We go together."

Pecos didn't hesitate. He stepped onto the first stair like it was familiar.

Mark followed.

The stairs were stone, slick with moisture. Mark kept one hand on the wall, and his fingers came away damp—not water. Something viscous.

He raised his hand to his light.

A thin smear shone dark.

Not purple.

Rust red.

"Keep moving," Alyssa said behind him, but her voice was strained, like she was speaking through a thick layer of cotton.

The air grew heavier the farther they went. The muffled cheering grew louder, then faded, then returned, like it was breathing.

Pecos stopped halfway down. He tilted his head, listening.

"What?" Mark whispered.

Pecos's eyes didn't focus on Mark. They focused on the wall.

There were roots there.

Not thick, tree roots. Fine threads, pale and vein-like, crawling between the stones. They pulsed faintly, as if they carried something.

Alyssa touched one with the tip of her pen. The root twitched away.

"Nope," Tommy muttered. "Nope nope nope."

Mark forced himself to keep moving.

At the bottom of the stairs, the tunnel opened into a corridor just wide enough for two people side by side. The walls were old brick, damp and sweating. The floor sloped downward, and the smell—iron and flowers— became almost unbearable.

Every few feet, the brick was broken, and roots threaded through like stitches.

Pecos walked ahead, barefoot-silent. Mark's footsteps sounded too loud, too human.

Alyssa's flashlight caught something carved into the brick.

Letters.

Not random. Not graffiti.

A name.

HARROW.

And beneath it, a handprint—darkened, smeared, as if someone had pressed a bleeding palm into the wall and left it there to dry.

Mark stared. His skin tightened like he'd stepped into cold water. "That's… blood."

Alyssa nodded, face pale. "My grandfather wrote about 'blood signatures.' He said the pact was… renewed. Marked."

Tommy swallowed hard. "So the Harrows signed it. With blood. In a tunnel under a cemetery."

Mark's jaw clenched. "Why?"

Pecos answered without turning. "Because blood and petals… gives access."

Alyssa jerked her head toward him. "You didn't read that."

Pecos's shoulders lifted in something like a shrug. "I don't need to. It's in the ground."

Mark felt a chill move through him that had nothing to do with the damp. Pecos wasn't guessing. Pecos was reciting.

Like the land had taught him the rules.

They reached a door at the end of the corridor.

Not wood. Not metal.

Stone.

A slab set into the brick, carved with the same shallow grooves as the hatch above—lines and circles, a play spiraling inward. In the center was a small depression shaped like a palm.

Alyssa's breath trembled. "It's asking."

Mark's hand twitched. He didn't want to touch it. He didn't want to give it anything.

But Pecos stepped forward.

"No," Mark snapped, grabbing his arm. "Don't."

Pecos looked at him then, and for a second, Mark saw the friend he'd known since middle school—the kid who laughed too loud, who ate spicy chips like it was a dare, who once cried when his dog died and tried to hide it behind jokes.

Then Pecos's eyes slid past Mark, and that friend drifted away behind something older.

"It already has me," Pecos said softly. "I'm just… closer to the signal."

Mark's grip tightened. "We go together. Remember?"

Pecos hesitated—just a blink, just a flicker of choice.

Alyssa stepped up beside them. "Wait," she said, voice shaking. "We don't give it blood. Not here."

Tommy's flashlight beam swung between them. "I'm begging you. Please. Can we use literally anything else? Sweat? Tears? I have plenty of both."

Alyssa swallowed. "There's another rule." She forced herself to speak the words like they mattered. Like they could form a shield. "Confession. Honesty. My grandfather wrote the land hates it."

Pecos's brow furrowed. "It… hates it," he repeated, like he was tasting the idea.

Mark's pulse thudded in his throat. He didn't know how to "confess" to a door. He didn't know how to be honest with a thing that had been lying to Lowridge for a century.

But he knew one truth like a rock in his chest.

"I'm scared," Mark said.

His voice echoed in the corridor, small and stupid.

Tommy's mouth opened, but no joke came out.

Alyssa stared at Mark like she hadn't expected him to say it out loud.

Mark kept going, because the words were out now and he couldn't shove them back in. "I'm scared because… because if this is real—if the heart is real—then Jason didn't just die. He got… taken." His throat tightened. He forced air through it. "And I've been pretending I can fix that. Like I can win a game against something that doesn't play fair."

The tunnel went quiet.

Even the muffled cheering paused, as if the sound itself had been interrupted.

Pecos's breathing hitched. The roots along the wall pulsed, then dimmed.

Alyssa whispered, "Mark…"

Mark shook his head, eyes burning. "I'm scared I'll go down there and see him and… I won't be able to do anything. And then it'll be my fault again."

He didn't know when he'd started crying. The tears felt hot against his cold cheeks.

The stone door didn't move.

But the pressure in the air eased, just a fraction. Like something had stepped back.

Alyssa stepped forward, placing her palm—clean, uncut—into the depression.

Nothing happened.

She closed her eyes. "I'm scared too," she whispered. "I'm scared I'll read the wrong thing and make it worse. I'm scared the answers my grandfather left me aren't enough."

Tommy swallowed hard, then said, "I'm scared I'm going to die in a tunnel because I followed you idiots." His voice cracked. "But... I'm more scared of leaving you alone down here."

Pecos stared at the stone. His jaw worked like he was fighting something inside his mouth.

Then he said, barely audible, "I'm scared that it's... inside me. That I don't know where I end and it begins."

The roots along the wall shivered.

The stone door rumbled.

A line appeared down the center—thin at first, then widening as the slab split apart. Not sliding. Unsealing.

The air beyond was colder. Deeper. And the sound that rolled out wasn't cheering.

It was a heartbeat.

Slow.

Immense.

The four of them stepped through.

The chamber beyond was cathedral-wide, carved out of earth and stone. The ceiling arched high overhead, lined with roots that hung down like chandeliers. Purple petals drifted lazily through the air, falling in slow spirals, landing on the floor like ash.

In the center of the chamber stood the heart.

It wasn't shaped like a human heart, not exactly. It was too big, too wrong. A massive knot of roots and muscle-like fiber, wrapped in layers of dark purple petals. Veins of pale thread ran across it, pulsing with faint light. Every slow beat made the floor tremble beneath Mark's shoes.

Mark's flashlight beam trembled on its surface, and he saw something that made his stomach turn.

Faces.

Not fully formed, not like statues. Impressions. Like people pressed into wet clay and pulled away too late. A jawline. A cheek. A closed eye. All half-swallowed by the living mass.

Tommy gagged, turning away. "Oh my God."

Alyssa's voice was barely there. "It's… it's a body."

"It's a mouth," Pecos said.

Mark stared at the heart, and the pressure returned—stronger now, direct. He felt it behind his eyes, pushing, pushing, like something trying to look through him.

Then Mark saw the altar.

It sat to the left of the heart, raised on a platform of stone. Ancient. Cracked. Carved with symbols Alyssa had shown them from the journal. At the center was another handprint, blackened with old blood.

And beside it, carved deep into the stone:

E. HARROW.

Alyssa's flashlight beam locked on it. "That's… that's not a grave marker," she whispered. "That's a signature."

Mark's mouth went dry. "So the Harrows weren't victims."

"They were…" Tommy's voice broke. "They were partners."

The heart beat again.

And something moved at the edge of Mark's vision.

Shadows—football-player shapes—stepped out from behind the hanging roots. They formed a circle around the chamber, silent as statues. Uniforms torn. Helmets cracked. Purple flowers sprouting from their ribcages like corsages.

Their faces were hard to see, but Mark felt their eyes.

All of them on him.

A cheer rose, muffled and distorted, as if the ghost players were celebrating a play only they could see.

Alyssa's breath hitched. "They're… guarding it."

Pecos took a step forward.

Mark grabbed his sleeve. "Pecos, no."

Pecos didn't stop. He walked toward the heart like he was walking toward a light in darkness. The ghost players didn't move to stop him.

They moved to stop Mark.

One of them stepped into Mark's path. It raised a hand—skeletal fingers wrapped in strips of old tape—and pointed.

Not at Mark.

At Pecos.

The message was clear as a whistle.

He belongs here.

Alyssa lifted the journal, flipping pages with frantic speed. "There's something—there has to be—"

Tommy's voice shook. "Maybe we're too late."

Mark's stomach dropped. "No."

Pecos reached the base of the heart. The roots there spread out like veins across the stone floor, slick and glistening.

He knelt, pressing his palm to the living mass.

The heart shuddered.

Purple light surged up the roots.

Pecos's shoulders went rigid. His mouth opened, but his voice didn't come out as a word.

It came out as a sound—half sob, half cheer.

Mark lunged forward.

The ghost player in front of him moved fast—too fast. A shoulder slammed into Mark's chest, sending him stumbling back. Cold hit him, like he'd been shoved into a freezer.

"Move!" Mark yelled, and it was useless. His voice was swallowed by the chamber's heartbeat.

Alyssa grabbed Mark's arm. "Don't fight them like they're people," she gasped. "They're not."

Mark's eyes darted to Pecos.

Roots were climbing his legs.

Not wrapping like vines.

Growing into him.

Pecos's jeans darkened where the roots pressed against his skin, as if they were sinking beneath it. His head tilted back, eyes rolled white.

Alyssa's voice rose, desperate. "Pecos! Look at me!"

Pecos's lips moved.

"No," he whispered.

Mark couldn't tell if Pecos meant no to them or no to himself.

Tommy stepped forward, voice cracking. "Pecos, please! Come back!"

The heart beat again, harder.

The entire chamber trembled.

A shower of petals fell, landing on Mark's shoulders, sticking to his skin like damp paper.

And then Mark felt it.

A sharp sting on his palm.

He looked down.

One of the petals had a thorn hidden beneath it. It had cut him, shallow but real. A bead of blood welled up.

The heart changed.

The light in its veins brightened. The faces pressed into its surface seemed to sharpen, like they were waking.

The ghost players' heads snapped toward Mark in perfect unison.

Alyssa's eyes went wide. "Mark—"

Blood and petals, Mark remembered.

Access.

The air thickened, pressing down on Mark's shoulders. The chamber seemed to lean in.

A shadow detached from the heart.

For a second, Mark thought it was just another ghost player—another dead boy in a uniform.

Then the shadow took a step into the light, and Mark's breath turned to ice.

Jason.

Not the Jason from Mark's memories. Not the boy who laughed too loud and tackled him in the backyard and stole his fries.

This Jason's skin was gray and translucent, like fog held in shape. Purple veins traced under his skin, pulsing in time with the heart. His eyes were not eyes. They were dark hollows lit from within by something hungry.

His mouth opened.

The voice that came out sounded like Jason's voice drowning.

"Leave," he rasped.

Mark's throat closed. "Jason."

Jason's head tilted, like the name hurt. For a moment, a flicker of something human crossed his face.

Then the heart beat.

Jason's expression snapped into something hard.

His body moved.

Fast.

He crossed the space between them in a blur and slammed Mark into the stone floor.

Mark hit hard, pain flashing up his spine. The air left his lungs in a strangled gasp. Jason's hand—cold as grave soil—clamped around Mark's throat.

Alyssa screamed. "Jason, stop!"

Jason's face hovered inches above Mark's. Purple light pulsed in his hollow eyes.

"Blood," Jason whispered, and Mark felt it—not as a word, but as a command. "You brought blood."

Mark clawed at Jason's wrist. It was like trying to pull away steel.

Tommy charged, tackling Jason from the side.

Tommy's body went through Jason like mist, but the impact still knocked Jason off balance. Mark rolled, coughing, gulping air.

Alyssa knelt beside Mark, hands shaking as she pressed cloth against his palm. "Don't bleed," she hissed. "Don't—"

Jason rose, turning toward Tommy.

Tommy scrambled backward, eyes wide. "Okay, okay, I'm sorry, man, I'm sorry—"

Jason lifted his hand.

The roots on the floor surged, snaking toward Tommy's ankles.

Tommy screamed as they wrapped around him, tightening.

Mark pushed himself up, fury burning through the fear. "Jason! This isn't you!"

Jason's head snapped toward Mark.

For a heartbeat, the cheering returned—louder now, hungry, as if the chamber itself approved of the violence.

Alyssa's voice cut through it, sharp. "Mark! Honesty!"

Mark froze.

Honesty. Confession. The thing the land hated.

He looked at Jason—at his brother's broken face—and the truth rose up in him like vomit.

"I couldn't save you," Mark shouted.

The words hit the chamber like a thrown rock.

The cheering stuttered.

Jason flinched.

Mark's voice cracked. "I keep thinking if I find the right secret, the right tunnel, the right spell, I'll get you back. But I can't." Tears blurred his vision. "And I hate myself for that."

The roots around Tommy loosened, just a fraction.

Jason's hand trembled.

Alyssa seized the moment. She held the journal up, flipping to a page covered in her grandfather's cramped writing. "Jason, if there's anything left of you—listen to him!"

Jason's face contorted, as if two expressions were fighting for control.

His mouth moved, and for a second the voice that came out was Jason's real voice, thin and terrified.

"Mark…" he whispered.

The heart beat.

Jason's eyes darkened again.

His body lunged toward Mark.

Mark braced, but Jason didn't go for his throat this time.

He went for his wound.

Jason grabbed Mark's bleeding palm, pressing it down onto the stone floor.

Pain flared—physical and something deeper, like Mark's blood was being pulled into the roots through the stone.

Alyssa screamed. "No!"

The heart's veins lit up like highways.

The faces in its surface shifted, pressing outward, mouths opening in silent screams.

Pecos convulsed, roots climbing higher, swallowing his thighs, his waist.

Mark felt the chamber's attention lock on him, the way a stadium locks on the quarterback right before the snap.

Jason leaned close, voice a harsh whisper. "Find… the hybrid."

Mark's breath caught. "What?"

Jason's eyes flickered, human for one second. "Marcus," he rasped. "He… escaped."

Alyssa's face went white. "Marcus? Who is—"

Jason's grip tightened, crushing Mark's fingers into the stone. Mark bit back a scream.

Jason's voice broke, urgent. "Pump station," he forced out. "Water tower. He's… hiding. He knows… how to run."

The heart beat again, and Jason's face twisted, the human flicker swallowed.

His voice dropped into something inhuman. "And you brought blood."

Jason shoved Mark's hand harder.

The roots surged.

Mark felt something wrap around his wrist, pulling, pulling, trying to drag him toward the heart.

Pecos screamed.

Not a word. A raw sound that echoed off stone and shook dust loose from the ceiling.

Mark yanked back with everything he had, but the roots held.

Tommy, free now, lunged forward and grabbed Mark's arm, pulling.

Alyssa threw herself onto Pecos, wrapping her arms around his shoulders, trying to keep him from sinking deeper into the root-web.

"Pecos!" she sobbed. "Fight it! Fight it!"

Pecos's eyes snapped open.

They were not white anymore.

They glowed faint purple, like embers behind glass.

His mouth moved, and when he spoke, his voice came out layered—Pecos and something else, whispering under it.

"It wants… a body," Pecos gasped. "It wants… to cross."

Mark's mind flashed to everything the town had been. Everything it wanted to stay.

"No," Mark growled.

He looked at Jason—at his brother being used like a weapon—and something inside Mark hardened.

He stared straight into Jason's hollow eyes and said the truest, ugliest thing he'd been avoiding for months.

"You're not the land," Mark said. "You're my brother."

The chamber went still.

The cheering died completely.

For a heartbeat, there was only the immense slow thud of the heart.

Jason's expression cracked. His mouth opened, and a sound like a sob tried to come out.

The roots around Mark's wrist slackened.

Alyssa's voice was hoarse. "Mark, keep going."

Mark's eyes burned. "I miss you," he said, voice shaking. "And I'm angry you left me. And I'm sorry I didn't tell you that when you were alive because I thought we had time."

The air in the chamber seemed to recoil, like the truth had teeth.

Jason's body shook.

He turned his head slightly, as if he could hear something else calling him.

The heart beat.

Jason's eyes flared purple.

His hand snapped up, grabbing Mark's throat again.

But his grip wasn't as strong.

Mark could breathe.

Alyssa shoved the journal toward Jason, pages fluttering. "If you're trapped in there—if you're still conscious—help us!"

Jason's mouth opened.

His voice came out as a strangled mix of commands and pleading.

"Hurry," he rasped. "It… learns."

Then he screamed.

The scream wasn't human. It was the sound of a hundred voices layered together—players, parents, coaches—cheers and cries mashed into one.

Jason staggered backward, clutching his head.

The roots holding Mark snapped back like severed cords.

Mark yanked his hand free, blood smearing the stone.

Alyssa grabbed his wrist, wrapping it tight with cloth.

"Move!" Tommy shouted, hauling Mark toward Pecos.

Alyssa clung to Pecos's shoulders, pulling with everything she had.

Mark grabbed Pecos's arm, and the skin under his fingers felt wrong—too warm, too alive, like it had a pulse separate from his own.

Pecos groaned, body jerking as the roots resisted. They tightened, digging in. Mark felt Pecos's muscles strain, felt the moment where Pecos's body almost gave up and let the land have him.

Tommy, face red with effort, grabbed Pecos's other arm. "Come on, man! Come on!"

Pecos's head lolled, eyes half-lidded. His lips moved.

"Marcus," he whispered.

Mark's chest tightened. "We'll find him," Mark promised. He didn't know who he was promising—Pecos, Jason, himself. "We'll find him and we'll get you out."

Pecos's eyes met Mark's for a second.

For a fraction of a heartbeat, they were normal.

Then Pecos screamed again, and the roots tore free of his legs with a wet, ripping sound that made Mark's stomach lurch.

Pecos collapsed into their arms.

The heart beat hard.

The chamber shook violently.

The ghost players finally moved—closing in, their bodies blurring, their hands reaching.

Alyssa grabbed the journal, voice ragged. "The door—back!"

They dragged Pecos toward the stone slab they'd entered through. Mark's shoes slipped on petals. The air felt thick with anger.

Behind them, Jason stood near the heart, trembling, half-human and half-hungry. His gaze found Mark.

For a moment, his mouth moved in a silent word Mark could almost read.

Run.

Then the heart pulsed, and Jason's body snapped into the shadows, swallowed.

They reached the stone door.

It was closing.

The split down the center narrowed, grinding together.

Mark shoved his shoulder into it, grunting as stone scraped his skin.

Tommy shoved with him. Alyssa half-carried Pecos, half-dragged, tears streaming down her face.

"Go!" Alyssa screamed.

Mark threw himself through the gap, scraping his ribs. Tommy followed, then Alyssa, dragging Pecos.

The stone slammed shut behind them with a sound like a coffin lid.

The cheering returned, muffled again, distant and looping—as if nothing had happened.

For a moment, they lay in the corridor, gasping, the brick walls sweating around them.

Pecos coughed, body trembling. Purple veins pulsed faintly under the skin of his calves, where the roots had been.

Alyssa wrapped her arms around him, sobbing. "You're here," she whispered. "You're here."

Tommy stared at Mark's hand, where blood still stained the cloth. "Dude," he whispered. "We just… we just got tackled by your dead brother."

Mark didn't answer.

He couldn't stop seeing the heart.

He couldn't stop hearing Jason's voice—Find the hybrid. Marcus. Pump station. Water tower.

Mark pushed himself up, ignoring the ache in his ribs. "We're not done," he said.

Alyssa looked up, face streaked with tears. "Marcus," she breathed. "Jason said Marcus."

Pecos's eyes fluttered. When he spoke, his voice was weak, but there was something steady beneath it now—like a wire pulled taut.

"Half-taken," Pecos whispered. "Half… free."

Mark nodded once, hard. "Then we find him," he said. "Tonight."

They stumbled up the stairs, the tunnel seeming longer on the way out. The air got warmer with each step, but the smell of violets clung to them like smoke.

When Mark shoved the hatch open, the fog above rolled toward them like it had been waiting.

They emerged into the cemetery like survivors crawling out of a grave.

The Harrow stone stood silent, innocent in the moonlight.

Mark glanced toward Jason's headstone.

In the pale light, purple flowers trembled at its base.

Mark's throat tightened, but he didn't look away.

"I heard you," he whispered, so quiet even Tommy couldn't tease him for it.

Somewhere beneath the earth, the heart beat.

But up here, in the cold night air, Mark felt something else too.

Not hope, not yet.

Just direction.

And that was enough to keep moving.

CHAPTER 15: THE HOLLOW NIGHT

The tunnel behind the visitor bleachers breathed them out like it didn't want them.

Mark hit the cold air and staggered, lungs scraping. Stadium lights hung above the fog in a sick half-glow—bright enough to turn mist into walls, dim enough to make the field look unfamiliar. Tommy doubled over, hands on his knees. Alyssa came out last, grimoire hugged to her chest, eyes darting back into the dark.

Pecos didn't come.

The space where he should have been pressed on Mark like a helmet pulled too tight. Down in that altar room, Pecos had gone rigid—eyes open, body held in place by something Mark couldn't see, like the earth had stitched him to the stone.

Mark forced himself to look away from the tunnel mouth and out across the turf.

The yard lines were faint. The numbers blurred under fog. And beyond the far fence, the cemetery glowed—soft purple light clinging to headstones the way dew clings to grass.

Two quick clicks sounded from the end zone. Cleats on concrete.

Tommy straightened too fast, panic flashing in his eyes. "Tell me that was you."

"It wasn't me," Alyssa said.

Mark's mouth went dry. The violet scent threaded the air—sweet, sharp—rimmed with something metallic that made his gums ache.

Then the stadium lights blinked.

When they steadied, someone stood on the fifty-yard line.

A man in a long coat that might once have been red, now dulled to rust. Purple petals layered around his neck like a collar—too many, too thick, some fresh, some wilted. He held a whistle between two fingers, and that small clean shine was the only thing that looked ordinary.

Alyssa lifted her chin. "Who are you?"

The man's smile was polite. "A traveler. A custodian. A witness, when it suits me."

Tommy let out a thin laugh. "That's not an answer."

"It is the only answer that lasts," the man said. His gaze moved to Mark and held there, as if he'd been waiting for him specifically. "You may call me the Wanderer."

Mark didn't step back. He didn't step forward. He kept his voice flat because if it cracked, he'd hear what fear sounded like. "Where's Pecos?"

The Wanderer's eyes flicked toward the ground. "Listening."

Anger sparked hot behind Mark's ribs. "Let him go."

"I can't release what the land has taken," the Wanderer said, still calm. "But I can offer you a path."

Alyssa's fingers tightened on the book. "We're not making deals."

"You already live inside one," the Wanderer replied. "You've simply enjoyed the benefits without reading the terms."

The fog thickened along the sideline, and the hum Mark had felt in the catacombs rose under the turf—one, two—like a buried drum keeping count.

The Wanderer lifted the whistle. "You found the heart. You saw the guardians. You learned the obvious truth."

"What truth?" Tommy demanded, trying for brave and landing on shaky.

"That you cannot reach it," the Wanderer said.

Mark's jaw tightened. "We'll reach it."

The Wanderer's smile thinned. "Not while the guardians stand."

Alyssa's eyes narrowed. "Then we get past them."

"How?" Mark asked, though he already felt the answer closing in.

The Wanderer pointed toward the cemetery fence. "By playing."

Tommy stared at him. "No."

"Yes," the Wanderer said, as if correcting a child. "One drive. One score. Your side against mine."

Alyssa didn't blink. "Rules."

The Wanderer's approval was subtle but present. "No leaving the boundaries. No outside help. No hiding beneath the earth. Win, and the guardians weaken. Lose…" He opened his hands. "And you become what Lowridge is built on."

Mark swallowed. "And if we refuse?"

"You delay," the Wanderer said. "And the land does not like delays."

Behind them, stone scraped—slow, deliberate—from the tunnel mouth.

Alyssa's flashlight snapped toward it.

A player stepped out.

Then another.

Then another.

Five figures moved onto the sideline, silent as film. Their uniforms didn't match—different eras stitched into shoulder pads and helmets. One wore a leather cap with no facemask. One's jersey looked decades old, the number half-faded. One was a lineman's bulk made wrong by time, pads too large, edges softened like they'd been underwater.

And one—

Mark's breath caught.

Number twelve.

Jason's number.

The figure moved into the half-light, translucent at the edges, and Mark saw his brother's face behind the bars of the helmet like an image trapped in glass.

Jason's eyes were violet.

For a heartbeat, something behind that violet flickered—recognition trying to breathe.

"Jason," Mark whispered.

Alyssa stepped closer to Mark, voice low. "That's a lure."

Jason's mouth moved without sound.

Don't.

The Wanderer raised the whistle to his lips.

The note that came out was too low to be heard properly. It vibrated through Mark's bones instead. The chalk lines on the field brightened bone-pale. The fog poured across the turf and hugged the ground like it belonged there. The cemetery fence shimmered, and the world narrowed to a boundary.

Deep under the field, a different kind of silence answered the whistle.

Pecos knelt in the altar room where the roots had pinned him, fingers pressed to stone. The note didn't reach his ears—it reached his bones, a low vibration that made the heart beneath the slab thump harder, eager. For one sharp moment, the roots lit with sensation: Mark's fear like a flare, Tommy's panic like a dropped weight, Alyssa's focus like a blade. Pecos tried to push back through the network, to send anything—a warning, a direction, a word—but the land held him tight, letting him watch and nothing more.

"Quarterback," the Wanderer said, pointing at Mark.

Mark's shoulders tightened with muscle memory and dread.

"Runner," the Wanderer said, pointing at Tommy.

Tommy's laugh cracked. "Of course."

The Wanderer's gaze landed on Alyssa. "Witness."

Alyssa's eyes flashed. "Excuse—"

"Someone must remember," the Wanderer said softly.

Then he stepped back, dissolving into fog until only the petal-collar and the pale whistle gleamed.

"One drive," his voice drifted in. "Begin."

The ball appeared in Mark's hands.

Cold. Heavy. Wrong.

For the length of one breath, it wasn't leather—it was a tight knot of purple petals bound by something dark and slick.

Mark blinked, and it was a football again.

Tommy leaned in, voice urgent. "Tell me you have a plan."

"We score," Mark said. "We don't bleed."

Alyssa snorted once, humor stripped to a thin edge. "Easy."

Across the line, the ghost-players shifted into position with the clean precision of people who'd run the same drill for decades. Jason stood slightly back, eyes fixed on Mark.

The field pressed at Mark's thoughts—routes offered like whispers. Cut here. Turn there. Follow the pattern. It would be smoother. Safer.

It would not be his.

"No," Mark breathed.

Alyssa heard it. "Choose, Mark."

Mark took the snap that wasn't a snap and shoved the ball into Tommy's hands. "Left. Hard cut at the twenty."

"That's not a play," Tommy hissed.

"It is tonight," Mark said.

Tommy ran.

Fog slapped at his shins. His cleats bit damp turf. For two seconds, it looked like a real breakaway.

Then the fast ghost-player moved—no sprint, no footsteps, just a stutter through space—appearing in front of Tommy like the film had skipped.

Tommy tried to juke. His foot caught.

Roots tightened around his cleat.

He hit the ground hard, and the sound didn't carry the way it should have, as if the fog swallowed impact.

Mark sprinted toward him.

The ghost-player knelt. A hand—half there, half shadow—pressed a purple petal to Tommy's exposed forearm where sleeve had ridden up.

Tommy's breath punched out. His body went still.

Then his eyes opened.

Violet.

Mark's stomach dropped. He'd seen that look once already in the cemetery, in the empty stare that wasn't Jason and yet wore his face.

"Tommy," Mark said, voice tight. "Look at me."

Tommy rose without effort, like someone had lifted him by a string. He turned and started running—not toward the end zone.

Toward the fence. Toward the graves.

Alyssa's voice snapped. "Mark—he's being pulled."

Mark caught Tommy by the shoulder pad and hauled him back. The cold under Tommy's skin made Mark's hand recoil, but he held on.

Tommy's mouth moved. No sound. His eyes stayed violet and blank.

Mark leaned close, desperation burning through him. Truth, he thought. The town chokes on truth. Maybe the land does, too.

"I'm scared," Mark said into Tommy's ear.

Tommy's stride faltered, just a fraction.

Mark pushed harder, words ripping out like they'd been caught in his throat for years. "I'm scared I'll end up like Jason. I'm scared I already am. I'm scared I want to win so bad I don't even know if it's me anymore."

Tommy stumbled.

The violet in his eyes flickered, thin as a candle threatened by wind.

"I hated it," Mark said. "I hated the way they turned him into a trophy. And I hated myself for being jealous of a dead person."

Tommy's mouth opened, and a sound broke through—raw, human. "Mark... stop."

Mark tightened his grip. "Fight. You're not a route."

The violet dimmed again.

Then petals drifted down around them, slow as snow.

Mark's scraped knuckles throbbed from the earlier climb, and when he looked down, he saw it—skin split, a smear of blood bright against his hand.

The scent sharpened instantly. Violet and iron.

A ghost-player's hand reached toward Mark's wound.

Alyssa was there before Mark could move. She flipped open the grimoire, struck her lighter, and whispered a single harsh word.

The flame jumped, becoming a thin ribbon that slid along the ground and curled around Tommy's forearm.

Tommy yelped. "Alyssa!"

"It's not for you," she snapped.

The fire kissed the petals and burned them black without touching Tommy's skin. Sweet smoke rose, choking and metallic. Tommy gagged and blinked hard.

His eyes returned—brown, wet, furious.

"I hate," Tommy coughed, "this town."

Alyssa's face had gone pale. A thin line of blood ran from her nose. She wiped it away like it was an inconvenience, but her hand shook.

"Can you do that again?" Mark asked.

Alyssa shot him a look that could have stripped paint. "Once. Maybe."

Mark turned back to the field.

The ghost-players regrouped in fog, patient, silent.

Jason stood at midfield, still watching.

Mark's chest tightened. He forced himself to meet those violet eyes. "I'm sorry," he said, not loud, not dramatic—just true.

Jason's shoulders jerked as if the words struck something inside him.

The violet dimmed for a heartbeat.

"Now," Mark said.

They moved as one.

Alyssa stepped forward, slammed the grimoire shut, and the fog around the defenders wavered—just enough, just long enough.

Tommy took the handoff again and sprinted, roaring like the sound could keep him alive. Mark ran beside him, ready to drag him back if the land tried to take the wheel.

The lineman ghost-player loomed ahead, massive.

The field whispered: cut right.

Mark refused.

He took the ball from Tommy in a quick pitch and cut left, hard, reckless, shoulder dropping.

His body collided with cold.

For a second, it felt like being tackled by winter itself. Something inhuman pressed against his mind, tasting fear, tasting guilt, searching for a door.

Mark shoved back with everything he had.

The ghost-player's form wavered.

Mark slipped past.

The seam of the end zone line waited ahead, pale as bone.

Jason moved.

He met Mark at the line, hands grabbing Mark's pads with a strength that wasn't fully human and yet felt achingly familiar.

Mark's breath caught. "Jason—"

The violet flared in Jason's eyes, and Mark felt the pull again—blood, petals, access—like the land was reaching through his brother to claim Mark's open wound.

Mark leaned in, forehead nearly touching Jason's helmet, and forced the words out before silence could steal them.

"I don't want your legacy," Mark whispered. "I want my brother."

Jason's grip tightened, then twitched.

The violet dimmed.

For the length of one heartbeat, Mark saw Jason—just Jason—eyes dark, grief pinned behind them.

Jason's mouth moved.

Run.

Mark didn't hesitate.

He broke free and dove across the line.

The stadium lights flared full bright for a single blinding flash. The fog recoiled. Mark hit turf and rolled, breath ripping out of him.

Silence fell hard.

Somewhere below, Pecos felt the flash as a jolt through the roots—like a score recorded in the only ledger the land cared about. The heart's pulse stuttered, then steadied, and for a moment he sensed a thin crack in the pattern, a weakness they had bought with breath and blood.

Tommy stumbled into the end zone and collapsed beside Mark, laughing like someone on the edge of a cliff. "We scored. We scored."

Alyssa limped in last, grimoire clutched tight, blood dried on her lip. "Worst touchdown in history," she muttered.

Mark pushed himself up and looked back.

The ghost-players remained—but their outlines flickered, weaker, as if someone had turned down the signal. Jason stood among them with his head bowed.

The Wanderer stepped out of fog, clapping slowly.

"Beautiful," he said. "Almost moving."

Tommy spat. "You're sick."

"I am old," the Wanderer replied pleasantly. "And you have won the game."

Mark's chest heaved. "Then the gate weakens. We go back down."

The Wanderer's smile held amusement and pity. "You still can't touch the heart."

Alyssa's eyes narrowed. "Why?"

"Because the heart is protected by more than strength," the Wanderer said. "It is protected by story. By rules you do not yet understand. By a hinge you haven't found."

Mark's stomach dropped. "Pecos."

The Wanderer's gaze slid to the ground. "The boy who listens. The one who can feel the routes beneath the town."

Alyssa stepped forward, voice cold. "You threaded him into it."

"The land threaded him," the Wanderer corrected gently. "I only opened the door."

Tommy's voice rose, fear turning into anger. "Let him go."

"I cannot," the Wanderer said. "But I can offer you a trade."

Alyssa's answer came instantly. "No."

The Wanderer's smile didn't waver. "Bring me the hybrid," he said softly. "Bring me the hinge. And I will show you the way in."

Mark's hands clenched. "We're not trading him."

"You already are," the Wanderer said. "You simply don't like the exchange rate."

Behind the Wanderer, at midfield, Jason lifted his head. His violet eyes met Mark's, and this time the recognition held—small, desperate.

Jason's mouth moved.

Find… the—

The violet flared, and the message drowned.

Jason's shoulders locked. The others stiffened in unison, like puppets waiting for the next pull.

The Wanderer lifted the whistle again. "You have until Hollow's Eve," he said. "Midnight. The field. The fog. You know the rhythm."

"And if we don't?" Mark asked.

The Wanderer's smile went hungry. "Then Lowridge plays its favorite game."

He stepped backward into the mist, petals rustling softly, and vanished as if the fog had always belonged to him.

The stadium lights steadied. The boundary shimmer on the fence faded, leaving only metal and darkness and the cemetery glow beyond.

Tommy drew a shaky breath and laughed once, helpless. "Okay. So. That happened."

Alyssa stared at the tunnel mouth like it was a wound in the world. "We go back for Pecos," she said. It wasn't a question.

Mark looked down at the turf near the sideline.

Tiny purple buds had pushed up through the grass.

On the field.

Where they weren't supposed to bloom.

He crouched without touching them and felt the hum beneath the grass —one, two—slow and patient.

A route beginning.

A prayer ending.

Mark stood.

"Now," he said.

And behind the cemetery fence, the flowers glowed softly, as if they were pleased to be remembered.

CHAPTER 16: THE ONE WHO ESCAPED

The stadium lights dimmed as morning came on, fog loosening its grip the way a hand pretends it isn't holding you.

Mark sat on the cold concrete behind the visitor bleachers, helmet in his lap, staring at the tape on his forearm. Beneath it, his scrape throbbed in a slow rhythm that didn't match his heartbeat.

Tommy paced until his steps started tracing the same loop—one-two, one-two—like his body wanted a tunnel to run through.

Alyssa stood at the fence with the grimoire tucked under her arm, eyes fixed on the cemetery beyond the far end zone. In daylight the headstones looked ordinary again. The purple glow was gone, sunk back into soil that never seemed to dry.

"We won," Tommy said at last, like he needed to hear the word out loud.

Mark tasted metal. "We survived," he corrected.

Alyssa didn't look away from the cemetery. "He said we would."

Mark heard the Red Wanderer's voice again—dry as leaves, amused as if the night had been entertainment.

You won the game, not the war. You still can't touch the heart.

Mark's stomach tightened. "This was never about 'winning,'" he said. "It's about keeping us busy until we break."

Tommy's face flickered at the mention of break—at the memory of Pecos still down there, half-swallowed by roots and stone. Mark didn't say the words. They all carried them anyway.

A small pressure gathered behind Mark's eyes, the familiar hum in the bones. Not loud. Not pulling. Just… testing. Like something in the ground had turned its head.

Then Mark's phone buzzed.

Unknown number.

He answered, and the speaker filled with static threaded through that same low vibration—earth turned into sound.

No voice came through.

But a text did.

WEBB.

Then a second message: coordinates.

Mark's throat went tight. He didn't know how he knew, only that he did.

"Pecos," he whispered.

The call cut off.

Alyssa leaned in, eyes snapping to the screen. "That's not random," she said. "That's a direction."

Tommy swallowed. "Who's Webb?"

Mark's forearm stung under the tape, like the scrape was listening. He remembered Jason's broken sentence under the cemetery, the way it had punched through the hum for one heartbeat.

Find the hybrid. He escaped.

"A player," Mark said. "One who got away."

*****

Alyssa didn't waste time on speeches. She drove straight to the library, into the back stacks where Lowridge kept its own mythology boxed and labeled.

Mrs. Hall hovered nearby, suspicious but flattered to be asked for "local history." Alyssa played the role perfectly—polite, earnest, harmless.

Mark opened a yearbook from fifteen years ago and saw the Lions logo wrapped in the familiar purple flowers, printed like a flourish instead of a warning.

Tommy flipped pages fast, muttering dates under his breath.

"Here," Tommy said, suddenly hoarse.

A senior photo. A wide receiver with a bright, practiced smile and eyes that didn't match it.

MARCUS WEBB.

Two pages later, a smaller picture under a headline about community outreach:

MISSING.

LAST SEEN AFTER A HOME GAME.

Mark's stomach dropped. "They printed it like a fundraiser," he said.

Alyssa turned the inside cover toward them. A donation stamp: DR. ELIAS MERRITT. Her grandfather.

In the margin beside Marcus's photo, faded ink in a familiar hand:

Find Webb. He knows the way out.

Alyssa's fingers trembled once, then stilled. "My grandfather suspected," she said. "He left breadcrumbs."

Mark typed Pecos's coordinates into the computer. A dot appeared over a patch of green far from any town name.

Distance from Lowridge: 198 miles.

Tommy stared at the screen like it was a door. "Two hundred miles," he whispered. "That's… that's outside the story."

Alyssa snapped the yearbook shut. "Exactly."

*****

The highway felt like a different world.

As Lowridge shrank behind them, Mark's lungs unclenched in slow increments. Tommy's bouncing knee finally stopped. Even Alyssa's shoulders lowered a fraction.

Distance mattered. Marcus had proven that much simply by existing.

Then they passed a rest stop, and Mark saw it—one purple bud pushing up through a crack where concrete met dirt. Not glowing, not dramatic, just stubborn and alive.

Alyssa saw it too. Her knuckles whitened on the steering wheel. "It's not just in town," she said.

Tommy tried to joke and couldn't. "Or we brought it with us."

Mark pressed his bandaged arm against his ribs. The scrape burned like an ember.

He didn't answer, because the truth was the only thing that seemed to make the hum hesitate.

And the truth was: he didn't know.

*****

The coordinates led them off the highway and onto gravel, then into woods thick enough to swallow light.

The GPS stuttered and froze. Alyssa parked anyway.

"We walk," she said.

A pale line crossed the road a few yards ahead, only visible when the sun hit it right.

Salt.

They followed it through the trees until a clearing opened and a small cabin appeared, windows darkened, porch still as a held breath. Another thick salt line circled the cabin like a boundary drawn by a trembling hand.

Alyssa stopped short. Mark did too, instinctively. Tommy exhaled hard.

The cabin door opened.

A man stepped out, mid-thirties, lean, flannel and work boots—ordinary until Mark's gaze caught on his left forearm.

Scar lines ran from wrist to elbow in thin slits, and within each slit, purple threads glimmered faintly, like flowers trying to live under skin.

The man's eyes locked on Mark's bandage.

"Don't come closer," he said.

Alyssa raised her hands. "We're not here to hurt you."

He didn't look at her. "Say your names," he ordered. "And say one true thing."

Tommy blinked. "That's—"

"Necessary," the man snapped. "Truth holds. Lies are doors."

Mark felt the hum twitch behind his eyes, like it approved of the sentence.

He swallowed. "Mark Rivers," he said. "And I don't want to be a symbol."

The man's gaze sharpened, not unkindly.

Alyssa's jaw worked. "Alyssa Merritt," she said. "And I'm scared I'm too late."

Tommy's voice came out small. "Tommy Decker. And I want my mom to stop looking at me like I'm already gone."

For a beat, the woods went even quieter.

Then the man nodded once, as if a lock had clicked.

"Good," he said, and finally looked up at them like they were people instead of threats. "Stay behind the line until I say."

Mark's throat tightened. "Marcus Webb?"

The man flinched at his own name, then nodded. "That's what they called me," he said. "Before Lowridge turned me into a story."

Mark gestured at his phone. "Pecos sent us. And… and Jason—"

Marcus's eyes went distant, as if listening to a voice under the wind. "Your brother's still fighting," he murmured. Then he focused again, hard. "Show me your arm."

Mark's first instinct was to deny it.

Marcus's stare cut through him. "Do not lie to me."

Heat rose to Mark's face. He peeled the tape back enough to show the scrape. The edges looked wrong—too dark, bruising too fast, a faint violet tint like ink under skin.

Marcus inhaled slowly. "You've been marked," he said. "Not chosen. Not blessed. Not anything people can pretend is pretty. Marked as noticed."

Alyssa's voice went tight. "Can you help him?"

Marcus's gaze flicked to the woods again, wary. "Inside," he said. "And don't bleed on my threshold."

*****

The cabin smelled of wood smoke and salt and something medicinal. Shelves held jars: petals suspended in clear liquid, dried roots, iron nails, black powder flecked with metal.

Marcus shut the door and slid a heavy bolt into place. "Don't open the book," he said, nodding at the grimoire.

Alyssa bristled. "We need it."

"It needs you," Marcus corrected. "It's a mouth."

Mark's skin prickled. "How do you know?"

Marcus lifted his scarred forearm and pressed two fingers to one slit. A tiny purple bud pushed through the skin like a tooth breaking gum.

Tommy made a choked sound.

Marcus pinched the bud and pulled. A petal came free, wet with something that wasn't blood, twitching faintly between his fingers.

"I'm not free," Marcus said quietly. "I'm a hybrid. Half mine, half signal. But I learned how to keep the signal from driving."

Mark's throat tightened. "How did you get away?" he asked. "From the field. From the fence."

Marcus's gaze slid to the bolted door as if he could still hear a crowd through it. "Same way you almost didn't," he said. "I cut against the play."

He spoke like it was simple, but his hand flexed once at his side, betraying memory. "It wanted me running toward the cemetery," he continued. "Routes in my muscles, a map in my skull. And then I saw my little brother in the stands—ten years old, wearing my number like armor. I realized if I crossed that fence, I wasn't just stepping into the flowers. I was setting the next kid's path."

Tommy swallowed audibly.

"So I ran wrong," Marcus said. "It felt like tearing myself in half. The pull fought me for every step. But I kept moving until the signal thinned— until distance made the hum stumble."

Alyssa's eyes sharpened. "Distance alone did it?"

"No," Marcus said, and his voice hardened. "Distance buys you breath. Truth buys you control."

He looked directly at Mark. "I said the thing I'd never said in Lowridge. Out loud. To nobody. I said: I'm scared. I don't want to die for this town. I'm running. I'm done being a symbol."

The words sat in the cabin like smoke.

"And the pull loosened," Marcus added. "Just enough for me to keep choosing steps."

Mark felt the ache in his chest twist, as if the confession had a physical weight.

"But the petals had already touched blood," Marcus said, lifting his scarred forearm. "By the time I made it out, it was inside me. The first time it tried to take me completely was in a motel room, two counties away. I didn't have a cemetery to anchor it, so it tried a different method—turning me into a moving receiver. I fought it with circles, with salt, with iron… and with truth. I didn't win clean. I merged. I survived."

He glanced toward the shelves of jars. "Survival leaves stains."

Alyssa leaned forward. "How?"

Marcus set the petal on the table and slid a shallow metal tray into view. On it was a circle drawn in dark powder mixed with salt and iron filings.

"Severance," he said. "It grounds the pull. Buys you time."

Mark's pulse hammered. "That's… a spell?"

Marcus's mouth twisted. "Call it survival," he said. "Ingredients matter —burned petal, salt, iron, a pinch of grave dirt. But what really matters is what you do inside it."

Alyssa's eyes narrowed. "What do you do?"

Marcus's gaze locked onto Mark. "You tell the truth," he said. "The one you keep swallowing. The one the town trained you to choke down so you'd keep belonging."

Mark remembered the roar of the crowd. The way it had shoved him downfield. The way his muscles had known the route before his mind.

Marcus's voice stayed steady. "The flowers are conduits," he said. "Blood opens the circuit. The cemetery is the strongest node. Distance weakens the station—but if you're marked, it will keep testing you until it finds a crack."

Tommy's voice trembled. "So truth… stops it?"

"Truth interrupts the current," Marcus said. "Denial is a highway. Truth is gravel."

He knelt and drew a fresh circle on the cabin floor, widening it with salt and iron. "Step in," he ordered Mark.

Mark hesitated. The hum rose behind his eyes like water behind a dam.

Alyssa's hand hovered near Mark's shoulder but didn't touch. "Mark," she said softly.

Mark stepped into the circle.

The pressure hit instantly—stadium lights behind his eyelids, fog in his throat, the command like a tide.

RUN.

His knees bent without permission.

Marcus's voice cut through like a whistle. "Say something true."

Mark opened his mouth and almost said I'm fine, because that's what he always said.

The hum surged, eager.

Mark swallowed hard. The truth that came out tasted like rust.

"I wanted to leave Jason behind," he said, voice shaking. "I wanted out so badly I… I was relieved when he was gone."

The cabin went still.

Alyssa's breath caught. Tommy made a small sound like grief startled into the open.

The hum faltered—just a stutter, but real. The pressure loosened enough for Mark to breathe.

Mark's eyes burned. He kept going because he had to. "I don't know how to save him," he whispered. "And I'm scared I'm next."

The hum receded another notch, pulling back like a tide that didn't like the shore.

Mark stood inside the circle, shaking, but still himself.

Marcus nodded once, fierce and satisfied. "That's severance," he said. "Truth cutting the line."

He looked at Alyssa. "Your turn."

Alyssa stepped in, jaw clenched. "I'm not scared," she snapped.

The hum surged hard, delighted.

Marcus's eyes narrowed. "Try again."

Alyssa swallowed, voice breaking. "I'm terrified," she said. "I'm terrified my grandfather died trying to fix this and I'm going to die too and it won't matter."

The pressure eased.

Tommy stepped in last, trembling. "I'm angry," he said, the words spilling fast. "I'm angry no one sees it, and I'm angry that the town loves the Lions more than it loves the boys."

The hum softened, grudging.

Marcus stepped back and regarded them like he was measuring whether they could survive their own honesty.

"Good," he said. "Now you know what it costs."

He slid a small pouch toward Mark. "Salt. Iron. Black ash. You'll need more, but this will start you."

"And listen," Marcus added, voice low. "Severance is not a cure. It's a window. When you use it on someone already taken, you may get them back for minutes—enough to speak, enough to pull information through the fog, maybe enough to choose something before the signal slams down again. But if you hesitate, if you feed it a lie, the snap-back is worse."

Tommy's hands clenched. "So it's dangerous."

"Everything is dangerous," Marcus said. "This is just honest about it."

He nodded toward Alyssa's grimoire. "And every time you cut the current, you make noise. You disturb the network. That's when Eoraziel pays attention. It can ignore denial for years. It doesn't ignore resistance."

Alyssa clutched the grimoire tighter. "We found the heart," she said. "We can't touch it."

Marcus's eyes went distant again, listening to something under the floorboards. "The heart can be attacked," he said. "But you need an anchor-breaker."

Mark's stomach clenched. "What is that?"

Marcus shook his head once. "A way to snap the signal at its source," he said. "Someone has to carry the weight long enough to break it."

Tommy whispered, "Pecos."

Marcus didn't deny it. His silence was answer enough.

Alyssa's voice shook. "We didn't choose that for him."

"No," Marcus said quietly. "And that's why you're not Lowridge."

He exhaled, long and tired, and looked out at the darkened window like he expected eyes in the trees.

"Here's the other cost," he said. "If I help you more than this—if I use what I am to reach into the network—Eoraziel will notice me."

The name made the air feel colder. Mark's skin prickled, as if the woods outside had leaned closer.

Marcus's mouth tightened. "I've stayed quiet for fifteen years so it wouldn't turn its face fully toward me," he said. "If I step back in... it will hunt."

Tommy's voice cracked. "Then don't."

Marcus gave a small, humorless smile. "Running only works until the road runs out," he said. "And it's marked your blood."

Mark's phone buzzed.

A text from his mom.

MARK. COME HOME. SOMETHING HAPPENED AT SCHOOL.

A photo followed—tile floor, lockers, and a smear of purple petals like someone had spilled a bouquet and dragged it.

Alyssa went very still.

Tommy's face drained of color. "It noticed," he whispered.

Marcus stared at the screen, and the purple threads in his scars pulsed faintly in response, like a tuning fork answering a note.

"Yeah," Marcus said softly. He grabbed a duffel bag from the corner. "It noticed."

Mark tightened his grip on the pouch of ash and salt.

"I'm scared," he said, and this time it wasn't a confession pulled out of him—it was a choice.

Marcus nodded once. "Good," he replied. "Let's go make it pay attention to the wrong things."

CHAPTER 17: THE PACT'S BREAKING POINT

The cabin's quiet felt earned, the way silence did after a close call—when your body finally realized you were still alive.

Mark rinsed his hands at the sink until the tremor in his fingers settled. In the window above the basin, the woods reflected back in dark layers, and beyond them, faint stadium lights bled through fog like Lowridge had left a nightlight on.

The town didn't sleep. It waited.

On the couch, Pecos lay half propped on a pillow. His eyes were closed, but he wasn't resting. His breathing came in careful pulls, and every so often his forearm twitched as if something under the skin was testing its range.

Mark tried not to stare. He failed.

Thin violet threads ran beneath Pecos's forearm—too straight to be veins, too deliberate to be fear. They pulsed in a rhythm that wasn't his heartbeat, like another clock had started inside him.

Alyssa paced with her grandfather's journal pressed to her chest, turning in tight circles like she could wear a new answer into the floorboards. Tommy sat on the other end of the couch with his helmet in his lap, fingers worrying the ring he always wore. He'd taken it off and put it back on twice since they'd arrived.

Marcus Webb set a book on the table and unwrapped it like it might bite.

The grimoire's cover looked like burned wood polished smooth, grain lines tight as fingerprints. Even closed, it made the room feel smaller.

"That's it," Alyssa said.

"That's it," Marcus confirmed.

Mark swallowed. "You said you could read it."

Marcus didn't look up. "I said I could try."

He opened a drawer and pulled out a tin of gray ash and a pouch of coarse salt. He poured both in a careful circle around the grimoire, leaving space between the boundary and the book, like he was naming the edges of something hungry.

Tommy shifted. "Does it… care about your circle?"

Marcus's voice stayed level. "We'll find out."

Pecos opened his eyes. "Before we do," he said quietly, "tell me what you're deciding about me."

The sentence cut clean through the room.

Alyssa stopped pacing. Tommy's fingers stilled on his ring. Mark felt heat rise behind his ears, because the answer had lived in their silence.

Marcus glanced at Pecos, then back to the book. "We're not deciding anything without you," he said.

Pecos held his gaze. "Good."

Alyssa stepped closer, her voice steadier now. "We're trying to find out how to break the pact," she said. "Not how to pay it."

Marcus rested both palms on the table—outside the ash and salt—and closed his eyes.

For a few seconds the cabin stayed a cabin: old wood, dust, pine, cold air.

Then the grimoire made a sound like a sigh.

Mark's stomach tightened. The pressure behind his eyes sharpened, the same wrong sensation that came with the flowers—like the air had become a thought you couldn't escape.

Marcus opened his eyes.

A faint wash of violet slid across them, as if moonlight had entered from the wrong direction.

Tommy made a small sound that might've been a curse if he'd had the energy. "Okay. Not a fan of that."

Marcus's voice didn't change pitch, but it changed texture—like two stations overlapping. "It wants a path," he said. "It always wants a path."

Alyssa leaned in despite herself. "Severance," she said. "What is it?"

Marcus's gaze drifted, unfocused. "Two steps," he murmured. "A door. Then a cut."

Mark forced himself to speak. "Explain."

Marcus's fingers flexed on the tabletop. "First step is the anchor-breaker."

Alyssa's breath caught. "My grandfather wrote that phrase."

Marcus nodded once, slow. "The pact isn't just roots and blood. It's tied to a person. A living throat. Someone who carries the town's lie so the land can hold the bargain steady."

Mark felt the words land in his ribs. Living throat.

Alyssa's voice went quiet. "Anchor-breaker breaks it by… confession."

"By truth," Marcus corrected. "Confession is just what truth sounds like when it hurts."

He inhaled sharply, like something tugged on his lungs. "The land feeds on what you hide. Shame. Denial. Everything you swallow so you can keep smiling. The anchor-breaker stands in the network and lets it try to take them. Then—when it believes it owns them—the anchor-breaker names the truth the town refused to name."

Tommy frowned. "So the anchor-breaker is bait."

"Bait that bites back," Marcus said. "If they hold on."

Mark's mouth was dry. "Second step."

Marcus's violet gaze drifted again. "The cut. Severance. Once the door is open, you reach the root-heart and you cut it."

"The root-heart," Alyssa repeated, writing it down like ink could pin it.

"It's a place," Marcus said. "Under Lowridge. Where the routes knot. Where the names are kept."

Mark pictured the cemetery like a grid. Marked stones. Space waiting.

Alyssa lifted her head. "So we go there after the anchor-breaker opens the door."

Marcus's voice went flat. "If the anchor-breaker fails, the land stops bargaining and starts taking openly."

Pecos exhaled, careful. "And you're looking at me like you already decided I'm the door."

No one answered fast enough.

Mark took a step forward. "No," he said.

Alyssa's eyes flicked to him. Tommy swallowed hard.

"We're not choosing Pecos because it's convenient," Mark said, louder this time. "We're not turning him into a tool."

Pecos watched him for a moment, then nodded once, like he was filing that away. "Good," he repeated.

Alyssa steadied herself. "My grandfather wrote that the anchor-breaker has to choose. If it's forced, it reads like payment, not defiance."

Marcus's violet eyes blinked. "That's right."

Pecos's jaw tightened. "Then I choose later," he said. "When I know what I'm choosing for."

Alyssa nodded. "We give you the choice now," she said. "We pull your consciousness back first—before we ask you to stand in the door."

Pecos's forearm pulsed. The violet threads brightened, then faded, like the land had noticed his name in the conversation.

Marcus's mouth tightened. "It heard that."

Mark's stomach dropped. "Because we said the truth?"

"Because we said anything it didn't choose," Marcus replied. "Truth is a blade. It's also a flare."

Alyssa looked at Pecos. "Stay with us," she said softly.

Pecos's eyes focused with effort. "I'm here," he said, but the words sounded like they'd traveled a long way to reach his mouth.

Marcus reached into his pocket and set a small glass jar inside the salt circle. A single dried petal lay curled at the bottom—purple turned nearly black.

"This came from the cemetery," Marcus said. "It still holds signal."

Mark stared at it. Even dead, it looked stubborn.

Marcus's gaze found Mark. "You want to save him?" he asked. "Then start with truth. Right now."

Heat rose behind Mark's eyes. "What does that have to do with—"

"It has everything to do with it," Marcus cut in. "The network holds you by what you won't say. It uses your silence like a handle."

Alyssa didn't soften it. "And you've got a lot of handles, Mark."

Mark wanted to argue. He couldn't. The truth sat in his throat like a weight.

He stared at the jar until the room stopped spinning. "I'm angry at Jason," he said.

Tommy's head lifted slowly.

Mark kept going because stopping would be worse. "I'm angry he left me with the town's expectations. I'm angry that people talk about his death like it's a story with clean edges. And I'm angry at myself because part of me still thinks if I win enough games, I'll make it right."

The cabin's air shifted, subtle as a held breath. Mark glanced toward the window.

Outside, between the trees, a faint purple shimmer flickered and went still—like something had opened an eye and closed it again.

Inside the jar, the dried petal trembled.

Then it dulled, the purple sinking as if someone had turned a dial down.

Alyssa inhaled sharply. "Okay," she whispered. "That's real."

"It can't hold what's named," Marcus said. The violet film on his eyes thinned. "Not for long."

Tommy stared at the jar like it had betrayed physics. "So… what do I do? Just say I'm terrified?"

Alyssa shot him a look. "You are."

Tommy's ears reddened. His fingers tightened around the ring until his knuckles went pale. "When I was little," he said, voice rough, "I saw something in the cemetery. My dad swears I don't remember because I was three, but my body remembers. Every time I smell that sweet violet stink, I want to run—and I joke because if I don't, I freeze."

The petal dimmed a fraction more.

Pecos let out a slow breath. "It hates honesty," he murmured.

Alyssa swallowed. "I have one too," she admitted. "My grandfather—he wasn't only warning me. He believed the pact was protecting the town. He wrote that the founders thought they were saving everyone by sacrificing a few."

Tommy shook his head. "That's still—"

"I know," Alyssa snapped, then softened. "I'm not defending it. I'm saying the rot survived because people called it necessity."

Marcus nodded once. "That's how it lasts centuries."

Pecos's breathing hitched. The violet threads under his skin brightened, pulsed, then flared wider for a heartbeat. His eyes unfocused.

Alyssa was beside him instantly. "Pecos," she said. "Stay. Stay."

Pecos blinked hard like he was pushing back through water. "I'm here," he repeated, and this time it sounded more like him.

Marcus drew a new line of ash on the table, reinforcing the circle. "No more flares," he said. "Not until we're ready to use them."

Alyssa's gaze snapped to Marcus. "How do we pull him back?"

Marcus's violet gaze went distant again for a moment. Then he exhaled and the double-texture in his voice faded, leaving only exhaustion. "The network is routes," he said. "Cemetery and field are the strongest nodes—grave soil and game soil. Glory and grief."

Mark's chest tightened. He could almost hear it: the crowd roar, the band, the hum under it all.

"To pull him back," Marcus continued, "we need an anchor that belongs to Pecos more than the land does. Family. Memory. Choice."

Alyssa nodded, already building steps. "We go to his grandmother's place."

Pecos's jaw tightened. "It's my uncle's now."

Tommy's brows lifted. "Does your uncle like midnight spiritual interventions?"

Pecos didn't answer. That was answer enough.

Marcus's voice turned hard. "We don't have time to be polite."

Alyssa looked at Pecos. "We bring a petal," she said. "We force the signal to compete with something truer. We call you back while you still can choose."

Pecos held her gaze, steady even with pain pulling at him. "And if I can't?" he asked.

Alyssa's throat worked. "Then we still don't decide for you," she said. "But we don't let it decide for you either."

Marcus tapped the grimoire with one finger—still outside the salt. "There's one more line," he said, voice low. "The book doesn't soften it."

Alyssa didn't blink. "Say it."

Marcus's gaze slid to Mark. "The land expects a Rivers," he said.

Mark's stomach dropped.

Tommy shook his head hard. "No. It expects the mayor. Or Coach. Or —"

"Bloodline matters," Marcus cut in. "Names matter. That's why your family is treated like Lowridge royalty. That's why it took your brother. That's why it keeps testing you."

Mark's mouth went dry. "Testing me how?"

Marcus's eyes narrowed. "On the field. In fog. In moments when you feel the play run through you like it isn't yours. That's Eoraziel checking the fit."

Mark's pulse hammered. He hated how accurate it was.

Alyssa's hand found his arm, light but steady. "You don't have to be what it wants," she said.

Marcus's voice went colder. "But if you step into the network as the anchor-breaker, it will try to wear you like a jersey. It will show you your brother. It will offer you relief if you stop fighting."

Pecos's voice came quiet, firm. "Choice changes the signal," he said. "Mark choosing matters."

Tommy's eyes were glassy with panic. "So we don't let him."

Alyssa's sarcasm flashed, brittle. "And how do you propose that? We hide him? We leave town? You think the land can't count?"

Mark exhaled slowly. The truth he'd said a minute ago still hurt in his chest, but it also felt like a door he'd finally opened himself.

"If it expects me," Mark said, "then I'll stand where it expects me to stand."

Tommy's head snapped toward him. "Mark—"

"I'm not volunteering to die," Mark said, forcing the words to stay steady. "I'm volunteering to choose."

Alyssa's fingers tightened on his arm, and for a moment the others blurred—Marcus over the book, Tommy hovering near Pecos like proximity could protect him.

Alyssa guided Mark two steps toward the sink, just out of the couch's orbit. Her voice dropped to something only he could hear.

"You don't have to prove anything to me," she said.

Mark let out a shaky breath he hadn't known he'd been holding. "It feels like I do," he admitted. "My last name—Jason—people look at me like I'm already part of the bargain."

Alyssa's gaze didn't flinch. "You were born into a story you didn't write," she said. "That doesn't make you the villain. It makes you... the person who can change the ending."

Mark's throat tightened. "And if I can't?"

"Then we don't let you do it alone," Alyssa said, and the words were steadier than anything she'd said all night. "We make your truth bigger than its lie."

Mark managed a small, tired sound that wasn't quite a laugh. "That's your pep talk?"

"It's the only kind I have," she said, and the corner of her mouth lifted—brief, real. Then her expression sobered again. "Also... I'm sorry. For coming at you like you're a locked door. I'm scared, and I turn fear into questions."

Mark met her eyes. "Keep asking," he said. "Just... don't let me hide."

Alyssa nodded once, like a promise. "Deal."

Marcus held Mark's gaze. "If you break," he said, "it won't stop at you."

Alyssa's shoulders stiffened. "Who?"

"The team," Marcus answered. "The ones closest to the field. If you fail, it will try to balance the loss of control by taking more pieces. It will turn a game into a harvest."

Silence hit the cabin like a weight.

Pecos closed his eyes for a second, then opened them. "Then we move fast," he said.

Alyssa nodded. "Tonight," she said. "We go to Pecos's family land. We pull him back as much as we can."

"And tomorrow," Marcus added, "we train."

Alyssa's eyes sharpened. "You teach us."

Marcus let out a quiet, humorless breath. "Some of what's in there might hurt you."

"We'll take hurt," Alyssa said. "We're done with helpless."

Tommy finally forced a half grin, thin but present. "Also, you look like a terrible substitute teacher, so you're probably qualified."

For a moment, Marcus's mouth twitched—almost a smile.

Mark looked at Pecos. "We get you your choice," he said.

Pecos nodded once. "Then we fight."

Mark crossed to the back room Marcus had offered and paused at the window one last time. Fog rolled through the trees like something rehearsing. Far off, stadium lights glowed steady, patient, as if they were already sure who would show up on Friday night.

Mark pressed his palm to the glass and let the fear settle without swallowing it. Truth as a blade. Truth as a flare.

Outside, between trunks, a faint purple shimmer rose and fell—like breathing.

Somewhere beneath the cabin floorboards, so subtle he would have missed it a week ago, the wood creaked in a cadence that wasn't his.

One-two.

One-two.

The land was counting down.

CHAPTER 18: THE GATHERING STORM

Lowridge was pretending again.

Morning traffic moved like it always moved. The diner's neon buzzed. The big downtown sign still bragged WHERE LEGENDS ARE MADE, and the purple flower curled around the Lowridge Lions logo like a harmless decoration.

Mark noticed the new bloom tucked behind the sign's metal edge anyway—real, velvet-dark, too fresh for late fall. Somebody had placed it there like a blessing.

He didn't touch it. He didn't trust anything in this town that wanted to be held.

By lunch, the fog had returned.

Not thick enough to shut down school, not strange enough to make the principal send a warning. Just a low, pale smear that hugged the football field beyond the cafeteria windows, clinging to the turf like a secret.

Tommy slid into the seat across from Mark and stabbed a fry like it had offended him. "Tell me you're seeing this."

Mark kept his voice low. "Seeing what?"

Tommy leaned closer. "The fog. In the middle of the day. My grandma would've nailed the windows shut for less."

Alyssa dropped her tray beside them without asking. "It's not weather."

Tommy made a face. "Cool. Love that answer."

Pecos sat last, quiet as always, shoulders slightly hunched. His eyes flicked to the windows and back, like he was listening to something none of them could hear.

Alyssa's phone buzzed. She glanced at the screen, then at Mark. "After practice. Same place. Bring your camera."

Mark's fingers tightened around his water bottle. He hadn't told her he'd started carrying it again. He wasn't sure he liked that she knew anyway.

Practice started clean.

For the first twenty minutes, it was just football: warm-ups, routes, the ball snapping into Mark's hands and leaving again. The kind of routine that tricked you into believing you could control anything if you repeated it enough.

Then Dylan Harrow ran the same slant three times without hearing a single whistle.

Coach Whitman's shout cut through the drill. "Harrow! Stop!"

Dylan didn't stop. He cut hard, caught a pass that wasn't thrown, and kept moving like the field had taken over his muscles.

Mark stood frozen under center, ball cradled against his ribs. Dylan hit the end zone, pivoted, and ran the route again—perfect timing, perfect angle, empty stare.

Tommy drifted near Mark, helmet on, voice barely moving his lips. "That's not normal."

"No," Mark said.

A second whistle. A third.

Dylan blinked mid-stride like someone had switched a light on inside his skull. He stumbled, then stopped, confused and embarrassed. "Coach? I thought you called it again."

Coach's face didn't soften, but his eyes did something else—something measured. "Water. Now. Shake it off."

Dylan jogged to the sideline, laughing too loud at a joke he hadn't heard.

Mark's gaze dropped to the turf. Near the numbers, a cluster of tiny purple buds pressed up between blades of grass, slick-looking even in daylight.

A flicker hit behind Mark's eyes—pressure, then clarity.

For one skipped heartbeat, he saw under the field.

Not dirt and pipes.

Lines.

A faint web of routes and branches stretching from the stadium toward the cemetery fence, then out toward town—toward the new tech park cranes on the far horizon.

Then his vision snapped back.

Mark threw the next pass too hard. Coach barked his name. Mark forced his shoulders loose and pretended nothing was wrong, because Lowridge rewarded denial like it was discipline.

They met behind the stadium by the old utility shed.

Alyssa was already there with her grandfather's journal and a canvas bag that clinked softly. Tommy paced. Pecos leaned against the shed wall, palm pressed to the metal like he could feel the hum through it.

Alyssa didn't waste time. "The buds are on the field. That's weaponization."

Tommy stopped pacing. "We're really saying that word like it's normal."

"It's accurate," Pecos said. His voice was calm, but his jaw was tight. "It's spreading faster."

Mark held up his camera. The strap around his wrist felt like a tether. "I saw… lines. Under the turf."

Alyssa's eyes sharpened. "Then it's starting. Your grandfather wrote about that—about the town becoming a map."

Tommy's laugh came out thin. "Great. So the land installed GPS."

Alyssa flipped open the journal and tapped a page. "He calls it an awakening. Not magic. A counter-current. He believed the pact didn't just bind the town—it changed people living on it. Slowly."

Tommy's ring flashed as he rolled it between his fingers. "So we're… changed."

"We're soaked in it," Alyssa said. "And the only way to fight it is to stop being passive inside it."

Pecos's eyes stayed on the ground. "That's why confession breaks the conduit."

Tommy frowned. "I still hate that the solution is feelings."

Alyssa ignored him and kept reading. "We need a place where the roots are close. Salt. A claim. And a token—something the pact recognizes."

Mark's stomach tightened. "You mean—"

"I don't mean Jason," Alyssa said quickly. "Older. Founders' era. The stones with the original plaques."

Tommy blew out a breath. "We're doing this tonight, aren't we."

Alyssa nodded. "Hollow's Eve is in four days. The fog is already showing up at lunch. We don't get more time."

Pecos finally lifted his hand from the shed. His fingers trembled. "The land's active. It's listening."

Mark didn't like the way that sounded.

They didn't go through the cemetery front gate.

Pecos led them along the creek trail where the air always smelled faintly sweet, then along the fence line to the older section where stones leaned like tired teeth. Here the flowers grew in deliberate rings, and the fog curled between markers like slow smoke.

Alyssa stopped at a half-sunken stone with a tarnished lion plaque at its base. "This one's in the journal."

Mark crouched. The screws were old, reluctant. The pocketknife shook in his hand as he turned them loose.

When the plaque came free, the flowers around the grave shuddered.

Response. Not wind.

Tommy made a sound that tried to be a joke and failed. "Yep. Love that."

Alyssa wrapped the plaque in red twine, knotting it tight. "We don't carry it bare."

"Why?" Mark whispered.

"Because it knows it," Alyssa said. "And we're about to tell it we know, too."

They followed Pecos deeper into the trees to a shallow depression where the ground felt softer, warmer—wrong. Pecos pressed his palm to the soil and inhaled like he'd touched a live wire.

"The roots are close," he said. "Here."

Alyssa poured salt in a circle, set the wrapped plaque in the center, and lit a stubby black candle. The flame burned steady in the fog as if it had its own air.

"We start with truth," Alyssa said. "Something you've never said here. Something the town trained you not to say."

Mark's chest tightened. Tommy stared at the trees. Pecos watched the ground.

Alyssa stepped into the salt circle first. "My name is Alyssa Dawson," she said. "And my family helped build the cage."

The candle flame bent toward her.

"I'm not crazy," Alyssa continued, voice hard. "I'm angry. And I'm done protecting a town that won't protect its kids."

A distant sound moved through the woods—like a cheer heard through water.

Mark stepped in next before he could lose his nerve. "My name is Mark Rivers," he said, and the words felt heavier than pads. "I'm supposed to want this—football, glory, all of it."

He swallowed. "I don't."

The air tightened.

"I want to leave Lowridge," Mark said, voice breaking on the last word. "And I think Jason died because the town was hungry."

Fog surged, then paused, as if something had turned its head.

Pecos spoke from the edge of the circle, voice low. "My name is Pecos Morales. This land knows my blood. I'm not a tool."

The hum under the soil deepened like a bass note.

Tommy hesitated, then stepped into the circle, shoulders squared like he was taking a hit. "My name is Tommy Blake," he blurted. "I'm scared."

The candle flame flared.

Tommy's cheeks flushed, but he pushed through. "I joke because if I don't, I freeze. And if I freeze, something gets in."

He squeezed his ring so hard his knuckles whitened. "And I didn't tell you something. When I saw it last week, I— I went to Coach. I didn't know what else to do."

Alyssa's head snapped up. "Tommy."

"I'm sorry," he said, and it came out real.

The ring vibrated in his palm.

The fog answered.

Between the trees, figures moved—old uniforms, cracked helmets, bodies threaded with faint purple light. They ran between stones in perfect routes, cutting and crossing, never colliding, never slowing. Faces hidden. Eyes empty.

One of them ran straight at the circle and stopped at the salt line like it had hit glass.

Mark raised his camera without thinking. The viewfinder sharpened what the night tried to blur.

A number on the jersey.

Eli Carter.

Mark's stomach dropped. He clicked the shutter.

The snap of the photo cut through the fog like a clap.

For one suspended instant, everything stalled—the running figures mid-stride, the candle flame stiff, the fog held in place.

In that pause, Mark saw behind the facemask.

Eli's eyes were open.

Aware.

Trapped.

Then the moment broke and the routes resumed, mechanical and hungry.

Alyssa's voice went tight. "Keep talking. Control it. Don't let it write for you."

Tommy stared at his ring like it had betrayed him and saved him at the same time. "I'm scared," he said again, louder. "And I'm still here."

The vibration in the ring surged into his wrist like a current.

The air inside the salt circle changed—thinned, clarified—like a huddle forming around them.

The nearest figure recoiled a step, not afraid, but resisted—like it had hit something it didn't expect.

Tommy blinked hard. "Did I—did I do that?"

"Yes," Pecos said, breath tight. "Hold it."

Mark's vision flickered again and the field-map returned—lines under the soil, branching outward. He saw routes from cemetery to stadium to town, and along those routes, dots—people—moving through their evenings unaware.

He saw Hollow's Eve week like a play drawn in advance: parade, bonfire, festival game night.

He saw fog on Main Street at noon.

He saw petals falling like confetti.

He saw players running perfect routes with empty stares.

He saw himself among them.

Mark's knees nearly buckled.

A whisper brushed the inside of his skull—familiar, fractured.

Don't let them write your ending.

Jason. Or something wearing Jason's voice.

Mark clenched his jaw and forced air into his lungs. "No," he said, and the word felt like a shove. "Not anymore."

Alyssa placed her hand over the wrapped plaque. "We're not offerings," she said. "We're awake."

Pecos pressed his palm into the soil and grimaced as if the ground pushed back. "It knows we can push now."

The fog thickened at the tree line and something larger shifted inside it —taller, wrong in its proportions, as if hunger had tried to borrow a body.

Mark lifted the camera. The lens refused to focus. Purple and black smeared across the viewfinder like the glass didn't want to admit what it was seeing.

The shape didn't cross the salt circle.

It didn't need to.

A thought pressed against Mark's mind, sweet and cold:

Glory feeds the roots.

Mark swallowed metal and answered out loud because silence was a door. "Then starve," he rasped.

Tommy's ring hummed louder. The thin protective air held.

Alyssa's eyes stayed locked forward. "This is our will," she said, voice steady. "Not yours."

The shape in the fog shifted—not anger, not hate.

Adjustment.

Like a disease noticing the body had started fighting back.

The fog retreated by inches. The running figures blurred and reformed deeper among the stones, routes continuing farther away.

The hum under the soil eased—not gone, never gone—just eased, like the land had taken a breath and chosen patience.

Mark exhaled, shaking.

Alyssa pinched out the candle with two fingers. Smoke curled up, thin and gray.

Tommy stared at his ring. "So… we just unlocked something."

Alyssa nodded, mouth tight. "The power was always inside us. The pact just kept it asleep."

Pecos's shoulders sagged with exhaustion. "Awake doesn't mean controlled."

They didn't speak until they were off cemetery ground and back on the creek trail, where the air smelled more like water than perfume.

Pecos stopped first. His knees bent as if the land had finally released him and his body remembered it was human. He braced a hand on a tree, breathing hard.

"You're anchored," Alyssa said, watching him closely. "You can feel the roots without falling into them."

Pecos swallowed. "Anchored isn't the word I'd use." He flexed his fingers. "It's like… a hook in my ribs. Like it knows where I am now."

Tommy blew out a breath that shook. "Okay. Cool. So the earth has your location."

Alyssa didn't laugh, but something like relief loosened her shoulders. She flipped her journal open in the dim light and stared at the page.

Then she blinked, startled. "That wasn't there before."

Mark leaned in. The ink on the page looked sharper, darker—as if the words had been rewritten while she wasn't looking. Beside his grandfather's notes, a faint line of symbols had appeared in the margin, delicate and precise.

Alyssa traced them without touching. "I can read it," she whispered, and the way she said it—half awe, half dread—made Mark's skin prickle. "It's not… English. It's not even Latin. But I know what it means."

Tommy's eyes widened. "You're telling me you just downloaded a cursed language pack?"

Alyssa ignored him. "It's a warning. And a list."

"What kind of list?" Mark asked.

Alyssa swallowed. "Components. Places. Nodes. It's like… the pact left instructions in the margins because we're finally looking."

Pecos's gaze lifted toward the dark trees. "Or because it wants us to follow them."

Mark's camera strap tightened around his wrist as his fingers curled. "Or because it's trying to predict us."

Tommy rubbed his arms as if he'd gotten colder. "Let's focus on the part where we didn't die. What did we just get?"

Mark hesitated, then lifted the camera and aimed it down the trail.

For a second, nothing.

Then the pressure behind his eyes sharpened and the world shifted into something like a play diagram. Faint lines ran through the woods—paths of least resistance, routes the fog preferred, places the ground felt thinner.

Mark lowered the camera quickly, heart racing. "I can see where it wants to move," he said. "Where it's already moving."

Alyssa nodded slowly. "I can hear it. Not like voices—like… intent. The way a crowd feels before it roars."

Tommy looked down at his ring. "And I can—" He swallowed, then slapped the ring against his palm like he was calling a huddle.

The air around them tightened.

Not visible. Not dramatic.

But the fog at the edge of the trail pulled back a fraction, as if it had hit a line on the ground it didn't like crossing. The chill in Mark's skin eased.

Tommy's eyes widened in the dark. "Oh. Okay. That's real."

Pecos exhaled, a shaky sound. "Protection."

Tommy lifted his chin like he'd won an argument with the universe. "About time I contributed something besides jokes."

Alyssa's voice softened. "It's still you, though. It's your will doing it."

Tommy's face flickered—pride, fear, something almost like grief. "Then I need reps," he said, suddenly serious. "I need... drills. If I lose focus and it gets in—"

Mark didn't finish the thought. None of them did.

Alyssa closed the journal carefully, like it might bite. "We practice control the way we practice football," she said. "Repetition. Rules. Signals. We don't improvise until we're ready."

Pecos pushed off the tree, steadying. "And we don't do it on the field," he added quietly. "Not yet. That's its home turf."

Mark's stomach tightened at the phrase. Home turf.

He looked past the trees toward town, where lights glowed warm and safe from a distance. Somewhere out there, Dylan Harrow was probably eating dinner, laughing, not remembering the moment his body had run on someone else's command.

Somewhere out there, the town was planning parades and fireworks and a "festival game night" like it was just school spirit with better decorations.

Mark swallowed and felt the metallic taste return, faint and threatening.

"Hollow's Eve is going to be a snap count," he said. "And whatever's under this town... it's already in formation."

As they turned to leave, a single purple petal drifted down through the branches and brushed Mark's cheek—cool as damp soil.

It clung for half a second, deciding if it had found blood.

Mark brushed it away.

This time, his hand didn't move on someone else's command.

He chose.

And somewhere under Lowridge, deep in the root network that held the town like a fist, something listened—and began to plan the next play.

CHAPTER 19: THE TRAINING GROUND

Mark slept in fragments.

Every time he drifted, the stadium lights returned—white glare through fog—and the field became a map again. Routes braided under the turf like veins. Dots moved along them: people, players, names he didn't know but his body recognized. The network didn't care if he was awake. It wanted his attention.

When he finally sat up, sweat cooling on his neck, he realized he was counting without meaning to.

One-two.

One-two.

He forced himself to stop. Forced air into his lungs. Forced his mind back into the cabin, into wood and dust and pine resin and the thin warmth of the propane heater.

Tommy was already awake on the couch, ring on, ring off, ring on again —like he couldn't decide if it was armor or a leash. Alyssa sat at the table with her grandfather's journal open beside the grimoire, copying symbols into a notebook with a steadiness that didn't match the circles under her eyes. Pecos leaned in a chair by the window, watching the trees like he could see the fog before it arrived.

Marcus Webb stood by the sink, hands braced on the counter, head bowed as if the day was already too heavy.

"You're up," Alyssa said without looking up.

"Was I ever down?" Mark's voice came out rough.

Alyssa's pen paused. "Did you see lines again?"

Mark hesitated. "In my sleep. But clearer."

Tommy's laugh was dry. "Cool. So even naps are haunted now."

Marcus turned slowly. His gaze flicked over Mark, lingering the way it had last time when he'd said the land expected a Rivers. "Then it's accelerating," he said.

Pecos's voice was calm, but the tension underneath it made Mark's skin prickle. "It's closer."

Marcus nodded. "Hollow's Eve is a pressure spike. The network tightens. It'll probe harder for doors."

Tommy lifted his ring like it was evidence. "So... training. We're training, right? Please tell me we're not just vibe-checking fog until it eats us."

Marcus's mouth twitched, not quite a smile. "We train."

Alyssa snapped her notebook shut. "We lock rules first."

Mark felt his shoulders loosen a fraction. Rules meant fairness. Fairness meant a chance.

Marcus pulled three objects from a cloth bag and set them on the table: a small jar with a dried purple petal, a strip of athletic tape, and a tarnished lion plaque wrapped in red twine—the one they'd taken from the founder's grave.

He placed them in a row like tools.

"This is how we keep you alive," he said.

Rule One: Never bleed on the field.

Marcus didn't soften it.

"Blood plus petals equals access," Alyssa said quietly, repeating the premise they'd already locked.

Mark remembered Eli's scraped forearm, the petal brushing fresh blood, the switch inside him. His stomach tightened.

Tommy raised his hand like it was class. "What if someone gets hit? It's football."

Marcus stared at him. "Then you pull them."

Coach Whitman would never allow it. Mark didn't say that out loud. The thought of trying made his chest feel tight.

Alyssa did say it. "Coach won't."

Marcus's gaze went flat. "Then you make him."

Tommy's eyebrows climbed. "Oh, sure. We'll just—what—outvote Coach with haunted bracelets?"

Pecos's voice cut in, calm and heavy. "It's not about Coach's permission."

Mark looked at Pecos. His forearm's violet threads were dimmer today, but they still pulsed beneath the skin like a second heartbeat. Pecos's eyes were steady, though, present.

"I'm anchored," Pecos said, "but it can still tug me. That means it can tug you. That means if you bleed on the field and it sees a path, it won't ask politely."

Mark swallowed.

Rule Two: Fog is cover. Fog is delivery.

Alyssa slid her notebook forward, showing a page of symbols she'd copied from the journal's changing margins. "It's spore behavior," she said. "Not metaphor. The fog carries it."

Tommy shifted. "We're saying spores now."

Pecos nodded once. "The sweetness in the air isn't just smell. It's contact."

Mark remembered the way his throat had tightened in the cemetery, how his eyes had stung. He'd thought it was fear and cold.

It hadn't been.

Marcus tapped the jar with the dried petal. "This is signal residue," he said. "When the fog is thick, it amplifies. It's like… the network turns up its own volume."

Rule Three: Truth breaks the grip—but it also draws attention.

Marcus looked at Mark when he said it.

"Truth is severance," Alyssa said. "But it's a flare."

Tommy's fingers tightened around his ring. "So we have to be brave and quiet at the same time."

Marcus's voice went low. "Brave and controlled."

Mark's pulse thudded in his ears. Controlled. That word mattered.

Rule Four: Do not touch a live bloom.

Alyssa's eyes flicked to Mark's hands, like she could see the old habit of reaching.

"Even through gloves?" Mark asked.

Marcus's answer was immediate. "Especially through gloves. You think you're protected. You relax. It slips in."

Tommy's mouth twisted. "This town is allergic to basic safety."

Rule Five: Your power is your will. Your will needs structure.

Marcus picked up Tommy's ring and held it up between two fingers like it was a relic.

"This isn't magic jewelry," he said. "It's a focus point. A ritual object made human. Your fear made it important. Your habit made it consistent."

Tommy blinked. "So I accidentally invented a talisman by being anxious."

Alyssa nodded. "Yeah. Pretty much."

Tommy stared at Marcus. "That's either inspiring or rude."

"It's usable," Marcus said.

He pointed at Mark. "Your camera is the same. You see patterns because you're trained to. You notice edges. Timing. Framing. When you shoot, you impose a boundary on what you're seeing. The network hates boundaries."

Mark's fingers tightened around the strap.

Marcus looked at Alyssa. "Your journal is an open channel. It's adapting because you're reading it like a weapon instead of a bedtime story. It's responding."

Alyssa's jaw tightened. "It's also trying to lead me."

Marcus nodded. "Exactly. Use it. Don't follow it."

Then he looked at Pecos, and his tone changed—more careful. "And you," Marcus said, "are the ground wire. If you don't choose how to conduct, it will choose for you."

Pecos didn't flinch. "Then we practice choice."

Tommy exhaled. "Okay. Rules are cute. When do we do the part where we don't die?"

Marcus lifted the tarnished lion plaque wrapped in red twine. "Now."

They moved out behind the cabin into the trees, away from the creek trail, away from any route that could be mistaken for the path to the cemetery or the field.

Marcus chose a clearing where the ground was packed hard with pine needles, where the air smelled clean. He scattered salt in a circle, then ash in a second circle outside it—two boundaries, like a double fence.

"This is your training ground," he said. "We make a pocket where the network can't fully stabilize."

Alyssa set her grandfather's journal open on a stump at the circle's edge. The pages fluttered once even though the air was still.

Mark raised his camera, then lowered it. The lens felt heavier out here, like the forest didn't want him using it.

Tommy stood in the circle and rolled his shoulders. "I feel like I'm about to do breathing exercises with a demon."

Marcus's gaze stayed flat. "Breathing exercises are how you keep your mind from becoming a door."

Tommy's face sobered.

Pecos hovered at the edge of the outer ash ring, jaw tight. "It's here," he murmured. "Not inside. Watching."

Mark's skin prickled. He lifted the camera again.

Through the viewfinder, the trees sharpened, and the clearing became a diagram. Faint lines ran under the needles, subtle as hair. They tried to braid toward the center, then hesitated at the salt and ash boundaries.

Mark's stomach dropped. "It's trying," he whispered.

Marcus nodded. "Good. That means we're doing it right."

He held up the jar with the dried petal. "This is your controlled trigger," he said. "Signal in a bottle."

Alyssa's voice went tight. "We're provoking it."

Marcus didn't deny it. "If you can't provoke it on your terms, it will provoke you on its terms."

Mark hated how true that felt.

Marcus handed the jar to Alyssa. "Stand outside the circle. Uncap it when I say."

Alyssa took it like it was a live grenade.

Marcus looked at Tommy. "Ring on."

Tommy slid it on, swallowing. "Ring on."

Marcus looked at Mark. "Camera ready."

Mark lifted it, finger near the shutter.

Marcus looked at Pecos. "Stay outside. Feel it. Don't let it pull."

Pecos nodded, shoulders tense. "I'm here."

Marcus stepped into the salt circle. He set the wrapped plaque at his feet. "We start with the smallest Severance," he said. "A tug. Not a possession."

Tommy frowned. "How do you measure that?"

Marcus's gaze flicked to him. "You'll know."

Mark felt his heartbeat. Felt the air thicken just slightly.

Marcus lifted his chin. "Now."

Alyssa uncapped the jar.

The moment the seal broke, sweetness flooded the clearing—violet and metallic. Mark's throat tightened. The world seemed to tilt like the camera had shifted in his hands.

The pine needles shivered.

A faint fog seeped between tree trunks—not rolling in like weather, but threading in like breath.

Pecos hissed softly, pain flashing across his face. "It's louder."

Tommy's eyes widened. "Yeah. Okay. That's—"

A low hum rose under the sound of the forest, too deep to be a normal vibration. Mark felt it in his teeth.

In the salt circle, Marcus's eyes darkened, then flashed violet.

His shoulders stiffened.

Mark's pulse spiked. "Marcus—"

Marcus raised one hand, palm outward. "Not yet," he said, voice rough.

His head tilted as if listening. His fingers flexed like someone else was testing them.

Then his mouth moved, and the words that came out sounded like Marcus but didn't belong to him.

Glory feeds the roots.

Mark's stomach turned. The same phrase. The same pressure behind his eyes.

Tommy took a step forward, ring hand raised like he was about to throw a punch at the air. "Nope. Don't like that."

Marcus's jaw clenched. His nostrils flared. For a second, his eyes cleared—Marcus again. "This is the tug," he rasped. "This is what it feels like."

He inhaled, slow. "Now—Severance."

Alyssa's voice went tight. "How?"

Marcus's eyes flicked to Mark. "Truth," he said. "Simple. Precise. No decoration."

Mark didn't want to say anything. Silence was his default defense. Silence was how he survived being watched.

But silence was also a handle.

Marcus's voice sharpened, like pain made it honest. "Mark."

Mark stepped forward, camera still raised. His mouth tasted metal. He forced the words out like he was pulling a splinter.

"My name is Mark Rivers," he said. "And my family benefited."

The hum spiked.

The fog swirled, thickening near the circle's edge like it was leaning in.

Mark forced himself not to stop. "Jason died and everyone called it tragedy," he continued, voice shaking. "But part of me thinks the town chose him."

Marcus's shoulders jerked.

The violet in his eyes flickered like a light losing power.

Tommy swallowed hard. "Keep going," he said, and for once he wasn't joking.

Mark's throat tightened. He felt the old guilt rise like a wave.

"I'm scared that if I stop winning," Mark said, "Lowridge will take someone else. And I hate that fear because it means I'm still playing the pact's game."

The words landed like a weight in the clearing.

For a breath, the fog stalled.

Marcus shuddered, then sucked in air like he'd been underwater. The violet drained from his eyes, leaving them dark again.

He exhaled hard and looked at Mark. "That's Severance," he said, voice hoarse. "Truth cuts the grip."

Alyssa's shoulders loosened. "It worked."

Tommy stared at his ring hand like it had witnessed something holy and disgusting. "So... we just did a practice possession."

Pecos's breath came in tight pulls. "And it's paying attention now."

Mark lifted the camera, heart pounding.

Through the lens, the clearing's boundaries glowed faintly—not light, but definition. The ash ring, the salt ring, the plaque at Marcus's feet. Mark could see how the network tried to route around them like water around stones.

Beyond the trees, deeper in shadow, a shape shifted—tall, thin, wrong. It didn't cross into the clearing. It didn't need to.

Mark's camera refused to focus on it.

A pressure pressed against his skull—gentle, intimate, like a hand on his cheek.

A voice threaded into his thoughts, not quite words, not quite sound.

Rivers.

Mark's knees nearly buckled.

Alyssa stepped closer, voice sharp. "Mark. Look at me."

Mark forced his gaze away from the trees. Alyssa's eyes were steady—sharp humor stripped away, leaving only fierce clarity.

"Anchor yourself," she said. "Name the now."

Mark swallowed, breathing hard. "Cabin," he whispered. "Pine. Cold. Alyssa's voice. Tommy's ring."

The pressure eased a fraction, like the network didn't like being ignored.

Tommy's ring hand lifted, fingers spread. "Huddle," he muttered, and the air around them tightened—a thin, protective tension that made the fog recoil at the ash line like it had hit a wall.

Marcus straightened, wiping sweat from his brow. "Good," he said. "That's it. Your powers aren't fireworks. They're stances. Anchors. A refusal."

Mark's hands shook around the camera.

Alyssa capped the jar quickly. The sweetness in the air thinned.

The fog didn't vanish. It lingered at the tree line, patient.

Pecos winced, clutching his forearm. The violet threads brightened briefly, then dimmed. "It tasted the cut," he whispered. "It didn't like it."

Marcus's voice turned grim. "It will adapt."

Tommy blew out a breath. "Of course it will."

Alyssa flipped her notebook open again, writing fast. "Limits," she said. "We lock limits."

Marcus nodded. "Mark—your map vision will intensify. But it can pull you into it. Don't stare too long. Don't chase the lines."

Mark swallowed. "And the camera?"

"It's a blade," Marcus said. "But blades cut both ways. If you fixate on what you see, you invite it to show you more."

Alyssa looked at Tommy. "Your ring—protection is focus. If you panic, it collapses."

Tommy made a face. "So no pressure."

Pecos's voice was low. "And me?"

Marcus looked at him carefully. "You're the conduit. Which means you're the most dangerous and the most valuable."

Pecos's jaw tightened. "That's not comforting."

"It's reality," Marcus said. "And reality is a kind of protection."

Alyssa closed her journal. The pages fluttered once, like something inside it didn't like the decision. "We practiced Severance," she said. "Next we practice the anchor-breaker moment. The stand."

Tommy's eyes widened. "We're rehearsing Mark's sacrificial hero speech now?"

Mark's stomach tightened. "It's not a speech."

Alyssa's gaze held his. "It's a choice."

Pecos's voice came quiet. "We do it before Hollow's Eve," he said. "Because that night, the land will try to make the choice for us."

Mark looked past the trees again. The fog still hovered, thin but stubborn, like a spectator who didn't want to leave.

In the distance, a sound drifted through the woods—so faint Mark almost missed it.

A cheer.

Not from the stadium.

From somewhere under the ground, as if the roots remembered what crowds sounded like.

Mark's mouth tasted metal again. He tightened his grip on the camera strap until the pressure steadied him.

"Okay," Mark said, voice low. "We keep training."

Tommy nodded, jaw set. "We keep training."

Alyssa's eyes sharpened. "And we keep telling the truth."

Pecos pressed his palm to the earth one more time, then pulled it away like it burned. "Because it hates the truth," he murmured.

Marcus looked toward the tree line, where the fog waited like a held breath. "And because it wants you," he said quietly—eyes on Mark. "So it will offer you every lie you've ever wanted to believe."

Mark swallowed hard.

He didn't answer.

But in the silence, he made a promise to himself—not a vow of victory, not a grand declaration.

Just a decision:

When it called his name again, he would choose the now.

And he would not let the land count him like a score.

CHAPTER 20: THE SHADOW REALM

The town had stopped pretending.

Sirens wailed somewhere near Main Street, but the sound came muffled, as if even noise was getting swallowed by the fog. Streetlights flickered in slow, sick blinks. Purple growth threaded up porch rails and mailbox posts like it had always belonged there, like Lowridge had always been a place where flowers climbed metal and ate paint.

Mark Rivers ran anyway.

He ran because running was the only thing his body knew how to do when the world turned hostile—when the play broke down and instinct took over. He ran because behind them, something heavy moved through the dark with a wet dragging sound, and when it hit the pavement it left a smear that glowed faint violet for half a second before dimming.

Marcus Webb ran beside him, not like a kid sprinting from trouble, but like someone who'd been chased for years.

Alyssa was between them, clutching the grimoire to her chest as if the book could shield her from teeth. Tommy brought up the rear, baseball bat in one hand, his other arm hooked under Pecos's shoulders.

Pecos didn't run.

Pecos stumbled, half-carried, his feet catching on cracks in the sidewalk. His head lolled forward like he was fighting sleep. Veins stood out dark against his neck, and every few seconds a faint purple shimmer rolled under his skin like something turning over in the mud.

"Keep him moving," Marcus snapped. His voice was tight, not panicked —compressed. "Do not let him touch the ground."

Tommy gave a strained, breathless laugh that didn't match the situation. "Sure, man. No problem. I'll just carry him through the apocalypse."

Mark glanced back once.

A thing unfolded out of the fog behind them—taller than a man, hunched, its limbs too long and jointed wrong. It didn't have a face, not really. Just a knot of petals and root-fiber where a head should have been, and in the center of it, a single glossy dark spot that caught streetlight like an eye.

Mark's stomach dropped.

The eye blinked.

The thing lunged forward, and the air filled with the sound of tearing vines.

Mark turned back and ran harder.

Marcus veered off the road, down a narrow cut between two houses. The yards were already ruined—flowers blooming in thick mats where grass should have been, petals slick with dew that looked too much like sweat. Mark's shoes skidded on damp soil. A purple bud brushed his ankle and trembled as if it recognized him.

Behind them, the creature hit the corner of the house with a dull thud and a splintering crack. Wood groaned. The structure shuddered. Somewhere inside, a dog barked once and then fell silent.

"Marcus!" Alyssa gasped. "Where are we going?"

"My place," Marcus said. "What's left of it."

They burst through another yard, hopped a low fence, and dropped into a shallow drainage ditch slick with mud. Mark's lungs burned. The fog pressed into his mouth and tasted sweet-bitter, like a crushed leaf and pennies.

Pecos made a sound that wasn't a groan and wasn't a word.

Mark looked back over his shoulder. Pecos's eyes had opened.

They were dark, but not normal-dark. They looked like the night sky reflected in water—too deep, too still—and in the center of each pupil, a tiny violet point pulsed like a heartbeat.

Tommy noticed too. His grip tightened, knuckles white. "Buddy," he said, voice shaking. "Pecos, you with us?"

Pecos's lips moved. For a second nothing came out.

Then, barely audible over the sirens and their own ragged breathing, Pecos whispered, "It's… moving."

Mark's throat went dry. "What's moving?"

Pecos's gaze slid past Mark, past the houses, past the streetlights. Past everything. "The routes," he breathed. "It's… opening the routes."

A cold sensation slid down Mark's spine.

Routes.

He'd heard that word in the grimoire, in Harold's warnings, in Marcus's half-finished explanations. Invisible lines beneath the town, lines that weren't just roots and water and soil but something like a nervous system—something that carried hunger.

Marcus stopped at the edge of a stand of trees that had once been part of a small wooded lot behind a closed-down daycare. Now the trees were webbed with purple blooms. Their branches sagged with petals like bruises.

Marcus shoved aside a curtain of vines and revealed a narrow gap between two trunks.

"There," he said. "In."

Mark didn't see a door. He saw a wall of roots. He saw purple flowers climbing bark and the dark beyond.

Marcus pushed through. The vines parted as if they knew him.

Mark's heart hammered once, hard. Then he followed.

Inside, the air changed.

It wasn't warmer. It wasn't colder. It was heavier, like the atmosphere had thickened by a degree. The smell was damp earth and crushed flowers and something faintly electrical—like the air right before a storm.

Marcus's hideout was less a room than a hollowed-out space beneath a fallen tree and a tangle of roots. Tarps and boards formed a crude shelter. A battery lantern sat on a crate, casting weak yellow light. Jars of salt, candles, and a bundle of dried herbs lay on a makeshift table. On the far side, a painted symbol—scarlet eye—stared from a board nailed to the root-wall, half-hidden by vines.

Tommy lowered Pecos carefully onto a folded blanket.

The second Pecos's back touched it, his body convulsed.

A sound tore out of him—sharp, strangled—and purple light flared beneath his skin, bright enough to paint the tarp ceiling violet.

Alyssa dropped to her knees beside him, grimoire already open. Her hands shook as she flipped pages. "Hold him," she said. "Hold his shoulders —don't let him thrash."

Tommy pinned Pecos gently but firmly, face pale.

Mark grabbed Pecos's wrist.

The skin beneath Mark's fingers felt wrong. Too cold. Too slick, like there was a thin film of oil between Pecos and the world.

Pecos's mouth opened, and for a terrifying second Mark thought petals would spill out—like Jason's mouthguard, like the stories. Instead, Pecos sucked in air in short, frantic bursts.

His eyes locked on Mark.

For half a heartbeat, the violet points in his pupils dimmed and Mark saw his friend—really saw him—behind the haze.

"Mark," Pecos whispered, and his voice sounded like it was coming from very far away. "It found… me."

"I'm here," Mark said, and hated how thin his own voice sounded. "You're here. Stay here."

Marcus paced once, then stopped. He looked at Pecos the way someone looked at a cracked bridge they still had to cross.

"We can't fight our way to the cemetery," Marcus said, voice low. "Not now. Not with those things on the roads."

Alyssa's head snapped up. "Then what do we do?"

Marcus didn't answer immediately. His gaze moved to the vines that threaded through the shelter, the purple buds that pulsed faintly as if breathing.

Then he said, "We go through."

Mark stared at him. "Through what?"

Marcus met Mark's eyes. In the lantern light, Marcus looked older than he should have—cheekbones sharp, shadows under his eyes. Purple veins traced faint lines under his skin, not like infection exactly, but like something that had mapped itself onto him and never left.

"The network," Marcus said. "The in-between. The place where the routes actually are."

Alyssa's fingers tightened on the pages. "The shadow realm."

Marcus nodded once. "Call it whatever you want. It's real."

Tommy let out a shaky breath. "That sounds like a horror movie nobody survives."

Marcus's mouth twitched. Not quite a smile. "Yeah. It does."

Mark looked down at Pecos. The violet pulse under Pecos's skin was brighter now, creeping up his neck, threading toward his jaw. Like roots searching for a seam.

"How?" Mark asked.

Marcus crouched beside the blanket, close enough that Mark could smell the damp earth on him. "I can walk it," he said. "Because I'm… this." He gestured vaguely at his own chest. "Because I didn't die all the way. I got stuck halfway between being fed and being free."

Alyssa swallowed. "And we're not like you."

Marcus's gaze flicked to the grimoire. "You have that."

Alyssa hesitated. "Spells won't—"

"They won't keep you safe," Marcus cut in. "Not safe-safe. But they can keep you whole. Shields. Anchors. The kind of thing that stops the network from pulling you apart."

Mark's pulse thudded in his ears. "And Pecos?"

Marcus's face tightened. "Pecos is already halfway in. That's the problem."

Pecos suddenly arched again, body tightening as if a hook had snagged him from the inside. His mouth opened in a silent scream. Purple light poured out from under his eyelids.

Alyssa slammed her palm on a page in the grimoire. "Circle," she said, voice turning hard with purpose. "We make a circle. Salt, candle, water. Now."

Tommy looked at Mark, eyes wide. "We're doing this?"

Mark didn't feel ready. He didn't feel brave. He felt like he was standing on the edge of something that didn't care if he lived.

But Pecos's fingers clenched around Mark's wrist with desperate strength, and Mark felt a pressure behind his own eyes—the same pressure he'd felt on the field, the same sense of being watched.

Pecos wasn't just sick.

He was being taken.

Mark swallowed hard. "Yeah," he said, and it came out steadier than he expected. "We're doing it."

They built the circle on the packed earth inside the shelter.

Alyssa poured salt in a ring, careful, hands shaking only slightly now. Tommy set candles at four points like compass directions. Marcus poured water from a jar onto the ground in a thin line that traced the salt, darkening the soil. The water didn't soak in. It sat on the surface like it was resting on glass.

Mark held Pecos's hand the whole time.

Every few seconds, Pecos's fingers spasmed. Each time, Mark felt a faint tug in his own chest, like a thread had looped around his ribs and someone somewhere had pulled.

Alyssa opened the grimoire to a page covered in tight, slanted handwriting. Old ink. Symbols. Notes in the margins, warnings underlined twice.

She looked up. "If we do this," she said, voice quiet, "we don't just… step into another room. We're stepping into the thing that's been feeding on this town for a century."

Marcus's eyes didn't leave Pecos. "It's already stepped into us."

Alyssa's jaw tightened. She nodded once. "Okay."

She began to speak.

The words weren't Latin. They weren't anything Mark recognized. They sounded like English that had been broken and reshaped until it fit a mouth that wasn't human. Alyssa's voice wavered at first, then steadied. The candles flared — small bright jumps of flame that turned purple at the edges.

The air thickened.

Mark's skin prickled.

Marcus knelt across from him, inside the circle. "You keep your mind on one thing," Marcus said, low enough only Mark could hear. "One anchor. Something that's yours."

Mark's throat tightened. "Like what?"

Marcus's gaze flicked to Mark's chest, where his Lions hoodie hung open. The captain patch on Mark's jersey underneath was visible in the lantern glow.

"Your brother," Marcus said.

Mark's breath caught.

Marcus didn't soften it. "Not the ghost. Not the puppet. Your brother. The real one. The one you remember."

Mark's eyes stung unexpectedly.

He thought of Jason laughing in the driveway, tossing a football one-handed like it was nothing. Jason stealing the last slice of pizza and grinning like he'd won something important. Jason's shoulder bumping Mark on the sideline, hard enough to bruise, gentle enough to mean I'm here.

Mark held that memory like a fist around a rope.

Alyssa's voice rose. The candles flared again, and the shadows in the shelter stretched.

Marcus took a breath and let it out slowly. "When it hits," he murmured, "don't fight it. Fighting is how it breaks you. Let it carry you, and hold your anchor."

Mark nodded, though his body wanted to do anything but.

Pecos's eyes rolled back. Purple light spilled out from under his lashes. His fingers tightened around Mark's.

The world lurched.

For a second, Mark felt weightless—like the moment at the top of a roller coaster when your stomach stayed behind and your body went forward.

Then the shelter disappeared.

The lantern disappeared.

The sound of sirens disappeared.

And Mark stepped into the shadow realm.

It looked like Lowridge had been turned inside out.

The shape of the town was still there—suggestions of streets, the faint outline of buildings—but everything solid had been replaced by a web.

Purple threads hung in the air like strands of spider silk, stretching in every direction. Some were thin as hair, trembling gently. Others were thick as ropes, pulsing with slow, heavy light. They ran through what should have been walls and trees and sky, forming a massive, living map.

Fog drifted between them in ribbons. It wasn't fog the way fog existed in the real world. It was presence—a soft, shifting substance that clung to the threads like breath on glass.

Mark's first thought was that it was beautiful.

His second thought was that beauty could be a trap.

Marcus stood beside him, half-solid in a way that made Mark's eyes hurt. Marcus's outline shimmered faintly, as if he was both here and not here, both boy and something else.

Alyssa was there too—her hair floating slightly as if underwater, her hands tight around the grimoire. Tommy stood a few steps away, eyes huge, mouth half open like he was trying not to scream.

And Pecos—

Pecos wasn't fully with them.

Pecos's body lay somewhere else. Mark could feel that, like a distant ache. Here, in the shadow realm, Pecos existed as a shape ahead of them— an ember behind layers of thread, deeper in the web.

A small pulsing point of light.

"Keep your shields up," Marcus said. His voice sounded wrong here, stretched thin. "If you feel something call you, don't answer."

Alyssa swallowed. "How do we—"

"Like this." Marcus lifted his hand.

Purple threads shifted around his fingers, parting like grass beneath a hand. He didn't cut them. He didn't break them. He coaxed them aside the way you'd coax a curtain open.

Mark's skin crawled. "You can… move it."

"I'm marked," Marcus said, flat. "It listens."

Tommy made a small sound. "I hate that sentence."

Marcus didn't laugh. He tilted his head, listening to something Mark couldn't hear. "We move slow," he said. "Stealth. The entity's attention here is like a patrol light. If it sweeps over you—"

Mark's chest tightened. "It sees us?"

Marcus's eyes flicked to Mark. "It always sees. The question is whether it notices."

They began to walk.

There was no ground, not really. Mark's feet found something firm enough to step on—a faint plane of darkness threaded with light, like walking across the surface of a still pond. Each step sent small ripples through nearby threads.

As they moved, Mark became aware of shapes in the fog.

At first they were just shadows—human outlines, barely there. Then one drifted closer, and Mark's breath caught.

It was a boy.

Not alive-boy. Not fully dead-boy either. A teen in an old football uniform, fabric torn, helmet missing. Purple threads wrapped around his wrists and throat like restraints. His eyes were open, glassy with panic.

He reached toward Mark with trembling fingers.

"Help," the boy mouthed.

Mark's stomach twisted. He took a half-step toward him without thinking.

Marcus grabbed Mark's arm hard enough to hurt. "No."

Mark's throat tightened. "That's—"

"That's bait," Marcus said. "Or it's real and it doesn't matter. Not right now."

The boy's mouth moved again. Mark couldn't hear the words, but his expression was pleading in a way that made Mark's ribs ache.

Alyssa's face went pale. "How many…"

Mark looked around.

There were dozens.

Hundreds.

Shapes suspended in fog and thread, bound to the web like insects caught in silk. Some wore uniforms from decades ago—leather helmets, old-numbered jerseys. Some looked more modern. Some were so tangled in thread they barely resembled human at all.

And all of them were awake.

Mark's anchor—the memory of Jason laughing—wavered under the weight of it. A sickness rose in his throat.

This wasn't just death.

It was storage. It was a collection. A trophy room no one had asked to see.

"This is what it does," Marcus said, voice low, almost bitter. "It doesn't let go."

Tommy's bat shook in his hand. "We can't—" he started.

"We can't save them," Alyssa finished, voice tight. Her eyes stayed on the grimoire like she couldn't bear to look too long at the trapped faces. "Not now."

Mark hated the words. He hated that they were true.

They moved deeper.

The threads thickened. The pulse grew stronger. Mark began to feel a rhythm in it—like a heartbeat, like a chant, like the roar of a crowd heard from far away.

He thought of the stadium.

The way the town sounded on Friday nights. The devotion that hit your chest like a wave.

Here, that sound existed as vibration in the web.

The route-lines weren't just roots.

They were wires. They were a system built on attention, on worship, on the town pouring itself into one thing over and over until the land learned how to drink it.

Mark's hands clenched.

Ahead, the pulsing point of light that was Pecos flickered—faint, struggling.

Mark tried to move faster.

Marcus hissed, "Slow."

Mark glared at him. "He's dying."

Marcus's face tightened. "And if you sprint through here like you're on the field, you'll light up every thread you touch."

Mark wanted to snap back, but then he felt it—

A shift.

The web trembled, subtle as a change in wind.

Somewhere far off, a thick bundle of threads brightened. The pulse deepened, like something taking a breath.

Marcus went still.

Alyssa's voice dropped to a whisper. "It felt us."

Marcus didn't answer. His eyes tracked something in the distance, something moving through the fog that wasn't a trapped spirit.

A light.

Not purple. Not warm. A cold, pale sweep—like a spotlight searching a stadium.

"It's looking," Marcus said.

Mark's heart slammed once.

"What do we do?" Tommy whispered.

Marcus's jaw worked. "We hide."

"How?" Mark demanded, and the word came out too loud.

The patrol-light shivered, as if hearing him.

Marcus grabbed Mark's hoodie and yanked him down toward a thick cluster of threads that hung like curtain strands. "Don't talk," Marcus hissed. "Don't think loud. Don't—"

Mark didn't understand what thinking loud meant until the web responded to his fear.

A nearby thread brightened, pulsing faster, as if reacting to Mark's panic like blood to a scent.

Mark clamped down on his thoughts the way he clamped down on pain during practice.

Jason laughing.

Jason laughing.

Jason laughing.

The patrol-light swept closer.

It passed over the trapped spirits, and they flinched as one. Their outlines shuddered, mouths opening in silent screams.

The light moved on.

Mark's breathing came shallow.

For a second, in the distance, Mark saw something else—something that made his anchor twist.

A thread that wasn't like the others.

It was thicker, braided, bright in places and fraying in others. It pulled away from the central pulse like it was trying to snap free.

And wrapped around it, fighting the pull—

Was a shape Mark recognized.

A broad-shouldered silhouette. A familiar stance. A presence that hit Mark in the gut like a fist.

Jason.

Not a ghost-boy begging.

Not a puppet standing in fog.

A thread of his brother, caught in the web and straining away as if even trapped, Jason was still trying to resist.

Mark's vision blurred. "Jason," he breathed, barely audible.

The patrol-light paused.

Marcus slapped a hand over Mark's mouth.

Mark's heart hammered. His eyes burned.

Marcus's eyes were furious. "Do you want it to find us?"

Mark nodded sharply, swallowing the taste of panic and grief.

The patrol-light moved on.

Marcus slowly removed his hand.

Alyssa's eyes were wet, but she didn't speak. She just tightened her grip on the grimoire until her knuckles went white.

Marcus exhaled through his nose. "We keep moving," he said, voice rough. "We keep quiet."

Mark swallowed hard. "That was him," he whispered.

Marcus didn't deny it. "Yeah," he said. "And if we don't get Pecos, that thread becomes a rope, and your brother becomes a leash."

Mark's stomach turned.

They moved again, faster now but careful—feet placing softly on the dark plane, shoulders hunched as if sound could be seen.

The web grew denser.

Threads converged ahead like highway ramps, merging and splitting in an endless pattern. Mark realized with cold clarity that he was looking at the town's true map—the routes beneath roads, beneath sidewalks, beneath graves.

And all of it led toward one place.

A heavier pulse.

A deeper glow.

The heart.

Pecos's light flickered near it, dim and fragile.

Then the web shuddered again.

This time, it wasn't subtle.

A cold ripple moved through the threads, like a tremor. The trapped spirits jerked, their outlines shaking.

Marcus froze.

Alyssa's lips parted. "That's—"

"Hunters," Marcus said.

From the fog behind them, shapes emerged.

They moved low and fast, not human, not animal exactly. Their bodies were built from thread and petal-mass, sleek and wrong, their heads pointed like snouts. In place of eyes, glossy dark spots reflected the patrol-light.

They didn't howl.

They listened.

Mark's breath caught.

Marcus grabbed Alyssa's arm. "Run."

Mark didn't question it.

They sprinted.

The shadow plane rippled under their feet. Threads snapped aside as they broke through them, and each contact sent a bright pulse along the web like a flare.

The hunters surged after them.

Mark could hear the sound now—a dry clicking, like bones tapping together. The web itself seemed to hum louder, as if their panic fed it.

Ahead, Pecos's light flared once, as if sensing them.

Mark ran harder, lungs burning even though this wasn't air. His anchor threatened to slip under the strain. Jason laughing—Jason laughing—he forced the memory down like a peg.

Marcus moved like he knew every turn. He veered left, then right, pulling them through narrow gaps in thick bundles of thread.

They burst into a wide open space where the web formed an enormous knot overhead—threads looping and spiraling like a cloverleaf interchange.

And in the center of it, suspended in a mass of pulsing thread—

Was Pecos.

Not his body. Not flesh.

A shape of him, lit from within, half-wrapped in purple strands that climbed over his limbs and throat. His face was turned toward them, eyes open, and for a second Mark saw both of him at once—the friend who cracked jokes and felt the land like music, and the conduit the town had been growing for.

Pecos's mouth moved.

Mark didn't hear the words.

But he felt them.

Hurry.

Mark lunged toward him.

The threads around Pecos tightened, pulsing hard, and the knot overhead brightened like an alarm.

Marcus grabbed Mark's shoulder. "Don't touch the main lines," Marcus said, voice sharp. "That's how it locks you."

"How do we get him?" Mark demanded.

Marcus's jaw clenched. "We pull his spark out of the tangle—just enough to keep him from sliding deeper. We don't free him. Not yet."

Alyssa's voice shook. "The hunters—"

They were already here.

The cold clicking surrounded them. Shapes moved through fog at the edges of the knot, circling, gathering, as if waiting for a signal.

The patrol-light swept closer, brighter now.

The web above them pulsed in response.

Mark felt it then—an attention turning toward him, slow and heavy, like an ancient thing lifting its head.

The entity.

Marcus's voice went low. "It knows."

The hunters crouched, ready.

Pecos's eyes locked on Mark, and for a second, the violet pulse in them dimmed.

Mark felt his friend's presence—small, battered, but still there.

Mark stepped forward anyway.

He reached out, not to the thick main lines, but to the smaller threads wrapped around Pecos's wrist. His fingers hovered a hair away.

The thread trembled.

It wanted him.

Mark's mouth went dry.

He thought of all the trapped spirits behind them. Of Jason's thread straining against the pull. Of Pecos collapsing in Marcus's hideout, body convulsing as the town's hunger used him like a handle.

Mark's voice came out rough. "Pecos," he whispered. "Hold on."

Pecos's lips moved again, and this time Mark felt the meaning like a punch.

It's taking me either way.

Mark's throat tightened. "Not without a fight."

The thread around Pecos's wrist tightened.

Mark didn't know the severance technique yet—not fully. That was supposed to come later, from Thalassa. But Alyssa had taught them shields. Marcus had taught them to see. Mark had learned, painfully, that sometimes you didn't need a perfect play—you needed a desperate one.

Mark clenched his anchor—Jason laughing—and with his other hand, he pressed his palm close to the thread without touching it.

He willed separation.

He pictured a line drawn clean through purple, like a blade through ribbon.

For a split second, nothing happened.

Then the thread snapped.

Not physically—there was no sound of breaking fiber. But the connection severed in Mark's mind, and the web flared bright, furious, like a nerve struck.

Pain lanced through Mark's chest. Not like a bruise. Like something inside him had been tugged out by roots.

He gasped.

Pecos's outline shuddered, and the threads around him loosened—just a fraction.

Enough for Pecos's hand to reach, trembling, toward Mark.

Mark grabbed it.

Contact sent a shock through Mark's arm. Cold and sweet and bitter all at once.

Pecos's mouth opened, and Mark heard his voice—not through ears but through bone.

"Don't let it—" Pecos tried.

The patrol-light slammed onto them.

The knot overhead pulsed violently.

The hunters lunged.

Marcus shoved Alyssa back. "Move!" he roared.

Mark didn't let go of Pecos's hand.

Pecos's outline flickered, struggling, and Mark felt the pull on Pecos intensify—like the web was yanking him back toward the heart.

Mark dug his heels in, body instinctively bracing the way he braced against a tackle.

"Mark!" Alyssa screamed.

The hunters hit.

They didn't bite like animals. They wrapped.

Thread and petal-mass coiled around Mark's legs, his waist, his arms. Cold pressure tightened, crushing.

Mark's grip slipped on Pecos's hand.

Pecos's eyes widened—human fear shining through violet haze.

Marcus slammed into the nearest hunter, hands glowing faintly purple as he tore at its thread-body like ripping tape. The thing shrieked without sound and dissolved into fog, only to reform a few feet away.

Alyssa raised the grimoire and shouted words that made the air crackle. A burst of heat flared—fire without flame—and a hunter recoiled, its petal-body curling as if scorched.

Tommy swung his bat and connected with something that felt like wet rope. The impact shuddered up his arms. "This is so not in my skill set!" he yelled.

Mark fought to breathe.

The patrol-light held steady on him now, pinning him like an insect.

And beneath that light, Mark felt the entity's presence settle fully—massive, patient, amused.

A chorus rose in the web, faint at first, then louder—voices layered over each other, hundreds of victims speaking at once, not words but sensation: hunger, devotion, want.

Pecos's outline began to slide backward, pulled toward the heart.

Mark's fingers slipped from Pecos's.

"No," Mark rasped.

He lunged forward, tearing through the coils around him with sheer panic strength, and grabbed Pecos's wrist again.

For a single heartbeat, Mark felt Pecos's mind press against his—a frantic flicker of thought.

If I go… I don't come back.

Mark's throat tightened. "Not yet."

The web pulsed.

The hunters tightened.

Marcus shouted something Mark couldn't hear. Alyssa's voice cracked on another spell.

And Pecos's outline jerked hard, yanked toward the deeper glow.

Mark was dragged with him.

The shadow plane dropped away beneath Mark's feet, and for a split second he was falling through a forest of purple threads into a darkness that felt bottomless.

Pecos's hand slipped.

Mark caught only air.

Pecos vanished into the deeper web like a light snuffed out.

Mark's scream tore out of him, raw and useless.

Then Marcus's hand clamped onto Mark's collar and yanked him back —hard enough that Mark's teeth clicked.

Mark hit the shadow plane, breath exploding out of him.

The patrol-light swung away, as if satisfied for the moment.

The hunters didn't retreat.

They circled closer, tightening the ring.

Marcus leaned close, eyes wild. "We're out of time," he hissed. "We have to go deeper—now—or we lose him."

Mark's chest heaved. His arms shook. The pain from that rough severance attempt still burned under his ribs like a bruise made of ice.

Alyssa stumbled to Mark's side, face pale, hair floating in the strange air. "Mark," she whispered. "If we go deeper—"

Mark looked at the knot overhead, at the pulse leading toward the heart.

He thought of Jason's resisting thread.

He thought of Pecos's eyes turning violet.

He thought of the trapped spirits begging in silence.

Mark's anchor tightened in his chest until it hurt.

"We go," Mark said.

The hunters lunged again.

And Mark, Marcus, Alyssa, and Tommy ran straight toward the darkest route in the web—toward where Pecos had been taken, toward the heart that pulsed like a waiting mouth.

Behind them, the shadow realm hummed louder, as if the town itself had started to cheer.

CHAPTER 21: THE ANCIENT OF DARKNESS

The dark route felt less like a path and more like a throat.

Mark ran anyway—because stopping in the shadow realm felt like kneeling on a highway with headlights bearing down. The plane beneath his shoes rippled like black water. Every footfall sent a faint pulse through the web above, and those pulses came back to him a heartbeat later, like the network was keeping score.

Behind them, the clicking followed.

Not one set of clicks anymore. Several. A rhythm of dry bones, petal-edges, and something that sounded too much like cleats on a locker-room floor.

"Don't—" Marcus started, then cut himself off.

Because even words had weight here. Mark could feel them, like sound was a lantern. He clamped down on his breathing, on the panic trying to flood his chest.

Anchor, he told himself. Jason laughing in the driveway. Jason's elbow in his ribs. Jason saying, Quit staring, little bro, you're gonna miss the catch.

But the memory kept fraying. Not because it wasn't real—because the shadow realm was crowded with other people's real.

Faces in the fog. Players in antique uniforms. A thousand mouths opening without sound as the patrol-light swept, searching.

Mark's stomach churned. He focused on Marcus's back instead — on the way Marcus moved like he'd run this route a hundred times, shoulders dipped, head slightly tilted as if he could hear where the web was tightest.

Alyssa kept pace beside Mark, the grimoire hugged to her chest like a shield that might turn solid if she squeezed hard enough. Tommy ran on Mark's other side, bat still in his hand like muscle memory had decided it mattered.

"Where—" Tommy whispered, then winced, like he'd felt his own word flare in the threads.

Marcus lifted a hand without looking back. Two fingers down. Quiet.

They crossed under a sagging bundle of thick conduit-lines that hung like cables in a storm. The lines pulsed violet and slow, and the fog clung to them like breath on glass.

Ahead, the web changed.

The purple threads thinned, and something darker took their place — long, hanging strands that didn't pulse. They absorbed light. They swayed like kelp in a deep ocean.

Mark's skin prickled. The air grew heavier, colder. Not cold like winter. Cold like the inside of a well.

Marcus slowed just enough to glance back at them, eyes sharp in the dim.

"This is her pocket," he said, voice barely a thread. "If we're lucky, the hunters won't follow."

"If we're lucky?" Tommy mouthed. No sound, but Mark read it anyway.

Alyssa's eyes were huge. "Her," she mouthed back.

Marcus didn't answer. He just turned and pushed forward into the hanging darkness.

The kelp-strands brushed Mark's cheeks as he followed. They were not wet. They felt like memory of wetness. Like your skin remembering rain even when you were dry.

And then—

The clicking behind them stopped.

Not faded. Stopped. Like someone had cut a cord.

Mark's lungs seized. He nearly stumbled, because his body had been bracing for impact and instead hit silence.

The web above them dimmed. The patrol-light, distant and pale, swept past the edge of the kelp-pocket and slid away, as if something here made it blink.

Tommy let out a breath that tasted like fear. His shoulders sagged for half a second before he snapped back up.

"Okay," he whispered. "Okay. I hate this place."

"Don't say that," Alyssa whispered, but it came out more like a plea.

Marcus raised one hand again, palm open. Not a stop this time—an offering.

Mark followed the gesture and saw it.

In the center of the pocket, where the dark strands hung like curtains, there was a shape suspended in the air.

At first, Mark thought it was a person drowning.

Then he realized it was a person held in place by chains.

Not metal chains.

Chains of flowers.

Purple blooms braided into thick links, petals fused into something stronger than steel. The links wrapped around the figure's wrists, her throat, her ankles. They pinned her to a crooked lattice of conduit-lines like a sacrifice nailed to a living cross.

The figure's body was almost an outline—woman-shaped, but not flesh. Inside her, darkness moved like slow water. Stars blinked and died in her ribs. Her hair floated around her head as if she were underwater, and when it brushed the kelp-strands, the strands recoiled.

Mark's heart thudded once, hard. He couldn't look away.

Alyssa's fingers tightened around the grimoire. "That's..." she breathed.

The figure's head tilted.

When she spoke, it wasn't sound in Mark's ears.

It was sound in his bones.

You brought children.

Mark flinched. The words vibrated in his teeth.

Marcus didn't flinch. He bowed his head—not in worship, but in something that looked uncomfortably like respect.

"We didn't have a choice," Marcus said. His voice was so quiet it was almost a thought. "He took Pecos."

The figure's darkness rippled, as if a current had passed through her.

Eoraziel takes what is offered. And what is not.

Mark had heard the name before—in Harold's warnings, in the grimoire's margins, in Alyssa's trembling explanations.

Eoraziel. The thing beneath the town. The hunger with a name.

Mark swallowed, throat raw. "Who are you?" he asked before he could stop himself.

The kelp-strands shivered, and Mark felt his words flare like a match. He expected the hunters to surge in.

But the pocket held.

The figure's gaze slid to him. There were no eyes, not really—just darker points within her darkness, like deep water looking back.

I was older when your founders still feared wolves, she said. I was old when the first stone was laid on this land. And I am tired of being chained in a child's garden.

Her head tilted again, and the flower-chains tightened as if reacting to her annoyance. A violet pulse crawled along the links, like a warning.

Marcus spoke the name like he was handing Mark a rope.

"Thalassa."

Alyssa sucked in a breath. "That's in the margins," she whispered. "The — the water-thing. The one who tried to—"

Thalassa's darkness flickered. Almost a laugh.

Tried to stop him, yes. Tried to cut the first thread before it became a net. Your Harrow bled and begged and named his hunger holy. The land listened. And the thing you call an ancient learned to drink.

Mark's stomach dropped at the word.

Harrow. The founder. The man whose name sat on plaques and banners like it was carved into righteousness.

"What do you mean, 'learned'?" Mark asked. He hated that his voice shook. He hated that he still sounded like a kid.

Thalassa's head tilted toward the violet threads beyond the pocket, toward the pulsing heart far away. Mark could feel Pecos's light out there—small, dim, still sinking.

Eoraziel is not what you fear him to be, she said. Not the oldest. Not the strongest. Not the first. He is… young.

Young. The word didn't belong with everything Mark had seen.

"Young?" Alyssa echoed, disbelief cracking through her whisper. "He feels—"

Like the whole town, Thalassa finished. Like a god. Because you have fed him for one hundred and fifty years.

Mark's brain snagged on the number.

"One hundred and fifty," he repeated. "That's it?"

Marcus's jaw tightened. "That's when the pact started," he said softly. "Harrow's time."

Thalassa's darkness pulsed like an ocean swell.

He was a seed, she said. A hungry little thing in the roots. Harrow watered him with desperation and blood and promise. The first sacrifice made the soil remember. Every victory after made the memory stronger. Every cheer, every prayer, every grave—another drink.

The pocket felt suddenly too small. Mark pictured the stadium, the roar, the way the whole town leaned forward like their breath could push a ball through the air.

He had always thought of it as tradition.

Thalassa called it feeding.

Alyssa's knuckles went white on the grimoire. "If he's young," she whispered, "then he can be beaten."

Thalassa's gaze slid back to Alyssa.

Yes, she said. And no.

Mark's spine went cold. "What does that mean?"

It means, Thalassa said, that a true ancient could cut the pact as a man cuts rope. It means I could have drowned him before he bloomed into this. It means others could have burned him to ash. But—

The flower-chains rattled without sound.

They are gone, she said. Or distant. Or trapped in wars you do not understand. This one has been clever. He grows in shadows. He feeds on small towns, on secrets, on pride. He hid from the old ones until it was too late.

Marcus's eyes stayed on Thalassa's chains, something bitter and familiar tightening his face. "He trapped you," Marcus said.

Thalassa's darkness sharpened, like a wave turning into a blade.

Yes.

The word landed like a stone.

He cannot allow interference, she said. So he wrapped me in his own language—petals, blood, devotion—and he pinned me here where I could watch him chew through generations.

Alyssa's voice broke. "Why didn't you... reach out? Warn someone?"

Thalassa's gaze went distant for a heartbeat, as if she was looking through Alyssa and seeing centuries.

I did, she said. A few. A handful. Each time, he killed them faster. Each time, your town called it accident, or tragedy, or "the price of a season." Humans are obedient when fed trophies.

Mark flinched like she'd slapped him.

Thalassa's attention returned to him. Her darkness slid over his face, and Mark felt the faint tug in his chest—the same tug he'd felt when he grabbed Pecos's wrist, when he tried to snap that thread.

Ah, Thalassa said softly.

Mark swallowed. "What?"

You have already cut once, she said.

Mark's mouth went dry. He remembered the moment: his palm hovering near the thread, his mind drawing a line, the snap that wasn't sound but...

separation. The ice-burn under his ribs afterward.

"That wasn't—" Mark started. "I didn't know what I was doing."

Thalassa's darkness rippled like approval and warning at the same time.

Good, she said. Then you have not killed yourself yet.

Tommy made a small choking sound. "Cool," he whispered. "Love that sentence."

Alyssa's eyes snapped to Mark. "You cut a thread?" she whispered, shocked. "Mark, how—"

"I don't know," Mark said, voice tight. "I just— I wanted him free."

Thalassa leaned forward as far as her chains allowed. The flower-links creaked, petals tightening, violet light pulsing brighter.

Want is not enough, she said. Want is how Eoraziel wins.

Her gaze fixed on Mark's chest, on the place where his anchor lived.

You will learn control, she said. Or you will become another face in the fog.

Mark's throat constricted. The trapped spirits flashed through his mind—hundreds of them, eyes open, mouths pleading. Jason's thread straining like a muscle about to tear.

Pecos's light sinking.

"What do we do?" Mark asked. The question came out raw.

Thalassa's answer didn't come right away. Her darkness shifted, slow and heavy, like she was choosing which pieces of truth to hand to a child holding a grenade.

You need a weapon that speaks the network's language, she said finally. Not fire. Not salt. Not bat and muscle. Those are human words.

She paused, and Mark felt the pocket tighten around the pause, like the shadow realm itself was leaning in.

You need severance.

Alyssa's breath hitched. "That's— that's what the grimoire calls it," she whispered. "In the back pages. It says it's… impossible."

Thalassa's darkness flickered. Another almost-laugh.

Impossible for humans who refuse to pay, she said. Everything is possible when you bleed for it.

Marcus stepped closer, careful not to touch the kelp-strands. "He's not ready," Marcus said. "He's just—"

A boy, Thalassa finished, and the words carried neither insult nor comfort. Yes. That is the point.

Mark's fists clenched. His nails bit his palms.

"You're going to teach me," he said. It wasn't a question.

Thalassa's gaze held him.

I will show you, she said. The technique is simple. The cost is not.

Mark's stomach twisted. "We don't have time."

Thalassa's head tilted toward the distant pulse again—toward the heart, toward Pecos.

No, she agreed. You do not.

Alyssa's voice shook. "Then teach him. Now."

Thalassa's darkness deepened, and for the first time Mark felt something like anger in her. Not at them—at the chains.

I can teach quickly, she said. The network will punish you quickly. This is fair.

Tommy swallowed hard. "I don't think 'fair' is what's happening," he whispered.

Thalassa ignored him.

Look, she said, and the word pulled Mark's attention the way gravity pulled a stone.

The kelp-strands in front of Thalassa parted, and something drifted into view between her and Mark.

A thread.

Not one of the thick violet conduit-lines. This one was thin, pale, almost silver. It trembled like a hair caught in water.

It came from the fog beyond the pocket—snaking in, curious, reaching.

Mark recognized the sensation immediately. That tug, that hunger.

"Is that—" Alyssa started.

A weak line, Thalassa said. A leash. One of Eoraziel's listening filaments. He sends them everywhere. They taste. They learn. They report.

Mark's heart kicked.

"So if we cut it—" Marcus began.

Thalassa's darkness rippled.

If you cut it incorrectly, she said, you will light your soul like a torch. He will see you. He will swallow you.

Mark's mouth went dry. "Then why show it to us?"

Because you need practice, Thalassa said. And because the filament is already here. Better to bleed with purpose than by surprise.

Alyssa's grip tightened on the grimoire. She looked like she wanted to argue, and couldn't find where to start.

Thalassa's attention returned to Mark.

You will not touch it, she said. Touch is what the network wants. Touch is surrender. You will see it. You will name it. You will cut it.

Mark stared at the filament. Up close, it wasn't just a line—it had tiny barbs along it, like thorns turned inward. It quivered as if it could feel him looking.

"How do I see it?" Mark whispered. "I can already—"

You see shape, Thalassa said. Not meaning.

Her darkness shifted, and the pocket dimmed further, as if someone had turned down the world.

Mark's vision adjusted. The filament brightened against the black, and then—

He saw it.

Not with his eyes.

With something behind his eyes.

A second outline, a faint glow around the filament that extended out into the web beyond, connecting to thicker threads like a capillary feeding an artery. He saw its intention—the way it pulled toward his chest like a hook searching for soft tissue.

Mark's breath caught.

"That's..." Alyssa whispered, seeing his face change.

Thalassa's voice pressed in.

Anchor, she said.

Mark's mind reached automatically for Jason laughing, but the memory wavered.

Not that anchor, Thalassa corrected, and the words were sharp. Your anchor is not grief. It cannot be.

Mark flinched. "Then what?"

Thalassa's darkness leaned closer. The water-in-her moved, slow and deep.

Anchor to choice, she said. Anchor to the moment you decided to fight. Not because you want your brother back. Because you refuse to be owned.

Mark's throat tightened. He thought of the town's roar. The way people wore rings and jerseys and called it loyalty.

He thought of Jason's grave.

He thought of Pecos's hand slipping from his.

He felt something hard settle in his chest—not a memory, but a decision.

No, he thought. Not anymore.

Thalassa's voice softened, just a fraction.

Good, she said. Now cut.

Mark raised his hand.

His fingers trembled. He hated that they trembled. He was a quarterback. He'd thrown game-winning passes with half the stadium screaming his name. He'd taken hits that left bruises like maps.

This was worse.

Because there was no playbook.

There was only a thin filament and a void behind it.

"How?" Mark whispered. "Do I—"

You do not pull, Thalassa said. Pulling is violence. Violence tangles. You slice.

Slice with what? Mark wanted to ask.

But as he stared at the filament's outline, he felt it—something in him that wasn't muscle. A thin edge of intent, like the first time he'd learned to throw a spiral and his wrist had found the motion before his brain did.

Mark pictured a line.

Not snapping.

Not tearing.

A clean cut.

He drew the line through the filament in his mind.

For a heartbeat, nothing happened.

Then the filament shuddered.

A soundless scream rippled through it, and the silver line split.

The moment it split, pain slammed into Mark's chest like a helmet to the ribs.

He gasped, stumbling forward. His vision flashed white, then black, then violet.

It felt like someone had reached inside his sternum and ripped out a strip of warmth.

Mark dropped to one knee, hand pressed hard against his chest.

"Mark!" Alyssa cried, catching his shoulder.

Tommy swore under his breath. "That— that looked bad."

Marcus crouched beside Mark, face tight. "Breathe," he whispered. "Breathe."

Mark tried. Air didn't feel like air here. It felt thick, like breathing through mud.

The pain eased a fraction, leaving behind a cold ache that spread through his ribs.

Thalassa watched him without pity.

That was one, she said.

Mark lifted his head, jaw clenched against the lingering burn. "One what?"

One severance, Thalassa said. One cut that cost you a piece.

Mark's stomach rolled. "A piece of what?"

Thalassa's darkness drifted closer. The flower-chains rattled, violet light crawling over the links like a heartbeat.

Life, she said simply. You spent it to cut his thread. That is why humans do not do this. You are built to bleed outward, not inward.

Mark's hands shook. He forced them still.

"How many?" he asked.

Thalassa's gaze held him.

Five, she said. If you are unlucky. Seven, if you are strong and careful and the network is merciful.

Merciful. Mark nearly laughed, and it came out like a cough.

Alyssa's face went pale. "That's— that's not enough," she whispered.

"It has to be enough," Marcus said, voice flat.

Tommy stared at Mark like he was seeing him from across a field. "So every time you do that," he whispered, "you— you lose…"

Mark swallowed hard. "Yeah."

Thalassa's darkness shifted, almost amused again.

Now you understand why heroes are rare, she said. Because the cost is always personal.

Mark forced himself to stand. His knees wobbled. He clenched his jaw until it hurt.

"Teach me properly," he said.

Thalassa's head tilted.

I just did, she said. But if you want to survive more than one cut, you must learn refinement.

Alyssa wiped at her eyes with the back of her wrist, furious at herself for it. "How do we make it... smaller?" she asked. "Less—"

Thalassa's attention slid to Alyssa.

You cannot make the price smaller, she said. You can only waste less.

Mark's stomach clenched. He pressed his palm to his chest again, feeling the ache. It felt like bruised ice.

"What did I do wrong?" he asked.

Thalassa's darkness moved, and for a moment Mark saw images in it— waves, deep water, pressure.

You cut with fear, she said. Fear is jagged. It tears what it touches. The network answered you in kind.

Mark's cheeks burned. He hated being called out like that, even if it was true.

"How do I cut without fear?" he demanded.

Thalassa's answer was immediate.

You don't, she said. You cut with fear beside you. You do not let it hold the blade.

Mark exhaled shakily.

Marcus's voice broke the pocket's hush. "Can you tell us how to get Pecos back?" he asked, blunt. "Or are we just— practicing while he disappears?"

Thalassa's gaze flicked to the distant pulse.

The conduit is deeper now, she said. Eoraziel is wrapping him. If you do nothing, his consciousness will dissolve into the network. He will become a function, not a person.

Mark's throat tightened.

But, Thalassa continued, and the word hit like a lifeline, you have already reached him once. He felt you. That matters.

Alyssa swallowed. "So we can reach him again."

Yes, Thalassa said. But not by force. Force is what Eoraziel expects. Force is his element.

Her darkness shifted, and Mark felt a faint chill sweep through the pocket.

Choice, she said. Consent. A willing thread is harder to twist. That is why Harrow's blood pledge was so potent—because it was offered.

Mark's jaw clenched. "Then we offer what?"

Thalassa didn't answer immediately. Her gaze drifted past them, past the kelp-strands, into the fog where trapped spirits hung like ornaments.

I cannot tell you how to save him without telling you how to lose him, she said finally.

Mark felt his stomach drop. "What does that mean?"

It means the network will demand a replacement, Thalassa said. It always does. It is a machine built on exchange.

Alyssa's face tightened. "No."

Thalassa's darkness turned toward Alyssa, and for a heartbeat it felt like the ocean staring at a raindrop.

You already know this story, she said. You have read it in your pages. You are simply hoping this time the ending changes.

Mark's chest hurt—not just from the cut.

"Then why help us?" he asked, voice rough. "If it's just a machine, if it always—"

Because Eoraziel is young, Thalassa said, and young things can be starved. Young things can be broken. The machine can be smashed if you cut the right gears.

Mark's heartbeat thudded in his ears. He stared at the violet threads beyond the pocket, trying to see what Thalassa saw.

"The right gears," he repeated.

Thalassa's darkness leaned closer again, and Mark felt the weight of her attention like pressure at the bottom of a pool.

The heart, she said. The central bloom where Harrow's blood signature still glows. The thread that ties every sacrifice to every victory. Cut that thread, and the network spasms. Cut enough key threads, and it collapses.

Alyssa's fingers tightened on the grimoire. "And we need severance for that."

Yes.

Tommy's voice wavered. "And he can only do it… five times."

Thalassa's darkness flickered, almost like sympathy.

Then you must choose which threads matter, she said. That is the real skill.

Mark swallowed. He thought of Jason's thread, thick and braided, straining away from the heart.

He thought of Pecos's spark.

He thought of all the trapped faces.

How do you choose?

Thalassa's gaze slid to him as if she could hear the thought.

You don't get to save everyone, she said. Not in this world. Not in any.

The words hit Mark like a shove.

He opened his mouth to argue, to refuse, to say something heroic.

But the shadow realm had already shown him the truth.

Hundreds.

A thousand.

A century and a half of hungry victories.

Mark's throat tightened until he couldn't speak.

Thalassa's voice softened again, and Mark hated that it made his eyes burn.

But you can save the living, she said. And you can free those trapped closest to the heart, if you are careful.

Marcus's voice went low. "You said you tried to stop him," he said. "How?"

Thalassa's darkness pulsed, and for a moment Mark saw a flash—water crashing through roots, purple blooms drowning, the web recoiling.

I opposed him, she said. Water against flower. Shadow against blood. I pulled his roots apart. I drowned his filaments. I would have ended him—

Her chains tightened, violet light surging.

—until he learned to bind me with the very thing I used against him. He took my own darkness and wove it into his net. He made my element a prison.

Alyssa's voice was small. "If we break him," she whispered, "can we free you?"

Thalassa's gaze held Alyssa for a long beat.

Perhaps, she said. Or perhaps I am already too entangled. I have been here too long.

Mark's stomach twisted. The idea of something like Thalassa—something ancient—being stuck, helpless, watching… it made the shadow realm feel even crueler.

Thalassa's attention returned to Mark.

You will not free me today, she said. You do not have the cuts to waste. You will use them on the heart, on the guardian threads, on what matters.

Mark's jaw clenched. "And you're okay with that?"

Thalassa's darkness rippled. A laugh this time, faint and cold.

No, she said. But I am not stupid.

She leaned forward as much as her chains allowed.

Listen, she said, and the word pressed into Mark's skull like a thumb.

Eoraziel is listening even now. The pocket dulls him, but it does not blind him. He knows you are here. He knows you seek a blade.

Mark's pulse spiked. He glanced back at the kelp-strands, half-expecting the hunters to burst through.

Nothing moved.

Thalassa's voice continued.

He will send your brother against you, she said.

Mark's heart stuttered.

Alyssa's breath caught. Tommy's grip tightened on the bat.

Marcus's eyes narrowed. "Jason," he said, quiet.

Thalassa's darkness pulsed.

Yes, she said. The thread you saw resisting is strong. It frustrates him. So he will tighten it. He will make your brother a leash.

Mark's throat went dry. He remembered the silhouette wrapped around the braided thread—Jason's stance, his presence, fighting the pull.

"He's still in there," Mark whispered.

Thalassa's answer came like a knife and a blessing.

He is, she said. And that is why he is dangerous. And why he is your key.

Mark swallowed hard. "How is he a key?"

Because Eoraziel's hold is not perfect, Thalassa said. He can puppeteer flesh. He can twist memory. But he cannot fully erase will—not when the soul refuses.

Mark felt something in his chest tighten—the same hard decision he'd anchored to earlier.

Jason refused.

Even trapped, Jason refused.

Thalassa's voice dropped lower, deeper.

When the moment comes, she said, you will hesitate. You will see your brother's face. You will want to believe the puppet is the person.

Mark's stomach clenched, because she was right.

Thalassa's darkness leaned closer, and Mark felt her words settle into him like cold water.

Do not waste your cuts on doubt, she said. Use your brother's resistance. Look for it. He will show you where to cut.

Mark's eyes stung. "You're saying—"

I am saying, Thalassa replied, that your brother fights. Use him. He is the key.

Silence held for a beat.

In that beat, Mark heard the distant pulse again—the heart. The network. Pecos sinking.

Time.

Alyssa's voice cracked. "Mark," she whispered. "We have to go."

Mark nodded, swallowing hard.

He looked up at Thalassa, at the flower-chains biting into her wrists, at the way her darkness moved like deep water held behind glass.

"Why tell us this?" he asked. "Why give me a blade?"

Thalassa's gaze held him, and for the first time Mark felt something under her coldness.

Not kindness.

Not mercy.

Something sharper.

Hatred.

Because I want him to choke, Thalassa said simply. Because I want his garden to burn. And because—

Her voice paused, and the kelp-strands shivered like they'd heard something.

Because I remember what it was to choose, she finished. Even if humans forget.

Mark's chest tightened.

He thought of Lowridge, of Friday nights, of trophies and chants. Of a town choosing season after season.

He thought of Pecos. Of Jason.

He thought of himself—of the moment he'd decided no.

He nodded once.

"Teach me one more thing," he said.

Thalassa's darkness tilted.

What?

"How to not waste it," Mark said. "How to cut clean."

Thalassa's gaze stayed on him for a long beat.

Then her darkness moved, and the pocket seemed to tilt with it, like the whole shadow realm leaned closer.

Listen to the thread, she said. Feel where it wants to go. Feel what it feeds. A cut is not just separation—it is denial. You deny the network what it expects.

Mark swallowed.

"And what does it expect?"

Thalassa's answer was quiet, and it landed heavier than any scream.

It expects you to be willing, she said.

Mark's throat tightened. He thought of Harrow bleeding and begging. Of a boy on a field, raising his arms to the crowd.

He nodded again, slow.

"Got it," he whispered.

Alyssa's hand found Mark's arm, steadying him. "Mark," she said, voice trembling but firm, "we're with you. Okay? Whatever it costs—we're with you."

Tommy nodded hard, eyes glassy. "Yeah," he whispered. "We're… we're not letting you do this alone."

Marcus's gaze held Mark's for a beat. "Choose your cuts," he said quietly. "Don't let pride pick for you."

Mark exhaled, shakily.

He looked back at Thalassa one last time.

"If we survive," Mark said, voice rough, "we'll come back."

Thalassa's darkness rippled, and the flower-chains tightened as if they didn't like promises.

Do not promise, she said. Promise is what made this. Act is what breaks it.

Mark nodded. He turned.

The kelp-strands parted as they moved, and the pocket's cold heaviness fell away behind them.

The moment Mark stepped back into the web, the violet pulse hit him again—louder now, heavier. The patrol-light swept somewhere far off, searching.

Mark felt it brush the edge of his awareness like a fingertip on a bruise.

He clenched his new anchor—choice, refusal, no—and kept moving.

Ahead, Pecos's spark flickered, dim and urgent.

And somewhere in the fog beyond, a braided thread strained like a muscle, still fighting.

Jason.

Mark swallowed hard.

He had a blade now.

And only so many cuts to spend.

CHAPTER 22: REACHING THE CONDUIT

The shadow realm didn't have a sky.

It had a ceiling of threads—purple veins braided through darkness—arching overhead like the underside of a living stadium dome. Every strand carried a pulse. Every pulse carried a memory. Mark could feel it in his teeth, in the soft spots behind his eyes where headache lived and waited.

Behind them, the hunters still clicked through fog like insects made of wet rope. Ahead, the web thickened into something almost architectural—ramps of light, junctions, convergences—routes stacked over routes until the whole town became one giant play drawn in nerves and root.

Marcus moved first, shoulders tight, listening. Alyssa kept the grimoire hugged to her chest like an organ she couldn't live without. Tommy walked with his bat raised, like it mattered here. Like it could hit a thing that was half-thought and half-hunger.

Mark kept one hand pressed to his sternum, not because it helped, but because it reminded him he still had a body.

Thalassa's warning echoed every time Mark looked at a thick bundle of lines and imagined cutting his way through.

Five to seven.

A number that wasn't a limit so much as a countdown.

He had already spent one in panic—his first severance, sloppy and desperate, back when he still thought the shadow realm was an emergency exit and not a mouth. Thalassa had guided his second and third, each one cleaner, each one leaving a different kind of bruise inside his ribs. Not muscle. Not bone. Something that felt like the part of him that believed tomorrow was guaranteed.

Now the web ahead of them tightened into a knot so dense it looked solid.

And somewhere beyond it—faint, blinking like a distant porch light through heavy rain—Pecos's signal throbbed in short, weakening beats.

Tommy swallowed hard. "Tell me we're close."

Marcus didn't look back. "We're close."

Alyssa's voice came out too steady, the way people spoke when they were holding the center of themselves with both hands. "If the heart is near the cemetery, the lines should converge like—"

"Like the stadium," Mark finished before he could stop himself.

The web reacted to the word.

Threads near his shoulder brightened, quickened, as if his thought had been a hand on a switch.

Marcus's head snapped toward him, eyes sharp. Not angry. Warning.

Mark clamped down, forced his mind back to his anchor.

Jason, sixteen, laughing with his mouth full of pizza because he thought it was funny to risk choking just to make Mark mad. Jason tossing a football in the driveway like he could do it forever. Jason saying You'll carry it next like it was a blessing.

Mark held the memory like a nail in wood.

The threads dimmed again.

They moved.

The ground under Mark's shoes wasn't ground. It was a dark plane stitched with light—like walking on a shadow stretched tight over a pit. Each step sent a faint ripple outward. Each ripple carried.

Don't think loud, Marcus had said. Mark finally understood what it meant: fear wasn't private here. Grief wasn't private. Want wasn't private. The web tasted intention the way bloodhounds tasted air.

They slipped between two thicker bundles of line, and the fog changed.

It turned sweet.

Not the sweet of candy or perfume—sweet like bruised fruit left too long in heat, like sap. Under it, the metallic tang Mark remembered from October hits and split lips.

Blood and petals.

Access.

It wasn't just a rule. It was a doorway.

Alyssa flinched, nostrils tightening. "That's… new."

Marcus nodded once. "You're smelling the conduit."

Tommy's voice went small. "So we're walking into the part that actually does it."

No one corrected him.

Because yes.

This was where Lowridge's "luck" lived. This was where the pretty purple symbol on letterheads and booster signs became a lockpick for human will.

As they pushed deeper, the trapped spirits thinned out. Fewer faces in the fog. Fewer silent mouths forming help. Not because the web had emptied—Mark could still sense them behind, layered in the lines like recordings—but because the closer they got to the center, the less the entity bothered with storage.

Here was function.

Here was feeding.

The threads overhead began to curve downward, funneling them forward like the throat of something patient.

Pecos's signal pulsed again—faint, stuttering.

Mark sped up without meaning to.

Marcus caught his sleeve and pulled him back a half step. "You rush and you light it up."

"I know," Mark said, and his voice came out flat from effort. "I know."

Tommy gave a shaky little laugh, too loud, then clapped a hand over his mouth like he could take the sound back.

The web shivered.

Somewhere behind them, the cold patrol-light swept. Not over their faces—there were no faces here the way there were in the living world—but over their presence, their heat.

A pale beam slid across the threads like moonlight over water.

Alyssa went rigid. Her fingers crushed the grimoire's spine.

Marcus angled them toward a sagging curtain of thicker line. "Hide."

They slipped into it. The threads draped across Mark's shoulders with a sensation like cobweb and wet grass. His skin crawled. He wanted to tear them off, but he knew better. Touch too hard, pull too fast, and the web would answer.

The patrol-light drifted nearer, slow and methodical.

Mark kept his anchor.

Jason laughing.

Jason laughing.

Jason laughing.

In the distance, a darker glow pulsed—deeper violet, thicker than light should be. It made Mark think of a bruise under skin.

The patrol-light hesitated.

Then moved on.

The web exhaled. Or maybe Mark did.

Marcus eased them back out.

Alyssa's voice was a whisper that still felt too loud. "It's guarding the heart."

Marcus nodded. "And it's getting smarter. It knows we've learned how to cut."

Mark flexed his fingers, trying to ignore the faint tremor that lived there now, the aftertaste of each severance. "Then we don't cut unless we have to."

Tommy's eyes flicked to Mark's hand. "How many more…?"

Mark didn't answer at first. He didn't want to give the number shape in his mind. But Alyssa was watching him, and Marcus already knew.

"Three," Mark said quietly. "Maybe four if I'm lucky and stupid."

Tommy's face tightened. "So we're doing this clean."

"Clean," Alyssa repeated, as if the word could make the plan holy.

They moved again.

The funnel opened into a space so wide Mark's breath caught.

It was a chamber—an absence in the web where the lines stopped being roads and became walls. Threads spiraled upward in ribs. The fog pooled thick along the perimeter. And at the center, hanging just above the shadow-plane like a suspended organ, was the conduit's heart.

It wasn't shaped like a heart the way drawings made it.

It was a root-knot the size of a small car, pulsing slow and heavy. Purple petals grew from it in thick mats, opening and closing in time with the thud. Veins of light ran through the knot and out into the web, feeding every route, every line, every whisper that kept Lowridge obedient.

And embedded within the knot—half-swallowed, half-held—was Pecos.

Not his body. His self.

A figure of him, faint, wrapped in thin strands that climbed his wrists and throat like vines. His head was bowed, and each pulse of the heart made his outline flare as if the conduit was using him like a battery.

Mark's stomach lurched. The chamber smelled like crushed violets and damp earth. It smelled like the cemetery after rain.

Alyssa's voice cracked. "Pecos."

Pecos's head lifted slowly.

His eyes were open, but they weren't normal eyes here. They looked like depth—darkness with a tiny violet point at the center, pulsing in time with the heart.

For a moment Mark couldn't tell if Pecos saw them… or if the conduit saw through him.

Marcus stepped forward carefully, as if approaching a sleeping animal. "We're here."

Pecos's mouth moved. No sound came out.

Then Mark felt it, not through ears, but through bone—the way he'd heard Pecos's warning before, the way the web carried intention.

You're late.

Tommy made a helpless sound. "We came as fast as we could."

Pecos's outline shuddered with something that might have been a laugh, if laughter could exist inside a trap.

Alyssa's hands tightened on the grimoire. "We can pull you out."

Marcus's eyes flashed. "No," he said at the same time Pecos's presence pressed a single clear message into the air:

You can't.

Mark stepped forward until the air near the heart prickled his skin. The threads at the edge of the knot brightened, interested. Hungry.

Mark stopped.

He didn't touch.

He swallowed the taste of violets and pennies and said the truth anyway, because truth was the only thing they'd learned that made the web hesitate.

"Tell us what to do," Mark said.

The heart pulsed once—slow, heavy.

Pecos's outline flickered, dimming, then brightening again as if he had to fight for each second of himself.

It's inside me, he sent. Not just on me.

Alyssa's voice went quiet, the sarcasm stripped away. "Can you push it out?"

Pecos's presence pressed back, weary and calm in a way that made Mark's throat tighten.

I've been trying since you found me. It doesn't work like that. It's not... an infection. It's a hand on a steering wheel.

Mark thought of Eli Carter's last route, of the way the body moved while the mind watched, trapped inside perfect footwork.

Mark's jaw clenched. "Then we cut the lines."

Marcus shook his head slightly. "Cutting the main routes here will ring the whole web. It will lock down. It will drag you in."

Alyssa flipped pages in the grimoire with shaking fingers. "There has to be a way. A ritual. Something—"

Pecos's presence spiked, sharp enough to make Mark flinch.

Stop reading. Listen.

Alyssa froze.

The heart thumped.

And then Pecos spoke with a clarity that didn't belong in a place like this.

I can collapse it from inside.

Silence pressed in.

Even the web seemed to hold its pulse for half a beat, like it was listening too.

Tommy's voice came out raw. "What does that mean?"

Pecos's presence shifted, and for a second Mark saw him—really saw him—like a memory lit from within: Pecos on the practice field, calm, watching the sky like it had answers. Pecos at lunch, quiet while the others filled the air with noise. Pecos pressing his palm to dirt like it was a friend.

It means I can pull the hunger inward, Pecos said without words. I can take what it spreads and hold it in one place long enough for you to break the heart.

Alyssa's breath hitched. "You'll die."

Pecos's presence didn't flinch.

Maybe. Or maybe I become what Marcus is. Stuck. Half-fed. Half-free. But if I don't—

The heart pulsed harder. The violet points in Pecos's eyes brightened.

Mark felt something press against the inside of his own skull, curious, tasting.

He steadied his anchor.

Pecos continued.

If I don't, it uses me anyway. It opens the routes all the way. It takes the whole team. Then the town. Then the road outside town. Then the growth corridor. It doesn't stop at Lowridge.

Mark's chest tightened at the mention of the road—the highway out, the bright new buildings, the optimism that had kept people moving in like moths to a porch light.

Alyssa whispered, "Pecos…"

Pecos's presence softened, just slightly.

You were right about one thing, he sent to Alyssa. The town doesn't know it's trapped.

Tommy's hands shook around the bat. "There has to be another way. We can— we can drag you out. Mark can cut—"

Marcus's voice cut in, low and brutal with experience. "If he cuts the wrong thing here, the web takes him too. Then you're down your cutter and your quarterback. That's not strategy. That's grief wearing a plan."

Tommy's face reddened, jaw working. He looked like he wanted to yell, but sound was danger here. So he swallowed it, and the swallow looked like it hurt.

Mark stared at Pecos's outline.

He wanted to refuse the choice because refusing meant Pecos stayed alive in Mark's mind. Because accepting meant admitting that sometimes there wasn't a win—only a trade that cost you something you couldn't replace.

Mark's throat tightened. He forced himself to ask, "What happens to you if you do it?"

The answer hit him like cold water.

I feel them.

Mark blinked.

Pecos's presence pressed the meaning in, steady and unflinching.

Every player it took. Every person it used as a host. Every victim. Every fear. Every night it sat inside someone's mind and made them watch themselves do things they didn't choose.

Alyssa's eyes filled, but she didn't wipe them. Her hands stayed on the grimoire like she was afraid letting go would make her useless.

It keeps them, Pecos sent. Not as ghosts. As pressure. As hunger. I'll carry it long enough to fold it inward. That's the only window you get.

Mark felt sick.

Tommy whispered, "That's not fair."

Pecos's presence held a calm that felt older than a high school kid had any right to carry.

Nothing about this town has ever been fair, he sent. It just looked like it was.

The heart pulsed again, and the threads at its edges brightened like nerves reacting to a needle. Mark felt the web's attention sharpen.

They didn't have much time.

Alyssa lifted her chin, voice trembling but clear. "If you do it, we break the heart. Physically. Not just... spiritually."

Marcus nodded once. "Salt and iron and flame. Anything that disrupts the root-mass in the living world will echo here."

Mark stared at the heart-knot, at the petals opening and closing like mouths.

And then he realized something that chilled him deeper than the shadow realm ever could.

The heart wasn't just a battery.

It was a conductor.

The flowers weren't decoration.

They were ports—little violet doors scattered across town, waiting for blood, waiting for adrenaline, waiting for game night to make people loud enough to be heard.

Lowridge's obsession had built a perfect machine.

Mark's voice came out rough. "If you collapse it from inside... can you keep it from using Jason?"

Pecos's eyes flickered.

For a second the violet points dimmed, and Pecos looked like himself again.

Jason is tangled deeper than I am, he sent. But he's fighting. That's why you still feel him. That's why the thread frays.

Mark's anchor trembled at the thought—Jason inside the web, resisting, straining away like a muscle that refused to tear.

Pecos's presence sharpened again.

But the heart has a guard.

Mark didn't need to ask what that meant.

The chamber cooled.

The fog at the far edge of the space pulled back in a slow, deliberate motion, like curtains opening.

And a figure stepped out.

It wore the shape of a football player, broad-shouldered, helmeted, uniform hanging wrong in the way old photos did—too stiff, too perfect. Purple petals clung to the facemask like dried bruises. Light threaded under the skin in faint routes.

Mark knew the stance.

He'd seen it in driveway throws, in old game footage, in the way Jason used to shift his weight before a snap.

The figure lifted its head.

The eyes were Jason's.

And they weren't empty.

They were crowded.

As if a hundred voices had learned how to look through one face.

Alyssa's breath hitched. "Mark…"

Tommy took a step back, bat raised, hands trembling. "No. No, no, no."

Marcus's shoulders tensed. "That's the leash."

Jason's mouth moved.

The sound that came out wasn't one voice.

It was layered—two, three, more—like wind trying to speak through a broken flute.

"Turn back."

Mark stood still.

His lungs forgot how to work for a second.

Then he forced air in, tasted violets, tasted copper, and took one step forward anyway—toward the heart, toward Pecos, toward the brother-shaped guard.

Jason's head tilted, as if considering him.

The heart thumped hard.

The web brightened.

And the brother-thing smiled beneath the facemask—slow and practiced—like something that had watched humans for a long time and finally learned the shape of cruelty.

Mark's hand flexed, readying the severance in his mind, even as pain already waited for the cut.

Pecos's presence pressed one last message into Mark's bones—quiet, unwavering.

Do it. While you still can.

And the chamber filled with a low, rising hum—like the first swell of a crowd before a kickoff—because the conduit had noticed them now, and it was eager to see who would break first.

CHAPTER 23: THE BROTHER'S BATTLE

The deeper routes didn't look like roads anymore.

They looked like nerve.

Purple threads thickened into bundled cords that ran in hard arcs through the fog—overhead, underfoot, through the ghost-shapes of houses and trees —each one pulsing with the slow, patient rhythm of something that had learned to feed without hurrying.

Mark kept his eyes on Marcus's back and kept his mind on one memory: Jason in the driveway, laughing, tossing a football with that effortless, careless grace that made everything else feel easy by comparison.

Hold the anchor.

Don't think loud.

Don't bleed.

They moved in a tight line. Marcus first, fingers lifted as he parted strands that would have snagged them. Alyssa followed, grimoire tucked under one arm, her other hand held out like she was feeling for heat. Tommy stayed close, bat gripped in both hands, ring tapping against the wood in a fast, nervous rhythm. Mark came last, because that's what quarterbacks did when the play broke—count heads, cover the exit.

Behind them, the clicking hunters skittered through fog. Not close enough to strike, not far enough to forget.

Waiting for one mistake.

Ahead, the web narrowed into a choke point where multiple route-lines converged—a braided knot of light and shadow that hummed like stadium speakers when the announcer leaned into the mic.

Marcus slowed.

Mark felt it too: a pressure behind his eyes, a heaviness in the air that wasn't air. The closer they got, the stronger the pull became, like gravity had decided to concentrate itself in one place.

"That's the throat," Marcus said.

Tommy's voice came out too loud. "The throat of what?"

Marcus didn't look back. "Of the thing that's been eating this town."

Alyssa swallowed. "And Pecos is past it."

Marcus nodded once.

Mark's stomach tightened. In the distance, beyond the knot, a faint violet glow flickered—small, unsteady, like a firefly trapped inside a jar.

Pecos.

Mark pushed forward instinctively.

Marcus's hand shot back, palm up. Stop.

Mark stopped. Every muscle in his body screamed to run anyway.

"Slow," Marcus said, low. "This is where it listens hardest."

Tommy gave a strained laugh. "Fantastic. We found the part of the nightmare with the best acoustics."

Alyssa's mouth twitched—almost a smile, almost not. "If it makes you feel better, you're definitely going to be the loudest ghost in here."

"Thanks. Comforting."

Mark breathed through his nose. Jason laughing. Jason laughing.

The choke point shimmered like heat over asphalt. Marcus stepped into it first.

The threads parted.

Not like a door opening.

Like a mouth choosing to unhinge.

On the other side, Lowridge was no longer a suggestion.

It was an altar.

The shape of the town rose in ghostly layers—street grids, rooflines, the faint skeleton of the stadium—all of it overlaid with thick, pulsing roots that webbed everything together. The routes ran toward a single central mass that glowed beneath a constant veil of fog.

A heart the size of a building.

No—bigger than that.

A heart the size of a need.

Mark's throat went dry.

The core wasn't just roots. It was flower, too—petal layers stacked in dark spirals, opening and closing with each pulse. Veins of violet light threaded through it like circuitry.

And in the petals, faces shifted.

Not fully formed. Not fully gone.

Eyes. Mouths. A cheekbone. A grin that almost looked like a grin until it didn't.

Tommy made a sound that might've been prayer if he believed. "That is… not okay."

Alyssa stared, blinking hard. "It's a network. It's been building itself under the town. Feeding. Wiring everything to one center."

Marcus's voice was flat. "Welcome to the pantry."

Mark's gaze snagged on the stadium's outline. In this place, it looked less like a field and more like a dish—wide, cupped, built to hold noise and devotion. Fibers ran from it straight into the heart, thick as cables.

Football wasn't tradition.

It was a pipeline.

Mark's hands curled into fists.

He thought of Friday nights. Of the roar hitting your chest. Of the way the town looked at you like you were proof that everything was fine.

And the heart pulsed, as if agreeing.

Alyssa's whisper was sharp with disgust. "It learned what we would offer without being asked."

Marcus turned his head slightly. "It didn't learn. It was taught."

Mark's eyes narrowed. "By who?"

Marcus didn't answer.

Because the fog ahead shifted.

And someone stepped out.

A player in a Lowridge uniform—older cut, older pads, the blue dulled like it had been washed too many times. A helmet shadowed his face. Purple petals clung to the facemask in stiff, dried clusters.

Mark's breath caught before he could stop it.

He knew the stance. The weight on the back foot. The way the shoulders angled like they were ready to throw a pass that only they could see.

Jason.

Not a clean ghost. Not a trick in moonlight.

Jason as the web held him.

Alyssa's fingers tightened around the grimoire. "Mark—"

Jason lifted his head.

For a moment, his eyes were just dark hollows in a shadowed helmet.

Then a faint violet point lit in each pupil.

The same pulse that had lived under Pecos's skin.

Mark's anchor jolted—grief and hope slamming into each other like helmets in a collision.

"Jay," Mark said. The name came out small.

Jason's mouth moved behind the facemask.

Two voices came out.

One was Jason's—familiar cadence, tired warmth.

The other was something layered beneath it—flat and hungry, like wind scraping over dead leaves.

"Little brother," Jason said, and something in Mark's chest cracked. "You finally made it to the end zone."

Tommy lifted his bat. "Nope. I do not like that sentence."

Alyssa's voice stayed level, but Mark could hear the tremor she was forcing down. "Jason, can you hear me?"

Jason's head tilted. "I hear everything."

A pause.

Then the lower voice slid in like a knife under skin.

"And I hear what you're afraid to say."

The web around them brightened.

Mark felt the routes tighten in response, like a net drawing closed.

Marcus moved one step forward, shoulders squared. "Don't play with him."

Jason's gaze snapped to Marcus.

For a heartbeat, the violet points in his eyes flared.

"Half-blood," the lower voice said. "Half-made. Half-mine."

Marcus's jaw clenched. "Keep talking and I'll rip your threads myself."

Jason smiled behind the mask. It didn't reach the eyes.

"Try."

The air thickened. Fog rolled in, and with it came that sweet-violet scent, rimmed with copper, like a mouthguard pulled from a bleeding mouth.

Alyssa's hand slid into her pocket. Salt. Candle stub. Something hard and familiar.

Mark saw it and understood: a circle wouldn't hold here. Not with the heart watching.

But rules were rules.

Confession and honesty broke the conduit.

And Mark had been swallowing truth for years.

Alyssa met his eyes for the briefest second. In that look was an entire sentence: If you want him back, stop lying.

Mark's tongue felt too big for his mouth.

"Jay," he said again, and this time he stepped forward, slow, hands open. "I'm not here for... whatever this is. I'm here for you. For Pecos. For everyone you—"

Jason lifted a hand.

The web vibrated.

Mark's lungs tightened as if a belt had cinched around his ribs.

"I remember you," Jason said. The Jason-voice softened, almost pleading. "I remember the driveway. I remember you watching me like I was the sun."

Mark's eyes stung.

"And I remember the look on Dad's face," the lower voice added, "when the council came to the house."

Mark froze.

Alyssa inhaled sharply.

Tommy's bat wavered. "The what now?"

Mark's heart slammed.

Jason took one step closer. Every thread in the air leaned toward him, hungry for the next word.

"Tell them," the lower voice whispered through Jason's mouth. "Tell them what you are."

Mark tried to breathe and found no space.

His father's study flashed in his mind: the drawer that never stuck, the ledger of old newspaper clippings, the envelope with wax stains. The way his dad went quiet whenever the cemetery came up. The way his mother shut conversations down with a smile that didn't match her eyes.

And Mark's own silence—his practiced, trained silence—had become part of the pact without him ever signing his name.

Alyssa's voice cut through, sharp and small. "Mark, the rule—"

"I know," Mark said, and his voice sounded like it belonged to someone else.

He turned his head, just enough to see his friends.

Tommy, shaking, still standing.

Alyssa, jaw tight, eyes wet but fierce.

Marcus, watching him like this was a fork in a road that only Mark could choose.

Mark looked back at Jason.

He saw, for a flicker, Jason's real eyes behind the violet points—tired, trapped, afraid.

Mark swallowed.

And then he did the thing he had avoided for years.

He told the truth.

"My family knew," Mark said, and the words hit the shadow realm like a thrown stone. "Not everything. Maybe not the worst of it. But they knew there was a council. They knew the town didn't win clean. They knew… the land took something."

The web shuddered.

Threads around Mark trembled, as if they'd been cut with an invisible blade.

Jason's shoulders jerked, like the confession had yanked on whatever held him.

Mark kept going. If he stopped now, the lie would knit back together.

"My dad—he never said it straight. He just… handed me the legacy like it was a blessing. Like playing quarterback would fix whatever he couldn't face. And I let him." Mark's voice cracked once, then steadied. "I wore it. I smiled. I took the pictures. I signed the posters. I stood in front of the trophy case like I belonged there."

Tommy's face went pale. "Mark…"

Alyssa didn't flinch. She looked almost relieved, like the world finally matched what she'd suspected.

Mark's gaze stayed locked on Jason. "And when you died, I told myself it was an accident because the truth was worse. Because if it wasn't an accident, then the town didn't just lose you—"

His breath hitched.

"It kept you."

The words landed.

For a moment, everything stilled.

The heart stopped pulsing.

The fog froze mid-drift.

Then the web screamed.

Not sound—vibration. A furious, tearing ripple that ran along every route line like a nerve reacting to pain.

Mark's chest flared with a sharp, cold ache, as if the confession had ripped something loose inside him.

Jason's helmet tipped forward. His hands clenched.

The violet points in his eyes flickered, unstable.

And for half a heartbeat, Jason's real voice came through—raw, human, unlayered.

"Mark," Jason whispered. "Don't—"

The lower voice slammed back in, louder, angry now. "Enough."

Jason lunged.

He moved too fast, not with muscle but with threads, pulled forward by the web itself. Purple fibers shot from the ground like whips, snaring Mark's wrists.

Cold pressure locked down.

Mark's knees buckled.

Alyssa shouted a phrase from the grimoire—words that tasted like rust in Mark's ears—and a bright crack of heat snapped through the fog. The fibers around Mark's left wrist recoiled, curling as if scorched.

Tommy swung his bat and smashed through a strand that had started to coil around Mark's ankle. The bat stuck for a fraction of a second—wet rope resistance—then tore free.

Tommy yelled, louder than fear. "If anyone wants to win a state championship right now, this would be the moment."

"Tommy!" Alyssa snapped.

"I am coping!"

Marcus grabbed Mark under the arm and hauled him up. "Keep your truth in your mouth," Marcus hissed. "It hates that."

Mark staggered, breath thin. Jason laughed—Jason's laugh, almost—and it broke Mark's heart because it was wrong, warped, missing the warmth.

Jason stepped closer, and the heart behind him began to pulse again, faster.

Alyssa moved to Mark's side, grimoire open. "Confession weakens the lines," she said, voice tight. "But it also makes you visible. It's like—like shining a light in here."

"Great," Tommy panted. "We're honest and we get murdered."

Marcus's eyes never left Jason. "If you're going to shine, shine all the way."

Mark's throat tightened. "What does that mean?"

"It means you don't stop at 'my family knew.'" Marcus's voice went colder. "You say what you want. Out loud. The thing you've been choking on since you were a kid."

Mark's chest rose, shallow. The words were there, behind his teeth, dangerous and true.

He looked at Jason.

Jason's head tilted as if listening. The violet pulse in his eyes steadied, as if the web liked where this was going.

Lowridge didn't celebrate champions. It kept them.

Mark felt that sentence in his bones.

And he finally understood: the land didn't just want blood.

It wanted devotion.

It wanted the part of you that said yes when you meant no.

Mark's hands shook.

He spoke anyway.

"I don't want it," Mark said. The words came out rough. "I don't want the legacy. I don't want the trophies. I don't want to be the town's proof. I wanted out before you died, and I was too scared to admit it."

The web jolted.

Jason jerked as if someone had punched him from the inside.

The violet points in his eyes dimmed.

Under the helmet, Jason's face—his real face—flickered into view for a split second, like a signal cutting through static.

"Good," Jason breathed. One word, pure Jason.

Then his expression twisted, and the lower voice snarled through his teeth. "You don't get to leave."

Behind Jason, the heart opened wider.

Petal layers peeled back like the iris of an eye.

Inside, something moved—thick roots turning, a slow churn like a stomach working.

And in that opening, Mark saw a glow that wasn't purple.

A small, steady ember-light, trapped deeper than the rest.

Pecos.

Mark's body surged forward.

Marcus grabbed his shoulder hard. "Not yet."

Alyssa's voice shook. "We have a window. It's open because your truth cut the tension. But it'll close fast."

Tommy wiped his sleeve across his mouth and stared at the heart. "Okay, so… do we jump into the giant flower-mouth or do we have a better plan?"

Marcus's eyes narrowed. "We take Pecos's spark. We anchor it to the living. Then we get out before it learns how to swallow us whole."

Mark's gaze stayed on Jason.

Jason stood between them and the heart like a gate.

Jason's hands trembled. The violet light under his skin pulsed and faltered, like the web was trying to retake control.

Mark stepped forward, slow.

"Jay," he said. "I'm sorry."

Jason's helmet dipped, almost a nod.

Then his voice split again, two layers fighting for the same air.

"Run," Jason whispered.

"Stay," the lower voice demanded.

Jason's shoulders shook.

Mark saw it—the battle inside the vessel, the boy trying to protect his brother and the hunger trying to use his mouth as a lure.

Mark didn't raise a weapon.

He raised the only thing that could sever the conduit.

Truth.

"I failed you," Mark said, and his voice was steady now, because the worst part was already out. "I let the town make your death into a story that fit their denial. I let them hang your jersey in glass and call it honor. I didn't ask what you were trying to tell me."

Jason's violet pupils flickered wildly.

The web trembled.

A thread snapped somewhere above them, and a thin shower of purple light drifted down like pollen.

Jason's gloved hand lifted—slow, struggling—and pressed two fingers to his own facemask, right over his mouth.

A gesture Mark remembered from childhood. A silent signal: Quiet. Listen.

Jason lowered his hand and took one step sideways.

Just enough to reveal a path to the heart.

Alyssa sucked in a breath. "Mark—"

"I see it," Mark whispered.

Marcus moved first, fast and controlled. He cut through the fog with his hand, parting threads as he went. Alyssa followed, grimoire up, murmuring a shield phrase that made the air around them shimmer faintly, like heat haze.

Tommy grabbed Mark's sleeve. "If we survive this, I'm never making jokes again," he said.

Mark looked at him. "That's a lie."

Tommy blinked, then let out a strangled laugh. "Okay. Maybe fewer jokes."

Mark stepped toward the opening.

Jason's head turned. For one fragile second, the violet points in his eyes were gone entirely.

Jason looked at Mark through the helmet like he could finally see him.

"Don't let them write your ending," Jason said.

It wasn't the lower voice.

It was his.

Mark's throat closed.

He nodded once.

And then the heart pulsed hard—angry now, aware—and the web snapped toward them like a fist closing.

Jason's body jolted, yanked back toward the heart by a surge of thread.

His arm shot out and caught Mark's wrist with desperate strength.

Cold flooded Mark's veins.

For a heartbeat, Mark saw through Jason's eyes: a tunnel of purple, endless faces, devotion pouring like water into a drain.

Jason's grip tightened.

"Go," Jason rasped. "Before it—"

The lower voice surged up, drowning him. "Stay."

Jason's fingers spasmed, and Mark felt the conduit try to hook into him through that contact—cold and sweet, like petals pressed into a cut.

Mark ripped his wrist free.

Pain flared, sharp and bright.

He didn't look back.

They ran.

Straight toward the open flower-mouth.

Straight toward the ember-light that was Pecos.

Behind them, the heart's pulse accelerated, and the shadow realm filled with a sound like distant cheering—Lowridge's Friday night roar, warped into hunger.

And somewhere behind the fog, a familiar laugh fractured into a scream.

CHAPTER 24: PANIC SETS IN

Harold Saan had lived in Lowridge long enough to recognize the town's lies by the way they sounded.

For decades, the lie had worn a friendly voice. It was the kind that came with casseroles and porch lights and "how's your mother doing?" It was the kind that called a boy a hero on Friday nights and called his funeral "a tragedy" on Monday mornings. A lie you could swallow because everyone else did.

Tonight, the lie didn't bother pretending.

The first scream came from the north end of Main Street, thin and sharp as a whistle, and then it doubled—another voice, then another—until it became a chorus that made the air tremble. Sirens tried to rise over it and failed. Wind pushed fog through the street like a living tide, and within that fog, purple petals spun and stuck to everything they touched.

Harold stood in the doorway of the hardware store with a revolver he hadn't wanted to pick up, watching the streetlights flicker in slow, sick blinks.

The flowers were learning new ways to grow.

They didn't just climb anymore. They built.

A mailbox post disappeared beneath a fast-blooming sheath of violet vines, thickening like muscle. A minivan at the curb sprouted blossoms along the windows as if the glass were soil. The blooms pressed outward, pushing the windows until they spiderwebbed and snapped. Someone inside pounded on the doors. The sound came muffled, like it was underwater.

Harold turned away before he could see what happened next.

Behind him, the hardware store had been converted into a refugee pocket—fifteen, maybe twenty people huddled between aisles of paint cans and lawn tools, faces pale in the battery-lantern glow. There were children crying into their parents' shirts. There were old men holding baseball bats like they still thought this was a burglary they could scare off. There were three teenagers with bruised knuckles and wild eyes who kept glancing at the door like the street might decide to walk inside.

Alyssa's mother sat on a plastic step stool near the back, shaking so hard her teeth clicked. She'd been one of the ones who showed up at Harold's house earlier, breathless and terrified, asking where her daughter was.

Harold hadn't had an answer.

He still didn't.

He gripped the revolver tighter. It felt wrong in his hand. Not because he'd never held one before—he had, years ago, for reasons he didn't revisit —but because tonight the threat didn't have a body a bullet could argue with.

A girl of maybe nine tugged his sleeve.

"Mr. Saan," she whispered, eyes swollen from crying. "Are we gonna die?"

Harold swallowed. The words wanted to come out as a lie, soft and reassuring and useless.

Instead he crouched so he could look her in the eye.

"I'm doing everything I can to keep that from happening," he said.

The girl stared at him like she didn't know what to do with honesty. Then she nodded, small and shaky, and backed away toward her mother.

A sudden crash echoed from outside—wood splintering, metal bending. The refugees flinched as one.

"Shut the lights," Harold said. "Now."

A man near the lantern hesitated.

Harold's voice sharpened. "Now."

The lantern went dark. The store fell into a thick, breath-held silence broken only by whispering sobs and the faint hum of a dying fluorescent sign outside.

Harold eased the door nearly shut, leaving only a thin gap to watch the street through.

The fog moved.

Something in it moved with purpose.

He saw a shape pass beneath the streetlight—broad shoulders, human outline, familiar gait.

For half a second relief flickered through him.

Then the streetlight blinked, and the shape became something else.

It was still wearing a jacket—red, like a flare in the fog—but the person inside it was no longer a person. The jacket hung off a frame that bulged in strange places, as if muscles had rearranged themselves. The neck was too long. The head angled wrong. And where the face should have been, there was a mass of petals and root-fiber, folded and layered like a grotesque flower.

In the center, a glossy dark spot reflected the streetlight.

An eye.

Harold's stomach turned cold.

The Red Wanderer.

He'd been a rumor for weeks. A stranger who showed up just as the town started coming apart—offering prayers that sounded like chants, offering "solutions" that felt like surrender. He drifted through gas stations and church basements, speaking softly to people already afraid, telling them the land was angry and would be soothed if they stopped resisting.

Harold had watched him once from the back row of a "community meeting" in the high school gym, when the mayor tried to keep everyone calm with practiced lies. The stranger had stood up and smiled and said, We've always known what the price is.

Half the room had nodded like they'd been waiting for permission.

Harold had wanted to drag the man outside and ask what he was.

He hadn't.

Now the Red Wanderer stood in the middle of Main Street like he owned it, and the fog around him bowed, as if the air itself recognized authority.

A cluster of townspeople shuffled out of the haze behind him.

They moved wrong.

They weren't stumbling drunk. They weren't running from danger. They walked with the synchronized steadiness of people being guided by something deeper than thought. Their faces were blank, mouths slightly open. Purple pollen dusted their cheeks and brows like bruising.

Harold's pulse thudded in his ears.

Possessed.

He'd seen it start earlier, subtle—people's eyes glazing during pep rallies, hands trembling while they clapped, voices slipping into the same rhythm when they spoke about the Lions. It had felt like hysteria, like a town building itself into a frenzy.

Tonight it was no longer hysteria.

It was control.

The possessed crowd stopped in the intersection under the dead traffic light, facing the direction of the football stadium. The Red Wanderer lifted both hands slowly, reverently, like a pastor raising a blessing.

The crowd lifted their hands too.

And from their mouths came one sound, layered and identical:

"Give."

Harold's skin prickled.

The word repeated, louder.

"Give."

Then, all at once, the crowd turned their heads toward the hardware store.

Not their bodies. Just their heads, snapping in unison like birds.

Harold froze.

Their eyes—every single one—caught the faint line of light in his door gap. The glossy dark spots in their pupils shone, too still, too reflective.

The Red Wanderer's petal-face folded as if smiling.

He spoke. His voice wasn't loud. It didn't need to be.

It carried through the fog like sound through water.

"Harold Saan," it said.

Hearing his name in that voice felt like being touched by cold mud.

Harold's grip tightened on the revolver until his knuckles ached. He didn't speak. He didn't move.

The Wanderer's head tilted, petals whispering against each other. "You have hidden them."

Harold's throat went dry.

Behind him, someone stifled a sob.

The Wanderer stepped forward.

Each footfall left a faint violet smear on the pavement that glowed for half a second and then dimmed, like a pulse fading.

"You think you can keep the town from its own hunger," the Wanderer said. "You think you can delay what is owed."

Harold's mouth tasted metallic. He wanted to shout that this wasn't hunger—it was theft. He wanted to scream that the town didn't get to owe its children.

But he'd learned long ago that monsters didn't argue.

They invited.

The Wanderer lifted one hand toward the stadium, and as if responding, the air shifted.

Harold felt it like pressure behind his eyes.

A vibration.

Far away, from the direction of the football field, a low roar rolled across town.

It wasn't crowd noise.

It wasn't wind.

It was something vast waking up.

The possessed people shuddered as if the roar moved through them like electricity. Their mouths opened wider.

And then the voice came.

Not from one throat.

From all of them.

Hundreds of voices speaking in perfect unison, words stacked on words until they became something that felt less like speech and more like a command carved into the world.

"GIVE ME THE BOY."

The hardware store erupted in panicked noise—gasps, muffled screams, someone whispering "Jesus Christ" over and over like it was a spell.

Harold's heart hammered once, hard enough to hurt.

Mark Rivers.

Even here, even now, everything came back to the captain of the Lions. The town's golden boy. The one the land had been circling since the season began.

Harold forced himself to breathe.

The possessed crowd didn't move closer yet. They held, waiting, like a wave paused at the edge of a shore.

The Red Wanderer lowered his hand, slow and gentle. "Willing," he said. "That is all that is asked."

Harold's fingers trembled around the revolver.

He had promised himself—promised whatever part of Alyssa's grandfather still existed inside his own memory—that if the day ever came, he would not offer up another child.

But the voices outside kept pressing, heavy as gravity.

"GIVE."

"GIVE."

The word hit the door like fists.

Harold turned, back to the gap, and faced the refugees in the dark.

They stared at him.

Some were crying silently.

Some looked at him with desperate hope.

And some—some had a different look, a flicker behind their eyes that made Harold's stomach twist.

Calculation.

A man in a Lions jacket stepped forward. Harold recognized him: one of the boosters, always front row at games, always shouting about tradition.

"Harold," the man whispered, voice shaking. "He said… he said if we give him the boy, he'll stop."

A woman clutched a toddler against her chest. "Make it stop," she pleaded.

Harold's jaw clenched. "You don't believe that."

The booster's eyes darted toward the door, toward the chanting. "What if it's true?"

Harold's voice dropped. "What if it isn't?"

The man's face twisted. "Then what? We all die anyway?"

The question landed like a stone.

A murmur rippled through the room, fear turning into something sharper.

Harold saw it happen the way you saw a crowd shift in a stadium—one chant starting, catching, becoming a roar. He'd watched thousands of people demand a touchdown like wanting it hard enough could change physics.

Now the same mechanism was turning inward.

The booster took another step forward. "Where is Mark?"

Harold's pulse jumped. "He's not here."

The man's eyes narrowed. "Then where is he?"

Harold didn't answer.

The booster's gaze swept the room, and Harold saw something in it that made his skin crawl.

Devotion.

Not to people.

To the town.

To the idea of winning, surviving, keeping the story going even if it cost blood.

A teenager near the back—one of the wild-eyed ones—spoke up, voice trembling. "My dad's out there," he said. "He's… he's one of them now. If giving Mark saves him—"

A woman snapped, "You want to trade someone else's kid for your dad?"

The teenager flinched. "I don't want— I just—"

The argument sparked, quick as dry grass.

Harold stepped between them. "Enough."

His voice cut through the room like a whistle. People went quiet, more from shock than obedience.

Harold forced his hands to stop shaking. "Listen to me," he said. "That thing out there? It is not bargaining. It is not negotiating in good faith. It is testing you. It is looking for the same choice this town has made for a century: sacrifice the few so the many can keep cheering."

The booster's mouth tightened. "So what's your plan, Harold? You got a better deal?"

Harold's eyes burned. "My plan is not to feed it."

A low rumble vibrated through the store shelves. Paint cans rattled. Something outside hit the building with a wet, heavy sound.

A child screamed.

Harold's heart lurched. He snapped his gaze back to the door gap.

The fog had thickened. Purple vines had begun to crawl across the sidewalk, sliding like snakes toward the storefront. Blossoms opened as they moved, petals unfurling in slow, hungry spirals.

The Red Wanderer had not advanced.

He didn't have to.

He raised his hands again, and the vines paused, as if waiting for permission.

Then the Wanderer spoke, softer now. Almost kind.

"Willing," it repeated. "And the rest are spared."

Harold swallowed bile.

A bargain written in a single word: surrender.

Behind him, the booster exhaled a harsh breath. "We can't just sit here."

Harold turned. "We're not giving him Mark."

The booster's face hardened. "Maybe you don't get to decide that."

Harold stared at him.

Around them, the room seemed to tighten—fear compressing into something dangerous.

The same mob psychology that filled bleachers could fill a room, and Harold could feel it building, could feel the moment coming when someone would lunge, someone would open the door, someone would offer the boy just to make the chanting stop.

Harold's voice dropped. "You open that door and you don't just give it Mark," he said. "You give it permission. You tell it we will always fold."

The booster's jaw worked. "If Mark were here, maybe he'd choose to —"

A sharp crack snapped through the air.

Not from inside.

Outside.

The revolver went up in Harold's hand instinctively.

Through the door gap, he saw a figure stumble out of the fog—one of Harold's small resistance group, a man named Ruiz who'd been helping evacuate people from the north end.

Ruiz slammed into a parked car, panting, eyes wide.

Behind him, a vine-beast moved through the fog—four-legged, hulking, made of root-mass and petals, its back studded with open blooms that pulsed like gills.

Ruiz raised his shotgun and fired.

The blast echoed.

The creature barely flinched.

It surged forward, slammed Ruiz against the car, and vines wrapped around his throat.

Ruiz's mouth opened in a strangled cry.

Harold's breath caught.

The Red Wanderer didn't look at Ruiz.

He didn't look at the creature.

He looked at the hardware store, at the thin line of light, and lifted one finger like a conductor cueing a section of orchestra.

The vine-beast tightened.

Ruiz's cry cut off.

Harold's stomach dropped, cold and heavy.

The message was clear: there would be no stalemate. No waiting. No hiding.

Give, or watch the town be consumed.

Harold's hand shook on the revolver. He wanted to shoot the Wanderer. He wanted to shoot the creature. He wanted to shoot the whole fog and the whole damn pact out of existence.

But the Wanderer was too far, and the crowd between made a wall of meat that Harold refused to turn into casualties.

And worse—

Harold saw, in the possessed faces, something that wasn't fully gone.

A flicker.

Tears on a man's cheek even as he chanted.

A woman's hands trembling, fingers digging into her palms, like she was trying to hold onto herself.

They were still in there.

Which meant this wasn't just possession.

It was coercion.

Harold stepped back from the door. He turned to the refugees again, voice forced calm.

"We move," he said. "Back exit. Alley. We take the side streets to the church basement."

The booster scoffed. "Side streets are blocked."

"Then we go through yards," Harold snapped.

The booster grabbed his arm. "Harold—"

Harold jerked free. "Don't touch me."

The man's eyes flashed. "You're gonna get us killed."

Harold leaned in close enough to smell the stale beer on his breath. "No," he said, low. "You're going to get us killed if you start believing in bargains with monsters."

A woman near the back—Mrs. Everly, the librarian—raised her chin. Her voice shook, but it held. "He's right," she said. "We've been doing this for generations. We keep losing boys and calling it destiny."

The booster glared at her. "You can say that because it's not your kid out there."

Mrs. Everly's eyes filled with tears. "It was my brother," she whispered. "In '94. And we clapped for him until his legs gave out."

Silence fell, thick as fog.

Harold felt something inside him loosen, just slightly. A thread of hope.

Not everyone would fold.

He pointed to the back door. "Go," he said. "Quiet."

They moved in a huddle, footsteps soft on linoleum. Harold stayed last, watching the front door, watching the thin seam of light.

Outside, the chanting continued.

"GIVE ME THE BOY."

"GIVE ME THE BOY."

The words made the glass tremble.

Harold reached the back door just as another crash sounded outside—this time close enough that the whole building shuddered. A shelf toppled. Cans clattered.

The fog wanted in.

Harold pushed the back door open.

Cold night air hit his face, carrying the sick-sweet scent of crushed flowers.

The alley behind the hardware store was dark, lit only by the faint glow of purple blooms creeping along dumpsters and chain-link fences. A cat darted under a bush, eyes reflecting violet.

Harold guided the refugees into the alley, one by one.

As the last woman slipped through, the booster hesitated.

He looked back toward the front, toward the chanting. His face was twisted with fear and devotion and something like grief.

Harold caught his gaze. "Don't," he said.

The booster's throat bobbed.

Then—slowly—he nodded and stepped into the alley.

Harold released a breath he hadn't realized he'd been holding.

Behind them, the hardware store's front windows exploded.

Glass shattered outward in a spray of glittering shards.

A roar of petals poured in like a flood.

The chanting surged, triumphant.

Harold grabbed the nearest child and ran.

*****

In the shadow realm, time didn't move like it did aboveground.

It didn't tick. It didn't count.

It pressed.

Mark felt that pressure even before Marcus said anything.

They were crouched behind a thick curtain of threads, the purple web around them trembling as if something enormous had just inhaled. The air —if you could call it air—tasted sharp, metallic, like lightning trapped in a jar.

Alyssa's hands were shaking around the grimoire. Tommy's bat hovered uselessly at his side, as if he could swing at a concept. Marcus's outline shimmered, half-solid, his eyes fixed on the distant pulse of the network.

And Pecos's light—Pecos's ember—glowed ahead of them, steady now, anchored in place like a star caught in a net.

"Something changed," Mark whispered.

Marcus's jaw tightened. "Yeah," he said. "It noticed."

Mark's chest burned where the severance cuts had torn through him earlier. He could still feel the phantom snap of Jason's thread breaking, could still hear the way his brother's voice had sounded—lucid, grateful, gone. Jason was free.

But freedom had consequences.

The web pulsed again, harder.

From the distance came the faint suggestion of sound—not voices, not words, but the feeling of a stadium chant translated into vibration.

Mark's stomach twisted.

"The town," Alyssa whispered, eyes wide. "It's—"

Marcus nodded once. "It's panicking. Aboveground. It's feeding it."

Tommy swallowed. "That's… that's possible? We're down here and it's —"

"It's one system," Marcus said. "One nervous system. You cut one nerve and the whole body reacts."

Mark's fingers clenched around his anchor—Jason laughing, Jason bumping his shoulder, Jason throwing a football one-handed. He held the memory like a rope.

The web shuddered again.

The patrol-light—cold and pale—swept across the threads above them. It felt closer now. Less searching. More certain.

Marcus shifted, listening. "We can't stay here," he murmured. "We go out. Now."

Alyssa stared at him. "Out? We haven't—"

Marcus's eyes flicked toward Pecos's ember. "Pecos is anchored," he said. "Ready. We've done what we came to do here."

Mark's pulse jumped. "Then why do I feel like we're losing?"

Marcus's mouth tightened. "Because you are. Not him. The town."

Tommy let out a shaky breath. "I'd love to not lose the town."

Marcus grabbed Alyssa's wrist, pulling her closer. "When we step out, don't listen," he said, voice low and urgent. "Don't listen to any voice that isn't ours. If it speaks through them, it will try to hook you."

Alyssa's throat bobbed. "We can resist."

Marcus's expression was grim. "Some can," he said. "Will matters. That's the only reason any of this isn't already over."

Mark looked at Pecos's ember again—steady, pulsing faint violet. His friend was still in there. Still choosing.

Mark nodded. "Let's go."

Alyssa began the return incantation, words scraping through the air like stones. The threads around them loosened, making a thin corridor. Marcus guided them through, hand coaxing strands aside.

Mark's last glimpse of the shadow realm was a field of trapped silhouettes watching silently as the patrol-light swept past. Faces he'd never known and now would never forget.

Then the world lurched.

Weight returned.

Air filled his lungs—real air, damp and thick with fog.

And the smell hit him like a punch.

Smoke. Dirt. Crushed flowers. Blood.

Mark stumbled as the shelter around them snapped back into existence —the tangle of roots, the tarps, the battery lantern now flickering weakly. The candles Alyssa had set were burned down to stubs, wax pooling like tears.

Tommy gagged. "Oh god," he rasped. "That's worse than down there."

Alyssa's eyes widened as she looked out through the vine-curtain that served as a door. "Harold's wards—" she started.

Marcus shoved the vines aside.

Mark's breath caught.

The lot behind the closed-down daycare was lit by an unnatural purple glow. The trees sagged under heavy blooms. Vines crawled across the ground like living cables.

And beyond that—

Lowridge was burning.

Not all of it. Not yet. But pockets of flame flickered where houses had been overtaken and then shattered, where someone had tried to fight back with gasoline and desperation. Smoke rose into the fog and made the sky look bruised.

The street beyond the lot was clogged with people.

They weren't running away.

They were moving toward something.

Toward the stadium.

A river of bodies, heads tilted the same direction, mouths moving in the same rhythm. Even from here, Mark could hear it.

A chant.

Layered. Hungry.

"GIVE ME THE BOY."

Mark's stomach dropped.

Alyssa's hand flew to her mouth. "No," she whispered. "No, no—"

Marcus's face went pale in the lantern glow. "It's doing it," he said, voice tight. "It's skipping steps. It's going straight to the offer."

Tommy stared at Mark. His eyes were wide, terrified, furious. "It wants you."

Mark's throat went dry. For a moment he couldn't speak.

Then, from the street, a new sound rose—sirens, closer now, and the crack of gunfire that didn't sound like police training.

A scream cut off abruptly.

Mark flinched.

Marcus's gaze flicked to the far end of the street. "They're hunting," he said.

Alyssa grabbed the grimoire tighter. "We have to get to Harold," she said, voice shaking. "My mom—"

Mark's heart clenched. "Harold was leading people," he said. "He'll—"

A shadow moved through the fog on the street, and Mark's words died.

A figure in a red jacket walked at the front of the river of bodies.

Even from a distance, Mark recognized the way the jacket caught the light.

The Red Wanderer.

But the way he moved now—no, not moved, glided—made Mark's skin crawl. The fog curled around him like it wanted to touch him.

Then the figure turned, slowly, and looked directly toward the lot.

Toward Marcus's hideout.

Toward Mark.

The distance should have made it impossible to see details.

Mark saw the eye anyway.

A single glossy dark spot in the center of a petal-mass face, reflecting purple light like a polished coin.

The Wanderer lifted one hand.

And the chant sharpened, as if the whole crowd took a breath at once.

"GIVE ME THE BOY."

Mark's legs went cold.

Alyssa whispered, horrified, "It knows we're here."

Marcus grabbed Mark's shoulder hard. "We move," he snapped. "Now. Cemetery. We don't get caught in the river."

Tommy's bat shook in his hand. "How do we get through that?"

Marcus's jaw clenched. "We don't," he said. "We go around. Yards. Back fences. Anywhere the crowd can't move fast."

Mark stared at the street.

The river of bodies shifted.

Some people stumbled, not from clumsiness but from internal struggle. Mark saw a woman press her hands to her temples, tears streaking down her face as she fought the chant. He saw a man fall to his knees, clawing at his own throat like he was trying to rip something out of himself.

Then another possessed person grabbed the man's shoulders, hauled him up, forced him forward.

Will matters, Marcus had said.

Mark saw both answers play out in real time.

Alyssa's voice cracked. "We can't let them take you."

Mark swallowed hard. "I'm not letting them," he said.

He didn't know if that was bravery or stubbornness. He only knew the alternative was becoming another thread in the web.

Behind the crowd, the fog thickened.

Something moved in it—low, hulking shapes, vine-beasts and petal-swarms, guardians made of the land's hunger.

They flanked the river like shepherd dogs.

Guiding.

Controlling.

Harvesting.

Mark's skin prickled with the same pressure he'd felt in the shadow realm, amplified here by real air and real sound. The entity's attention was closer now, heavy as a hand on the back of his neck.

The chant rolled again.

"GIVE ME THE BOY."

Alyssa's fingers tightened around the grimoire until her knuckles went white. "Mark," she whispered, and there was raw fear in it. "If the town turns on you—"

Mark forced himself to breathe. He clenched his anchor—Jason laughing—and used it like a nail through his panic.

"We go to the cemetery," he said, voice steadier than he felt. "We finish it. Then the chant stops."

Marcus's eyes flicked to him, sharp. "You understand what it's asking," he said.

Mark nodded once. "Yeah," he said. "It's asking the town the same question it always has."

Tommy swallowed. "And what's the answer?"

Mark looked at the river of bodies, at the people who still had tears on their faces even as they marched, at the ones fighting and the ones folding, at the Red Wanderer's raised hand.

He didn't have a full answer.

He only had a choice.

"We make a different one," Mark said.

Marcus nodded, grim approval, and shoved the vine-curtain aside farther. "Then run," he said.

They slipped out of the hideout into the bloom-choked lot, crouched low beneath sagging branches. The purple flowers brushed their shoulders, cold and damp, trembling as if sensing prey.

Mark kept his eyes on the gaps between fences, on the backyards beyond, on the route that would keep them out of the river.

Behind them, the chant followed like a hunting call.

Ahead, the cemetery waited—dark, sealed, and pulsing with the heart they still hadn't reached.

And somewhere in Lowridge, the land held its breath, listening to see whether the town would offer up its captain again.

CHAPTER 25: THE DEPTHS OF THALASSA

Lowridge was coming apart in layers.

Not all at once—not in a Hollywood collapse where buildings folded neatly and the sky did something dramatic. It was subtler than that, which made it worse. The town still looked like a town. The same porches. The same mailboxes. The same banners strung for Homecoming and left up too long because nobody ever wanted the season to end.

But everything was wrong at the seams.

Fog rolled through the streets like a living spill, slow and patient, pooling in ditches and curling around tires. Streetlights blinked with a tired rhythm, as if the power grid was breathing. Purple growth climbed porch rails and wrapped mailbox posts, threading itself through rusted chain-link and eating paint in thin, deliberate lines—like handwriting.

The flowers were everywhere now.

Not just the cemetery.

Not just the old graves outside the fence that nobody admitted existed.

They had started claiming the town the way mold claimed bread: quiet at first, then sudden, undeniable. On the corner of Main and Hawthorne, a cluster had burst through a crack in the sidewalk, petals slick with dew that looked too much like sweat. Outside the diner, purple vines had crept up the window frame, pressing against the glass as if the building had lungs and the flowers wanted in.

Mark Rivers stood at the edge of the street with Alyssa, Tommy, and Marcus, the air heavy in his throat, and realized with a slow, sinking clarity that Lowridge wasn't pretending anymore.

The town had stopped dressing its rot in school colors.

Now it wore the rot proudly, like a crown.

Across the intersection, a crowd had gathered—too many people for this hour, too close together, faces lit in the sick blink of the streetlights. They weren't screaming. That was the problem. They weren't panicked in a way Mark understood. They were… aligned.

As if the same thought had been dropped into a hundred minds and left there to bloom.

A man in a booster jacket stepped forward. Mark recognized him—Mr. Harlan, who ran the print shop and always waved too hard. His eyes were glassy, pupils wide. Purple petals clung to the cuff of his sleeve like confetti.

"Mark," Harlan called, voice carrying in the fog.

Mark's stomach clenched. He didn't answer.

Behind Harlan, a woman near the curb lifted her hand in a small, slow wave. Mark recognized her, too. Mrs. Keene, who used to bring brownies to away games, who always smelled like flour and perfume. She smiled as if she was greeting him at the grocery store.

And when she smiled, Mark saw the faintest shimmer under her skin— like violet light moving beneath the surface, rolling up her neck in a lazy pulse.

Alyssa's fingers tightened on the grimoire against her chest. "They're coordinated," she muttered, sarcasm strained thin. "That is… new."

Tommy shifted, gripping his bat. He tried a laugh and only managed a short breath that sounded like it hurt. "This is the part where I say 'nope' and we all go home, right?"

No one responded.

Because there was nowhere to go home to.

Marcus Webb stood half a step ahead of them, shoulders squared like he was bracing for a hit. The fog made his outline look softer than it should have, as if the world couldn't decide where Marcus ended and the night began.

"Don't talk to them," Marcus said. "Not yet."

"Not yet?" Alyssa whispered. "We're surrounded."

Marcus's eyes flicked over the crowd. "They're not here to tear you apart," he said. "Not physically. Not right now."

Mark felt the hair on his arms rise. "Then why?"

Marcus's jaw tightened. "Because the entity learned a new move."

The crowd shifted closer in a single, subtle step. Like a tide.

Harlan smiled wider. "We don't want trouble," he called, and his tone was gentle enough to be insulting. "We just want you to do the right thing."

A young woman stepped forward from the second row—someone Mark didn't know, hair in a ponytail, hoodie pulled tight. Her voice rose, clear and bright.

"Give him to the land."

Mark's heart slammed once, hard.

The sentence hung there—simple, clean, almost rehearsed.

A ripple of agreement moved through the crowd, not shouted, not chanted. A sound like breath shared between mouths.

Alyssa swallowed. "That's it," she said softly. "That's the offer."

Tommy's voice came out rough. "What offer?"

Marcus didn't look away from the crowd. "Trade," he said. "A sacrifice with a face."

Mark's throat tightened. The old, familiar guilt tried to rise—Jason's grave, his family's legacy, the unspoken knowledge that his name mattered in Lowridge in a way it shouldn't. In a way that made the town feel like it owned him.

He wanted to say something. He wanted to demand why him, why not the mayor, why not the men who had kept the town's secrets like family heirlooms.

But his default under stress was silence, and his body obeyed before his mind did. Mark stood still, jaw clenched, hands empty, as if stillness could make him invisible.

The crowd moved again.

From somewhere behind them, a siren wailed and then muffled out, swallowed by fog.

A boy near the front—maybe fourteen—stared at Mark with flat curiosity. Purple buds trembled at the edge of his collar, as if they had found a warm place to root.

Mark's spine went cold.

He saw it then, the mechanism.

This wasn't just fear.

It was recruitment.

The flowers weren't simply blooming in the town—they were functioning. Acting like conduits, carrying influence, sliding into people's minds and running them like plays.

Mark's chest tightened with a strange, awful familiarity.

A route.

A pattern.

A current.

Alyssa leaned closer, voice low. "They're not all gone," she said. "Look."

Mark followed her gaze.

Near the back of the crowd, an older man stood with his hands clenched at his sides, face sweating despite the cold. His eyes flicked between Mark and the others like he was trying to make a decision.

And then the man did something small and brave.

He spoke.

"This isn't right," the man said, voice shaking. "This is—this is wrong."

The words were plain. Honest. A confession, not in the church sense, but in the truth sense. And the moment he said them, the purple shimmer under his skin faltered. Like the signal stuttered.

The crowd turned toward him.

Not with anger.

With attention.

The flowers on the streetlight pole behind him brightened, petals trembling.

The man's face tightened as if something inside him resisted. "I remember," he said, and his voice cracked. "I remember my brother. I remember what happened to him."

For half a second, Mark saw the man's eyes go clear.

Then the fog thickened between breaths, and the man's expression softened into a smile that didn't belong to him. He nodded slowly and stepped back into the crowd like a man walking into water.

Alyssa's whisper was fierce. "Will matters. Truth breaks the grip—briefly."

Marcus nodded once, grim. "It does," he said. "But they'll learn. They adapt fast."

Harlan lifted his hands again, palms out, peaceful. "Mark," he said, voice kind as a knife. "You know what you have to do. Your brother knew. Your father knew. Your family has always—"

"Don't," Mark said.

The word came out quiet, restrained, but it cut through the fog like a blade.

Harlan's smile twitched.

Mark's hands curled into fists at his sides. He didn't raise his voice. He didn't threaten. He just held Harlan's gaze and let the silence sharpen.

"I'm not a symbol," Mark said, and his voice stayed steady even as something in his chest shook. "I'm not yours."

For a heartbeat, the crowd hesitated.

Like the town itself had blinked.

Then, from somewhere deeper in the fog, a voice rose—layered, wrong, more than one throat speaking at once.

He is.

The sentence wasn't shouted. It wasn't even fully heard.

It was felt. Pressed against Mark's skull like a thumb.

Tommy flinched. Alyssa's shoulders went rigid. Marcus's eyes narrowed.

"Back," Marcus hissed.

The crowd surged.

Not running. Not attacking.

Just closing the distance in a single, unified motion like a net tightening.

"Move," Marcus snapped.

They moved.

They cut down a side street where the fog was thicker, where porch lights glowed weak behind purple-laced curtains. Mark's feet hit pavement in quick rhythm—one-two, one-two—and he hated how familiar the count felt. Like the town had trained him for this, too.

Behind them, the crowd followed. Not fast. Not frantic.

Confident.

Alyssa clutched the grimoire to her chest and kept pace, breath tight. Tommy ran beside her, bat tucked close, eyes darting like he expected something to leap out of the fog.

Marcus led them toward an alley behind the closed pharmacy, where a chain-link fence sagged under the weight of vines. Purple buds trembled on the wire, glowing faintly under streetlight.

Mark felt the pressure behind his eyes—the early warning, the sense of being watched by something that didn't need eyes to see.

"This way," Marcus said, and didn't bother to explain.

Alyssa didn't ask. She trusted Marcus the way you trusted a person who had already been through the fire and come back smelling like smoke.

They slipped behind the fence where the vines parted like they recognized Marcus.

And Mark knew—knew in his bones—that the town wasn't just growing flowers.

It was building doors.

*****

The shadow realm hit like cold water.

No gradual shift. No gentle slide.

One second Mark was in an alley behind the pharmacy, breath burning, fog in his mouth. The next second the world inverted and thickened, as if he had stepped into a place where air had weight and silence had texture.

Purple threads stretched in every direction—thin lines trembling like nerve endings, thick ropes pulsing like veins. The shape of Lowridge was still there, but it was hollowed out and rewired. Streets were suggestion. Buildings were absence. The true structure was the web.

Mark's stomach rolled. He steadied himself the way he steadied himself on the field—feet planted, shoulders squared, mind searching for an anchor.

Jason laughing.

Jason in the driveway, tossing a football one-handed like it was nothing.

Jason stealing the last slice of pizza and grinning like it mattered.

Mark gripped the memory like a rope.

Alyssa stood beside him, hair lifting slightly as if underwater. The grimoire's pages fluttered in a breeze that didn't exist in the real world. Tommy made a thin sound in his throat and then swallowed it.

Marcus didn't stumble. He moved like he belonged here, which was its own kind of nightmare.

"We go down," Marcus said.

Mark swallowed. "Down where?"

Marcus pointed—not to the ground, but into a denser region of web where the threads tightened and twisted, forming a spiral that disappeared into fog like a drain.

"The depths," Marcus said. "Where the water is."

Tommy's voice cracked. "There's water in… in this?"

Marcus's eyes flicked to him. "There's everything," he said. "This place is the town's underside. Whatever Lowridge buried, it buried here too."

Alyssa's gaze sharpened. "Thalassa," she said, like the name had weight. "If she's real—if she's chained—she's in the depths."

Marcus nodded. "And she's the only thing down there that doesn't belong to Eoraziel."

Mark's pulse hammered at the name.

Eoraziel.

The entity had finally been given a face in their minds, even if it didn't have one in the world.

A hunger wearing the town like clothing.

A parasite that had learned to speak in booster slogans and civic pride.

Mark's jaw tightened. "We free her," he said.

Alyssa's eyes flicked to him, quick and assessing. "We try," she corrected, sarcasm back like armor. "And it will be awful."

Tommy muttered, "I would like to officially submit a complaint."

Marcus started toward the spiral.

They followed.

The web thickened as they moved. Threads brushed Mark's shoulders like cobweb. Some tightened around his wrists for a heartbeat and then loosened, as if testing him. The fog here tasted sweeter, heavier, carrying that violet-metal tang that made Mark think of pennies pressed against his tongue.

The count in his head returned—one-two, one-two—like cleats in a tunnel, like a prayer he didn't want.

The spiral drew them in.

And then the world dipped.

Mark's stomach dropped, and the shadow plane became something like a slope. The threads around them slanted downward, deeper, denser, darker. Purple pulses became fewer but stronger, as if the web's heartbeat grew louder the closer they got to the source.

Alyssa's voice came tight. "Do you feel that?"

Mark did.

Pressure.

Not behind his eyes this time.

In his chest.

Like something below them pulled at his ribs, gentle at first, then with growing insistence.

Marcus moved faster. "Don't stop," he said. "If you stop, it catches."

"What catches?" Tommy asked.

Marcus didn't answer.

He didn't have to.

As they descended, Mark began to hear it—not sound exactly, but a sensation like distant surf. A slow, heavy rhythm that wasn't the web's pulse.

Something else.

Water, but not the kind you drank.

Water that drowned.

Ahead, the threads gathered into a shape like a cage.

And inside the cage, suspended in the thickest knot of the web, was a woman.

Not a woman the way Mark understood the word. Not human, not entirely. Her hair drifted in long dark ribbons like kelp. Her skin had the muted sheen of river stones. Her eyes were open and furious, and the gaze hit Mark's chest like a shove.

Chains held her.

Not metal. Not rope.

Root-chains.

Twisted bundles of purple-veined fiber that wrapped around her wrists, her ankles, her throat. They pulsed faintly, feeding, drinking from her like parasites.

Thalassa.

She didn't speak with her mouth.

Her voice arrived inside Mark's skull like cold water poured into a cup.

You came late.

Alyssa inhaled sharply, like she'd heard it too. "We came as fast as we could," she said aloud, and her voice shook once and then steadied. "We need your help."

Thalassa's eyes flicked to Alyssa, then Marcus, then Tommy. Then they locked on Mark.

Rivers.

Mark's throat went dry. "You know me."

Your blood knows this town. Her gaze sharpened. And this town knows your blood.

Marcus stepped forward, stopping just short of the cage. "She's bound to the network," he said quietly to Mark. "Eoraziel keeps her here to drink her power. Keeps her from flooding the roots."

Alyssa's fingers tightened on the grimoire. "If we free her, she can push back."

Tommy's voice came out small. "Can she… kill it?"

Thalassa's expression shifted—something like bitter amusement passing across her face.

No, her voice said, and the word carried the certainty of tides. Not yet. Not in your time. Not while the town still feeds it.

Mark's chest tightened. "Then what can you do?"

Thalassa's eyes burned. I can buy you breath.

Marcus nodded. "That's what we need," he said. "A window."

Alyssa swallowed. "How do we free you?"

Marcus looked at Mark.

Mark already knew the answer. He felt it in the way the root-chains tightened when he stepped closer, as if the web recognized him as a tool.

Alyssa's voice dropped. "Mark—"

Mark held up a hand, silencing her without looking at her. His default wasn't speeches. His default was action, quiet and deliberate.

He stepped toward the cage.

The root-chains trembled.

Thalassa's voice pressed harder into his mind.

This will cost you.

Mark's jaw tightened. "Everything costs now."

Alyssa's eyes flicked down to the grimoire, then up. "You have one severance cut left," she said. "One. If you spend it here—"

"I know," Mark said, voice low.

Tommy shifted. "We can't just—can't we do something else? Like… cut the chains with an axe or something? I have a bat. It's kind of like an axe's cousin."

Marcus didn't smile. "Those chains aren't in the world," he said. "They're in the system. Only severance breaks system ties."

Mark stepped closer until the threads brushed his skin like cold fingers.

He lifted his hand.

The root-chain around Thalassa's wrist pulsed brighter, as if excited.

Mark's stomach turned.

He thought of Eli Carter's last route, the way blood and petal had opened a door.

Blood + petals = access.

This was the rule. The cruel simplicity.

Mark pressed his palm against the air a hair away from the chain.

He didn't touch it.

Not yet.

He closed his eyes and grabbed his anchor.

Jason laughing in the driveway.

Jason's shoulder bump on the sideline.

Jason's last look, the way his words had landed wrong once Mark knew the truth.

Mark held the memory tight.

Then he reached into the thing Alyssa had taught him to feel—the invisible line where connection became control.

The severance wasn't a weapon like a knife.

It was a decision.

A refusal to be tied.

Mark drew an invisible line through the chain.

Clean.

Final.

He didn't say the words aloud, but he felt them in his bones.

Separate.

The chain snapped.

Not with sound—with sensation. Like a tendon cut. Like a pressure release.

Pain lanced through Mark's chest so hard he saw white. His knees buckled. He caught himself with a sharp breath that tasted like pennies and crushed petals.

Alyssa grabbed his elbow. "Mark—"

"I'm fine," he lied, because lying was easier than letting the truth crack him open right now.

Thalassa's wrist jerked free.

The web shuddered.

The remaining chains tightened in panic, pulsing brighter as Eoraziel's network reacted—like a body flinching from pain.

Thalassa's eyes widened.

For the first time, her expression wasn't fury.

It was relief sharp enough to look like rage.

Again, her voice hissed.

Mark swallowed hard. The pain under his ribs throbbed like a bruise made of ice.

He raised his hand again.

This time, the web fought him.

Threads tightened around his forearm, clinging, trying to pull him back like roots in mud. Mark clenched his teeth and held his anchor tighter.

Jason laughing.

Jason laughing.

Jason laughing.

He drew another line.

Severed.

The chain around Thalassa's ankle snapped.

The web convulsed.

A low tremor rolled through the depths like distant thunder. Fog thickened, pressing against Mark's mouth, sweet and bitter.

Tommy swore under his breath and then caught himself, face twisting with the effort of keeping his own rules. "This is—this is bad, man."

Marcus's voice sharpened. "It's noticing."

Alyssa's eyes were wide. "Mark, we said one cut left—"

Mark's hands shook.

He realized, dimly, that he hadn't used the severance twice.

He had used it once.

But the act of severing was like pulling a thread from cloth—the cut ran, splitting connections that had been braided together.

The network didn't do clean edges.

It did knots.

And Mark had just sliced into a knot.

Thalassa's chains loosened in a cascade.

Her throat freed.

Her other wrist freed.

Her body dropped—not down, because there wasn't a real "down" here, but into the space, like a creature released from a net.

She landed on the shadow plane with bare feet that didn't make sound.

And the moment Thalassa touched the web, the depths changed.

The air thickened with pressure that wasn't fog.

It was water, sudden and invisible, swelling around them like a tide rising in a room.

Thalassa lifted her head.

Her eyes went black as deep river pools.

Eoraziel, her voice said—not inside Mark's skull this time, but everywhere at once, a current running through the web.

The purple threads around them tightened, pulsing in response.

Something in the far distance stirred.

A heavy attention turning.

The entity lifted its head.

The web brightened in thick bundles, and a cold light began to sweep across the depths like a searching eye.

Thalassa's lips curved—not a smile, not quite.

A promise.

She lifted both hands.

And the water came.

Not liquid water in the human sense.

It was pressure and weight and drowning memory. It poured through the web in thick surges, flooding the threads, smothering purple pulses in waves of dark.

Mark gasped as the sensation hit his skin: cold, crushing, clean.

The purple glow around the cage dimmed.

Root-threads shuddered as if choking.

Thalassa stepped forward and drove her palm into the web.

A shockwave rippled outward.

Far above—far away—Mark felt the cemetery respond.

Not the place he'd walked in, but the place as the network understood it: a node. A mouth. A heart.

The purple pulses that fed it faltered.

Alyssa's voice came tight with awe. "She's… she's hitting the conduit."

Marcus's face was grim. "She's drowning the routes."

Tommy's eyes went huge. "Good. Yes. Drown them. Drown everything. I like drowning."

The cold searching light swept closer.

Thalassa didn't flinch.

She reached into the web like someone grabbing an artery.

And the depths roared with silent pressure.

For a heartbeat, Mark saw it—through the threads, through the fog, through the network's layered structure.

A shape like a massive bloom.

Petals layered over petals, roots braided into a body without form.

Eoraziel wasn't a person.

It was a system's hunger given shape.

It leaned toward them, its attention tightening like a fist.

Thalassa lifted her chin.

You have drunk long enough, her voice said.

And then she struck.

Water slammed into the purple bloom like a wave hitting a cliff.

The web screamed—not sound, but vibration. Threads snapped and reformed. Purple pulses spasmed, bright and furious.

Mark's teeth rattled.

Alyssa clutched the grimoire against her chest, eyes squeezed shut. "Hold!" she shouted, more to herself than anyone else.

Marcus grabbed Tommy's shoulder and anchored him, keeping him from stumbling as the shadow plane rippled.

Thalassa stood at the center of it, hair whipping like kelp in storm current, hands raised as she pushed, pushed, pushed.

The purple bloom recoiled.

Not retreating.

Not defeated.

But disrupted.

And in that disruption, a new sensation opened in the web—an absence.

A gap.

A door.

Mark felt it like a sudden breath in a sealed room.

Marcus's head snapped toward it. "There," he said.

The gap shimmered in the threads, a narrow passage where the purple pulses had dimmed enough to reveal what lay beneath: a darker route that led straight toward the cemetery node—toward where the physical heart-chamber waited behind soil and stone.

Alyssa's eyes widened. "She made an opening."

Thalassa's voice slammed into Mark's mind, sharp as ice.

Go.

Mark hesitated.

Because behind Thalassa, the cold searching light swept again, stronger now, and the purple bloom surged forward like it had learned how to swim.

Thalassa's shoulders shook with strain.

Marcus's face tightened. "She can't hold this," he said. "Not long."

Alyssa swallowed. "Thalassa—"

Thalassa didn't look at her. Her focus was locked on Eoraziel, on the web, on the drowning routes.

I can hold seconds, her voice said. Not minutes.

Mark's chest tightened.

He saw, in the edges of the web, something else—something he hadn't expected here.

A braided thread, bright in places and fraying in others, straining against the pull.

A silhouette fighting inside it.

Jason.

Not the puppet-ghost.

Not the bait-spirit.

A piece of his brother—caught and resisting, even now.

And then, as Thalassa's water surged again, Jason's thread snapped forward, loosening, just enough to slip like a hand reaching through a crack.

Mark felt it like a touch on his ribs.

A familiar presence, brief and steady.

Not words.

A push.

Go.

Mark's throat tightened so hard it hurt.

He nodded once, silent.

Marcus grabbed Mark's shoulder. "Move," he said.

Tommy lifted his bat, eyes wild. "We're really doing this. We're really—okay."

Alyssa tightened her grip on the grimoire and stepped toward the opening.

The web trembled violently.

Eoraziel's purple bloom surged again, forcing itself through the water, petals shivering, roots tightening like fists.

Thalassa made a sound that wasn't human—a low, furious exhale that turned into a wave.

She threw herself forward and locked onto the bloom like a wrestler grabbing a giant made of vines.

Water and flowers collided, tangled, fought.

Thalassa's voice—ragged now—slammed through the depths:

NOW!

Marcus shoved them toward the opening.

Mark ran.

The shadow plane rippled under his feet. Threads snapped aside as he broke through them, each contact sending bright signals along the web like flares. Mark felt the entity's attention tighten behind them, felt its hunger pull like a hook.

Alyssa ran ahead, grimoire clutched tight.

Tommy ran beside Mark, breath ragged, eyes darting back once like he couldn't help it.

Mark glanced back too, just once.

He saw Thalassa wrapped around the purple bloom, water pressure surging around them like a flood held back by sheer will.

He saw the cold searching light sweep toward her and stall, held.

He saw, for a heartbeat, Jason's thread press against Thalassa's shoulder like help given with the last of a hand.

Then the web shuddered.

The opening began to close.

Thalassa's voice was a ragged blade inside Mark's skull.

GO. DO NOT LOOK BACK.

Mark didn't look back again.

He ran into the gap, into the darker route that led toward the cemetery's heart.

Behind them, the depths roared with silent drowning as Thalassa held Eoraziel in a grapple that shook the town's underside.

And above, in the real world, the cemetery began to flood.

Not with rain.

With something deeper—something that made the purple flowers sag and dim, petals trembling as if they had finally, for the first time in a century, tasted fear.

CHAPTER 26: THE FINAL DESCENT

Thalassa's flood hit the cemetery like a held breath finally released.

Water poured over the hill in sheets, rolling between headstones, turning the rows into a shallow, gleaming sea. The purple flowers didn't like it. They shuddered as if the cold shocked them awake, petals folding inward, stems bowing, the glow dimming in pulses—bright, then faint, then bright again—like a throat struggling to swallow.

Mark came out of the shadow realm on his knees in the mud behind the far fence, the world snapping back into weight and sound so hard it made his teeth ache. Sirens wailed somewhere in town. The stadium lights were gone now—either dead or eaten—and the night was lit by lightning that didn't strike and by the violent, silver sheen of water under moonlight.

Alyssa stumbled beside him, the grimoire hugged to her chest. Tommy landed on one hand, spat, and immediately looked for something to hit. Marcus appeared last—half a second late, like the real world had to decide whether it would accept him—and when he straightened, the rain on his hoodie steamed faintly against his skin.

"Move," Marcus said, and his voice sounded raw, as if he'd screamed himself hoarse in the in-between. "She bought us seconds."

As if on cue, the air above the cemetery tore with a sound like an ocean pulling back from shore.

Mark looked up.

Out beyond the trees, where Lowridge's edge dissolved into fields, the sky had cracked open—not with light, but with depth. The clouds churned in a wide, rotating bruise, and through that bruise a shape moved. Water. Not rain-water, not river-water. Something older, heavier, purposeful. It spiraled around a second presence that was all thorn and petal-glare, the purple in it burning so bright it made the water look black by comparison.

Thalassa's voice didn't come from her mouth. It came from the ground and the water and the bones in Mark's ears.

GO NOW.

Her words tasted like salt.

Mark pushed himself up, legs sliding in mud that smelled like turned graves. "Where's the opening?" he shouted over the roar.

Marcus pointed with a jerk of his chin toward the oldest corner of the cemetery—the part no one used anymore, the part fenced off with rusted iron and a sign that had been replaced so many times the posts were layered with nails like scabs.

The flood had ripped the earth open there.

A sinkhole yawned between leaning stones, a dark throat that drank rain and returned nothing. Roots as thick as arms writhed around its rim, not reaching upward now but curling inward, retreating, drowning.

"The tunnels," Marcus said. "That's our route. Physical route. The one she forced open."

Alyssa's face was pale in the moonlight. "And the flowers?"

"They're alive," Tommy said, voice tight, eyes flicking to a cluster of purple heads bobbing in the water like drowned candles. "So... yeah. They're gonna be mad."

Mark felt the severance cuts in his pocket like heat through fabric—two thin bones of power he could not waste. Each one felt heavier than the last, as if the future itself was trying to pin him to the ground.

"We don't fight unless we have to," Mark said.

Marcus gave him a look that said he admired the idea and hated reality. "We run."

They ran.

The cemetery hill was slick, and the water made it worse. Mark's cleats dug in, tore free, dug in again. The scent of the purple flowers was everywhere—sweetness drowned in iron, perfume turned rotten by cold water.

As they reached the sinkhole, something moved beneath the surface.

A ripple, wrong-shaped. A shadow that didn't belong to the current.

Tommy raised his bat. "Mark—"

The water exploded upward.

A body came out of it—human outline, football pads, helmet—except the pads were fused to the torso by root-fiber, and the helmet's facemask was braided with purple stems that twitched like whiskers. The thing landed on the mud with a wet slap and came up running, too fast for something that should've weighed that much.

Ghost-player.

Not a spirit in the in-between.

A physical avatar. A corpse piloted by flowers.

It tackled Tommy.

Tommy hit the ground hard and yelled—half rage, half pain—as the thing's hands scrabbled for his throat. Purple buds burst along its wrists like knuckles.

Alyssa's voice snapped sharp. "Shield!"

She slapped her palm against the grimoire, and light flared—thin and gold, not warm but clean—and arced around Tommy in a trembling dome.

The ghost-player slammed into it and recoiled, petals sizzling at the barrier's edge like leaves thrown onto a stove.

Mark grabbed Tommy's shoulder and yanked him back. "Up!"

Tommy scrambled, coughing. "I hate—everything—about this town!"

More shapes broke the surface.

Two. Three. Five.

They came from between stones, from under water, from places the ground should've been solid. Jerseys from different eras. Numbers Mark had seen on plaques in the hallway. Names etched into the stadium wall.

They didn't speak.

They surged.

Marcus stepped forward, and for a second Mark saw what the in-between had made of him.

The purple under Marcus's skin brightened, not like infection now but like circuitry. His eyes went glassy and distant, as if he was listening to a frequency only he could hear.

"Don't touch them," Marcus said softly, and it sounded like he wasn't talking to the group at all.

He lifted both hands.

The roots around the sinkhole shivered. Then they snapped outward like ropes yanked by an unseen winch.

They caught three ghost-players mid-charge, wrapped their legs, and jerked them sideways into the flooded grass. The bodies hit hard, thrashing. Purple flowers burst from their mouths as they tried to rise.

Marcus clenched his fists.

The roots tightened.

The ghost-players stilled, pinned like insects.

Alyssa stared. "Marcus—"

"Go," Marcus rasped, and when he turned his head, a single streak of gray had appeared at his temple like frost. "Before it figures out I'm stealing its hands."

Mark didn't argue. He shoved Alyssa toward the sinkhole. "Down!"

A rusted ladder was bolted to the inner wall, half-buried. Mark grabbed it and started descending, mud sliding off his gloves. The air that rose from the hole was cold and damp and smelled like wet stone…and underneath it, the sweetness of the flowers, concentrated to a nauseating intensity.

Tommy went next, keeping himself between Alyssa and the hole's edge like he could body-block gravity. Alyssa clutched the grimoire with both arms, lips moving in silent rehearsal.

Marcus dropped last.

As Mark's boots hit the first narrow ledge below, he heard a new sound above—thin, high, almost like laughter.

The pinned ghost-players weren't staying pinned.

The roots Marcus had used were turning black at the tips, petals blooming along them like blisters. The network was learning. Adapting. Punishing.

Mark looked up.

The edge of the sinkhole was a ring of water and shadow now, the world above reduced to a moving coin of moonlight. A ghost-player's helmet filled part of it as it leaned over, staring down.

Then it jumped.

Mark jerked back.

The body slammed onto the ladder above him, metal groaning, and began to climb down toward them with frantic, jerky hunger, as if it understood—on some animal level—that the heart below was calling and it couldn't be left behind.

Alyssa raised her hand, her voice cracking on an incantation.

Heat flared.

Not flame, not fire that needed air. A clean burn that ran along the ladder like a fuse.

The ghost-player seized, petals shriveling. Its hands spasmed. It fell.

Mark watched it tumble past him into darkness, hitting wet stone below with a sickening thud. The purple glow down there swallowed it like a mouth.

"Keep moving," Mark said, though his voice sounded far away.

They descended into the cemetery's throat.

*****

The tunnels were older than Lowridge.

Stone walls curved in a way that didn't match human design, more like something had hollowed them out slowly over centuries—water, roots, hunger. The floor was slick with floodwater, ankle-deep, rising in waves whenever something moved in the earth above.

Purple flowers grew here too, but not like the ones on the surface. These were paler, almost translucent, petals thin as skin. They bloomed out of cracks in the rock, trembling with every vibration, their glow wavering like a pulse seen through tissue.

Mark's breath made fog in the cold air. Each exhale tasted sweet-bitter.

Tommy muttered, "I can't believe I'm gonna die in a sewer under a graveyard."

"It's not a sewer," Alyssa whispered. "It's… catacombs."

"Great," Tommy said. "Classy dying."

Marcus limped behind them, one hand pressed to his ribs like something inside was trying to tear free. He didn't complain, but Mark could hear it in his breathing—shallow, strained. Marcus's skin looked tighter on his face, as if the bones beneath had shifted forward. Another gray streak had appeared at his hairline.

The cost.

Every time Marcus pulled on the network, it pulled on him harder.

Mark kept his eyes forward.

The tunnel sloped down, deeper, and with every step the hum in the ground grew louder. Not a sound exactly—more like pressure against the inside of his skull. The same pressure Eli Carter had felt in the prologue, the pressure that meant the town's hidden map was waking up.

The heart was close.

Ahead, the tunnel forked.

The left path was narrower, clogged with collapsed stone and braided roots. The right path was wider, half-flooded, and lined with old, cracked tiles stamped with an emblem Mark recognized from booster club banners —the Lowridge Lions logo, but older, more severe, the lion's mouth open in a silent roar.

Alyssa's eyes widened. "That's not supposed to be down here."

"It's always been down here," Marcus said. His voice was rough. "They built on top of it. They always do."

A shape moved in the right tunnel's water.

Mark stopped. "Hold."

Something rose.

Not a full body this time—just a helmet, floating, and beneath it, a face.

A boy's face, pale and bloated from water, eyes open and glassy. Purple veins threaded across his cheeks like cracks in porcelain.

Mark's stomach lurched. The face was familiar.

Not personally. Not from school.

From photographs.

From trophy cases.

A champion from the eighties. Dead at seventeen. The town had called it a "heart condition." The paper had called it a tragedy. Mark had called it a warning he'd been too young to read.

The boy's lips moved.

Mark didn't hear words.

He heard need.

Behind the floating helmet, more faces drifted up in the water—like bodies tied below, trying to surface.

Tommy's grip tightened on his bat. "Nope."

Alyssa whispered a shield again, and a thin, gold shimmer spread outward, just enough to keep the water's surface from breaking toward them.

But the faces didn't press against the shield.

They watched.

They watched like the wall-spirits in the shadow realm had watched.

Hope and hunger mixed together until Mark couldn't tell which was which.

"Mark," Marcus said quietly. "Don't look too long."

Mark tore his gaze away, jaw clenched. "They're not… freed."

"No," Marcus said. "Thalassa's flood weakens the network, but it doesn't break it. Not by itself."

Mark's fingers brushed the severance cuts in his pocket.

Two.

And every part of him wanted to use one right now—use it on the water, on the faces, on the whole damn tunnel.

He forced his hand away.

Later. Not yet.

They moved into the right tunnel.

The water climbed to mid-shin. Cold sank through Mark's socks, numbing. The flowers on the walls trembled faster, like something was counting down.

Alyssa glanced up at the ceiling. "Do you feel that?"

Mark nodded.

The ground above them shook, distant but heavy.

Thalassa and Eoraziel—water and flowers—wrestling for the surface of the cemetery. Every impact sent a tremor down the tunnels like a warning.

Go now.

Seconds.

Not minutes.

They rounded a bend and the tunnel widened into a chamber that looked like a chapel stripped of everything holy.

Stone benches lay toppled in the floodwater. A crude altar stood at the far end, stained dark, covered in carved grooves. Purple roots ran through those grooves like veins filled with light. Above the altar, a line had been cut deeper than the rest—letters gouged by hand.

GLORY FEEDS THE ROOTS.
ROOTS DRINK THE BLOOD.

Mark's throat went dry.

Alyssa stared at the words as if seeing them was a wound. "That's it," she whispered. "The original line."

Tommy's voice cracked. "This is under the cemetery?"

"Under everything," Marcus said.

The water in the chamber shivered.

Then it boiled—not with heat, but with movement.

Ghost-players rose out of it like drowning men who had found a reason to breathe again.

Seven of them. Then more.

They climbed onto benches, onto stone, onto each other. Their helmets were cracked, their jerseys fused to skin, their hands threaded with roots. Purple flowers bloomed at their throats like corsages meant for funerals.

They didn't roar.

They didn't need to.

The chamber itself roared—hundreds of tiny pulses in the roots, in the walls, in the water, answering their emergence with a rhythm that sounded too much like a stadium crowd.

Mark stepped back, heart hammering.

Alyssa lifted the grimoire, voice steadying. "Tommy—shield!"

Tommy planted his feet. "On it."

He raised his free hand, fingers splayed the way Alyssa had taught him, and a shimmer formed—faint at first, then solidifying into a translucent barrier between them and the advancing dead.

The ghost-players hit it.

The barrier bowed under the impact, trembling, but it held.

Alyssa spoke and heat flared again, streaking across the surface of the shield like sunlight on glass. The flowers on the ghost-players' wrists curled and blackened, but the bodies kept pushing.

Mark looked at Marcus. "We can't stay."

Marcus's jaw clenched. "We don't."

Marcus stepped past the edge of Tommy's shield, into the water, and lifted his hands again.

The roots in the altar-grooves surged outward like snakes.

They slammed into the ghost-players' legs, their waists, their arms—wrapping, yanking, dragging them sideways, away from the barrier. The shield stopped bowing as pressure eased.

But Marcus flinched as if someone had punched him in the chest.

Mark saw it—saw the way Marcus's skin tightened, saw the way his shoulders sagged for a fraction of a second under invisible weight.

A harsh line appeared beside Marcus's mouth, deepening into a wrinkle that hadn't been there before.

Marcus's eyes flicked toward Mark, and in them was something older than a teenager's exhaustion.

"We go," Marcus said, voice hoarse. "Now."

Mark nodded.

They sprinted.

Tommy kept the shield moving with them, a trembling dome that shifted as he ran, protecting Alyssa's flank. Alyssa clutched the grimoire with one hand and used the other to throw bursts of heat behind them—enough to slow, not enough to stop.

Mark ran point, eyes scanning for collapse, for dead ends, for anything.

The tunnel sloped down again.

The pulse grew louder.

And then—

The walls changed.

They weren't stone anymore.

They were… something else.

Translucent in places. Veined. Soft-looking, like the inside of a living throat. Purple threads ran beneath the surface in thick bundles, glowing in slow, heavy waves.

Tommy gagged. "Tell me we're not inside it."

Marcus didn't answer.

Because ahead, the tunnel opened.

And Lowridge's heart opened with it.

*****

The chamber was too big to belong underground.

It rose like a cathedral carved by a patient hand that loved horror more than symmetry. The ceiling disappeared into darkness threaded with purple light. Columns of root and stone twisted upward like ribs. Floodwater pooled across the floor in rippling sheets, reflecting the glow in broken mosaics.

And at the center—

A massive organ of flowers pulsed.

It wasn't a flower the way anything above ground was a flower. It was a bloom made of hundreds of layered petals, each one thick and wet-looking, each one edged with faint luminescence. Roots the size of sewer pipes fed into it from every direction, disappearing into the petals like veins.

The pulse in it was slow.

Heavy.

A heartbeat.

Mark's knees nearly buckled, not from fear alone but from recognition: every cheer he'd ever heard in Lowridge, every Friday night roar, every stadium chant—this was where it had gone. This was what it had been feeding.

The heart beat.

The water trembled.

And the walls—

Mark's gaze snapped to the walls and his stomach turned over.

They weren't smooth stone.

They were filled.

Faces pressed from within them, suspended behind petal-resin like insects trapped in amber. Boys. Men. Some young. Some older. Some wearing uniforms. Some wearing work shirts. Their eyes were open.

Awake.

Watching.

Hundreds of them.

Alyssa made a sound that was half sob, half choke. "Oh my God."

Tommy's shield wavered.

Mark caught Tommy's elbow. "Tommy—keep it."

Tommy swallowed hard, eyes glassy. "I'm trying."

Pecos.

Mark's gaze locked on the center.

Pecos's body was there, half-sunk into the flower-organ like a sacrifice laid into a mouth.

His skin was pale, slick with water. Purple threads crawled over him, entering at his wrists, his throat, the soft places under his ribs. Flowers bloomed along his sternum like a grotesque chestplate. His eyes were closed.

But his chest rose.

Barely.

A shallow breath, stolen from a thing that didn't want to give it.

Mark's throat tightened. "Pecos."

A ripple ran through the heart.

A response.

Not from Pecos.

From the network.

From Eoraziel.

The air in the chamber thickened until Mark felt it press against his teeth.

Marcus staggered, one hand bracing against a root-column. His face had gone gray. His hair—Mark realized with a jolt—was not just streaked now. It was peppered, as if years had fallen into it in the space of minutes.

Marcus looked at Pecos, then at Mark. "That's him," he said, voice barely above the heartbeat. "Physical."

Alyssa's hands shook on the grimoire. "We can do it. We can start the ritual."

Tommy's shield flickered as something slammed into it from behind.

The ghost-players had followed.

They poured into the chamber's mouth like a tide of bodies, their purple glow brighter here, their movements faster. The heart fed them power, and in return they threw themselves at the barrier like desperate defenders protecting their end zone.

Mark's breath hitched.

This wasn't just the town's dead.

This was the town's last stand.

Alyssa's voice rose. "Hold them—just hold them—"

Tommy's face contorted with strain. "I'm holding! It's like pushing back a truck!"

Marcus pushed off the column, jaw set.

"Marcus—" Mark started.

Marcus lifted his hands.

This time, he didn't coax the roots.

He tore.

The root-columns shivered and then snapped inward, bending toward Marcus like iron pulled by a magnet. The thick bundles of purple threads in the ceiling brightened, and for a second the entire chamber looked like a living nervous system lit from within.

The ghost-players froze mid-charge.

Their bodies jerked.

Then the roots surged out of the floor and walls, wrapping them in violent coils, yanking them backward, pinning them against the cathedral ribs.

The shield stopped shaking.

Tommy gasped, relief crashing through his expression for a heartbeat.

Then Marcus made a sound like a cough that couldn't find air.

He dropped to one knee.

Mark lunged. "Marcus!"

Marcus's skin had changed.

Not rotted. Not possessed.

Aged.

Lines had carved deeper around his eyes. His hands trembled, veins standing out like raised cords. He looked—impossibly—like an older version of himself, the future he'd been stealing time from.

Marcus lifted his gaze to Mark, and the intensity in it cut through the chamber's horror.

"I can't do it again," Marcus rasped. "That was… everything."

Alyssa looked between Marcus and the heart, eyes shining with panic. "We need you."

Marcus shook his head once. "You don't. You needed a door."

He swallowed, hard, like it hurt.

"Finish it," he said. "I've done what I can."

Mark's chest constricted. He wanted to argue. He wanted to grab Marcus and drag him back from whatever bargain his hybrid blood was paying.

But the heart pulsed again, and Mark felt something in it turn toward him with the calm certainty of a predator that had finally cornered prey.

The chamber's purple glow deepened.

The faces in the walls widened their eyes as if they could feel it too.

A sound rose through the roots—low at first, then swelling into a roar that wasn't made of air.

It wasn't a voice.

It was will.

Eoraziel.

Mark's mouth went dry as the flower-organ swelled, petals parting, opening like a wound.

From within it, something began to rise.

Not a human body.

An avatar.

A mass of petal and root shaping itself into shoulders, into arms, into a head crowned with blossoms that bled light. Where a face should have been was a shifting knot of flowers, and in the center of that knot a single dark spot formed—glossy, reflective, an eye that held the moon in miniature.

The eye focused on Mark.

The roar inside Mark's skull sharpened into meaning—an ancient hunger translating itself into language.

CHAMPION.

The word hit like a cheer.

Mark's hands curled into fists.

Behind him, Tommy's shield trembled.

Beside him, Alyssa's breath hitched, and Mark felt the grimoire's pages flutter in a wind that wasn't wind at all.

Pecos's chest rose once, shallow.

As if he was trying to remind Mark he was still here.

Mark took one step toward the heart.

The severance cuts in his pocket burned like coals.

Eoraziel's avatar lifted one root-armed hand, and the flowers along its wrist bloomed open—wide and wet and hungry.

The chamber held its breath.

And in the wall of faces, a familiar glow detached itself—faint, clean, human.

Jason's spirit drifted forward from the resin like a thread pulled free, his outline flickering in the purple light.

He looked at Mark.

Not like a puppet.

Not like bait.

Like a brother.

"Hey," Jason whispered, and his voice sounded like memory. "Don't let it write you."

Then he turned, and with a sudden burst of pale light, he slammed himself into the nearest pinned ghost-player, shattering the purple restraints long enough for the thing to stumble back, disoriented.

An opening.

A chance measured in heartbeats.

Marcus's head lifted a fraction, eyes burning. "Now," he breathed. "Mark—now."

Mark nodded once, jaw clenched so tight it hurt.

He stepped into the floodwater and toward the pulsing flower-organ where Pecos lay merged, breathing, waiting—while Eoraziel's eye watched him like the end zone line.

And the heart beat again.

Louder.

Like the town itself had begun to cheer.

CHAPTER 27: THE HEART EXPOSED

The tunnel ended the way a throat ends—suddenly, and not gently.

Mark stepped into a chamber that didn't feel built so much as grown. The ceiling arched like the underside of a ribcage. The walls were slick with brine from Thalassa's flood and webbed with roots that pulsed faint violet, as if the stone itself had learned to breathe.

And in the center of it all, the heart waited.

It wasn't shaped like a human heart. It was too big for that. More like a swollen hive of petals and muscle, a living knot of purple mass that rose from the ground in slow heaves. Veins—routes—ran outward from it into the walls, into the floor, into the tunnels behind them, branching like highways. Every pulse sent a tremor through the chamber, and with each tremor the flowers embedded in the stone shivered, releasing a sweet scent rimmed with metal.

Pecos's body was fused to the heart's center.

Not buried. Bound.

His back was pressed against the thickest part of the organ like he'd been pinned there, arms spread, wrists swallowed by vines. Purple growth threaded under his skin in delicate lines that looked almost beautiful until Mark remembered what they were—routes, nerves, hunger made architecture. Pecos's head drooped forward. His chest rose and fell in shallow, stubborn breaths.

He was alive.

Tommy stopped beside Mark, bat dangling from his fingers. His voice came out small. "That's... that's not okay."

Alyssa stood with the grimoire open in her hands, pages warped from moisture but still legible, ink dark as bruises.

Marcus staggered in last.

He'd been holding himself together on will alone for the entire descent. Now, under the weight of the chamber, his knees buckled. He caught himself on a jut of rock, breath coming hard. In the dim violet light, Mark saw the changes that had been creeping up on Marcus accelerate—fine lines deepening, shadows carving under his eyes, a trembling fatigue settling into him like age finally collecting its debt.

Marcus looked up at Mark. His eyes were bloodshot and sharp.

"This is it," he rasped. "No more running."

Mark swallowed. The pressure behind his eyes—the thing he'd felt on the field—was constant now, like a hand on the back of his skull.

"What do we do?" Tommy asked, and hated himself for sounding like he needed an adult.

Marcus forced air into his lungs. "Same plan. Shields up. Fire clears the growth. Mark—" His gaze locked on Mark like a hook. "You do the cuts. You don't hesitate."

A pulse rolled through the chamber.

The heart answered with a heavier thud. The walls responded—faces pressed from stone as if the rock had turned to skin for a second. Mouths opened, silent. Eyes rolled under closed lids.

Mark's stomach turned.

They weren't floating ghosts. They were inside the place. Stored. Held.

Alyssa's voice shook. "They're all—"

"I know," Marcus said. "Don't look at them too long."

Mark crossed the wet stone toward the heart anyway. Every step made the routes under the floor hum—like a stadium crowd heard through concrete. He focused on one thing: Pecos's breathing.

Pecos's eyelids fluttered.

"Pecos?" Mark whispered.

Pecos didn't open his eyes, but Mark felt it—an answering presence, faint and frayed, reaching back along whatever thread still connected them.

A whisper pressed against Mark's thoughts.

Don't. It's listening.

Mark froze.

The chamber's pulse slowed, as if the heart had leaned in.

Then the heart beat again—harder.

And the flowers along its surface unfurled.

At first Mark thought it was just the organ reacting. Then the petals shifted into shape. A body rose out of the heart like a person standing from deep water.

It wasn't human, but it wanted to be.

A torso made of layered blossoms. Arms woven from root-fiber and vine. A head forming in slow, deliberate cruelty—petals arranging into something like a face, empty sockets filling with glossy dark, and in the center of its forehead, a thin red line that looked like a cut.

Its mouth opened.

And when it spoke, the chamber spoke with it—voices stacked together like a crowd chanting from far away.

"You made it," Eoraziel said.

Tommy stepped forward half a pace, bat raised like it mattered. "Back off."

The avatar turned its head toward Tommy with slow amusement. "Shield-bearer," it said. "How brave you are, holding a stick against a god."

Alyssa lifted the grimoire, hands steadying. "You're not a god."

Eoraziel's mouth curled. "I am what you fed."

It lifted one arm, and the veins along the walls brightened. The trapped faces in the stone twitched. A low moan rose—not from any single mouth, but from the entire chamber, a sound like grief pulled through a pipe.

Mark's throat tightened. "Stop."

Eoraziel's eyes fixed on him. "Make me."

Marcus shoved himself upright, swaying. "Now!" he barked. "Shields. Fire. Move!"

Tommy snapped into motion like a practiced lineman. He stepped between Mark and the heart, raised his free hand, and the air shimmered.

A translucent barrier formed—thin at first, then thickening. Faint lines rippled across it like chalk marks on a coach's board.

"Okay," Tommy muttered, eyes wide. "Okay, okay."

Alyssa drew a quick symbol in the air. Heat flared around her palm—no flame yet, just the promise of it. "Mark," she said, voice tight. "Tell me where."

Mark looked at the heart, and his vision shifted the way it always did now when he focused—peeled back into threads.

The heart wasn't just flesh. It was a knot of routes, a central interchange where every line in Lowridge converged. The thickest thread ran straight into Pecos's chest, braided tight around his ribs like a seatbelt that had become part of him.

And beneath the purple, Mark saw a different color.

A rust-dark line, almost black, pulsing faint red in time with the heart. It didn't look like a route. It looked like a scar.

A signature.

Mark's stomach clenched. "There," he said. "Under the outer layer. There's a red thread. A blood mark."

Eoraziel's gaze sharpened. "Ah."

The avatar's arm whipped forward.

Vines erupted from the heart's surface like spears and slammed into Tommy's shield. The barrier bowed inward with a sound like glass flexing. Tommy's knees bent.

"NOPE," Tommy grunted. "Not today."

Alyssa's fire finally caught. Flame bloomed from her hands—bright orange at its core, tinged violet at the edges. She swept it along the heart's surface, and blossoms blackened instantly, curling into ash that hissed as it hit the wet floor.

Eoraziel hissed—not pain, offense. "You burn your inheritance."

Alyssa's eyes flashed. "I burn the leash."

Mark didn't wait.

He stepped to the heart and raised his hand. Not a knife. Just his palm, fingers spread like he was about to catch a pass.

The thread-lines brightened, sensing him. Eoraziel's attention tried to hook into his thoughts like a root into soft soil.

"Mark," it said softly. "You don't have to do this."

Mark held onto his anchor—the memory of Jason laughing in sunlight, the easy warmth of a brother who hadn't yet become a symbol.

Then he made the cut.

Reality resisted. Pain snapped through his skull like a helmet-to-helmet hit. White flashed behind his eyes. His nose filled with warmth.

Blood ran down his upper lip.

Mark gritted his teeth and finished the motion.

The heart's outer layer split—cracked like a shell. A dark fissure formed across the petal-mass, and purple fluid seeped out, thick and glossy, pooling in the brine like ink in water.

The chamber shuddered. The trapped faces in the wall jerked as one, as if the crack had tugged their strings.

Eoraziel screamed.

Tommy's shield wavered. Alyssa's flames sputtered.

Mark stumbled, wiping blood from his mouth.

Marcus's hand clamped on Mark's shoulder. "One down," Marcus rasped. "Don't stop now."

Mark blinked hard. "That was—the second-to-last."

Marcus's grip tightened. "Then you know what the last feels like."

The fissure glowed faintly red. The blood signature underneath it had been exposed.

The chamber's scent shifted—less flower-sweet, more iron-heavy.

Alyssa's eyes locked on it. "That's—"

"The pact," Marcus said. "The name it was signed in."

Mark's breath came shallow. "Harrow," he murmured, the word pressed into him by the red line's recognition.

Eoraziel's voice turned pleased. "Yes. Harrow's gift."

Tommy swallowed. "Who the hell is Harrow?"

"Doesn't matter," Alyssa snapped. "It's a lock."

"And you want to break it," Eoraziel said, tilting its head. "Undo what made you winners."

Mark's pulse hammered. "What made us offerings."

Eoraziel lifted its hand again and the walls brightened with impressions —trophies, banners, a stadium roaring like devotion made weather.

"You were worshipped," it whispered. "And worship is food."

Alyssa flung fire at its face. The flames struck petals and the head burned—briefly—before reforming with a wet floral shuffle.

"Mark!" Alyssa shouted. "That crack won't stay open!"

Mark stared at Pecos, still pinned in the center.

Pecos's eyes opened.

They weren't fully his anymore—pupils ringed with faint violet—but he was looking at Mark. Really looking.

And Mark felt his voice inside him again, stronger now.

Mark… you can't pull me back without pulling them.

Pecos's gaze flicked to the wall.

To the trapped faces.

Mark understood in a sick flash. Pecos wasn't just linked. He was the anchor holding every victim in place.

Eoraziel smiled. "There you are."

Tommy's voice cracked. "Pecos—what's happening?"

Pecos's body trembled as the heart beat again, and the routes under his skin flared like purple lightning.

Then Pecos screamed—inside Mark's mind.

It wasn't one voice. It was hundreds, flooding through him. Mark saw flashes: a boy in an old leather helmet collapsing; a mother crying at a purple-bloomed grave; a scholarship letter signed with shaking hands because no one knew how to refuse the town.

Mark staggered back, clutching his head.

Alyssa grabbed Mark's arm. "We don't have long," she said, voice harsh. "If he's pulling the network into himself, he'll burn out."

Marcus's face went grim. "Anchor-breaker's active."

Eoraziel's voice slid into velvet. "I can stop his pain."

Mark's fingers twitched.

"I can pull the suffering back," it whispered. "Let him live. Let your town keep its miracles."

Then, softer—crueler—"I can bring your brother back."

The chamber went still.

Mark's chest tightened so hard he thought he might crack.

He heard Jason laughing—then saw Jason on the field with purple petals stuck to his facemask, that empty smile in the fog. The lure. The puppet.

Mark's knees threatened to buckle.

Eoraziel leaned closer, its scent drowning the air. "One cut and you sever the last tether holding him. He will be gone. Truly gone."

Something cold brushed Mark's shoulder.

A hand.

Mark turned.

Jason stood at the edge of Alyssa's firelight, half-formed in the mist. Jersey number faint as a memory. Purple threads tugging at his wrists and ankles like cobwebs.

But his eyes were his.

He looked at Mark the way he used to when Mark was about to do something stupid—half warning, half trust.

"Don't," Jason said.

Eoraziel snapped toward him, petals rippling with fury. "You."

Jason lifted his hand—pale, translucent—and fire blossomed around his fingers.

Not Alyssa's flame.

Something whiter. Colder. A light that didn't burn like heat but like release.

Jason flicked it toward the heart. Where it touched, flowers didn't ash.

They unmade.

Petals fell away into nothing, as if the chamber had forgotten they were ever there.

Eoraziel screamed again.

Jason's gaze stayed on Mark. "It lies," he whispered.

Mark's throat worked. "Jason—"

Jason shook his head once. "Finish it."

Mark nodded, eyes stinging. Words crowded behind his teeth—sorry, please, I miss you—but there was no room for them.

Mark faced the fissure.

The red thread pulsed.

The last severance cut waited like a loaded tackle.

Mark's hands shook. He could feel the cost hovering in his nerves.

Pecos's scream surged again, and through it came one clear thought—raw and human.

Hurry.

Mark swallowed, tasting iron.

"We choose ourselves," he said, voice low and shaking.

Eoraziel's eyes narrowed. "You choose death."

Mark lifted his hand. "We choose consent."

He pictured the red thread as a route someone else had drawn for him.

And he pictured stepping off it.

He made the cut.

The world went silent for one heartbeat.

Then pain tore through him—bright and deep, like lightning under skin. It started behind his eyes and shot down his spine. His knees buckled. His vision narrowed to a tunnel rimmed in white.

Blood flooded his mouth.

But the cut held.

The red thread snapped—not with sound, but with a sudden release, like a rope finally breaking after years of strain.

The blood signature flared crimson in the fissure, then dimmed like an ember starved of oxygen.

Eoraziel shrieked.

The heart convulsed. Purple fluid surged out of the crack and splashed across the floor, steaming where it hit Alyssa's flames. Vines spasmed. Blossoms wilted.

Mark collapsed to one knee, coughing dark blood onto wet stone.

Tommy's shield shimmered as the vine attacks faltered. Tommy let out a strangled laugh. "Did… did we do it?"

Eoraziel's avatar staggered, petals shedding like dead skin. "You don't understand," it snarled.

The routes in the walls began to retract—threads pulling inward, like veins yanked toward the heart. The trapped faces shuddered, outlines loosening as if the glue holding them had softened.

Pecos's scream peaked so hard Mark thought his skull would split.

Then Pecos's voice cut through—clearer than it had been since this started.

Mark.

Mark lifted his head, blinking blood out of his eyes.

Pecos's eyes were wide. Tears streamed down his cheeks, mixing with violet light.

It's working.

Relief hit Mark so hard his whole body shook.

But I can't hold much longer.

The vines around Pecos tightened—not as restraints now, but as conduits—dragging the collapsing network into his chest.

Eoraziel's voice turned cruel. "He will carry your guilt into nothing."

Jason stepped closer, pale fire burning brighter around his hands, and looked at Pecos with something like grief. Then he looked at Mark.

Mark understood what Jason couldn't say.

This was the line.

A pulse answered Mark's next breath—angry, off-tempo. The heart didn't stop just because the signature broke. It spasmed, trying to remember the rhythm it had lived on for a century.

Eoraziel's avatar straightened, shedding petals that hit the brine like wet confetti. Its voices weren't layered now; they were unraveling, threads snapping, the chorus splitting into individual tones.

"You cut the name," it rasped, and the sound was almost human for a second—wounded, hateful. "You did not cut the hunger."

Mark's vision swam. He wiped blood from his chin, but it kept coming. "We cut the lock."

Eoraziel laughed, hoarse. "A lock," it sneered. "Child. This whole town is the door."

It flung its arms wide, and for an instant the chamber's walls turned translucent.

Mark saw Lowridge above them—not as streets and houses, but as routes: glowing lines running under sidewalks, under Main Street, under the school, under the stadium. Every line converged here. Every line was throbbing, searching for a new command.

And above that, like a storm cloud made of sound, Mark felt it:

Devotion.

A distant roar, muffled and huge, as if the crowd was still chanting somewhere in the living world and the chant was leaking down through the ground like rainwater.

Eoraziel's eyes shone wet and dark. "They will feed me anyway," it whispered. "Friday or funeral. Win or grief. They always come. They always give."

A vine snapped forward—thin as a wire, fast as a whip—aimed straight for the blood on Mark's mouth.

Mark flinched.

Tommy threw himself in front of it.

The vine struck the shield first, then punched through with a wet pop and caught Tommy's forearm. Tommy grunted, teeth clenched. Purple light crawled under his skin from the impact point, branching like a bruise made of lightning.

"Tommy!" Alyssa shouted.

Tommy yanked his arm back, panting. "Still—good," he lied, and his eyes betrayed him. "Just... stings like a—like a thousand bees."

The shield around them fractured with a spiderweb crack, but it held. Barely.

Alyssa's hands moved fast. She didn't have salt anymore—everything in the chamber was wet, everything was slipping. So she used what she had: ash and brine and ink.

She dipped her fingers into the purple fluid leaking from the heart, then drew a circle in the air around them, whispering words that made Mark's ears ring. The circle didn't glow bright. It darkened—like the light around them was being told to behave.

Eoraziel recoiled a step, snarling. "That book is a wound."

"It's a record," Alyssa snapped. "And records can be rewritten."

Marcus lurched forward, one hand pressed to his ribs like the inside of him was trying to come apart. He looked at Mark with a kind of furious urgency that felt older than him.

"It's telling the truth," Marcus said, voice raw. "You broke the signature. Good. But the heart is still a battery. Still a pump. The routes will try to reboot."

Mark swallowed. "Then we cut more."

Marcus shook his head once, hard. "No time. There are too many lines. You'd bleed out before you made it halfway."

Eoraziel lifted its arms again, and the heart responded—routes tightening, pulling inward, dragging the loosened victims back like fish on a net.

Pecos screamed in Mark's skull, and Mark felt the weight spike so violently his knees threatened to fold.

Alyssa's voice broke. "Pecos—"

Pecos's thought came through like a sob pressed through teeth.

I'm holding them. I'm holding all of them.

Mark's stomach turned. "How?"

Pecos's eyes rolled toward Mark. Tears streamed. His lips moved, and for the first time, the words crawled out of his actual mouth—ragged, barely there.

"Routes… through me," he gasped.

Mark felt it then—felt the network trying to use Pecos as its new signature, its new blood mark. The lock had been cut, so it grabbed the nearest living hinge.

Pecos.

Marcus's voice went low. "Anchor-breaker means the collapse doesn't snap outward. It folds inward—into him. He's acting like a fuse."

Tommy's breathing hitched. "That's not—dude, that's not a fuse. That's my friend."

Marcus's eyes flicked to Tommy, and for once there was something like apology in them. "I know."

Eoraziel's avatar leaned closer, petals trembling, voice silky again—temptation returning like a habit.

"You can stop," it murmured to Mark. "Let the fuse burn quietly. Let the town keep its pride. Let the dead stay where they belong."

Jason stepped forward, pale fire burning brighter in his hands. He looked at Eoraziel like he wanted to punch it, even without fists.

"Liar," Jason whispered.

Eoraziel's gaze snapped to him, hate sharpening. "You should be grateful," it hissed. "I kept you."

Jason's expression hardened. "You kept my number. Not me."

He lifted his hand, and the pale fire swept across the vines binding Pecos. The vines didn't fully sever, but they loosened—just enough for Pecos's fingers to twitch free of one strand.

Pecos's hand reached—weak, trembling—toward Mark.

Mark grabbed it.

Pecos's skin was cold and too damp, like he'd been swimming in something that wasn't water. The moment their hands met, Mark felt the whole network surge against Pecos's chest.

Pecos's eyes squeezed shut. "Mark," he breathed, voice breaking, "I… can't… keep—"

Mark tightened his grip. "Then we don't keep it. We end it."

Marcus's shoulders sagged. He nodded once, like he'd been waiting for Mark to say it.

"You break the heart," Marcus said. "Not cut. Break. Shatter it, and the routes lose their pump."

Alyssa stared. "If we shatter it—what happens to—" Her gaze flicked to the walls. To the trapped faces.

Marcus's voice was rough. "Either they release… or they tear. I don't know. Nobody's done this and lived long enough to write it down."

Eoraziel's smile returned, small and vicious. "Hear that?" it whispered. "You want to be heroes, and you will become killers."

Mark's chest tightened.

He looked at the wall again. At the faces slipping, half-loosened, half-stuck—like a chorus held between inhale and exhale.

Jason's voice came soft behind him. "They're already hurting."

Mark turned. Jason's edges flickered. Purple threads tugged harder at his ankles, like the entity was trying to drag him back into storage. But Jason stood anyway, pale fire lighting the chamber in brief white breaths.

"You don't have time to do this clean," Jason said.

Mark felt his throat burn. "I don't want to do it dirty."

Jason's gaze held his—brother to brother. "Then do it honest."

Pecos's grip tightened around Mark's fingers—barely, but enough to matter. His thought came through one last time, thin and fierce.

I'll hold the wave. Just—do it fast.

Mark's vision blurred. He looked at Alyssa—at her jaw set, her hands shaking but steady on the grimoire. He looked at Tommy—arm bruising purple, shield still up because he refused to be the first one to drop. He looked at Marcus—half a person and half a warning, standing here anyway.

Mark tasted blood.

He faced the cracked heart, its fissure leaking purple like a wound that wouldn't close. The red signature under it was dim now, cut. Vulnerable.

He lifted his hand again—this time not to slice a line, but to feel for the heart's rhythm.

It beat wrong.

It beat hungry.

"Next," Mark said again, and the word felt like a vow he couldn't take back, "we break the heart."

Pecos cried out inside Mark's mind—one last surge of unbearable weight—and Mark felt the echo ripple outward through the tunnels, through the cemetery above, through the entire town.

Somewhere far away, Lowridge's flowers shivered.

And began, slowly, to wither.

CHAPTER 28: THE BREAKING

The heart didn't beat like an organ.

It pulsed like a crowd—slow, heavy, insistent—pushing through the chamber stone and into Mark's teeth. Each thrum carried a memory that wasn't his: Friday nights, fog, cleats on damp turf, voices chanting until a name stopped being a person and became an offering.

Roots webbed the ceiling in thick ropes, braided with purple veins that brightened every time Pecos pulled. The altar sat at the center like a fossilized tongue—black rock slick with moisture, carved with a scarlet eye. On it lay the heart: not flesh, not flower, but both at once. Petals packed tight as muscle. Root-fiber flexing with each pulse.

Pecos was on the floor beside it, half-propped against Marcus's discarded tarp cloak. His body trembled in waves. Purple light rolled under his veins like storm-light trapped in blood.

"Pecos," Alyssa said, voice raw. "Talk to me."

Pecos tried to answer. It came out as a broken exhale. Too much reality jammed into one body.

"I'm here," Mark said, more to himself than anyone. The severance cut in his chest still burned—Thalassa's teaching etched into him, every slice a price.

He looked at the heart.

A hairline fracture ran through the petal-mass where he'd cut—thin as spider thread, bright with purple light. Every pulse widened it, like the thing was trying to knit itself back together and failing.

Alyssa lifted her hands. Heat shimmered around her fingers. "When you say go, I burn."

Tommy crouched near Pecos, hands hovering like touch might shatter him. Marcus sat slumped against the far wall, sweat shining, his hybrid glow reduced to a bruised shimmer.

"Can you feel it?" Mark asked Pecos.

"All of them," Pecos whispered—too quiet, too old. His eyes weren't on the chamber. They were on the town. "They're stuck. In walls. In roads. In the grass."

Alyssa's throat worked. "We're going to get them out."

"No," Pecos said, sharper. "I'm getting them out. You're breaking it."

Mark's hands clenched. "I'm not leaving you."

Pecos's gaze found him. For one heartbeat the violet pulse in his pupils dimmed and Mark saw his friend—wet-eyed, exhausted, still himself.

"Not leaving," Pecos breathed, promise and goodbye braided together. "Just don't waste it."

The chamber shook—not from an earthquake, but from a scream.

Eoraziel's scream didn't use air. It vibrated through the root-webbing and into Mark's bones. The ceiling veins flared, flickered, flared again in a panicked stutter.

The heart pulsed harder.

The crack widened.

Purple light leaked from it, dripping down the altar like sap—then crawling across the stone floor toward Mark's shoes.

Marcus's head snapped up. "It's trying to bond."

Mark's skin went cold.

Thalassa had warned them: if the heart was damaged, Eoraziel would anchor to the nearest strong line—someone with blood on the routes, someone who had cut the network and survived.

Mark.

The purple thread thickened into a rope. It rose like a vine and opened at the end—petals unfolding, wet and gleaming, like a mouth.

It didn't speak.

It offered.

Relief poured into Mark's mind like warm water: Lowridge winning forever; his mother never crying again; Jason alive, laughing; Mark's grief flattened into silence.

All he had to do was stop fighting.

He wanted it.

That was the worst part.

Behind the offer was the hunger—ancient, patient, certain humans always chose comfort over truth.

The petal-mouth brushed Mark's wrist. Cold seeped into him: wet soil, a grave left open. Pressure tightened behind his eyes until his vision smeared.

Thalassa's lesson rose up—not words, a shape: water sliding off stone.

Don't wrestle. If you fight, you give it a grip.

Deflect.

Mark closed his eyes. He didn't shove the hunger away. He let it pass through him like wind through an empty hallway—then turned it, rotated it sideways, and let it slide into the cracks already splitting Eoraziel's own failing heart.

The petal-mouth recoiled.

Purple thread snapped back across the altar, lashing into the heart-mass.

Eoraziel screamed—furious now, half-formed words buried in the sound.

MINE.

Mark opened his eyes, breath shaking. "No."

Pecos arched, muscles locking. Purple light blasted out of his eyes like headlights.

Alyssa grabbed Mark's sleeve. "Now?"

Mark stared at Pecos, watching his veins darken as if ink were being poured into them from the inside.

Pecos bared his teeth. "Go. GO."

Mark turned. "Burn it."

Alyssa snapped her hands forward.

Fire bloomed—not red-orange, but white at the center, violet at the edges. The heart blackened instantly. Root-fiber curled like worms in salt.

Tommy surged forward, grabbing a fallen stone shard. He drove it into the crack and twisted.

The heart convulsed.

Purple light poured out, clinging, reaching.

The chamber walls flickered—stone thinning for a breath, and Mark saw shapes pressed inside it: faces, helmets, hands. Victims stored like trophies.

Pecos choked. Purple strands streamed from the chamber into him in thick cords. His fingers began to turn translucent at the edges, like smoke.

"Pecos—" Alyssa whispered.

"Keep going," Pecos rasped.

Inside the split heart, something knotted and pale twisted—a central root thick as Mark's wrist, pulsing with a slow stubborn beat. The main line. The last tether.

"Alyssa," Mark said, hoarse, "hold the flame."

She did, shaking.

Mark raised his hand.

He didn't need a blade. He needed intention.

He pictured the route as a line drawn from that root into everything above—into the stadium roar, into the cemetery grid, into every chant that had ever fed the land.

Then he pictured the line ending.

Not ripped. Not torn.

Ended.

Pain flared under his sternum, sharp enough to steal breath.

Mark brought his hand down, stopping a hair above the root.

Something snapped—inside the root, inside the air, inside Mark's ribs.

The heart spasmed. Petals whipped like a creature trying to crawl away.

Eoraziel screamed, and the scream tore open the world.

Lowridge changed in the same heartbeat. Mark didn't see it, but he felt it like nerves firing: purple flowers sagging on porch rails; blooms curling on headstones; vines falling limp from metal; buds in grass turning gray from the center outward.

The network was collapsing.

Pecos's body jerked as the weight of it slammed into him. His mouth opened and a sound poured out—pure agony big enough to hold a century.

Not just his pain.

All of them.

He held it.

He held it so no one else had to.

The heart cracked again. Alyssa's fire flared brighter, hungry now.

Marcus lifted his head, eyes glassy. "Finish it," he murmured.

Eoraziel struck again—not with vines, but with a mind.

BELONG.

Pressure doubled, then tripled. Mark staggered, knees buckling, as the town's need tried to pour itself into him like a mass possession.

His vision went white.

Then cool presence touched him—familiar as a hand on a shoulder in the dark.

Mark blinked hard.

Jason stood beside the altar.

Not flesh. Light. A thin luminous outline in a worn Lions jersey, eyes calm, not begging—present.

Jason looked at Mark, and Mark heard it the way he'd heard things in the shadow realm.

Stay.

Jason lifted one hand and guided the pressure—not fighting it, redirecting it—tilting the swarm away from Mark's center and into the broken lines Mark had severed.

Enough.

Mark sucked in air like he'd been underwater.

He turned back to the heart. It sputtered now, dying.

"Alyssa!" he shouted. "Push!"

Alyssa screamed—effort, fury, grief—and collapsed her fire inward.

The flame slammed onto the heart like a fist.

Petals ignited violet-white, burning so hot the air cracked.

The heart convulsed once.

Then it shattered.

A silent shockwave rippled out in a perfect circle. Root-webbing overhead snapped like puppet strings cut. Purple light burst outward and then imploded, sucked inward as Pecos pulled the last of the network into himself.

For a heartbeat the chamber went utterly dark.

Then ash began to fall.

Gray flakes settled on Mark's hair, on Alyssa's shoulders, on Tommy's shaking hands. It looked like snow. It smelled like burnt earth.

The purple glow was gone.

From the walls, the trapped shapes loosened.

Spirits rose—dozens, then hundreds—lifting through the ceiling as if gravity had forgotten them. They didn't scream now.

They exhaled.

Relief.

And in the midst of them, Jason moved like a guide, turning the freed toward the upward path with gentle touches, like he knew the route out.

Pecos convulsed one last time.

His skin was turning to ash from the fingertips inward, slow and inevitable, like frost creeping across glass. His eyes were clear now. No violet points. Just Pecos.

"If I stop," he whispered, barely there, "it snaps back."

Alyssa's sob broke loose. Tommy made a sound like someone punched him.

Mark dropped to his knees and took Pecos's brittle hand. "I'm sorry."

"Don't," Pecos breathed. "You did it."

"We did," Mark said.

Pecos smiled—faint, real. "Yeah."

His fingers loosened.

Ash spilled between Mark's knuckles.

Pecos looked up one last time, tracking the rising spirits, and Mark heard the final word like a blessing.

"Free."

Then Pecos was gone—dispersing into gray dust that drifted away on air that shouldn't have moved.

The chamber trembled from absence.

And the recoil hit Mark—psychic backlash, the snap of a town unplugged from its own obsession.

His vision tunneled.

Alyssa's face blurred.

Tommy's mouth opened in a silent shout.

Jason, farther away now, lifted his hand in a small farewell—less goodbye, more reassurance.

Darkness surged up like floodwater.

Mark tried to stay upright.

Tried to hold Pecos's smile in his mind so it wouldn't be swallowed by the same denial Lowridge had always used to bury its dead.

But the world tilted.

And Mark fell.

CHAPTER 29: EMPTY CEMETERY - ASH AND SILENCE

The heart did not explode.

It answered.

It answered the way the town answered the announcer on Friday nights —one body, one voice—except this voice wasn't made of lungs. It was made of routes and roots and everything Lowridge had poured into the ground for a century without admitting it.

Mark felt it in his teeth first. A vibration that turned his molars into tuning forks.

Then the web around them tightened.

The shadow realm's threads—purple, braided, pulsing—drew inward like a net cinching around prey. The trapped silhouettes hung in the fog beyond, dozens and then hundreds, their outlines twitching with the same flinch of panic, as if the heart had just snapped a leash.

Pecos was gone into the deeper dark.

But he wasn't gone in the way death was gone.

Mark could feel him.

A faint pull under Mark's ribs—like a hook sunk into the same place the curse had been tugging since the night of the first blood, the first petal, the first promise nobody ever wrote down. Pecos was still a light in the network, smaller now, swallowed by thicker threads, but there.

Marcus's hand locked on Mark's shoulder. Not gentle. Anchoring.

"Breathe," Marcus said. His voice sounded thin here, like it had to cross a long distance to reach Mark. "You don't sprint blind in this."

Mark didn't answer. If he opened his mouth, the only thing that would come out was Pecos's name—and Marcus had already shown him what names did down here. Names were signals. Names were flares.

Alyssa stood close, the grimoire pressed to her chest like a shield she didn't fully trust. Her face was pale in the purple light, eyes fixed on the web the way a person stared at a crack in ice under their feet.

Tommy hovered on the other side, bat still in hand like the wood could negotiate with hunger. His breathing came too fast, too loud.

He tried to swallow it down and failed. "This is… this is not… normal," he managed, like saying it plainly might make it less true.

The hunters circled at the edge of the knot, low and patient.

And above them, the patrol-light—cold, pale attention—paused like it was tasting the air.

Marcus's eyes flicked to that light, then to the darker route ahead.

"There," he said. "We go where it took him."

Alyssa's voice came out rough. "That's the heart."

Marcus didn't deny it. "That's the only door that matters now."

Mark looked toward the deepest pulse. The threads ahead thickened into something like arteries. The glow wasn't brighter; it was heavier. As if light could have weight, and the weight could press through skin.

He felt it turning its attention again—slow, amused.

Like the town watching a kid line up for a play he wasn't ready to run.

Marcus leaned closer, eyes hard. "Anchor," he said. "Right now. Don't let it rewrite you."

Mark clenched the memory he'd been using like a rope: Jason laughing in the driveway, tossing a ball one-handed, the sound loose and real.

The moment held.

Barely.

"Move," Marcus ordered.

They ran.

Not a sprint. A controlled push forward, like they were crossing thin ice and every heavy step would crack it. Mark kept his eyes on the pulse and his mind on Jason's laugh, on his brother's shoulder bump that meant I'm here.

Threads brushed Mark's arms like cobweb. Each contact sent a tiny shiver through the web. Each shiver felt like a notification.

The hunters followed.

Their clicking grew louder. Not coming from mouths—coming from joints, from thread-bones tapping together in rhythm.

One-two.

One-two.

A cadence.

Mark hated how familiar that cadence felt.

Ahead, the route narrowed, then opened into a hollow space beneath an enormous knot of interlaced strands. The knot hung overhead like a storm cloud made of veins.

And below it—

A deeper darkness, shaped like a doorway.

It wasn't a doorway in the human sense. There was no frame. No threshold.

Just an area where the web dipped, where the fog grew thick enough to look solid, where the pulse sounded like a heartbeat pressed against an ear.

Marcus stopped at the edge.

Alyssa came up beside him, lifting the grimoire as if the book could see what they couldn't.

Tommy edged behind them, bat trembling. "Tell me we don't have to —"

"We do," Marcus said.

The patrol-light shifted. The cold sweep slid closer, lingering on the knot overhead.

The web trembled.

The trapped spirits beyond jerked as one, faces turning toward the same point like flowers seeking sun.

The heart had noticed.

Mark stepped forward anyway.

The darkness grabbed at his skin—not cold, not hot—something like pressure underwater. His vision blurred and sharpened, blurred and sharpened, as if the world couldn't decide which version of itself to show him.

Then he was through.

*****

The heart-space was not a room.

It was a field.

Not grass. Not turf. A stretched plane of shadow threaded with purple, like the under-skin of a living thing. The routes ran here in dense lines, converging, splitting, braiding, looping back on themselves in patterns that made Mark's eyes ache if he stared too long.

And in the center—where midfield would be if this were a game Lowridge understood—

There was a mound.

A swelling knot of roots and petals and old hunger, rising like something trying to become a body. It did not have a face, but it had a focus: a single dark, glossy point embedded in the mass, catching the purple pulse like a pupil.

It blinked.

Mark's stomach dropped.

The blink wasn't an eyelid. It was a shift in the web—the entire network tightening for a fraction of a second, then loosening. Like a creature adjusting its grip.

And somewhere within the mound—

A flicker of light, weak and human.

Pecos.

Not flesh. Not bone.

A spark tangled in the heart's threads, wrapped so tight he was more idea than person, more signal than boy.

Mark saw Pecos's outline strain, saw his mouth open as if trying to speak.

No sound came out.

But Mark felt the meaning anyway, pressed into his skull like a hand.

Don't come closer.

Marcus's voice came behind Mark, tight. "We're too late to pull him clean."

Alyssa stepped forward, eyes locked on the grimoire. "Then we do what we said we'd do," she whispered.

Tommy gave a short, broken laugh. "We said a lot of things. I don't remember agreeing to walk into… this."

The heart-space pulsed.

The pupil fixed on Mark.

And Mark felt it—an interest, slow and hungry and personal.

Like the land had finally picked him the way it picked flowers: stubbornly, with purpose.

A pressure built behind Mark's eyes.

His vision smeared white for a split second, like a stadium light dragged across a camera lens.

And in that smear, he saw it.

A player.

Old uniform. Cracked helmet. Purple petals stuck to the facemask like dried blood.

Jason's jersey number.

Mark's anchor wavered.

Marcus's hand shot out and clamped Mark's wrist. "No," Marcus hissed. "It's bait or it's him and it's still bait. Either way—no."

Mark's throat tightened. He forced himself to look away from the illusion and back to the real problem: Pecos's spark, dim and struggling inside the heart.

Alyssa opened the grimoire on a page crowded with tight handwriting and symbols like warning signs. Her voice steadied in a way that felt unnatural—like she'd moved past fear into the clean violence of focus.

"This isn't a fight," she said, mostly to herself. "It's a severance."

Marcus nodded once. "You cut the routes. You cut the access."

Tommy's gaze snapped to Alyssa. "And Pecos?"

Alyssa's mouth tightened. "He's the anchor it's using. If we break the lines wrong—"

Her eyes flicked to Mark.

Mark understood without her finishing.

Backlash. Insanity. Hybrid. Haunted in daylight. Hollow at night. A person who could see too much and never rest.

Alyssa swallowed and kept going. "If we break them right… we still need a lock."

Mark looked at Pecos's spark.

Pecos looked back.

Even wrapped in thread, Pecos's expression was calm in a way that didn't belong here. Not peaceful—just certain. Like a kid who'd grown up with the land whispering at his ear and finally understood what it had been asking for all along.

His mouth moved again.

This time the meaning hit Mark hard and clean.

I can hold it.

Mark's chest tightened. "No," he said aloud before he could stop himself.

The heart's pupil shivered.

Marcus's grip on Mark's wrist went iron. "Do not talk," Marcus snapped. "Not here."

Mark forced his mouth shut, but the word had already escaped.

Alyssa's eyes went wide—then narrowed with decision. "Mark," she said, voice low. "This is where the story stops repeating."

Tommy's breathing hitched. "What does that mean?"

"It means," Alyssa said, "we don't get a version where everyone walks out clean."

The heart-space pulsed, and the routes around Pecos tightened like a fist.

Pecos's spark dimmed.

Mark moved without thinking.

He stepped forward, hands raised—not touching the thick main lines, not grabbing at the central knot like an animal in a trap. He reached for the thinner threads around Pecos, the smaller bindings that reacted to attention, to intention.

The moment his fingers got close, the threads trembled.

They wanted him.

Mark felt the pull in his ribs again. The curse recognized his bloodline. The Rivers legacy. The way the town had trained him to obey calls without questioning who was calling.

Alyssa's voice cut through the pressure. "Anchor," she said. "Now."

Mark forced his mind back to Jason—the real Jason—laughing in the driveway. For a heartbeat it steadied him.

Then Mark did the thing the curse hated most.

He told the truth.

Not with words—words were too slow here—but with a decision so clear it felt like a blade.

I am not yours.

The threads around Pecos's wrist flared bright, furious.

Marcus barked, "Now, Alyssa."

Alyssa began to speak the severance words.

Not Latin. Not a church prayer. Something older and rougher, shaped by desperation and ink-stained warnings in margins. The candles she'd used as anchors back in the shelter weren't here, but the grimoire itself seemed to carry their memory—small points of steadiness in a place built to unravel.

The routes around them pulsed.

The heart's pupil widened slightly, like surprise.

Mark's fingers brushed the thin binding thread.

Pain snapped through his arm, sharp and intimate, like a needle under skin.

He didn't let go.

He pictured the line again—the clean cut through purple, the separation of signal from flesh.

The thread did not snap like string.

It unhooked.

A ripple ran through the web, outward in all directions, and Mark heard it—

Not a scream.

A crowd inhaling.

Every trapped spirit in the distance jerked, heads lifting, as if they'd felt the leash loosen for the first time in decades.

Pecos's spark flared.

For one second, Pecos was there—fully there—eyes clear, expression human.

Mark grabbed his hand.

Cold and sweet and bitter slammed through Mark's palm. Not petals. Not rot. Something like raw soil and rain and a storm about to break.

Pecos's voice hit Mark's bones instead of his ears.

"Mark," he said, calm as ever, "don't lie to yourself."

Mark's throat closed.

Because he knew what Pecos meant.

The curse fed on denial. It fed on silence. It fed on the town pretending everything was fine while it buried boys and called them legends.

And Mark had been silent.

For years.

About Jason. About guilt. About his family's part in the legacy.

About how he'd felt the town's hunger and still walked onto the field anyway.

Alyssa's voice rose, severance words tightening like a rope around the heart's access points.

Marcus stepped closer to Pecos, hands lifting—not to save, but to stabilize. His fingers glowed faint purple, the mark in him responding.

Tommy hovered, bat raised like he could swing at a concept. "Tell me what to do," he demanded, voice cracking. "Give me a normal task. I am excellent at normal tasks."

Alyssa didn't look away from the grimoire. "Tell the truth," she said.

Tommy blinked. "What?"

"Out loud," Alyssa snapped, and now her sarcasm had teeth. "The thing feeds on what you don't say."

Tommy's mouth opened and closed.

Then, because he was Tommy and fear made him louder, he blurted, "I remember the woods."

Mark's head snapped toward him.

Tommy swallowed hard, eyes wet. "I remember being little. I remember something watching me and my dad telling me it was just fog and me believing him because I wanted to believe him. I remember lying about it because I didn't want to be the kid who was scared."

The web shivered.

The heart's pupil narrowed.

Alyssa's voice sharpened, the severance words clicking into place like a lock.

Mark felt it then—the route-lines loosening, the pressure behind his eyes easing just a fraction.

Truth hurt.

But it worked.

Mark drew breath and forced his own truth to the surface.

"My family knew," he said, and his voice sounded wrong here, thin and loud. "They knew something was off. They called it tradition. They called it sacrifice. And I kept playing anyway because I thought if I played perfect enough, I could make it not matter."

The heart-space pulsed hard.

The pupil blinked again—fast, irritated.

Pecos's grip tightened on Mark's hand.

Pecos's expression didn't change, but Mark felt the meaning:

Keep going.

Mark swallowed, throat burning. "Jason told me I was next," he said. "And I thought he meant the team. But he meant the debt."

A wave of cold moved through the web.

Not from the heart—from the routes breaking.

Alyssa's voice hit the final line.

The severance landed.

For a split second, everything went silent.

No pulse.

No hum.

No clicking hunters.

Just stillness so complete Mark could hear his own heartbeat and realize, with a sick twist, that the heart had been keeping time with him.

Then the heart-space cracked.

Not stone. Not glass.

Something more basic.

The mound of roots and petals shuddered, and the glossy pupil in its center widened—then fractured down the middle like a mirror splitting.

Purple light poured out.

The web around them lit up, every route-line flaring at once, like the entire town's nervous system firing its last signal.

Mark saw the trapped spirits beyond jerk free—some falling, some dissolving, some simply lifting like breath released after being held too long.

He saw a braided thread in the distance—thicker, fraying—pull away from the central knot.

Jason's thread.

It strained once, hard.

Then it snapped free—not erased, not consumed—released.

Mark's chest seized.

He felt, for the first time in years, a clean grief.

Not guilt. Not the curse twisting his memory into punishment.

Grief.

He almost collapsed under it.

Pecos squeezed Mark's hand once.

A goodbye.

Mark's eyes flew to Pecos, panic rising.

Pecos's spark brightened—then steadied into something new. Not trapped. Not struggling.

Anchored.

"Pecos," Mark tried to say.

Pecos shook his head, small, firm.

His voice hit Mark's bones one last time. "If it goes loose," Pecos said, "it finds another door."

Mark's throat closed.

Alyssa's eyes were wide, shining. She didn't speak, but her face said the same thing: This is the lock.

Marcus stepped forward, pain etched into the lines around his eyes. "You don't have to—"

Pecos looked at Marcus, calm as ever.

And in that look Mark saw something that wasn't surrender.

It was choice.

Pecos lifted his free hand—toward the fractured pupil, toward the spilling light—and pressed his palm into the air as if feeling the shape of the routes.

The heart-space shuddered again.

Purple threads whipped toward Pecos like vines seeking a trellis.

They wrapped him—not tight like a prison.

Tight like a harness.

Pecos's spark flared once, bright enough to make Mark squint.

Then the light folded inward, collapsing into Pecos like a door closing.

The heart-space sagged.

The routes dimmed.

The hunters at the edge of the field-space faltered, their forms unraveling, petals dropping away like dead leaves.

Mark's fingers slipped from Pecos's hand.

Not because Pecos pulled away.

Because Pecos was no longer in reach.

He was part of the lock now—threaded through the severed routes, holding the scar closed with his own signal.

Mark stood there, shaking, staring at the place Pecos had been.

Alyssa's voice cracked. "Pecos..."

Marcus's jaw clenched so hard it looked like it hurt. He didn't blink.

Tommy let out a sound like a laugh that had nowhere to go.

Then the heart-space collapsed.

The shadow plane fell out from under them.

And Mark was falling again—through purple threads and fog—except this time the web wasn't grabbing him.

It was letting go.

*****

Mark hit wet ground hard enough to knock the air out of him.

Real air.

Cold. Sweet. Bitter.

Fog.

He rolled onto his side, coughing, palms sinking into damp soil. For a second he didn't know where he was.

Then he saw the iron fence.

Saw the cemetery stones.

Saw moonlight on brass plaques.

And saw the flowers—

Not glowing.

Not pulsing.

Just... there.

Purple petals sagging as if they'd suddenly remembered they were only plants. Some already browning at the edges. Some collapsing into the mud like drained ink.

Alyssa lay a few feet away, gasping, grimoire clutched to her chest like it had saved her from drowning.

Tommy was on his back staring up at the sky, whispering, "Nope. No. I am never doing that again," like repetition could make it true.

Marcus was upright faster than the rest, scanning the cemetery like a soldier checking for incoming fire.

And beyond the fence—

The stadium lights flickered.

Once.

Twice.

Then steadied.

The fog began to thin. Not vanish—Lowridge didn't let go that clean— but thin enough that Mark could see the field again, the outlines of people moving, the chaos of a town that had been running on denial suddenly tripping over reality.

Sirens wailed in the distance—sharp now, not muffled.

Mark pushed himself onto his hands and knees.

His chest hurt in a way that wasn't injury. A hollowness where the curse's pressure had been, like someone had removed a splinter that had been in too long and left raw nerve behind.

He looked back into the cemetery.

The older stones sat quiet.

No figures moving between them.

No helmets in fog.

Just headstones and damp soil and the smell of crushed petals.

Mark's throat tightened.

He realized, with a sudden sick clarity, that he couldn't feel Pecos anymore—not as a pull, not as a presence under his ribs.

Not here.

Alyssa crawled closer, eyes searching Mark's face before she said anything. "He—"

Mark shook his head once. Small. Controlled. Because if he did anything bigger, he'd break.

Tommy sat up, face streaked with dirt and fog moisture. He looked around wildly, then fixed on the flowers sagging near a grave. "Are we... did we...?"

Marcus's voice came quiet. "It's done."

Alyssa swallowed. "Is it dead?"

Marcus stared at the cemetery like he was listening for an echo. "The hunger's not a person," he said. "You don't kill a disease with one swing. But you cut off its access."

Mark's hands clenched in the mud.

"Then why do I feel like—" Alyssa started.

"Because the land remembers," Marcus finished. "And now it remembers the cut."

Mark stared at the dying flowers.

Conduits.

Not pretty symbols.

Wires.

And for the first time in his life, Lowridge's symbol looked tired.

Mark pushed to his feet, legs shaking. He looked toward the stadium, toward Main Street beyond it, toward the places that would wake up tomorrow and try to tell a story small enough to fit inside denial.

A tragic accident.

A freak fog.

A bad night.

Something that didn't require anyone to admit what they'd fed.

Mark drew breath.

He tasted iron.

He thought of Pecos's last message.

Don't lie to yourself.

Mark turned to Alyssa, to Tommy, to Marcus, and forced the next truth out of his mouth like pulling a thorn.

"We tell it," he said.

Alyssa's eyebrows lifted. "Tell what?"

Mark's voice steadied—not because he felt steady, but because he'd finally chosen the thing the curse couldn't digest.

"All of it," Mark said. "We tell the town what it's been paying for."

Tommy stared at him like Mark had suggested walking back into the shadow realm for fun. "They won't believe—"

"Then we keep telling it," Mark said, and his voice surprised him with its calm. "Not because they'll thank us. Because it's the only way the cut stays clean."

Marcus looked at Mark for a long moment, measuring.

Then he nodded once. "That," he said, "is how you keep it from finding a new door."

The wind moved through the cemetery, cold and real.

Purple petals lifted from one grave in a small spiral and drifted away, not glowing, not mesmerizing—just leaves in moonlight.

Mark watched them fall.

And in the space they left behind, the night felt quieter.

Not safe.

Not healed.

But quieter in the way a stadium went quiet after a bad hit—when everyone held their breath and remembered, briefly, that bodies were fragile and glory wasn't free.

Mark looked at the sagging flowers again and made himself speak the name that hurt most.

"Pecos," he whispered.

The cemetery didn't answer.

But somewhere far under the ground—beneath routes and roots and scar tissue—the land held its breath.

And for the first time, it sounded less like hunger—

And more like restraint.

CHAPTER 30: THE FIRST LOSS

A week after the heart shattered, Lowridge still moved like it was walking on a bruise.

Morning came the way it always did—school buses coughing at corners, sprinklers clicking on, commuters streaming toward the new glass buildings down the highway where the growth corridor kept promising a future—but the town's old rhythm had been replaced by something thinner. A hesitation. A listening pause between sounds, as if Lowridge expected the ground to speak and didn't know what to do with the silence.

The cemetery looked wrong in daylight.

Not haunted-wrong. Not fog-wrapped wrong.

Just… empty.

The fence still ran along the back of the football field, and beyond it the headstones still stood in their patient rows like they always had, but the purple was gone. No petals on the wind. No blossoms tucked against stone. No stubborn patches that refused to die when everything else browned for winter.

Only scorched soil in places, dark as old charcoal, as if the earth had been cauterized.

Mark stood at the fence with his hands in his jacket pockets and tried to make his chest stop tightening every time his eyes went to that blackened ground.

Tommy came up beside him, shoulders hunched, fidgeting with the ring he always wore. He slid it off, rolled it across his knuckles, slid it back on. Off. On. Off.

"Feels like somebody stole the town's face," Tommy said.

Mark didn't answer right away. His throat was doing that thing it did when he had too much to say and no clean place to put it. He watched a groundskeeper in the distance rake the edge of the cemetery path like routine could erase memory.

"It was never its face," Mark said finally.

Tommy made a sound that was almost a laugh and almost a swallow. "Yeah. I know. Still. You ever get used to seeing the truth after you've lived with the lie your whole life?"

Mark's fingers curled inside his pockets. He thought of Pecos—how Pecos had looked the last time Mark had seen him fully himself, the violet point in his eyes dimming just enough to let Mark back in. Not without a fight.

He thought of ash falling like strange snow in the underground chamber. Thought of that psychic shockwave—like the town exhaling after holding its breath for a hundred years.

"I don't want to get used to it," Mark said.

Tommy's eyes flicked to him. "That's the most honest thing you've said since September."

Mark's mouth twitched, but it didn't turn into a smile.

Alyssa's voice cut across the quiet behind them. "You two are going to freeze out here."

She stepped up with her hands tucked into the sleeves of her sweatshirt, hair pulled back, face pale in the cold. She looked like she'd slept, technically, but not the kind of sleep that repaired anything. The kind that just restarted the day.

In her other hand, she carried the grimoire wrapped in a towel like it was something that could stain if it touched bare skin.

Tommy's gaze snagged on it. "You're still carrying that around like a haunted lunchbox."

Alyssa's mouth sharpened with her usual sarcasm, but her eyes didn't commit. "It is a haunted lunchbox."

Mark looked at the towel-wrapped book. "You shouldn't bring it to school."

Alyssa's voice went dry. "It's not like I can leave it on my nightstand and hope it learns manners."

Mark didn't push. He understood obsession in his own way—understood how your mind grabbed the only lever it believed could move the world back into something understandable. For Mark, it was replaying moments, searching for the exact second everything went wrong, like guilt could become a map. For Alyssa, it was ink and paper and proof.

Tommy nodded toward the empty cemetery. "So. This is it, huh? Lowridge without its... accessories."

Alyssa followed his gaze. Her sarcasm flickered, then softened into something quieter. "The flowers were conduits," she said, mostly to herself. "Every grave marker was a socket. Every petal was a wire."

Mark closed his eyes for a second. He saw Eli Carter running through fog, eyes empty, body too perfect, like the route belonged to something else. He tasted that sweet-metal air again, that feeling of being watched from inside his own skin.

When he opened his eyes, the cemetery was still empty.

"What now?" Tommy asked, and even his joking tone couldn't hide the fear underneath. "We just... go back to normal? Do algebra? Apply to college? Pretend we didn't walk through something that wanted to wear us?"

Alyssa's fingers tightened around the grimoire. "Normal's not waiting for us," she said. "Normal has a price."

Mark looked at the stadium, the bleachers, the banners that still hung in school colors like the town hadn't gotten the memo. "Then we pay it."

Tommy stared at him. "Man, that sounded like something a coach would say before halftime."

Mark's eyes stayed on the field. "No," he said. "It sounded like something Pecos would say."

That shut Tommy up.

For a moment the three of them stood there, the wind cutting through jackets and the silence inside them louder than any Friday night roar. Behind the fence, the headstones watched without purple glow, without a pulse, without that sense of hungry attention.

Just stone.

Just names.

Just grief that belonged to the living now, and not to the land.

*****

Friday came anyway.

Lowridge didn't cancel games because Lowridge didn't know how to stop being Lowridge. The banners went up. The marching band rehearsed. The booster club set up the trailer painted with a purple flower that suddenly looked like an accusation.

The fog showed up at sunset like it always did in October, rolling low across the grass.

But it didn't feel thick the way it had before.

It didn't feel like cover.

It felt like weather.

Mark noticed that first, standing on the sideline with his helmet under his arm, watching the other team warm up. Their jerseys were red and white, their parents clustered in a smaller section of bleachers, their band trying hard to fill the gaps in sound.

Lowridge's crowd was still big. Still loud. Still devoted.

But something in the sound had changed.

It wasn't a chant anymore.

It was just cheering.

Coach Whitman walked the sideline like he always did, jaw tight, clipboard in hand, disappointment already loaded behind his eyes like a weapon. Coach Williams stood with him, whispering something about coverage schemes, about reading the safety.

Old Lowridge would've listened.

Old Lowridge would've leaned in through the roots.

Now the coaches were just men.

Mark found Tommy near the bench. Tommy was bouncing on his toes like he could trick his body into feeling normal by pretending it was just another game. His ring flashed under the stadium lights as he fidgeted with it.

"Ready?" Tommy asked.

Mark's instinct was to say yes. To give the town what it liked.

But the last week had ripped too much open for him to keep lying out of habit.

"I don't know," Mark said.

Tommy blinked at him. Then, surprisingly, he smiled—small and real. "That might be the healthiest answer you've ever given."

Alyssa stood near the track, bundled in a coat, grimoire bag slung across her shoulder like a weight she refused to set down. She raised two fingers at Mark in a casual salute that tried to play as normal.

Mark nodded back.

The coin toss happened. The kickoff sailed. The game began.

And for the first time in decades, Lowridge looked like any other good high school team.

Good.

Not blessed.

Not fed.

Not carried by something beneath the turf.

Mark played clean. He made smart throws. He took hits and got up. Tommy broke a couple runs that should've lit the crowd on fire.

But the other team tackled. The other team adjusted. The other team wasn't an "outsider" stumbling into Lowridge's trap—it was just a team doing its job.

In the third quarter, on a third-and-short that Lowridge normally converted without even thinking, Mark handed the ball off and watched Tommy get swallowed at the line.

No invisible gap opened.

No perfect lane appeared.

Just bodies. Just physics. Just a hard stop.

The crowd made a confused noise, like they didn't recognize what they were watching.

Late in the fourth, the score was tied. The air was sharp with cold. Mark's hands ached inside his gloves. He stepped back in the pocket, scanned the field, and saw a receiver break open down the seam.

For a breath, it looked like the old miracle—the kind of play the town told stories about for decades.

Mark threw.

The ball sailed.

And the safety—an ordinary kid with ordinary reflexes—read it perfectly and jumped the route.

Interception.

The stadium didn't go silent at first. It didn't know how.

It made sound out of habit—shouts, gasps, a rising complaint—but underneath it was something new: the sudden realization that the script had been rewritten without permission.

The other team drove. Kicked a field goal.

Won.

When the final whistle blew, the sound that followed wasn't outrage, exactly.

It was grief disguised as confusion.

Parents stared like they'd been personally insulted by reality. Old men in faded Lions caps shook their heads as if the universe had committed a clerical error. The booster club trailer sat under the lights, the purple flower painted on its side looking too bright and too innocent for what it used to mean.

Mark walked off the field with his helmet in his hand and felt something he hadn't expected.

Relief.

Not joy. Not peace.

Relief the way you felt when you finally stopped holding something up that was never supposed to be yours.

Tommy jogged beside him, breath steaming. "We lost," he said, like he needed to test the words out loud.

Mark nodded. "We lost."

Tommy waited for the world to punish them for saying it. For the air to thicken. For the fog to roll in like a curtain.

Nothing happened.

Tommy's shoulders sagged.

Then he laughed—soft and stunned. "It's… just a loss."

Mark looked at the empty cemetery beyond the far fence.

"Yeah," he said. "It's just a loss."

*****

The town council meeting the next Monday was held in the gym because the council chambers couldn't hold the crowd.

Lowridge showed up in jackets and scarves, in work boots and polished shoes. People from the new developments near the tech parks stood beside people whose families had been here since before the town had a name worth printing.

The mayor sat at the folding table with the council members lined up beside him like a defensive front. The faces behind them were tight, angry, afraid.

Mark walked in with Tommy and Alyssa and felt the heat of attention hit him harder than any tackle.

Not admiration.

Not devotion.

Blame.

Alyssa leaned in, voice low and sharp. "Do not speak unless you have to."

Tommy whispered back, "That's funny, coming from the girl who argues with ghosts."

Alyssa shot him a look. Tommy shut up.

The mayor cleared his throat and started talking about "the tragedy," about "unprecedented events," about "community resilience." Words designed to sound like control.

Then someone shouted from the bleachers, "We were winners before you kids started digging!"

Another voice: "My family's business is already bleeding!"

A third: "The crops—have you seen the crops?"

A man stood—one of the older boosters, a face Mark recognized from every fundraiser photo. "We've had success here for generations," he said, voice shaking with something that wasn't just anger. "And now we've got nothing but loss and rumors and people talking about curses like we're some backwoods joke."

Alyssa's jaw tightened.

Mark looked at the man and saw it clearly: he wasn't mourning football. He was mourning certainty. He was mourning the feeling that the town was protected by something bigger than consequence.

The mayor raised a hand. "We are investigating—"

Alyssa stood up.

Mark's heart jumped. Tommy's eyes went wide.

Alyssa's voice cut through the noise like a blade. "There's nothing to investigate."

The gym quieted—not completely, but enough.

The mayor stared at her. "Miss Dawson—"

"You want the old ways back," Alyssa said, and the words came out steady, almost calm. "Say it."

Murmurs rippled. Faces tightened.

Alyssa held up her chin. "You want the purple flowers back because you liked what they gave you. You liked winning. You liked perfect weather. You liked crops that grew like miracles. You liked a town that looked blessed from the outside."

Her eyes swept the crowd. "But those flowers were conduits. They were how it got into people. How it drove players like puppets. How it took lives and hid the cost under trophies."

Someone shouted, "That's not true!"

Alyssa's gaze snapped to the voice. "Then explain Eli Carter."

The name hit the room like a dropped weight.

Mark felt Tommy stiffen beside him.

Alyssa's voice didn't rise. It didn't need to. "Explain the players who died and the graves that glowed under moonlight. Explain the fog that wasn't fog. Explain why this town has a cemetery that watched Friday nights like an audience."

Silence pooled.

Then the mayor spoke, voice tight. "Even if—even if—there was something… unnatural… the town thrived."

Mark heard it then.

Not the lie.

The confession.

Lowridge had always known something was wrong. It had just decided the trade was worth it.

Mark felt something shift inside him—anger, maybe, or grief finally finding a target.

He stepped forward.

He didn't want to talk. Silence was his defense. But silence was also how the town had survived.

"No," Mark said, and his voice came out low but clear. "It didn't thrive. It fed."

He looked at the crowd, at the boosters, at the parents, at the kids in letterman jackets who didn't understand why their world felt smaller now.

"It fed on players," he said. "It fed on fear. It fed on all of you cheering like worship. It took people and made it look like glory."

The mayor's face tightened, like he wanted to deny it even now.

Mark kept going. "You're mad because you're average now. Because you have to earn what you get."

A few people gasped. A few people bristled.

Mark nodded once, as if agreeing with them. "Yeah. That hurts. But it's real. And real is what we have left."

The mayor's hands trembled on the table. He looked suddenly exhausted, older than he had a week ago.

He leaned into the microphone.

"I can't lead a town that doesn't know what it wants," he said, voice rough. "And I won't lead a town that wants blood bargains back."

A stir ran through the room.

The mayor swallowed. "I'm resigning. Effective immediately. We will hold an emergency election."

For a second, nobody moved.

Then the room erupted—not into celebration, not into unity, but into the chaotic sound of a town realizing it could change and being terrified of what change meant.

Alyssa sat back down slowly, like her legs had finally remembered they were shaking.

Tommy leaned in, whispering, "Well. That went… polite."

Alyssa gave him a look that almost smiled. Almost.

Mark didn't feel victorious.

He felt hollow.

But hollow wasn't the same thing as trapped.

*****

That night, Alyssa asked them to meet her behind her aunt's old trailer on the edge of town—where the woods began to thicken and the streetlights stopped trying.

Her aunt wasn't there. Not physically. She'd left Lowridge again the day after the heart broke, slipping out like someone who'd learned that staying was another kind of possession.

Alyssa stood by a rusted fire pit with the grimoire in her hands, towel unwrapped now. The book looked older than paper had any right to look. The cover seemed to drink the porch light.

Tommy stopped short. "Oh no. You're doing a thing."

"I'm doing a thing," Alyssa confirmed.

Mark stepped closer. "Alyssa."

She looked at him, and for once her sarcasm didn't show up to protect her. "If I keep it," she said quietly, "I'll read it forever. I'll chase the next answer. I'll convince myself I can control what happened by understanding it."

Mark didn't argue. He'd seen obsession in her eyes every day since the cemetery. He'd also seen how close she came to letting that obsession become a new chain.

Alyssa swallowed. "And that's how this starts again. Someone thinking they can handle it."

Tommy's voice softened. "You sure?"

Alyssa nodded once. "No. But yes."

She set the grimoire in the fire pit like she was laying something to rest. Then she looked at Mark.

"My family helped start this," she said, and the confession landed like a stone. "Not directly, maybe. But we were part of the story. Part of the keeping-quiet. I told myself I was exposing the truth for justice, but part of me wanted to prove I wasn't crazy. Wanted to win."

Her eyes glistened. "I'm tired of winning."

Mark felt his throat tighten. He nodded. "Then don't."

Alyssa struck the match.

The flame took a second to catch, like the book resisted. Then the corner of a page curled, blackened, and the fire began to climb.

For a moment, the air smelled sweet—faintly floral, faintly metallic— and Mark's muscles went rigid, his body bracing for a surge of pressure behind the eyes.

But it didn't come.

The sweetness thinned into ordinary smoke.

The pages burned.

Alyssa watched without blinking. Tommy shifted from foot to foot like he wanted to crack a joke but didn't trust his voice.

When the book collapsed inward with a soft whoof, Alyssa exhaled like she'd been holding her breath for years.

Mark looked at the fire and thought of Pecos.

He thought of the way Pecos had carried the network into himself—how the flowers across town had withered in the same instant, as if the land's nerves had been severed.

Pecos had paid for this.

The least they could do was not rebuild the same trap with new tools.

*****

Mark walked home alone.

Lowridge was quieter at night now. Not safer—quiet didn't equal safe— but uncharged. The streetlights didn't flicker like they were blinking messages. The shadows lay where they belonged.

He passed the booster club trailer and didn't look at the purple flower painted on its side.

He passed the cemetery road and did look.

The fence glinted under moonlight. The headstones stood. The blackened patches of soil looked like scars.

Mark didn't go in. He wasn't ready for that kind of stillness yet.

He turned toward home, hands in his pockets, and felt something brush his glove.

Soft.

Light.

He stopped.

Pulled his hand out.

On his palm lay a single purple petal.

Not paper.

Not paint.

Velvet-soft, cool as damp soil.

Mark stared at it so long his eyes started to sting.

The world stayed quiet.

No pressure behind his eyes. No hum under the pavement. No fog thickening like a curtain.

Just the petal, resting there like a question that hadn't been fully answered.

Mark's fingers curled slowly around it—not tight, not possessive. Just enough to keep it from blowing away.

He thought of what Alyssa had said. Normal has a price.

He thought of what he'd said in the gym. Real is what we have left.

Mark opened his hand again and let the petal sit on his palm under the streetlight.

Then, carefully, like handling something that could still burn, he slid it into an empty film canister from his camera bag—an old habit from his art life, a way of keeping fragile things safe without pretending they were harmless.

He snapped the lid shut.

And kept walking.

Behind him, Lowridge breathed—ordinary, wounded, free.

And somewhere beneath that ordinary, a possibility waited in the dark, patient as a root.

CHAPTER 31: THE SILENCE AFTER

Mark woke up with his hands tangled in the sheets like they were vines.

For half a second he didn't know where he was. The room was dark, the air cold, and his throat tasted like dirt and pennies. In the dream, the purple flowers had pushed up through his mattress. Petals had pressed against his lips, soft as velvet, and the moment he tried to spit them out, they had turned to roots—thin threads that slid down his throat and pulled.

He sucked in air hard enough to make his ribs ache.

His ceiling fan was still. His phone on the nightstand glowed 3:17 a.m. In the hallway, the house made its usual old noises—pipes settling, wood clicking—except now every sound had a second meaning. Every creak could be a footstep. Every hush could be a crowd holding its breath.

Mark sat up slowly. The room spun at the edges. His heart wouldn't stop sprinting, like it hadn't gotten the memo that the game was over.

He swung his feet to the floor and felt the carpet under his toes—dry, boring, normal. He waited for the pressure behind his eyes, for the faint hum in his bones that used to come when the routes were near.

Nothing.

That nothing should have been a gift. Instead it felt like standing in an empty stadium after the lights went out—quiet so big it could swallow you.

Mark padded to the bathroom, turned on the faucet, and drank straight from the tap. The water was cold and clean, and still he couldn't stop imagining it as something filtered through soil.

When he looked up, his reflection stared back like a stranger. His face had thinned since the night everything broke. Shadows lived under his eyes. A healing cut marked his forearm where a thread had burned him through the skin. His hair stuck up in a way his mom would've fixed before school, back when school was the only kind of pressure that mattered.

He gripped the sink until the tremor in his hands eased.

Breathe in. Count to four. Breathe out.

He'd read that online—how to calm a body that didn't trust the world anymore. It worked sometimes. It worked tonight, barely.

When he went back to his room, he didn't crawl under the blankets. He sat on the edge of his bed and listened to the silence of Lowridge.

A month ago, silence didn't exist in this town. Even on weeknights, you could hear it—someone revving a truck down Main, someone practicing with the marching band, somebody's dad yelling at a referee on TV like the refs could hear him through the screen.

Now there were gaps. Whole stretches where nothing moved. Like the town was learning how to be quiet without being watched.

Mark's eyes burned. He blinked hard and stared at the window until the sky softened from black to bruised gray.

By the time the sun came up, he'd already been awake for hours.

*****

Lowridge looked wrong in daylight.

Not because it was ruined—most of the damage had been cleaned up, boarded up, painted over. People in town were good at repairs. They'd been patching things for generations.

But there were places where the world still showed its seams.

On Oak Street, a mailbox post was still wrapped in dead vine, brittle and gray as rope. In the ditch behind the elementary school, the grass grew in uneven squares, like someone had laid sod and forgotten to water half of it. A black mark streaked the sidewalk near the gas station where one of the flower-things had hit the pavement; the stain wouldn't wash away, no matter how much bleach Mrs. Alden poured on it.

Mark jogged past it anyway, his breath fogging in the cool morning. He ran because his body needed something to do with all its leftover adrenaline. He ran because running was a language he understood: start here, end there, keep going, don't stop.

He turned onto the road that led toward the cemetery.

He told himself it was coincidence. He told himself his feet just knew the route.

He told himself a lot of things.

The cemetery fence was new. Someone—probably Harold, or the church committee—had replaced the warped old chain link with black iron bars that looked like they belonged on a postcard. The gate stood open. There were no purple flowers curling around the hinges, no petals caught in the metal like bruises.

Just dew. Just grass.

Mark slowed to a walk. His lungs burned in a clean, honest way. He stood outside the gate for a long moment, the way you stand outside a locker room door before a game—knowing once you step through, you're committed.

He stepped in.

Pecos's memorial wasn't big. That was the point.

No marble statue. No giant plaque. Just a flat stone set into the ground near the back row, where the older graves leaned like tired teeth. Someone had etched his name—PEDRO "PECOS" GARCIA—along with the years he'd lived and a simple line beneath:

HE HELD THE LINE.

At the base of the stone sat a small bronze bowl, darkened by weather. Inside it was a thin layer of ash.

Mark stared at it until his vision went soft.

A month later and his brain still kept trying to rewrite the ending. Still kept looking for the version where Pecos got up, shook off the dirt, and cracked a joke about how they all owed him tacos.

Mark crouched. The grass around the memorial was greener than the rest of the cemetery, like the earth had decided to try harder right here.

He didn't touch the ash. He didn't know if that was a rule or just superstition.

"Hey," he said anyway, the word rough in his throat.

The morning air didn't answer. A crow called once from a far branch.

Mark swallowed and forced himself to keep talking, because if he didn't, the silence would fill the space with other voices.

"I don't know what you saw in there," he murmured. "In the web. In the… whatever that place was." His jaw tightened. "But I'm sorry you were the one who had to do it. I'm sorry you were the one who had to be brave first."

He stared at the ash like it could hear him.

"And thank you," Mark said, and his voice cracked on it. "For not letting it keep us."

He bowed his head, breathing through the ache in his chest.

When he finally stood, he noticed something new: a small bouquet of white daisies resting on the stone next to the bowl.

Not purple. Not special. Just daisies.

Alyssa.

Mark wiped his face with the sleeve of his hoodie and headed back toward town.

*****

Alyssa's room at her grandpa's house had turned into an archive.

Books were stacked on the floor in uneven towers—town histories, botany guides, old football yearbooks with cracked spines. Notebooks were spread across her desk like she'd exploded a filing cabinet. A handheld recorder sat beside a mug that said LOWRIDGE LIONS MOM even though Alyssa had never been anyone's mom and had never cared about the Lions until they tried to eat her friends.

Mark leaned against her doorframe and watched her write.

She didn't look up right away. Her pen moved fast, scratching across paper with an intensity that made Mark think of the way she used to underline passages in the grimoire, like if she marked it hard enough, it couldn't lie.

"You didn't sleep," she said finally.

Mark blinked. "How do you—"

"You're doing the thing." She glanced at his face. "The too-still thing. The 'I'm fine' thing."

Mark tried to smile. It came out crooked.

Alyssa set her pen down, rubbed her eyes, and tapped the recorder. "I'm cataloging everything before people decide it didn't happen."

"People already decided," Mark said.

She gave him a look—flat, tired, sharp. "Not us."

Mark exhaled and stepped inside. The room smelled like paper and old dust and the lemon cleaner her grandpa used on Sundays.

Alyssa pushed a notebook toward him. On the page was a timeline—dates, locations, names. She'd written PECOS in all caps, circled it twice. She'd listed the words they'd learned, the rituals that almost worked, the things that did work, and the things that cost too much.

"Why?" Mark asked, though he knew the answer.

"Because history gets rewritten by whoever's still standing," Alyssa said. "Because if I don't put it down, someone's going to call it a gas leak or a mass hallucination. Because in twenty years the booster club will be selling shirts that say SURVIVED THE FOG and people will laugh about it like it was a haunted house attraction."

Mark's throat tightened.

Alyssa's voice softened, just a little. "Because Pecos deserves better than a rumor."

Mark looked down at the timeline again.

There was a blank space at the bottom, like she'd left room for the future.

He didn't know if that was hope or dread.

"What are you going to do with it?" he asked.

"Keep it," Alyssa said. "For now. Maybe one day... I don't know. Maybe it becomes a warning. Maybe it becomes the only honest thing Lowridge ever produced."

Mark nodded once, because he didn't trust his voice.

Alyssa reached under her desk and pulled out a small envelope. "This came for you yesterday. I forgot to give it to you."

Mark took it. The return address was a post office box in town. No name.

His stomach went tight. For a second he smelled purple petals again, sweet and metallic.

"What is it?" he asked.

Alyssa shrugged, but her eyes were wary. "Probably a bill. Or a hate note. Or Harold trying to be dramatic."

Mark slid the envelope into his hoodie pocket without opening it.

Some things could wait.

*****

Tommy had stopped going to practice.

Coach Whitman texted him anyway—short messages that read like commands: You coming? Need you. Don't bail now. As if loyalty could be summoned like a dog whistle.

Tommy didn't answer.

Mark found him behind his garage, sitting on an upside-down bucket with his elbows on his knees. A pile of football gear lay on the concrete beside him: shoulder pads, cleats, his jersey, all of it looking suddenly like costume pieces from a life that belonged to someone else.

Tommy didn't look up when Mark approached.

"You should be in school," Mark said, because sometimes it was easier to say the wrong thing than the real thing.

Tommy gave a humorless snort. "So should you."

Mark sat on the edge of the concrete step. The morning sun warmed the back of his neck, but it didn't reach inside.

Tommy stared at his hands. His fingernails were bitten raw. "I keep thinking," he said quietly, "that if I'd swung the bat faster. If I'd paid attention sooner. If I'd—" He swallowed hard. "If I hadn't made it a joke all the time."

Mark's chest tightened.

"It wasn't a joke," Mark said. "Not to you."

Tommy's mouth twisted. "It was how I didn't break."

Mark looked at the jersey on the ground. Purple and gold, still bright. Still proud.

"They named the memorial after him," Tommy said suddenly. "They say his name out loud now like it's a donation."

Mark didn't answer.

Tommy's voice shook. "I should've been the one."

Mark turned to him sharply. "Don't."

Tommy flinched, like the word hit.

Mark forced his tone down. "Pecos made his choice," he said. "He didn't do it so you could trade places with him in your head forever."

Tommy blinked fast. His eyes were red-rimmed. "Then what am I supposed to do with it? With the fact that I'm still here and he's—"

"Carry it," Mark said, and hated how simple it sounded. "Carry it without turning it into a punishment."

Tommy laughed once, broken. "Easy for you to say, Captain."

Mark felt the old title land on him like a weight. He used to like it. He used to believe it meant something good.

Now it just meant the town expected him to keep taking hits.

Mark stood. "Come with us tonight," he said.

Tommy's brow furrowed. "Us?"

"Me and Alyssa," Mark said. "We're going to the cemetery."

Tommy swallowed. His throat bobbed. He nodded once.

"Okay," he whispered. "Okay."

*****

Marcus left on a Tuesday.

It felt wrong that it wasn't dramatic. No sirens. No fog. No purple glow in the trees like a warning. Just a gray bus in the station parking lot and a duffel bag slung over his shoulder.

Mark, Alyssa, and Tommy stood with him under a flickering overhead light. The station smelled like old coffee and diesel. A woman at the counter watched them like she expected trouble, which in Lowridge was a safe assumption.

Marcus looked healthier than he had when Mark first found him—less hollow, less haunted. The purple veins that used to map his skin had faded to faint lines you could miss if you didn't know where to look.

He rubbed the back of his neck, eyes on the bus door. "Feels weird," he admitted.

Tommy snorted. "Everything feels weird. That's the new normal."

Marcus's mouth twitched. Not a smile, exactly, but something close. "Yeah."

Alyssa stepped forward and hugged him before anyone could say something and make it awkward. Marcus stiffened for a second, like his body didn't know how to accept comfort, then his arms came up around her.

"Don't let them rewrite it," Alyssa murmured against his shoulder.

"I won't," Marcus said, voice rough. "You either."

She pulled back. Her eyes were shining. "Send letters," she demanded. "Not texts. Letters. Proof you exist."

Marcus huffed. "Okay, historian."

Mark watched, throat tight.

Marcus turned to him last.

For a moment neither of them spoke. Too much history lived between them—Marcus as the half-ghost who knew the routes, Mark as the one who'd dragged his friends into hell and back.

Marcus held Mark's gaze. "You did good," he said quietly.

Mark scoffed before he could stop himself. "Pecos did good."

Marcus nodded. "Pecos did the impossible. But you?" He lifted his chin slightly, like a coach spotting a player who didn't know he'd earned the starting spot. "You kept moving. That matters."

Mark's voice came out flat. "So you're just… gone."

Marcus exhaled. "I'm going to try being a person. A normal one."

"Do you even know how?" Tommy asked, half-bitter, half-awed.

Marcus shrugged. "Guess I'll learn."

Mark's chest tightened. "Where will you go?"

"Anywhere the ground doesn't know my name," Marcus said.

The bus driver called boarding.

Marcus picked up his duffel.

He looked at all three of them. "If the purple comes back—" he started.

"It won't," Alyssa said, too fast.

Marcus's eyes flicked to her, then softened. "If it does," he corrected gently, "call me. Don't try to be heroes alone."

Mark nodded.

Marcus climbed the steps, hesitated, then turned back once more. "Mark," he said.

Mark's throat tightened. "Yeah?"

Marcus's gaze was steady. "Leaving doesn't make you a traitor."

The words hit Mark hard enough that he forgot to breathe.

Before he could answer, Marcus was inside, and the bus door folded shut between them.

The engine rumbled. The bus pulled out of the station and turned onto the road like it had every right to go somewhere else.

Mark watched until the taillights disappeared.

Tommy wiped his eyes with the back of his hand and swore he wasn't crying. Alyssa stared at the empty space like she was memorizing it for later.

Mark just stood there, listening to the absence.

*****

That evening, the cemetery air was warmer than it had been in the morning, the sun low and gold through the trees. The world smelled like cut grass and exhaust and something faintly sweet from the wildflowers that had started to creep back in.

Alyssa carried the daisies. Tommy carried his jersey folded tight like a flag. Mark carried nothing but the weight in his chest.

They stopped at Pecos's memorial.

Mark crouched again, the way he had that morning, and this time he didn't force words right away. He let the silence be there. He let it hurt.

Alyssa knelt and laid the daisies on the stone.

"Normal flowers," she said quietly. "Like you wanted."

Mark glanced at her. "Did he tell you that?"

Alyssa's throat bobbed. "Not in words. But... you know. He always hated the purple."

Tommy stepped forward, hands shaking, and set his jersey beside the bowl. The gold numbers caught the light. For a second, it looked like any other memorial at any other cemetery.

Then Tommy's shoulders collapsed. He covered his face with both hands.

"I'm sorry," he whispered into his palms. "I'm sorry I didn't see it sooner. I'm sorry I made you do it."

Mark stood and put a hand on Tommy's shoulder. Tommy flinched, then leaned into it like he'd been waiting for permission to fall apart.

Alyssa wiped her face, furious at her own tears.

Mark stared at the ash.

He imagined Pecos's laugh. Pecos's calm voice. Pecos standing barefoot in the grass in the early chapters of this nightmare, eyes closed, listening to the land like it was music only he could hear.

"You held the line," Mark said softly. "You did. For all of us."

The words didn't fix anything. They didn't bring him back.

But they landed in the air like a promise.

As they turned to leave, a breeze moved through the cemetery. The daisies trembled. Tommy's jersey fluttered slightly.

For a split second, Mark felt something warm brush the back of his neck —like a hand, like a presence.

Not a voice. Not a ghost in the fog.

Just… a quiet acknowledgment. Like the field after a good play, when the world pauses and you know you're not alone out there.

Mark inhaled slowly and let the sensation pass without grabbing at it.

*****

His parents were in the kitchen when he got home.

That alone made Mark's stomach tighten. Lately, they moved around each other like strangers sharing a space they didn't understand. His mom cooked and cleaned and tried to keep routines alive. His dad worked longer hours at the auto shop, came home smelling like oil, and sat in front of the TV without turning the volume up.

Tonight, they sat at the table together.

Two mugs of coffee sat between them. It was almost funny, the effort. Like they'd rehearsed.

Mark stopped in the doorway.

His mom's eyes lit with a cautious hope that hurt to see. "Hey, honey."

His dad cleared his throat. "Mark."

Mark's hands curled into fists at his sides. "What's going on?"

His mom glanced at his dad, then back. "We... we wanted to talk. If that's okay."

Mark's heartbeat picked up, stupid and quick, like his body smelled danger in kindness.

His dad shifted, looking at the tabletop. "We've been—" He stopped. Started again. "We've been thinking. About everything. About Jason. About... what you went through."

Mark's throat tightened. The name still hurt in a place he couldn't reach.

His mom reached across the table, like she meant to take his hand. Mark stepped back before she could.

Her face fell.

Mark hated himself for it and couldn't stop.

"We just want to be a family again," she said, voice small.

His dad's jaw worked. "We weren't there," he admitted, and the words sounded like they cost him something. "We should've been there. We should've listened."

Mark swallowed hard. His mind flashed: his parents cheering in the stands while something beneath the field counted his brother's steps. His mom talking about scholarships like they were salvation. His dad telling Jason to toughen up after a hard hit.

They hadn't meant harm.

But the town didn't need villains. It needed people who would look away.

Mark's voice came out harsh. "I'm trying," he said. "I'm trying to be here, okay? But I can't—" He shook his head, searching for the right words and finding only the wrong ones. "I can't do the pretend thing."

His mom's eyes filled. "We're not pretending."

Mark flinched, because she believed that.

He stared at them, at the careful coffee mugs, at the way his dad's hands were clasped too tight, at the way his mom's shoulders were hunched like she was bracing for impact.

He could feel love in the room. He could also feel everything it couldn't erase.

"I'm not ready," Mark said, quieter now. "I don't know when I'll be ready."

His dad nodded once, stiff. "Okay."

His mom wiped her cheek fast, as if tears were another mess she could clean up. "Okay," she echoed.

Mark backed out of the kitchen and went to his room, closing the door behind him.

In the dark, he sat on his bed and listened to his own breathing.

He wasn't angry at them. Not exactly.

He was just tired.

*****

Friday came anyway.

Lowridge had tried to cancel the game. There were meetings. There were arguments. People said it was disrespectful. People said it was necessary. People said football was the only thing that kept the town from falling apart, which would've been funny if it hadn't been true for so long.

In the end, the lights came on.

They weren't as bright as they used to be. Some bulbs had burned out and hadn't been replaced. The scoreboard flickered. The band played with a kind of caution, like music might summon something.

Mark sat in the bleachers with Alyssa and Tommy, halfway up, far enough that he could see the whole field and the cemetery beyond the fence.

The cemetery was dark.

No purple glow. No pulsing light.

Just headstones and shadows and the shapes of trees.

A part of Mark waited for the pressure behind his eyes. Waited for the hum. Waited for the routes to wake up and remind him that nothing ever really ends.

The kickoff happened.

The ball arced through the air, clean and normal, and landed in a player's hands like it always had.

The crowd cheered—smaller, uneven. More human.

Mark watched the game like someone watching a movie of his own life. The new quarterback threw two interceptions. The defense missed tackles they would've made last season like their bodies had been guided by something stronger than practice.

Lowridge was… mediocre.

And every time they messed up, no purple flowers bloomed to reward them anyway. No perfect luck bent the play into place.

They lost by seven.

When the final whistle blew, there was a stunned pause, like the town didn't know what to do with failure without tragedy.

Then someone clapped.

A single clap, slow.

Another joined it.

Soon the bleachers filled with applause—not the roaring worship that used to shake Mark's ribs, but something quieter. Something real.

Mark felt his breath leave his lungs in a shaky exhale he hadn't realized he'd been holding for years.

Tommy turned to him, eyes shining. "We lost," he whispered, like it was a prayer.

Mark nodded, throat tight. "Yeah."

Alyssa's smile was small and sad and proud all at once. "And the sky didn't fall."

Mark looked past the field, past the fence, to the cemetery.

The headstones sat in the dark like they always had.

No audience. No hunger.

Just rest.

For the first time since Jason died, Mark believed—just a little—that the town might learn how to live without feeding something.

He stood to leave, and his hoodie pocket bumped against his thigh.

The envelope Alyssa had given him earlier.

His stomach tightened again.

As the crowd filed out, Mark pulled it out and stared at it under the weak stadium light. The paper was plain. The seal unbroken.

He should've waited until he got home.

He opened it anyway.

Inside was a letter. Official. Crisp. The kind of paper that felt expensive.

At the top, a crest. A college name that wasn't Lowridge. A place on a map that existed beyond this town's borders.

Mark's hands went cold.

CONGRATULATIONS, it began.

Mark's vision blurred. He read it again, slower, as if his brain didn't trust good news.

Admitted.

Scholarship consideration.

Orientation dates.

A life that wasn't here.

Alyssa leaned in, reading over his shoulder. Her breath caught. "Mark…"

Tommy stared, then let out a disbelieving laugh. "Dude," he said softly. "You're out."

The word out landed like a door unlocking.

Mark looked up.

Across the field, the highway beyond the stadium was visible in the distance, a strip of dark road reflecting faint light. A route that led somewhere else. A route the land didn't own.

The night wind moved through the bleachers, cool against Mark's face. For a moment, the air smelled like grass and popcorn and fall—normal Friday night things.

And beneath it, faint as memory, he felt that same warm brush at the back of his neck.

Not a ghost.

Not a command.

Just a presence that felt like approval. Like forgiveness. Like his brother, somewhere beyond the routes, finally letting him go.

Mark folded the letter carefully and held it against his chest.

He didn't know how to leave. He didn't know how to be a person outside the town's hunger.

But he knew, in the quiet after the whistle, that staying wouldn't bring anyone back.

And leaving didn't mean the story was over.

It meant the story was finally his.

CHAPTER 32: ECHOES OF SACRIFICE — FINAL POLISH

The fog didn't vanish when the sirens stopped.

It thinned the way a bruise fades—slowly, unevenly—leaving patches of gray in the low places and a sweetness in the air that didn't belong to any season. When Mark Rivers stepped out onto his porch, the neighborhood looked almost ordinary again: wet leaves pasted to sidewalks, holiday lights still hung from gutters because nobody had the energy to take them down, and a crow perched on the power line as if it had always owned the street.

But the purple was everywhere if you knew how to look.

A vine had crept up the mailbox post and died there, shriveled into a black thread that glittered faint violet when it caught the light. A cluster of petals clung to the curb at the edge of the storm drain like something that had washed up and refused to be washed away. And down by the old water tower, the trees still leaned inward, listening.

Mark stood very still and let the quiet settle into his bones.

Some part of him expected to feel the pull again—the faint tug behind his eyes, the sensation of routes opening under his feet like hidden trapdoors. He expected the town to inhale and hold its breath, counting the way the stadium counted, one-two, one-two, like a cadence that could start a play or start a prayer.

Nothing happened.

That should have been relief.

Instead it made him uneasy, as if he'd woken in a house where the fire had gone out and couldn't remember whether it died on its own or whether something had put it out.

His mother's car sat in the driveway, dew beading on the hood. She hadn't slept. Mark could see that in the way the curtains moved upstairs—small, restless shifts—like she was pacing room to room, looking for something to fix even though the part that needed fixing wasn't a thing you could hold.

Jason's photo still sat on the entryway table. Someone had dusted it. Someone had straightened the frame.

Mark hadn't.

He couldn't decide if he was afraid to touch it, or afraid of what it meant that he no longer felt afraid.

A knock came from the side of the house—soft, then firmer.

Tommy stood at the gate with a paper bag in one hand and his ring in the other, pulling it off and sliding it back on like the metal was the only thing keeping his fingers from shaking. His eyes were bloodshot, his hair still damp as if he'd showered for the first time in days and hadn't felt any cleaner afterward.

"You eat?" Tommy asked.

Mark shook his head.

Tommy held up the bag. "I stole breakfast from my own kitchen. It's either heroic or criminal. Hard to tell anymore."

Mark almost smiled. Almost.

Tommy looked past him toward the street, toward the thin fog pooling in the gutters. "They're doing it at the field," he said.

Mark didn't ask what "it" was. He knew.

The town had always used the field as its altar. They might never call it that, but they knew where to gather when they needed to feel like one body. When the land had been hungry, the crowd had fed it without noticing. When the land had started taking openly, the town had panicked and splintered and called it an emergency.

Now, with the immediate terror gone, Lowridge was doing what it did best: turning catastrophe into ceremony.

"Harold called," Tommy added. His voice tightened around the name, not from respect or dislike exactly—something older, like a kid saying the principal's name out loud. "Said we should come. Said we… should be seen."

Mark's throat went dry. "Be seen doing what?"

Tommy's mouth twitched. "Standing in front of everybody while they decide what story to tell."

Mark looked at the bag in Tommy's hand. Grease had soaked through in one corner. The smell was familiar—eggs, sausage, something fried. Normal life. An attempt.

He took the bag and held it like it weighed more than it should.

"Where's Alyssa?" Mark asked.

Tommy's gaze slid away. "Library," he said. "She's been there since dawn. Like if she finds the right paper, the right line, she can prove to the town that it has to stop lying."

"That won't work," Mark said, quiet.

Tommy shrugged. "Yeah. She knows. She's doing it anyway."

Mark nodded once. He understood that kind of stubbornness. He'd worn it like shoulder pads.

They walked together down the street, not talking much. Every few houses they passed a porch with a candle on it, flame steady in daylight because people were afraid to let the dark come back. A couple of yards had fresh ribbons tied to trees—purple and gold, of course—because Lowridge couldn't mourn without branding.

At the end of Maple, the road opened into the main drag. The new tech corridor lay farther out, glass and steel and optimism, the place the town advertised when it wanted investors and new families. You could almost see the future from here: clean sidewalks, chain coffee, bright signs promising growth.

Closer in, Lowridge looked like it always had—old brick, old wood, old money tucked into corners where it could watch.

And on Main Street, taped to the window of the diner, someone had written in thick marker: WE LOST GOOD KIDS.

Under it, smaller and sharper: NOT THE TOWN.

A second note had been slapped over that one at an angle: THE TOWN MADE THEM.

Tommy stopped and stared. His ring slid down his finger and clinked softly against his knuckle. "We're really doing this," he said, like he couldn't believe the town was capable of arguing about the dead in public.

Mark kept walking. "It was always there," he said. "We just didn't have a reason to look."

The stadium parking lot was half full. People moved in clusters, speaking in tight voices, glancing over their shoulders as if the fog might still be chasing them. A few news vans had slipped in from out of town, hungry for a "small-town horror" segment they could package and forget.

Mark saw the mayor near the gate, wearing a neat coat and a face that had practiced sympathy in the mirror. Booster club men stood nearby, shoulders squared, arms folded, measuring the crowd like they were counting votes. A group of teens from the band huddled together, eyes wide, whispering. Some wore black armbands. Some wore their Lions hoodies like armor.

In the middle of it all, the field lay green and damp under a thin wash of sunlight.

The cemetery fence was visible beyond the far end zone.

The flowers at the edge of the graves were dimmer than they'd been on Hollow's Eve, but they were not gone. They held their color the way an old stain held. They waited.

Mark felt something in his chest tighten—not a pull, not a command. More like recognition. A scar remembering what cut it.

They entered through the side gate and found Alyssa near the fifty-yard line, jaw set, hair pulled back, the grimoire tucked in her bag like contraband. She looked up when she saw them, and her expression softened for a fraction of a second.

"Please tell me you slept," Tommy said.

Alyssa's smile was all teeth. "Please tell me you've met me."

She pointed with her chin toward the temporary podium set up near the sideline. A microphone. Folding chairs. A row of framed photos on easels— faces of boys and men who had once worn the blue and gold.

There were too many.

Mark's gaze caught on Eli Carter's photo—captain's grin, bright eyes that didn't know what was coming. A photo of Marcus Webb too, younger, before the town had half-killed him and made him something in-between. Mark's stomach clenched when he saw Jason.

His brother looked like a joke Jason would have made about himself: all confidence, all light, as if he could outrun anything.

Mark swallowed. "Where's Pecos's family?" he asked.

Alyssa glanced toward the bleachers. "Front row," she said. "His mom hasn't stopped holding his jersey. Like if she puts it down, she has to admit there's nothing inside it."

Tommy's hand tightened around his ring.

Mark looked across the field.

Pecos wasn't here. Not in a body. Not in a chair. Not in any way the town could point to and pretend. Pecos was a name in the air, an absence big enough to shape everything around it.

"He's not dead," Tommy said, too quickly, as if saying it loud could make it true.

Alyssa didn't answer right away. Her eyes flicked to Mark. "He's not here," she said finally, which was the only honest version.

They stood in silence as the crowd filled in.

Harold Reed moved through it like someone who belonged to both halves of the town. He wore his sheriff's jacket, but the badge looked heavier than it used to. He paused near the mayor, said something low. The mayor's smile tightened.

Then Harold approached them.

His gaze went to Mark first. "You're here," he said.

Mark nodded.

Harold's eyes moved to Alyssa. "And you," he said, and there was something like apology in it. "Your grandfather would've…"

Alyssa cut in, voice flat. "He would've wanted the truth. Not a speech."

Harold flinched, then nodded once as if accepting the hit. "We're going to try," he said. "That's why I asked you to come. People trust you." His gaze returned to Mark. "They trusted Jason. They trust you."

Mark felt the old weight settle—legacy, expectation, the town's hands on his shoulders.

He didn't move.

Harold lowered his voice. "They're going to tell a story today," he said. "If you don't speak, it won't be your story."

Alyssa leaned in. "And if he speaks, they'll boo him."

Harold's mouth tightened. "Some will," he admitted. "Some will listen."

Tommy raised a hand, ring glinting. "And some will act like this was a weather event."

Harold's eyes flicked to Tommy, and for the first time he looked tired enough to be human. "Yeah," he said. "That too."

A whistle sounded—sharp, familiar. A reflex ran through Mark's body like muscle memory.

Coach Whitman walked onto the field.

His posture was still military-straight, but his face had aged in the last week. Lines had carved themselves deeper around his eyes, not from time but from strain. He took the microphone, and the speakers popped.

"My people," Coach began.

A ripple moved through the crowd—approval, discomfort, devotion. Coach had always spoken like he owned the field, like the field owed him answers.

"We're here today to honor the boys and men we lost," he said. His gaze moved over the photos. "Champions. Lions. Sons. Brothers."

Mark's hands clenched at his sides. He could feel the town leaning in, hungry for familiar language. For comfort.

Coach continued. "We've been through a hard season," he said, and the word season landed wrong, too close to football, too close to harvest. "We've seen things that don't make sense. We've seen tragedy. And we've held together because that's who we are."

A murmur of agreement.

"The investigators—" Coach started.

Alyssa muttered, "Here we go."

Coach's tone stayed steady. "—are still looking into what happened. We don't have all the answers yet."

That was a lie that sounded like professionalism. A lie with clean edges.

"But what we do have," Coach said, lifting his chin, "is our community. Our faith. Our tradition."

The crowd clapped. Not everyone. Not the front row where Pecos's mother sat with her hands locked around cloth.

Coach held up a hand. "We will not let outsiders turn our pain into their story," he said, eyes cutting toward the news vans. "We will not let rumors poison our kids."

Mark felt his stomach twist. Rumors. Like the flowers were gossip.

Coach's voice softened, as if offering mercy. "We will heal," he said. "We will move forward. We will honor them the way we always have—by being proud."

Proud.

Pride had been the town's favorite drug. Pride was what made people swallow questions.

Coach stepped back from the microphone. "Mayor Callahan will speak," he announced.

The mayor came forward and took the mic, hands clasped, face solemn. His speech was polished, full of words like resilience and progress and partnership. He mentioned grants. He mentioned safety improvements. He mentioned a memorial plaque that would be installed near the stadium entrance, like metal could substitute for honesty.

He did not mention the flowers.

He did not mention the graves.

He did not say the word pact.

Mark could feel Alyssa vibrating beside him, a contained rage that wanted an outlet.

Tommy whispered, "If he says 'moving forward' one more time, I'm going to move forward into his microphone."

The mayor finished to polite applause. Then he stepped aside and looked toward Harold.

Harold took the microphone like it was a weapon he didn't want to draw.

"Most of you know me," Harold said. His voice was rougher than usual. "You know my family. You know I've served this town a long time."

A few nods. A few mutters.

Harold's gaze swept the crowd. "I can't tell you everything," he said, and Mark felt the old system push back inside that sentence—law, liability, the town protecting itself. Harold inhaled, then corrected himself, and the honesty in the shift hit harder than any confession Mark had heard. "No. Let me say it right. I can tell you everything. I'm choosing to."

A ripple ran through the bleachers.

Harold continued, voice steadying as if he'd made his decision and now he could breathe. "A lot of people are going to want easy answers," he said. "Accidents. Weather. Panic. Anything that lets us pretend this was nobody's fault."

A man in a booster jacket called out, "It wasn't!"

Harold's eyes fixed on him. "It wasn't?" he asked. "Then tell me why I have twenty-seven open files in my office—twenty-seven—full of young men who died in ways nobody investigated because we didn't want to see the pattern."

Silence fell.

Harold's jaw tightened. "We told ourselves it was random," he said. "We told ourselves it was bad luck. We told ourselves it was the price of playing hard."

Mark felt his pulse tick in his throat.

Harold's voice dropped. "It wasn't random," he said. "And it wasn't luck."

Alyssa's breath caught beside Mark.

Harold looked at the photos—Jason, Eli, the others—and for a second his face cracked. Then he leaned into the microphone.

"There is something wrong with this land," he said.

The crowd reacted like someone had stepped on a nerve. Voices rose. A laugh, sharp and disbelieving. A woman whispered, "Oh Lord." Someone hissed, "Don't say that."

Harold didn't stop. "I'm not asking you to believe in ghosts," he said. "I'm asking you to believe in evidence. In history. In what we've all watched and refused to name."

He lifted a folder—thin, cheap paper, a symbol of authority. "We have records," he said. "We have stories. We have graves."

His gaze lifted, and for the first time he looked straight toward the cemetery fence, as if willing the town to do the same.

"Those flowers," Harold said, and the word landed heavy, "are not decoration."

A woman in the stands stood up. "Don't," she said, voice shaking. "Don't make this about that."

Harold's eyes softened. "Ma'am," he said, gentle, "it's been about that the whole time."

The crowd swelled with noise—anger, fear, denial.

The mayor stepped toward Harold, face tight. "Sheriff," he said into the mic, too quiet for the speakers but loud enough for those close. "This isn't appropriate."

Harold looked at him. "Appropriate is how we got here," he said, and stepped back.

Alyssa's hand touched Mark's sleeve. "They're going to stop him," she whispered.

Harold turned his head toward Mark. No words. Just a look that said: Now.

Mark's legs felt heavy.

He didn't want the microphone. He didn't want the eyes. He didn't want the town's hunger to settle on him again.

But he thought of Pecos, not here. Thought of Jason's thread in the web, straining. Thought of Eli Carter stepping off the field like he'd been called.

Mark walked forward.

Some people clapped because they thought this was the part where the quarterback gave a hopeful speech. Some people groaned. Some people watched with the cold interest of a jury.

Mark took the microphone.

The field smelled like damp turf and old sweat and something floral that wouldn't leave.

He looked out at the bleachers and saw his mother, face pale. Saw his father's rigid posture. Saw Pecos's mother holding fabric like it was flesh. Saw Alyssa's aunt at the back, half-hidden under a scarf, eyes sharp as knives.

He saw kids his age with phones half-raised, ready to record. Ready to turn truth into content.

He saw old men who had watched decades of championships and wanted to keep watching.

Mark's throat tightened.

He could lie. He could give them comfort. He could say moving forward, healing, proud.

He could protect them from the ugliness of what they'd helped build.

He remembered the rule—confession and honesty broke the conduit. Not like salt broke a curse in a movie. Not clean. Not instant. But real.

The land fed on what was hidden, what was swallowed.

Mark inhaled and felt the air scratch his lungs, sweet and bitter.

He spoke.

"My brother died three years ago," he said.

The crowd went quiet in a way Mark had never heard during a game. Even the news cameras seemed to still.

Mark kept his voice level. Thoughtful. Restrained. "They told us it was an accident," he said. "They told us there was nothing to investigate. They told us to honor him by winning."

His father flinched.

Mark continued. "I believed them," he said. "Because believing them meant I didn't have to ask what it cost."

A murmur rolled through the crowd, uncomfortable.

Mark's hands tightened on the sides of the podium. "I've stood on this field my whole life," he said. "I've heard you cheer like you were part of us. Like you loved us."

He looked at the booster men. The mayor. Coach Whitman.

"And maybe you do," he said. "But love isn't what kept this going."

A sharp intake of breath. Someone muttered, "Watch your mouth." Mark didn't.

Mark's voice stayed steady. "We all knew something was wrong," he said. "We joked about it. We whispered about it. We told our kids the flowers were lucky."

He glanced toward the cemetery fence. "We used them as a symbol," he said. "We put them on our signs. We painted them on our trailers."

Alyssa's smile flashed, quick and fierce.

Mark leaned forward. "Those flowers aren't lucky," he said. "They're doors."

The crowd reacted—confusion, anger, fear.

Mark's jaw tightened. "They're how it gets in," he said. "Blood and petals. That's how it starts."

A cry rose from somewhere in the stands. A woman sobbed.

Mark kept going, because stopping would be mercy and mercy was how the town survived.

"Some of us got taken," he said. "Some of us got used to take others. Some of us got buried, and then the flowers grew, and everybody pretended it was pretty."

He paused. The silence stretched.

Mark's voice softened, not into comfort but into something raw. "Jason tried to warn me," he said. "Pecos tried to warn me. People have been warning us for a hundred years."

He looked at Harold, who stood with his jaw clenched like he was holding back a storm.

Mark faced the crowd again. "If you want to heal," he said, "you stop asking for a story that lets you stay innocent."

The mayor stepped forward, face hard. "Mark," he said, and his tone carried a warning.

Mark ignored him.

"You want to fix this?" Mark asked the bleachers. "You say it out loud. You admit what you did. You admit what you let happen."

He swallowed. His next words tasted like blood even though his mouth was dry.

"My family benefited," Mark said. "From the legacy. From the attention. From the scholarships. From the pride."

His mother's hands went to her mouth.

Mark's voice cracked for the first time, barely. "And I hated it," he said, "but I still took it."

A shiver ran through the crowd—not everyone, but enough that Mark felt it like a wave.

He heard it then, faint and strange: the hum under the field, the old vibration of the routes.

Not commanding. Listening.

Mark forced the truth through anyway.

"You're not cursed because you're special," he said. "You're cursed because you kept feeding it."

A man shouted, "That's not true!"

A teenage girl yelled back, "Yes it is!"

The crowd began to split in real time—voices rising, people turning to argue with neighbors. It didn't look like a riot. It looked like a town finally seeing itself in a mirror and not liking the reflection.

Coach Whitman strode forward, face red. "That's enough," he snapped, reaching for the microphone cord.

Harold stepped between them.

Coach stopped short, stunned, as if the sheriff's refusal was more shocking than any monster.

Harold's voice was low. "Let him finish," he said.

Coach's jaw worked. His eyes flashed toward the mayor, toward the boosters, toward the crowd. For the first time, Mark saw fear in him—not fear of the supernatural, fear of losing control.

Mark took one more breath.

"I don't know what happens next," he said, and that was the most honest sentence he'd spoken on that field in his life. "Pecos is missing. People are dead. The flowers are still there."

He glanced toward the cemetery, toward the purple that wouldn't fade. "This isn't over because we want it to be," he said.

He looked back at the town. "But it won't get to hide in us anymore," he said. "Not if we stop hiding from each other."

He stepped back.

For a second, nobody moved. Then the noise came—some applause, sharp and furious; some boos; some sobs; some arguments that broke into shouting.

Mark felt strangely hollow. Not relieved. Not proud. Just emptied out, like he'd finally opened a fist he'd kept clenched for years.

Alyssa grabbed his elbow as he stepped off the platform. "You just set the town on fire," she said, voice tight.

Mark looked at her. "It was already burning," he said.

Tommy let out a breath that was almost a laugh. "He did it," he whispered, and slid his ring onto his finger with a shake.

They moved off to the side as the crowd churned.

Pecos's mother stood up slowly from the front row. She walked to the fence between the bleachers and the field like she was walking to a grave.

Coach Whitman tried to speak again, voice raised, but people were talking over him now. The mayor's face had gone flat, calculating.

Harold stayed near the podium, hands at his sides, not reaching for his gun, not reaching for control. Just present.

Pecos's mother looked at Mark. Her eyes were swollen, but clear.

"My boy," she said, and her voice cracked on the word, "is he…"

Mark's throat tightened. He could have lied. He could have given her comfort.

Instead he gave her the only thing he had left that might matter.

"We're still looking," he said. "He's still… there. Somewhere."

Her hands tightened around the jersey. She nodded once, as if she'd expected no less than uncertainty. "Bring him back," she said. Not a plea. A command. A mother's faith in anger.

Mark nodded. "I'm trying," he said.

She leaned forward, close enough that Mark could smell laundry soap on the cloth. "And those flowers," she whispered, eyes flicking toward the cemetery. "If they take him… I'll burn this town down myself."

Mark didn't doubt her.

Alyssa's aunt moved closer from the back, face shadowed. The scarf fell away enough for Mark to see the faint tremor in her hands, the way her eyes tracked something behind the living crowd.

"They're still listening," she murmured, voice like gravel. "Even if they're quieter."

Alyssa stiffened. "Aunt May," she said, and the name sounded like a warning and an anchor all at once.

May's gaze met Mark's. "Truth helps," she said. "It weakens the grip. But it also wakes the ones who've been sleeping."

Tommy frowned. "Great," he said. "So honesty is both the cure and the alarm system."

May's mouth twitched. "Welcome to Lowridge," she said.

The mayor pushed back toward the microphone, voice tight with damage control. "This gathering is not—" he began.

Alyssa stepped forward before she could stop herself. She didn't grab the mic. She didn't need to. Her voice carried anyway, sharp as a snapped branch.

"Then make it something," she said. "You're going to put up a plaque, right? You said it yourself. A memorial at the stadium entrance."

The mayor's eyes narrowed. "That will be handled by the committee—"

"Committee," Tommy repeated, disgusted.

Harold lifted a hand—not for silence, exactly. For order. It worked in a way Mark hadn't expected. People knew that gesture. People had obeyed it their whole lives.

"This isn't a court," Harold said, voice loud enough to cut through the chatter, "but it is the town. And the town gets a say."

A ripple moved through the bleachers. Suspicion. Hope. Anger.

Harold looked at the framed photos again, and his voice roughened. "We're not burying them twice," he said. "Not with words."

The mayor took a step forward. "Sheriff, you can't just—"

Harold stared him down. "Watch me," he said, and there was no heat in it, only fatigue and resolve.

Pecos's mother lifted her son's jersey higher, like a flag. "No more pretty lies," she said, and the tremor in her hands didn't make the words smaller. It made them heavier.

A man near the booster club shouted, "You want to put superstition on a memorial?"

A teenage girl snapped back, "You want to put nothing?"

The argument rose—two sides forming the way teams formed across a line. Some people started leaving, faces hard, muttering about outsiders and hysteria. Others stayed rooted, like something in them had finally decided to stop being polite.

Harold's voice cut through again. "Listen," he said. "This isn't about believing in monsters. It's about refusing to lie."

He pointed toward the cemetery fence. "If the plaque says 'tragic accidents' and 'unexplained events,' then it's another program. Another keepsake. Another way to keep feeding it."

Coach Whitman's face went rigid. "We honor them with tradition," he said.

Harold's gaze flicked to him. "Tradition is what killed them," he said, and the silence that followed was immediate and brutal.

Harold turned back to the crowd. "We vote," he said. "Right now. Not a committee vote. A town vote."

The mayor sputtered, "This is not—"

Harold didn't look at him. "Show of hands," Harold said, voice steady. "All in favor of the memorial acknowledging the truth—no euphemisms, no 'accidents'—the truth about what happened here and what the flowers mean… raise your hand."

For a heartbeat, nobody moved.

Then Pecos's mother raised her hand, arm shaking, jersey in the other.

Alyssa's hand went up.

Tommy's hand went up.

Mark's hand went up—slow, deliberate, as if he was signing something in blood.

A scattering followed. Teenagers first. Then a few parents. Then a couple of older men who looked like they'd swallowed their pride and found it bitter.

Booster club men glared around, counting. Some raised their hands anyway, furious at themselves for it.

Harold scanned the crowd, jaw clenched. He counted under his breath. Mark could see it in his eyes—numbers, not hope.

Harold lowered his hand. "Hands down," he said.

A wave of movement as arms dropped.

"All in favor of keeping the memorial… neutral," Harold said, and the word neutral sounded like a coward's prayer, "keeping it a standard tragedy memorial—raise your hand."

More hands rose than Mark expected. Fast hands. Confident hands. Hands attached to faces that looked relieved to be given permission to stay asleep.

The two sides hung there for a moment, arms up, like the town was split down the fifty-yard line.

Harold counted again.

His face tightened.

The mayor's mouth curved into something like victory.

Then Harold exhaled, long and hard, and lowered his own hand.

"Truth," Harold said, and his voice didn't lift, it just settled. "Wins. By three."

A sound rose—half cheer, half sob, half anger. People shouted. People cursed. A few stormed out, shoulders hard like they'd been betrayed. Others hugged, tight and shaking, like they'd been holding their breath for years and didn't know how to breathe right.

Coach Whitman stared as if someone had taken his playbook and lit it on fire.

The mayor's face went pale, then blank again, already recalculating.

Harold lifted his chin and spoke once more, quieter now but clear. "Put the truth on it," he said. "If we're going to build anything, we build it on what actually happened."

The ceremony broke apart into clusters—families hugging, people arguing, old friends turning away from each other. The town's unity had always been a performance. Now the stage was showing its seams.

Mark walked with Alyssa and Tommy toward the far end zone where the fence separated the field from the cemetery.

The ground near the fence looked… different.

Not healed. Not clean. But altered.

Patches of purple growth had turned gray, brittle. In other places, the petals still held color, but they no longer glowed with that private light. They looked like flowers again—beautiful, stubborn, wrong.

Mark's eyes dropped to a strip of turf near the track where the purple had once threaded like veins.

A thin blade of grass there was green—real green, bright in a way that didn't match the season, the kind of green you saw in early spring when the world decided to try again.

Mark stared at it too long.

Alyssa crouched and studied a clump near the fence line. She didn't touch it. She didn't have to.

"They're still conduits," she said softly. "Even if the signal is weaker. It's like… the network lost its voice, but the wires are still in the walls."

Mark stared at the cemetery beyond. Headstones. Rows. A grid that used to be an audience.

He felt, faintly, the routes under his feet—not pulling, just present. Like veins in stone.

Alyssa reached into her bag and pulled out a small bottle of water—clear, ordinary. Mark recognized it: the water they'd used in the circle, the water that hadn't soaked into the ground like it was sitting on glass.

"I filled it from the creek," Alyssa said. Her voice was quiet. "The one that runs past the old church. The one May says still remembers what the land used to be."

Tommy glanced at her. "You're going to bless the field?" he asked, half-mocking, half-hopeful.

Alyssa's eyes flicked to him. "Don't start," she said. "Not today."

Mark understood. Not because he believed in magic the way a story believed in it, but because he'd seen rules. He'd seen the way honesty snapped threads. He'd seen the way water could sit on soil like a boundary.

Alyssa uncapped the bottle. She looked at Mark. "You said it out loud," she said. "Now we do something with it."

Mark nodded once.

Alyssa stepped close to the fence and poured a thin line of water along the base, slow and steady. The water didn't spread. It drew a clean dark line in the earth like ink.

For a second, nothing happened.

Then a breeze moved through the cemetery—a small, real wind, not the breath of the fog. The brittle gray petals shivered and collapsed like ash. A faint sweetness lifted, as if the ground exhaled.

And along the edge of Alyssa's dark water line, the green showed again —one more stubborn blade pushing up through the place where purple had clung.

Mark's skin prickled.

Not with fear.

With sensation—like a limb waking up after numbness.

He could feel the routes shift, minute, like a muscle unclenching. He didn't see the web the way he'd seen it in the shadow realm. He didn't want to.

But he felt something ease.

Tommy swallowed. "Did we just... do something?" he asked.

Alyssa's smile was faint, exhausted. "Something small," she said. "And small is all we get for now."

Mark stared at the line of water. "Will it come back?" he asked.

May's voice drifted from behind them. "If you feed it," she said. "It always comes back if you feed it."

Mark turned.

May stood at the edge of the track, hands in her coat pockets, eyes fixed on the cemetery like she could see through dirt. "The land doesn't forget," she said. "But it can heal if you stop making it carry your lies."

Alyssa's jaw tightened. "And if we don't?" she asked.

May's gaze shifted to the field, to the bleachers, to the people still arguing in knots. "Then the next time the fog rolls thick," she said, "you'll hear the old cadence again."

Mark's mouth went dry.

He looked back toward the crowd. Toward Coach Whitman. Toward the mayor. Toward the booster men already pulling each other into tight circles, already working on the next story—except now they had to work harder. Now the town had voted.

Lowridge would try to forget. Lowridge would try to clean its hands.

But Mark had said it out loud. The conduit had heard.

And the town—by three shaking hands' worth of courage—had chosen to write the truth where everybody entering the stadium would have to see it.

Mark turned to Alyssa and Tommy.

"We're not done," he said.

Tommy's ring clicked against his finger as he nodded. "No," he said, voice low. "We're not."

Alyssa shouldered her bag. "Next step," she said, sarcasm returning like armor, "we find out what the town buried besides bodies."

Mark looked toward the cemetery, toward the stubborn purple that still clung to stone.

In the pale daylight, the flowers didn't glow.

But Mark could feel them listening.

And somewhere—somewhere behind the fence, somewhere under the ground, somewhere in the routes that still ran like veins through Lowridge —a missing boy waited.

The crowd began to thin, leaving behind scattered programs and trampled grass and a silence that felt like the end of a game and the beginning of something worse.

Mark took one more look at Jason's photo on the easel.

Jason's grin didn't change.

But for the first time in years, Mark didn't feel like the grin was a command.

It was just a memory.

And memories, Mark realized, could be anchors—or they could be chains.

He turned away and walked off the field with his friends, into a town that was no longer allowed to pretend.

CHAPTER 33: THE JOURNEY FORWARD

Three months later, the cemetery looked like a place you could breathe.

The first time Mark Rivers noticed it, he didn't trust it. He stood at the chain-link fence where the football field ended and the graves began, and he waited for the air to turn sweet-bitter again—waited for the faint pressure behind his eyes, the sense of something listening through the ground.

It didn't come.

Instead, wind moved through the grass like it was allowed to. Real grass. Green in uneven patches where the earth had been blackened and tired, pushing up through the scar like stubborn hair. Dandelions dotted the edges of the headstones. A couple of daffodils—bright, ordinary—had been planted near the newer graves, their yellow heads nodding like they didn't know the rules Lowridge used to live by.

There were still places where the soil looked wrong if you stared too long. A faint gray sheen under the surface. A stubborn line of dirt that wouldn't take seed. It wasn't magic anymore—at least not the way it had been. It was damage. The kind you couldn't sweep off a sidewalk.

But it wasn't purple.

Mark kept his hands in his hoodie pocket and watched a groundskeeper —Mr. Doran from the parks department—push a wheelbarrow of mulch along the fence line. He moved slower than he used to, shoulders a little rounded, like the last few months had put a weight in his spine. He paused, wiped his forehead with the back of his wrist, and looked out over the field with an expression that was half grief and half stubborn irritation.

"Never thought I'd see the day," Mr. Doran muttered, not looking at Mark, "when this town spent money on a cemetery before it spent money on new bleachers."

Mark almost smiled.

"Bleachers were falling apart," Mark said.

"Bleachers always fall apart," Mr. Doran replied. He jabbed a shovel into the mulch like it offended him personally. "They just usually fall apart after a championship, not after… all that."

All that.

That was what people called it when they couldn't stand saying the real words.

Mark turned his gaze back to the field.

The far end zone didn't look like an end zone anymore.

It was still painted—faint lines, faded numbers, the ghost of the Lions logo you could see if the light hit at the right angle—but the town had carved a new shape into it. Wooden planters sat where the tackling dummies used to be. A half-circle of stone benches faced a small, simple plaque that didn't have a sponsor's name on it.

Behind the plaque, a garden had been planted.

Not purple flowers. Not anything that tried too hard.

Wildflowers. Native stuff, Mrs. Lowell from the high school science department had insisted. Coneflowers and black-eyed Susans. Milkweed because she said the monarchs needed it and because Lowridge needed to remember that something could survive without being fed blood and attention.

A memorial garden at the edge of the altar.

It would have felt symbolic if Mark didn't know how literal it was.

Tommy came up behind him, stepping light on the track as if he didn't want to make noise in the wrong place.

He held a plastic bag from the gas station—two bottled waters and a pack of gummy worms, because Tommy's idea of emotional support was always sugar and something stupid.

"How's it look?" Tommy asked, then immediately added, "Don't say 'better.' Better feels like a trap."

Mark took a bottle of water. The plastic crackled in his grip. "It looks… different," he said.

Tommy's shoulders loosened a fraction. "Different I can handle."

They stood there in the early afternoon sun while the town moved in the background—cars passing, people pretending they weren't watching, kids on bikes cutting through the parking lot even though the sign said NO TRESPASSING. The sign had been there for years. Nobody had ever listened to it. Lowridge didn't listen to rules unless they were painted on the field.

"Coach Whitman drove by my house yesterday," Tommy said.

Mark glanced at him. "In his truck?"

"Yeah," Tommy said, mouth twisting. "Real slow. Like he wanted to see if my lawn was still loyal."

Mark snorted once, then caught himself. Humor still felt wrong sometimes. Like laughing too loud might wake something up.

Tommy popped a gummy worm into his mouth and chewed with unnecessary aggression. "My dad says the boosters are broke," he said. "Not broke-broke, but… broke enough that they're mad."

"That's good," Mark said.

Tommy raised his eyebrows. "You just said good."

Mark shrugged. "Yeah. It's good."

Tommy looked out at the garden, at the plaque. "The town's income dropped," he said, like he'd been reading numbers the way Alyssa read old journals. "No playoffs, no big sponsorships, fewer tourists. People don't come here to watch high school football if the headline on Google is 'CURSED TOWN.'"

Mark's throat tightened at the word cursed, spoken out loud in daylight. It still felt like daring.

"But," Tommy continued, "my mom says the diner's been busier on weekends because people from the highway stop in now. Not for games. Just… because it's there. It's normal. And Mr. Patel opened that little hardware spot where the trophy shop used to be."

Mark stared. "He actually did it?"

Tommy nodded. "Yeah. He said he was tired of selling foam fingers in a town where fingers got taken."

Mark swallowed.

The trophy shop had been a shrine. Rows of shiny cups and framed photos of smiling boys, all of it polished until you could see your own face reflected in the lie. Mark hadn't been inside since Jason died.

A hardware store was… practical.

Boring.

Necessary.

It made something in Mark's chest unclench.

Alyssa arrived late, as usual, because Alyssa had been late to everything except the truth.

She walked across the track with her bag slung over one shoulder, hair pulled back, eyes sharp. The grimoire was gone—burned, buried, whatever version of ending they'd chosen for it—but Alyssa carried something else now: notebooks. Legal pads. Folders. The weight of someone who'd decided the way to fight a curse was to document the town so it couldn't lie about itself again.

She stopped beside them and looked at the cemetery. Her expression softened in a way that didn't happen often anymore.

"It's working," she said quietly.

Mark didn't ask what she meant. The land. The honesty. The small things.

Tommy flicked a gummy worm at her. She caught it without looking.

"Don't celebrate," Tommy warned. "Celebrating feels like a trap."

Alyssa popped the gummy worm into her mouth anyway. "You're both exhausting," she said, and it was almost normal enough to hurt.

They walked the fence line together.

A few people were out there planting—quiet volunteers, mostly older women and teenagers who looked like they didn't know how to be teenagers anymore. Sheriff Harold Reed stood near the gate, hands on his hips, talking to Mr. Doran with the exhausted patience of a man who'd spent his whole life trying to keep a town safe from itself.

Harold spotted Mark and lifted his chin. Not a smile. Not a speech. Just acknowledgment.

Mark nodded back.

They didn't talk about the night the town fractured. They didn't talk about the way the mayor's office had tried to spin everything and failed because too many people had heard the truth in real time. They didn't talk about the meetings afterward, the arguments, the vote—narrow, ugly, honest—that decided the memorial would include the real story, not the sanitized version.

Mark could still hear it sometimes: the crowd splitting into two halves, the sound of a town realizing it wasn't one body anymore.

He didn't miss the unity.

Unity had been the lie.

*****

Mark's room looked like it belonged to a person who was leaving.

Boxes stacked against the wall. Posters peeled down. A duffel bag open on the bed like a mouth waiting to be fed. His football cleats sat by the door, mud still in the grooves, because Mark hadn't been able to bring himself to clean them yet. Cleaning them felt like deciding what they were.

Were they just shoes?

Or were they a relic?

Downstairs, his mother moved in the kitchen—soft footsteps, cabinets opening and closing with careful quiet. She didn't ask him to stay anymore. She didn't tell him he was abandoning the family. She didn't say, "Jason would've—" the way she used to, as if Jason's memory was a leash she could pull to keep Mark in place.

Instead, she cooked.

She made food and left it on the counter like an offering, like if she fed Mark enough he would forgive her without her having to ask.

Mark stood in front of the open closet and stared at his jerseys.

The Lions colors still made his stomach twist. Not with pride. With history.

He reached for the captain's jersey—the one with his name stitched across the back—and paused.

He remembered standing on the field with a microphone, telling the town the truth, and feeling the routes listen beneath his feet.

He remembered the water Alyssa poured by the fence, the way the brittle petals collapsed like ash.

He remembered Pecos's mother standing up and saying, Bring him back, like grief was a command.

He shut the closet door and walked to his desk instead.

On the desk sat an acceptance letter.

He'd read it three times the first day it came, like repetition would make it more real. State school, two hours away. Not some dream scholarship paid for by booster money and pride. A scholarship, yes—but one that came from grades, from hard work, from a counselor who'd looked him in the eye and said, "You're allowed to have a future that isn't built on dead boys."

Mark picked up the letter now and ran his thumb along the edge.

Leaving felt like betrayal.

Leaving also felt like breathing.

His phone buzzed.

TOMMY: bonfire. creek. tonight. last one before we scatter.

Mark stared at the text until his eyes burned.

Scatter.

Like seeds. Like ash.

He typed back ok and shoved the phone in his pocket before he could change his mind.

As he turned, something clinked softly inside the top drawer of his desk.

Mark froze.

He hadn't touched that drawer in weeks.

He opened it.

Inside was a small glass vial.

Not big—about the size of his pinky finger. Cork stopper. A strip of masking tape wrapped around it with handwriting in black ink:

PECOS

Mark's throat tightened so hard he couldn't swallow.

He remembered the memorial after the memorial—the one the town didn't put on the news. Pecos's mother had stood by the garden with a plain metal urn in her hands, because there had been no body to bury, no clean ending to pretend to understand. Just the absence and the story and the stubborn need to put something in the ground.

Alyssa had said the words. Harold had stood nearby, silent, like a man guarding a line.

Tommy had held Mark's elbow the way he always did when Mark didn't know if he could keep standing.

And after, when nobody was looking, Mark had taken a small amount.

Not because he wanted to steal his friend.

Because some part of him couldn't stand the idea of Pecos belonging to Lowridge, even in death, even in disappearance, even in whatever the truth was.

Pecos had been the first person in their group who'd felt the land for what it was. Pecos had tried to warn them. Pecos had been taken because he was connected.

Mark stared at the vial.

The ash inside wasn't purple.

It was gray-black, fine as dust, with the faintest sparkle if the light hit it right—like ground-up glass.

Mark closed his fist around it and pressed it to his palm until it hurt.

Downstairs, his mother called softly, "Mark? Dinner's ready."

Mark didn't answer right away.

He slid the vial into his pocket like a secret.

"Yeah," he said finally. "Coming."

*****

The creek behind the old church still ran clear.

That had been Alyssa's point, back when everything was still actively falling apart: the creek remembered what the land used to be. The church was old enough that its foundation had been poured before the pact got carved into the town's bones. The water came from somewhere beyond Lowridge's hunger.

Mark didn't know if that was true.

But when he stood at the edge of it now, watching the current slip over stones, it felt… clean in a way the rest of the town still didn't.

Tommy built the fire like he was angry at the wood.

Alyssa sat on a fallen log with her notebook open, but she wasn't writing. She was just holding the pen between her fingers like it was an anchor.

Marcus Webb showed up late.

Not the Marcus who used to move like someone hunted. Not the Marcus whose skin sometimes shimmered with purple veins and wrongness.

Just Marcus.

Older-looking now. Not old-old. But the kind of older that came from catching up to years your body hadn't been allowed to feel. His hair had grown out. His face was thinner. His eyes still held that half-in, half-out expression sometimes—like he could see a map beneath the world if he tried hard enough—but the hunger in the air didn't respond to him anymore.

He walked up to the fire, held his hands out to the heat, and said, "If this is a support group, I want it on record that I hate all of you."

Tommy's laugh cracked out of him, sharp and surprised. "There he is."

Mark felt something loosen inside his chest.

Alyssa looked up. "You're late," she said.

Marcus shrugged. "Time's fake," he replied. Then his gaze flicked to Mark's bag sitting near the log, half-packed. "So. It's real."

Mark nodded once.

Tommy poked the fire too hard and sent sparks snapping up into the dark. "I'm leaving too," he said, like if he said it fast enough it wouldn't hurt.

Alyssa's pen stopped moving. "Where?"

Tommy shrugged. "My uncle's in Kansas City. Construction. He said I can work with him. Get out of here. Not… forever. Just—"

"Distance," Marcus said quietly.

Tommy nodded. His jaw clenched. "Yeah. Distance."

Alyssa's gaze turned to Mark. "And you're going to school."

Mark stared at the fire. "Yeah."

"And I'm staying," Alyssa said, and there was no hesitation in her voice. She said it the way she said facts she'd written down. "Someone has to."

Tommy frowned. "You don't have to be the historian for a town that tried to eat us."

Alyssa's eyes flashed. "That's exactly why someone has to," she said. "Because if I leave, they'll rewrite it. They'll pretend it was weather.

They'll say the flowers were a 'mass hallucination.' They'll do what they always do."

Mark watched her face in the firelight.

Alyssa had changed. Not in the dramatic way the movies did, with new clothes and confidence. In the quiet way of someone who'd seen the skeleton under a town's skin and decided to keep looking anyway.

"You're going to burn yourself out," Mark said.

Alyssa's mouth tightened. "Maybe," she said. "But I'd rather burn out than go numb."

Marcus stared into the flames. "Numb is how this started," he murmured.

Silence settled for a moment.

The creek kept running.

Far off, someone's dog barked.

Tommy cleared his throat and dug into his backpack. He pulled out four cans of soda—cheap cola from the gas station, because none of them were in a champagne mood.

He tossed one to Mark. One to Alyssa. One to Marcus.

Then he held his own up, hand shaking a little.

"To... not dying," Tommy said.

Alyssa lifted her can. "To telling the truth," she corrected.

Marcus's can hovered in the air. "To never joining the booster club," he said, deadpan.

Mark looked at the fire.

He thought of Jason.

He thought of Pecos.

He thought of all the names on that plaque at the field, carved into stone so the town couldn't pretend those boys had never existed.

"To leaving," Mark said finally. "And it not meaning we lost."

Tommy's eyes shone in the dark. "To leaving," he echoed.

They clinked cans.

The sound was small.

It still mattered.

After a while, when the fire had burned down into a steady bed of coals, Tommy got quieter. Alyssa stopped pretending she wasn't tired. Marcus leaned back on his hands and watched the sky like he was checking for patrol lights that weren't there anymore.

Mark stood.

No announcement. No speech. He just walked away from the fire and followed the creek path toward the cemetery, because some part of him had known he was going to do this all night.

The grass grew thicker as he got closer. The air cooled. The smell of damp earth and water replaced smoke.

He found Jason's grave the way he always did—like a magnet.

The headstone was clean. Someone had replaced the old wilted flowers with something simple: white daisies. Mark didn't know who had done it. Maybe his mom. Maybe a neighbor. Maybe one of the families who'd started leaving offerings for all the dead now, not just the ones who wore blue and gold.

Mark stood over the stone.

Jason's name was carved deep. The dates underneath looked too short for a life.

Mark didn't talk to the grave like some people did. He didn't say, I miss you out loud, because the words felt too big for air.

Instead, he reached into his pocket.

His fingers brushed the small glass vial.

He pulled it out and held it in his palm, moonlight catching the faint sparkle in the ash.

Mark stared down at Jason's name and thought, I'm leaving you here.

It felt cruel.

It also felt honest.

"I'm going," he said softly, barely above the creek's whisper.

No wind answered. No fog rolled in. No purple light flickered under the ground.

The quiet didn't feel empty.

It felt earned.

Mark swallowed hard and tucked the vial back into his pocket.

Then he did the only thing he could think of that didn't feel like a lie.

He placed his hand on the cold stone and held it there until his fingers stopped shaking.

When he walked back toward the fire, the path felt less like a trapdoor and more like a road.

Tommy looked up when Mark returned, eyes searching his face like he was checking for injuries.

Mark shook his head. I'm okay, the gesture said, even if it wasn't fully true.

Alyssa scooted over on the log to make room without making a big deal of it.

Marcus threw another stick on the coals and watched it catch.

They sat together until the fire burned down and the night got cold enough to force them to move.

When they finally stood to leave, it didn't feel like closure.

It felt like the beginning of a life that had to be lived without the town's hands on their throats.

Mark walked home under a sky that didn't look like a bruise anymore.

And for the first time since Jason died, the silence behind him didn't feel like something stalking.

It felt like space.

Like a future.

CHAPTER 34: THALASSA'S GIFT

The first thing Mark noticed was the absence of purple.

Not gone everywhere—not yet—but absent in the way a headache is absent after you've lived with it so long you forget what silence feels like. The morning air over Lowridge carried wet leaves and chimney smoke and the faint mineral bite of winter runoff. Ordinary scents. Honest ones. No violet sweetness threading the cold like a lie.

He stood at the edge of the creek behind St. Michael's and watched the water move.

It didn't glow.

It didn't hum.

It didn't feel like a mouth waiting to open.

It just ran—clear over stones, carrying dead grass and a single brown leaf that spun in place, then surrendered and drifted on.

Alyssa's text had come in before sunrise.

Found the entrance. Not sealed. Not safe. We should go.

He'd stared at it for a long time, thumb hovering, a familiar pressure blooming behind his eyes—the old instinct to delay, to pretend there wasn't one more thing to check. One more place to face.

Then he'd read it again and understood what she meant.

If they left anything unfinished, Lowridge would finish it for them. With denial. With ceremonies. With new paint on old rot.

Tommy's truck rumbled up behind him, tires crunching on the dirt shoulder. Tommy climbed out without slamming the door, like loud noises still felt like invitations. His hair was longer now—two months of not caring—and his ring sat on his finger like an anchor he didn't trust.

"You look like you're about to propose to the creek," Tommy said.

Mark didn't smile, but something in his chest loosened anyway. "It texted first."

Tommy came to stand beside him, hands shoved into his jacket pockets. He stared at the water like he expected it to do something clever.

"Is this where she thinks it is?" he asked.

Mark nodded. "She said the old route. The one May used to—"

"—use to scare kids," Tommy finished, though his voice didn't make it a joke. "Yeah. That one."

A crunch of footsteps in wet leaves. Alyssa emerged from between the bare brush and the low pines, hair tucked into a beanie, backpack slung across her shoulder. The grimoire's shape was obvious beneath the canvas like a secret she no longer bothered to hide.

Her face looked different these days—not softer, not harder exactly. Just steadier. Like she'd stopped expecting the town to become decent and started expecting herself to be.

"Morning," she said, and the word sounded like a truce.

Tommy lifted two fingers in greeting. Mark stepped forward and hugged her, quick and awkward the way they always did, like they were afraid contact might trigger something old.

Alyssa's hand pressed briefly to his jacket, right over his ribs. "You okay?" she asked, quiet.

Mark looked down at the creek. "I don't know what okay means anymore," he said. "But I'm here."

Alyssa nodded like that was enough. "Good," she said. "Because it's open."

She led them along the creek's bend, past a stand of cedars that smelled sharp and clean, past a fence that had collapsed sometime during the fog weeks and hadn't been repaired because nobody wanted to admit how small their control had always been.

The ground grew softer underfoot. The trees leaned closer. Mark felt an old reflex rise in him—the urge to count his steps like a cadence.

One-two, one-two.

He stopped himself and listened instead.

Nothing counted back.

They reached the place where the creek split around a low hump of earth —an old mound half swallowed by roots. Two stones jutted from the hillside like broken teeth, carved with faint shapes that were neither crosses nor letters. Alyssa crouched and brushed dead leaves aside.

"There," she said.

A crack in the earth.

Not a dramatic cave mouth. Not an iron door. Just a narrow, dark seam between roots and stone, the kind of thing you could miss a hundred times if you weren't looking for the ways a town hid its own sins.

Tommy stared. "That's it?" he asked, voice thin. "We fought monsters for… a crack?"

Alyssa stood, hands dirty, eyes sharp. "That's how it started," she said. "Small. Quiet. Easy to pretend it was nothing."

Mark stepped closer. The seam smelled like damp stone and old soil. No sweetness. No violet tang. But the air that breathed out of it carried something else—cool and clean, like water in a shaded well.

Alyssa pulled a flashlight from her pocket. "It's not deep," she said. "But the chamber is... wrong now. Collapsed in places. Like the land finally decided it was done holding it up."

Tommy shifted his weight. "And if it's not done?" he asked.

Alyssa's gaze flicked to Mark. "Then we'll know," she said.

They went in one at a time.

Mark first, because that was how it always ended up—captain going first, symbol going first, boy with the dead brother going first. He ducked into the seam and felt the temperature drop around him. The earth pressed close on both sides, roots like ribs overhead.

His flashlight beam caught old scratch marks on stone. Runes that had once looked alive now looked like dried scars.

A few feet in, the passage widened.

And the chamber opened around them like an empty throat.

Mark stopped.

He remembered it from the worst nights—the smell of blood and flowers, the altar slick with offerings, the black roots writhing like they wanted to become hands. He remembered purple light pulsing in the cracks, remembered the sense of attention.

Now—

Now the altar was shattered.

Stone split in three pieces. One slab leaned against the wall at an angle like it had finally given up. The runes were there, but faded, broken by fractures that ran through the carvings like lightning cracks.

The roots were dead.

Not rotting with that wet, hungry smell. Just dead—dry cords curled against stone, brittle as old rope.

And in the center of the chamber, where the altar's shadow used to feel like a trap, there was a pool.

A shallow basin carved into the floor, filled with clear water that reflected the flashlight beam in a steady, unafraid shine.

Alyssa stepped beside Mark. Her breath caught. "It wasn't here before," she whispered.

Tommy shuffled in behind them, ducking his head. He stared at the pool like it might lunge.

"This feels like the opposite of everything else," he said.

Mark crouched at the edge. The water didn't ripple until his shadow crossed it—then it moved gently, like it acknowledged him.

He reached one hand out and stopped, hovering. Old instinct screamed don't touch. Every lesson they'd learned had come from touching the wrong thing.

Alyssa's voice was quiet. "May called it Thalassa," she said, like she was afraid the name itself might wake something. "Not the land. Not the hunger. The thing beneath—what the land was before it got… trained."

Tommy swallowed. "A water goddess?" he asked, half-mocking, half-hopeful.

Alyssa shook her head. "Not a goddess," she said. "A current. A memory. A way the land heals."

Mark stared into the pool.

For a second, he saw his own reflection: pale, tired, eyes older than they should've been at seventeen. He saw Alyssa's face in the angle behind him, Tommy's behind her.

Then the reflection shifted.

Not like a hallucination snapping into place—no dramatic shimmer. Just a change in depth, as if the water remembered other light.

The chamber brightened.

Not with purple. With something pale-blue and clean, like moonlight on snow.

Mark's throat tightened.

Across the pool, a figure stood.

A boy in a football uniform, but not torn and wrong like the ones in the web. This uniform looked… normal. The colors were muted, like a photograph left in sunlight too long, but the lines were right. The stance was right.

Jason.

Not a puppet in fog.

Not a shadow with empty eyes.

Jason the way Mark remembered him—shoulder relaxed, one hand on his hip like he was listening to a coach's speech he'd heard a thousand times and still didn't believe.

Jason smiled.

It wasn't slow and empty. It was quick and real, the grin that used to show up when Jason stole the last slice of pizza and dared Mark to complain.

Mark's breath left him in a shaky exhale. "Jay," he whispered.

Alyssa's hand found Mark's sleeve, steadying him without pulling him back. Tommy made a sound that might've been a sob or a laugh; it died in his throat.

Jason didn't speak. He didn't have to.

Behind him, other shapes gathered—not crowds, not trophies—just people. Kids. Players. Some older, some younger. Faces Mark didn't know, but the posture of them felt familiar: shoulders squared, hands on knees, the way boys looked when they were waiting for the whistle.

And among them—

Pecos.

Pecos stood slightly apart, hands shoved into his hoodie pockets, chin tilted the way he always did when he was listening to something under everybody else's words. His eyes weren't violet now. They were just his.

He looked at Mark and lifted two fingers in that half-salute he'd always used instead of waving.

Tommy choked. "Pecos," he said, voice cracking on the name like it had a hook in it.

Pecos smiled—small, tired, but real.

Mark's chest hurt. Not the sharp pain of panic. The slow ache of grief finally being allowed to exist without being used against him.

Jason's gaze moved to the broken altar. Then to Mark.

Mark understood, suddenly, the shape of the message.

It's done.

Not because they were brave enough. Not because they'd earned it. Because something older than the pact—something that did not bargain, did not hunger in the same way—had moved in the quiet after their truth and said: Enough.

Mark's eyes burned. "I'm sorry," he whispered, and he didn't know who he meant it for first.

Jason's smile softened. His hand lifted, two fingers pressed briefly to his own chest like a promise.

Then the figures began to fade—not dragged away, not swallowed. Just… letting go. Like a fist unclenching.

Pecos's gaze held Mark's for one last beat.

And Mark felt it—clean and unmistakable—peace.

The water in the pool rippled once.

The chamber dimmed back into stone and shadow and flashlight beam.

Mark was still kneeling at the edge, hand hovering over the water like he'd been caught mid-prayer.

Tommy wiped his face with the heel of his palm, angry at his own tears. Alyssa's eyes were wet, but she looked almost calm, as if she'd been carrying this moment in her pocket for years.

Mark finally lowered his hand into the pool.

The water was cold.

Not shock-cold. Wake-you-up cold. Honest cold.

The instant his skin touched it, he felt something move through him— gentle, not invasive. A current sliding through the tight places in his chest, into his throat, behind his eyes.

For a heartbeat he saw the routes again—not the web of the shadow realm, not the hungry network—just faint lines under the town, like veins under skin.

And he felt them settle.

Not vanish. Not erase history. Settle, the way a body settles after fever breaks.

Alyssa whispered, "Do you feel that?"

Mark nodded. He couldn't speak yet.

Tommy leaned closer, eyes wary. "Is it… safe?" he asked.

Mark lifted his hand out of the pool. Water dripped from his fingers onto dead roots. The drops soaked in. No sizzling. No purple flare. Just absorption, slow and natural.

"It's safe," Mark said, voice hoarse. "For now."

Alyssa exhaled like she'd been holding her breath since the cemetery first glowed. She pulled the grimoire from her bag and set it on the broken altar slab. Not ceremoniously. Not dramatically. Just… placing it down like a burden.

"We should leave it?" Tommy asked.

Alyssa shook her head. "No," she said. "It's ours. Not the town's. Not the land's." She glanced at Mark. "But we don't need it to keep the door shut anymore."

Mark looked around the chamber one last time.

The carvings on the stone looked like scars that had stopped bleeding. The dead roots looked like proof something had once tried to be a chain.

The pool looked like a gift you didn't deserve and had to learn how to accept.

They backed out slowly, one at a time, leaving the chamber to its quiet.

Outside, the creek kept running.

The trees didn't lean in the same way.

The air smelled like winter and soil and woodsmoke, and the absence of violet felt like a mercy that might not last unless they earned it every day.

They stood for a moment on the bank, looking down at the water like it might speak.

Tommy broke the silence first, because he always did when silence got too heavy. "So," he said, voice shaky but trying, "we just got blessed by… whatever that was."

Alyssa gave him a look. "Don't start."

Tommy shrugged. "I'm coping," he said. "Let me cope."

Mark's phone buzzed in his pocket. A message from his mom.

Where are you?

He stared at it, thumb hovering.

He could say out.

He could say with friends.

He could say finishing something.

He typed: By the creek. I'll be home soon.

He looked up at Alyssa and Tommy. "We should go," he said. "People will be looking."

Alyssa's mouth tightened. "They always are," she said.

They walked back along the creek. When they reached the road, Mark glanced once toward the cemetery beyond the trees.

From here, he couldn't see the grave rows. He couldn't see the stones.

But he could feel the place, faintly—like a scar that would always remember what cut it, even if it stopped aching.

Tommy's truck waited at the shoulder like a promise of movement.

Alyssa paused with one foot on the step, turning back to Mark. "You're still leaving," she said. It wasn't a question.

Mark swallowed. The future had been a highway out of town in his head for so long it had stopped feeling real. Now, with the land quieter, with Jason's grin no longer a command, he could feel the grief under everything —and the possibility under that.

"Yeah," he said. "But not running."

Alyssa nodded once, satisfied.

Tommy glanced between them. "You two are being weird," he said. "Get in the truck before I have to have feelings again."

Mark climbed into the passenger seat. The engine started. The tires rolled.

As they drove, Mark felt the town around them like an old stadium after a game—lights still on, trash scattered, the echo of cheers fading into something that sounded a lot like wind.

Lowridge would try to turn healing into ceremony. It would try to put the purple flower back on its letterheads and pretend it meant something harmless.

But beneath all of that, something had changed.

Not erased.

Changed.

And as the creek slipped past in the side mirror, Mark understood the shape of Thalassa's gift—not power, not protection, not a weapon.

A warning system.

A way to feel when the land started to tighten again. A way to know when silence was peace and when silence was a breath being held.

He rested his head against the cold window and let his eyes close for one long, quiet beat.

One-two.

One-two.

Not a play.

Not a prayer.

Just a heartbeat.

And somewhere behind them, in a chamber broken open to the truth, the water kept running—clear and ordinary—like the land had finally remembered what it was allowed to be.

CHAPTER 35: THE LAST PETAL

The morning after the ceremony, Lowridge looked like it had been rinsed and left damp.

Sunlight came in thin sheets, as if the sky was still afraid of what it might reveal if it got too bright. The fog had pulled back from the streets but refused to leave entirely, pooling in ditches and clinging to the bottoms of fences like a habit. There were places on the sidewalks where the purple growth had turned to brittle gray, and other places where it held its color stubbornly, petals bright against mud, like the town couldn't decide whether it had been cured or merely warned.

Mark Rivers carried a cardboard box to the trunk of his car and set it down carefully, like it might break open and spill memories across the driveway.

Inside: clothes, a duffel bag, the scholarship paperwork, and the framed photo of Jason that had sat on the entryway table for three years. Mark had almost left the frame where it was—like leaving it behind could count as moving on—but he'd taken it anyway. Not because he wanted a shrine on the passenger seat.

Because he didn't want to leave Jason in a house that still smelled like denial.

The street was quiet. No kids walking to school. No lawnmowers. No music. Even the birds sounded cautious, their calls shorter, clipped, as if the trees had taught them the value of shutting up.

Across the way, Mrs. Halverson stood on her porch with a mug in both hands, staring at her garden bed where something purple had tried to bloom and then shriveled. She didn't wave. Mark didn't either. Their relationship had always been built on polite distance and football scores, and now there were no scores anyone trusted.

Mark climbed into the driver's seat and sat with the door open, breathing the air.

It still tasted faintly sweet.

Not the fresh sweetness of spring. Not the clean sweetness of rain. The other kind—the kind that clung to the back of your throat and made you think of a cut lip, pennies, and violets crushed under cleats.

He checked the rearview mirror out of habit.

For a second, he expected to see purple threads in the air, invisible routes lit up like a map no one had asked to read. He expected the hum under the town to answer him, to tug behind his eyes and remind him that leaving was never as simple as driving away.

Nothing happened.

Silence should have felt like freedom.

Instead, it felt like the moment right before a snap—everything held in place, waiting for motion.

From inside the house, a cabinet closed softly.

Mark stayed where he was until his mother's footsteps reached the front door.

She stepped out onto the porch, hugging her arms across her body like the morning air hurt. She had put on makeup, just enough to cover the bruised look sleep deprivation left under her eyes, but it didn't fool Mark. He'd learned, young, that Lowridge women could paint grief into something presentable and still feel it rot beneath.

"You're really going," she said.

Mark nodded. "Yeah."

She didn't argue. She didn't ask why. She'd watched him speak in front of the town. She'd watched the reaction. She'd watched the way certain people looked at him afterward—like he had thrown a rock at a stained-glass window and ruined something sacred.

She stepped down the porch stairs, slow, and stopped at the passenger-side door.

"Where will you be?" she asked.

Mark swallowed. "Huntsville," he said, because it was easier than saying: somewhere new, somewhere bright, somewhere the land doesn't know my name.

His mother's mouth tightened. "The scholarship?"

"Still good," Mark said. "They called last night. Said… said they're sorry. Said I can start in January if I want."

Her eyes flicked to the boxes in the trunk, then back to him. "They don't know what happened here," she said softly.

Mark stared past her, toward the end of the street where the town sloped down toward Main. "Some of them do," he said. "They're just far enough away to treat it like a story."

His mother's hands twisted together at her waist. "Your father—"

"Will be fine," Mark said, too quickly.

She flinched like he'd slapped the air between them. Mark exhaled and tried again, softer. "He'll be angry," he said. "And then he'll be embarrassed. And then he'll pretend he was never angry."

His mother's gaze dropped to the driveway, to the crack running through the concrete like a fault line. "He thinks you made Jason's death mean something else," she whispered.

Mark felt that old pain flare—sharp, familiar. "It already meant something else," he said. "We just didn't want to look."

His mother's eyes shone, but no tears fell. Lowridge taught you to keep your tears inside until they became something useful—fuel, performance, prayer.

"What if leaving doesn't fix it?" she asked.

Mark reached across the seat and pulled the passenger door open, the motion too quick, too reflexive, like he was responding to a blitz. "It won't fix it," he said. "But staying won't either."

His mother looked at the open seat, then at him. "When you were little," she said, voice thin, "Jason used to tell me you'd go farther than him."

Mark's throat tightened. "Jason said a lot of things."

She gave a small, broken smile. "He did," she agreed. Then her expression steadied, the way it always did when she decided to be brave because there was no other option. "Call me," she said. "Even if it's just… silence on the line."

Mark nodded.

She leaned in and kissed his forehead. Her lips were cool. Her hands trembled against his cheek for half a second, then pulled away.

"Be careful," she said.

Mark wanted to tell her there was no such thing as careful anymore, not in a world where land could listen and hunger could learn your name. But he just nodded again, because his mother needed some version of comfort, and he couldn't take that away too.

She stepped back. "Go," she said, voice firm now. "Before you change your mind."

Mark closed the door.

The latch clicked like the start of a countdown.

*****

Lowridge's "growth corridor" sat on the edge of town like a promise made to outsiders.

It had started with a single new building—glass, steel, a logo that looked like an arrow shooting forward. Then a cluster. Then a whole stretch of road widened and repaved, new streetlights installed, banners hung from poles announcing the future in cheerful fonts.

WELCOME TO LOWRIDGE — WHERE TRADITION MEETS INNOVATION.

Mark drove that road now because it was the quickest way to the hospital, and because part of him wanted to see if the town's shiny new skin looked different after everything that had happened.

It didn't.

The same manicured lawns. The same brand-new apartment complex with a name that tried to sound like nature: Violet Ridge Lofts. The same coffee shop with a chalkboard sign promising "community" and "craft." The same fenced-in lot where a data center was being built, its walls pale and windowless, like a bunker someone hoped would pass for progress.

The old Lowridge still clung to the edges: rusted chain-link fences behind the new development, abandoned fields left unplanted, a strip of trees that leaned inward as if the land didn't care what humans called its surface.

And there—right at the base of a bright new streetlight—Mark saw a thin, dead vine curled up like black thread. It glittered faint violet when the light hit it, just like the one on his mailbox had.

Not gone.

Just quieter.

He gripped the steering wheel until his knuckles went pale.

At the intersection, a billboard had been erected in the last month. A smiling family, a golden retriever, a kid holding a football like it was an extension of his hand.

LOWRIDGE: A GREAT PLACE TO GROW.

Someone had spray-painted over the bottom in angry black letters:

AT WHAT COST?

Mark drove past without slowing.

His phone buzzed on the seat beside him. Tommy's name flashed across the screen.

Mark answered. "Yeah."

Tommy's voice came through, rough. "You on your way?"

"Hospital," Mark said.

A pause. "We're already here," Tommy said. "Alyssa's with me."

Mark swallowed. "Okay."

Tommy hesitated like he wanted to say something else—like he wanted to make a joke to keep the air from feeling too real—but then he just said, "See you."

The call ended.

Mark's hands tightened again on the wheel.

He wasn't sure when Tommy had stopped sounding like he expected the world to bounce back. Maybe it was when he'd watched Pecos disappear. Maybe it was when he'd watched Mark tell the town the truth and realized there was no going back to Friday nights as entertainment.

Maybe it was both.

*****

The hospital smelled like antiseptic and old coffee.

It was the kind of building built for function, not comfort, with fluorescent lights that made everyone look slightly haunted. The lobby TV played a morning news segment about "unexplained events" in a "small southern town," careful to avoid words that would make sponsors nervous.

Mark didn't watch it.

He walked down the hallway to the wing where Pecos's room was and felt his body slip into that quiet hyper-awareness that had kept him alive on the field—every sound cataloged, every movement measured, every exit noted.

As if danger still lived in the vents.

Tommy was leaning against the wall outside Pecos's room, arms folded, eyes fixed on the floor. Alyssa sat in one of the plastic chairs, the grimoire bag at her feet like she'd brought a weapon to a place that didn't believe in weapons unless they came with paperwork.

She looked up when Mark approached. Her face was pale, and there were faint purple shadows under her eyes that didn't come from makeup. She had that look she got when she'd been awake too long, running on adrenaline and stubbornness.

"You packed?" she asked.

Mark nodded.

Tommy's gaze flicked up. "You really leaving today," he said, like he was still trying to make the sentence fit in his mouth.

Mark shrugged, which wasn't an answer so much as a refusal to make this into a speech.

Alyssa stood. "He's asleep," she said, and Mark could hear everything she wasn't saying: not dead, not awake, not free.

They went inside.

Pecos lay in the hospital bed with an oxygen tube under his nose and electrodes stuck to his chest. He looked smaller than Mark remembered, not because he'd changed physically but because he'd always carried himself like he belonged to the land—solid, rooted, immovable. Now he looked like someone the world had picked up and shaken until the insides didn't settle right.

His skin was normal color. No violet pulsing. No veins mapped dark under his throat.

But Mark saw the flowers anyway—not literal, not visible to anyone else, but in the way Pecos's fingers rested, curled slightly, as if they still remembered thread.

Pecos's mother sat beside the bed, hands clasped around her son's jersey like she'd been doing at the ceremony. When she saw Mark, her eyes sharpened.

"You're leaving," she said, no greeting, no softness.

Mark stopped at the foot of the bed. "Yes," he said.

Her jaw tightened. "And my boy stays," she said, like she was testing him to see if he would pretend that was fair.

Mark swallowed. "We're still working," he said. "Alyssa—"

Alyssa stepped forward, voice controlled. "We're not done," she said. "Not with the land. Not with the town. Not with whatever it used Pecos for."

Pecos's mother stared at Alyssa like she was weighing her. Then her gaze returned to Mark.

"You brought him back," she said. "Or you brought something back wearing his skin."

Mark's stomach dropped. He hadn't expected her to say it out loud, not in a hospital room with nurses walking past. But grief made you honest in ways politeness never allowed.

Mark stepped closer and looked down at Pecos.

He remembered Pecos's eyes in the shadow realm—violet points pulsing like a heartbeat—and the way Pecos had looked at him like he already knew what losing meant.

"He's here," Mark said quietly. "He's not… whole. But he's here."

Pecos's mother's hands tightened on the jersey until the fabric wrinkled. "If he wakes up wrong," she whispered, voice shaking now, "if he wakes up and he's not my boy—"

Alyssa's gaze softened. "Then we'll know," she said. "And we'll deal with it."

Tommy let out a breath that sounded like a laugh made of pain. "That's our new motto," he murmured. "We'll deal with it."

Pecos's mother stared at them for a long moment, then looked back down at her son. She reached out and brushed his knuckles with the tips of her fingers.

"He was always stubborn," she said, almost to herself. "Always thought he could carry more than he should."

Mark felt something twist in his chest. He stepped to the side of the bed, careful not to crowd her, and spoke into the quiet.

"Pecos," he said.

No response. Just the steady beep of the monitor.

Mark swallowed and tried again. "I'm leaving," he said, voice low. "Not because I'm done. Because I'm not. But because I can't… stay in the middle of it anymore."

He paused, the words sticking. Then he forced them out like a confession, because confession was the only thing that had ever cut the thread.

"I'm afraid," Mark said. "I'm afraid the town will turn me into a symbol again. I'm afraid I'll let it. I'm afraid I'll get used."

His voice cracked on the last word, and he hated himself for it.

Alyssa's eyes flicked up. Tommy shifted, uncomfortable, like he wanted to shield Mark from being seen even here.

Mark looked at Pecos's face. "I promised I'd bring you back," Mark whispered. "I'm still trying. I swear I am."

For a second, Pecos's fingers twitched.

It was so small Mark almost thought he'd imagined it.

Tommy leaned forward, breath held. "Did you see that?"

Alyssa's hand went to the bedrail. Pecos's mother's head snapped up, eyes wide.

Pecos's fingers twitched again—one small motion, like a muscle remembering a signal.

Then stillness.

The monitor beeped on, steady as ever, indifferent.

Pecos's mother swallowed hard. "That's him," she whispered, and the certainty in her voice was fierce, protective. "That's my boy."

Mark exhaled, slow.

He reached into his pocket and pulled out something he'd carried all morning without looking at it: a small iron football charm from Jason's keychain, the one Mark had found in a drawer months ago and thought he'd lost. The metal was worn, edges smooth from years of handling.

He set it on the bedside table.

"I don't know if iron matters," he said, glancing at Alyssa, thinking of May's rules, thinking of salt and fire and water and honesty. "But... it matters to me."

Alyssa nodded once. "It matters," she said. "Sometimes that's enough to make the routes hesitate."

Tommy's mouth twitched. "Great," he whispered. "We're fighting ancient hunger with sentimentality."

Mark almost smiled. Almost.

He looked at Pecos one last time.

"Hold on," he said quietly. "Don't let it write you."

Pecos didn't answer. But Mark thought he felt something in the air shift —minute, like the tightening of a shoelace. Like a boundary being drawn.

*****

On the way out of the hospital, Mark saw May Dawson in the hallway.

He hadn't heard her approach. She was just there—leaning against the wall in a dark coat, hands in her pockets, eyes fixed on the far end of the corridor like she was listening to something beyond the building.

Alyssa stiffened immediately. "Aunt May," she said, as if naming her was both a greeting and a warning.

May's gaze slid to Mark. "You're leaving," she said. Not a question.

Mark nodded. "Today."

May's mouth twitched. "Good," she said, and Mark didn't know whether to be offended or relieved.

Alyssa's voice sharpened. "We're not abandoning it," she said.

May's eyes flicked to her niece, and there was a tired affection there, hidden under the gravel. "I know," May said. "You're the kind that stays to argue with the dark. I was too, once."

Tommy shifted. "You got a point, or you just lurking in hospitals for the vibe?"

May's eyes narrowed. "I have a point," she said.

She pushed off the wall and stepped closer, lowering her voice. "The town will try to fix this by painting over it," she said. "By building something shiny and calling it healing. That corridor out there? It's not just investment. It's distraction. The land likes distraction."

Mark's throat went dry. "It's quieter," he said. "But it's still… there."

May nodded. "Quieter is not gone," she said. "Quieter is waiting."

Alyssa's jaw tightened. "So what do we do?"

May's gaze moved from Alyssa to Tommy to Mark, as if weighing which of them could carry what truth.

Then she reached into her coat pocket and pulled out a small book of matches. The cover was old, the kind that came from diners or motels, with faded printing. St. Michael's Church — Lowridge, it read.

May held it out to Mark.

Mark stared at it. "A matchbook?" he asked.

May's eyes didn't soften. "Fire is honest," she said. "It doesn't negotiate. It doesn't pretend. It doesn't care what story the town tells about it."

Mark took the matchbook. The cardboard was worn, edges bent. It felt too small to matter.

May leaned in slightly, voice lower. "If the land offers you something on the way out," she said, "don't take it."

Mark's skin prickled. "Offers?" he asked.

May's eyes held his. "It's losing control," she said. "It will try to regain it. Sometimes it does that with teeth. Sometimes it does it with gifts."

Tommy's face tightened. "Gifts like what?" he asked.

May's gaze shifted, almost unwilling. "Like the thing you want most," she said.

Mark's throat tightened.

May stepped back, pulling her hands into her pockets again. "Go," she said to Mark. "And don't be polite to the dark."

Alyssa opened her mouth, ready to argue, but May was already walking away down the corridor, shoulders squared like she'd learned long ago that staying too close to people made you responsible for their pain.

Mark held the matchbook in his hand until the cardboard warmed.

*****

He drove back through the corridor toward home, and the future kept smiling at him.

New signs. New pavement. New banners. New names: Lionheart Parkway. Violet Ridge Lofts. Field & Bloom Market.

Field & Bloom.

Mark's fingers tightened on the steering wheel. He could almost hear the town's marketing committee patting itself on the back, proud of its "branding," proud of the way it could turn even the thing that tried to kill them into an aesthetic.

A thin gust of wind lifted dust across the road. Mark caught the scent again—sweet, metallic, floral.

He checked the rearview mirror again.

Still nothing.

Then—at a stoplight—something tapped the inside of the windshield softly.

Mark's eyes snapped up.

A single purple petal clung to the glass, stuck there as if it had been placed deliberately. It was too vivid to be dead, too intact to be from one of the brittle gray vines. The color looked wet, fresh, like it had been cut from a living flower seconds ago.

Mark's mouth went dry.

The petal didn't flutter. The air inside the car was still. It just stayed there, pressed to the glass like a fingerprint.

Mark forced himself to breathe.

He reached out slowly, the way you reached for a live wire when you didn't have gloves.

His fingers hovered an inch from the petal.

The pressure behind his eyes returned—faint at first, then sharper, like a lens clicking into focus.

The world dimmed by half a shade.

Not enough for anyone else to notice. Enough for Mark to feel it.

The petal brightened.

And in that brightness, Mark saw movement at the edge of his vision—someone standing on the sidewalk across the street, just beyond the reach of the new streetlight.

A figure in a red cloak.

Tall. Still. Hood shadowing the face.

Mark's stomach dropped.

The light turned green.

Cars behind him honked. The future wanted him to move.

Mark didn't.

He stared at the figure.

The figure didn't move, didn't wave, didn't gesture. It just stood there like a memory that refused to be forgotten.

And then a voice slid into Mark's mind—not words exactly, but meaning shaped like language.

You could keep them safe.

Mark's fingers tightened on the steering wheel. His heart thudded once, hard.

You could keep him.

Jason's name didn't appear in the thought. It didn't have to. Mark felt it anyway, like a hook snagging a scar.

The petal on the windshield pulsed.

Mark saw, for a fraction of a second, the stadium field at night—fog rolling, lights burning down through it, the crowd roaring like a living thing. He saw Jason on the sideline, helmet tucked under his arm, grinning.

Not ghost-Jason. Not thread-Jason.

Jason the way Mark remembered him.

Jason's grin widened.

Come on, little brother, the memory seemed to say. One more season.

Mark's throat tightened. His hands shook.

He could almost feel the weight lift if he said yes. The town would love him again. The town would stop looking at him like a traitor. The land would stop hovering at the edge of his dreams.

And maybe—maybe—Pecos would wake up whole. Maybe the trapped spirits would rest. Maybe Jason would stop straining against the web.

All Mark had to do was feed it one last time.

The thought was smooth. Seductive. It slid into the shape of Mark's guilt like it belonged there.

Mark's breath came shallow.

Then he remembered Pecos's mother holding the jersey like it was flesh.

He remembered Coach Whitman saying proud.

He remembered the mayor talking about grants like money could patch over rot.

He remembered the trapped spirits begging in silence in the shadow realm.

And he remembered what May had said in the hallway.

Fire is honest.

Mark's gaze locked on the petal.

He took his hands off the wheel.

The honking behind him intensified. Someone shouted through an open window. Mark didn't care.

He opened the glove compartment, fingers clumsy, and grabbed the matchbook May had given him.

St. Michael's Church — Lowridge.

His thumb slid along the striker.

The pressure behind his eyes surged, as if the town itself had inhaled.

Don't, the meaning pressed into him.

Mark's jaw clenched. "No," he said out loud.

The word felt like stepping over a line.

He struck the match.

The flame flared bright and ordinary—yellow, simple, human.

For a second, Mark almost laughed at how small it looked against everything he'd seen.

Then he leaned forward and touched the flame to the corner of the petal.

The petal didn't burn like paper.

It hissed.

The smell that rose was sweet and rotten at the same time, like fruit left too long in heat. Purple light flared along the edges, and Mark felt a tug under his ribs—like something tried to yank him backward through his own spine.

Mark held the flame steady.

He spoke again, voice shaking. "You don't get me," he said. "You don't get him. You don't get any of us."

The petal curled in on itself, blackening, the purple color collapsing like a bruise fading under pressure. The tug in Mark's chest loosened, then surged again, more frantic.

The figure across the street shifted—just a fraction, like the dark had blinked.

And then the streetlight flickered.

For half a second, the world looked like the shadow realm—threads in the air, lines under pavement, the corridor a web dressed up in glass.

Mark kept the flame on the petal until it was nothing but ash stuck to the glass.

The pressure behind his eyes snapped.

Air rushed back into his lungs like he'd been underwater.

The honking behind him was suddenly loud again, real again. The future demanded motion.

Mark wiped the ash away with his sleeve.

When he looked across the street, the red-cloaked figure was gone.

Only a man in a business jacket stood there now, staring at his phone, unaware of anything except whatever app told him where to park.

Mark's hands trembled on the wheel.

He forced himself to breathe.

Then he drove.

*****

By the time Mark pulled into his driveway again, his body felt like it had been hit hard and left upright out of spite.

He killed the engine and sat for a long moment with both hands on the steering wheel, staring at the house.

The curtains upstairs were still. His mother was probably in the kitchen, washing something that didn't need washing because keeping hands busy was easier than keeping a mind still.

Mark opened the door and stepped out.

A breeze moved through the street—real wind, not route-hum—and for a moment Mark thought he heard it: one-two, one-two, the old cadence, the count that started a play and ended a prayer.

Then it faded into ordinary leaves shifting.

Mark went to the trunk and lifted the last box.

His phone buzzed again.

Alyssa: You okay?

Mark stared at the message.

He didn't want to tell her about the petal. He didn't want to give the dark more shape by naming it. But Alyssa had built her whole life on refusing to let things stay unnamed.

Mark typed: Almost got offered something. Burned it.

A pause. Then: Good. Keep burning.

Mark swallowed, shut his phone off, and carried the box inside.

*****

He left at noon.

His mother stood on the porch again, arms folded tight, face composed. Mark hugged her once, quick and hard, and told her he'd call. She nodded like she believed him and like she didn't.

Mark didn't go to the stadium.

He didn't go to the cemetery.

He didn't need to. Those places were already in him, mapped under his skin the way routes had mapped themselves under the town.

He drove toward the highway.

Out past the old water tower, the road rose slightly, giving him a view of Lowridge spread out behind: the older downtown brick and worn roofs, the stadium lights visible even in daylight, the cemetery beyond like an extra bleacher section built for ghosts.

Farther out, the growth corridor gleamed, glass catching sun, banners snapping in wind, the future smiling hard.

Mark kept his eyes on the road.

At the last stoplight before the highway, he glanced in the rearview mirror one final time.

For a second, in the distance, he thought he saw a violet flicker along the tree line—one stubborn bloom refusing to die.

Then a truck passed and blocked the view, and when the view returned, it was gone.

Mark exhaled.

He didn't know if the land would let him leave clean.

He didn't know if the town would ever stop feeding it.

He didn't know if Pecos would wake up and be himself or something else wearing his face.

But he knew one thing.

He knew what the dark offered him, and he knew what it took to refuse.

Mark merged onto the highway.

The road stretched ahead like a route he had chosen for himself.

The town fell behind him.

And for the first time in a long time, the silence in his head didn't feel like waiting.

It felt like space.

EPILOGUE: FREEDOM IN THE REARVIEW

Mark Rivers woke before sunrise because his body still thought mornings meant practice.

For a few seconds he lay still and listened for the town's old rhythm—the hidden cadence under everything, one-two, one-two, like cleats in a tunnel and prayers in a throat. The house was quiet. No whistles. No distant roar from the stadium. Just the ordinary creak of settling wood and the soft, faraway hiss of a shower running upstairs.

His mother.

Mark stared at the ceiling and let the quiet sit on him until it stopped feeling like a trick.

The air smelled like coffee and cold December rain and something faintly floral that shouldn't have been there anymore. Not the heavy, suffocating sweetness of the bloom—nothing that made your teeth ache with it. Just a whisper of violet that drifted in and out like a memory trying to decide if it still had permission.

He sat up.

His duffel bag lay open on the floor, half-filled with clothes he didn't care about and things he did. The scholarship letter was tucked inside the front pocket like a ticket. His phone sat face-down on the nightstand, dark and mercifully silent. His captain patch rested on top of a stack of folded shirts, the blue-and-gold thread catching the pale light from the window.

On the dresser, Jason's framed photo leaned against the mirror.

Mark had moved it there last night. Not because he was ready, but because leaving it behind felt like lying.

Jason's grin looked the same as it always had—bright, cocky, like the world couldn't take him down.

Mark tried to hold that grin as an anchor, not a chain.

He pulled on a hoodie, grabbed his keys, and carried the duffel down the stairs.

His mother was at the kitchen sink, hands braced on the counter as if she needed the edge to keep from falling. The overhead light was off; the only illumination came from the weak blue glow of the microwave clock and the gray dawn seeping through the window.

She turned when she heard him.

Her eyes were red but dry. In the last month she'd cried until tears felt like a luxury she couldn't afford anymore.

"Morning," she said.

Mark's throat tightened. "Morning."

She looked at the duffel bag like it was a betrayal and a relief at the same time. "You don't have to go today," she said, and even as she said it, Mark could tell she knew it wasn't true. If he stayed, the town would find a way to put its hands on him again. It always did.

"I do," Mark said quietly. "If I don't... I don't think I'll ever leave."

His mother's jaw worked. Her gaze flicked to Jason's photo, then away, like she couldn't bear to meet his eyes even in glass.

"He would've left," she whispered.

Mark nodded. "Yeah," he said. "He tried."

Silence hung between them, filled with all the words they'd never said when the town was still winning and the flowers were still "lucky."

His mother reached for the coffee mug on the counter and pushed it toward him. "Eat something," she said, which was her version of I love you, which was her version of don't die.

Mark wrapped both hands around the warm ceramic and let it steady him.

Then he felt it.

Something small, dry, and wrong against his palm.

He froze.

The mug sat half-lifted. His breath caught in his throat. His fingers opened slowly, like he was afraid of what he'd find there.

A petal.

Purple. Velvet-soft. Cool as damp soil.

It lay against his skin like it had been waiting.

Mark's stomach turned.

He hadn't touched one in weeks. Not since they'd cut the routes and sealed what they could and watched the town's devotion collapse into argument and grief. Not since Pecos—

He stopped that thought before it could sharpen.

His mother noticed the change in him, the way his shoulders went rigid.

"What is it?" she asked.

Mark closed his fist around the petal so tight it creased. "Nothing," he lied automatically.

Then he heard himself. The old reflex. The old habit.

He loosened his fingers.

"It's not nothing," he corrected, voice rough. He opened his hand again. Let her see.

His mother stared at the petal, and for a second she looked like she might drop the mug.

"How—" she started.

"I don't know," Mark said. "But it's here."

The petal glistened faintly in the gray light. Not a glow that would draw eyes. A private shine, like something smiling in the dark.

And beneath that shine, Mark felt it—a pressure behind his eyes, so subtle he almost missed it. A small tug, the way a fishing line trembles when something on the other end tests the hook.

His mother backed away from the sink as if the counter might bite her. "Get rid of it," she whispered.

Mark stared at the petal and tasted metal at the back of his mouth—old nosebleeds, autumn hits, the copper rim of a cut lip.

In his head, a thought rose that wasn't his.

You could keep it.

A memory of roar. Of stadium lights. Of being important.

You could make sure no one else ever takes from you again.

The kitchen seemed to tilt by a degree. The air thickened. Dawn light in the window felt farther away.

Mark's fingers twitched with the old pre-snap tap, thumb to palm, as if his body wanted to line up behind center and let somebody else call the play.

His mother's voice cut through. "Mark," she said, sharp with fear. "Don't."

Mark blinked. The pressure behind his eyes pulsed once.

In the quiet, he heard it—faint as wind in a vent: one-two, one-two.

The cadence.

A promise disguised as a habit.

Mark's chest tightened.

He thought of the altar in the woods, the old stories Alyssa had dug up, the way blood had made roots move like hands.

He thought of the shadow realm, the web of routes lit by devotion, and the way truth had snapped threads like brittle bone.

He thought of Pecos's eyes turning violet as he fought to stay himself.

And then, without meaning to, he thought of Jason—not the ghost in fog, not the thread trapped in a knot, but his brother on the driveway with a ball tucked under his arm, grinning like he'd stolen the world and was offering half of it.

Jason's voice in Mark's memory: Don't let them make you stay.

Mark's hand stopped shaking.

He looked at his mother. "I'm not doing it," he said, and the words felt like a door opening.

His mother's breath hitched. "Then—"

Mark set the mug down carefully, as if sudden movement might wake something. He walked to the junk drawer, pulled it open, and took out a cheap lighter someone had used for candles. He didn't look at the drawer long enough to see what else was inside—old keys, dead batteries, the small clutter of a family trying to live normal.

He carried the lighter and the petal to the back door.

His mother followed, two steps behind, silent.

Outside, the backyard was wet and gray. The fence line sagged where purple vines had once climbed. Most of the growth had withered after the rupture, leaving behind black threads that glittered faintly when they caught the light—scar tissue on wood.

Mark stepped onto the patio.

For a moment the petal lay innocent in his palm, just a piece of something beautiful.

Then the pressure behind his eyes sharpened again, and Mark knew innocence was one of the town's favorite lies.

He flicked the lighter.

The flame caught with a small, ordinary click.

He held it beneath the petal.

The purple didn't ignite right away. It warmed. Curled. The scent lifted —sweet as crushed violets, rimmed with iron, like a bruise you couldn't see.

Mark's skin prickled. The cadence in his head rose like a chant.

One-two, one-two—

Mark let the flame touch the petal fully.

It caught.

Not with a whoosh. With a slow, deliberate burn, like paper that didn't want to admit it was paper. The edges blackened, and the purple turned briefly bright, then collapsed into ash.

The pressure behind Mark's eyes shuddered and snapped—like a line breaking under strain.

Silence rushed in, sudden and clean.

Mark exhaled hard, breath fogging in the cold air.

The ash drifted off his palm in a thin spiral and landed on wet concrete.

His mother made a sound that was half sob and half laugh, like her body didn't know what emotion belonged here.

"It's gone," she whispered.

Mark stared at the last flecks of black. "Yeah," he said, though his voice didn't hold victory. Only relief and the strange ache of choosing.

His mother reached out and gripped his wrist, firm. "Don't come back," she said, and Mark knew she didn't mean it like abandonment. She meant it like a blessing. Like a command to live.

Mark nodded once.

"I'm going to the cemetery," he said.

His mother's grip tightened. "Alone?"

Mark hesitated, then shook his head. "Alyssa said she'd meet me," he said. "Tommy too."

His mother released him slowly, like letting go of a railing. "Okay," she said. "Okay."

The cemetery gate creaked the way it always had, a familiar complaint in a place that had swallowed too many names.

Fog lingered low between the stones, thin now, daylight-diluted, but still present in the dips of earth as if the ground liked to keep secrets close. The flowers along the older rows were dim and brittle. Some had gray petals that crumbled if the wind touched them. Some still held their color, stubborn and wrong, but none of them glowed the way they used to.

None of them sang.

Mark walked the gravel path with his hands in his hoodie pocket, fingers still smelling faintly of smoke.

Alyssa waited near the back, beside the marker they'd placed for Pecos.

It wasn't a grave. They didn't have a body to bury. The town had offered paperwork—missing person, presumed dead—words that tried to make absence manageable. Pecos's mother had refused the finality of it. So they'd chosen a stone anyway, a placeholder for a boy who had been taken into the routes and hadn't come back in anything they could carry.

The marker was simple. PECOS MORALES. BELOVED SON. FRIEND. LION.

Underneath, in smaller letters Alyssa's aunt had insisted on carving: HE LISTENED.

Tommy stood on the other side of the stone, hands shoved into his coat pockets, ring glinting when he shifted. His face looked older than it should have. The town aged you in ways nobody talked about.

Alyssa's eyes flicked to Mark's hands. "You smell like smoke," she said.

Mark nodded. "It tried," he said. He didn't have to explain what.

Alyssa's jaw tightened. "Of course it did."

Tommy swallowed. "On your last day," he muttered. "That's low. Even for… whatever that is."

Mark stepped up to the marker and knelt. The ground was damp. Softer than it should've been in December, but not turned. Not hungry.

He pulled a small jar from his pocket—one Alyssa had given him at dawn. Inside was a pinch of ash. Not from the petal he'd burned on the patio. From the last of the bloom they'd managed to scorch away at the creekbank, the night the routes collapsed. They'd kept it for this, like you kept a match after a fire just to prove it could be lit.

Mark held the jar over the soil and hesitated.

The old pact had started with blood on stone.

Mark didn't want to offer anything to the land. He didn't want to feed it. He didn't want to bargain.

He wanted to honor a friend.

Alyssa crouched beside him. "This isn't an offering," she said softly, as if reading the hesitation in his hands. "It's a burial. We're not giving. We're ending."

Mark swallowed. "Yeah," he whispered. "Ending."

He poured the ash into a shallow hole he'd dug with his fingers, letting it fall like black snow. Tommy stepped closer and held out something in his palm: Pecos's old whistle from practice, the one he used to call out cadence when Coach wasn't looking, the one he'd carried like a joke and a duty.

"I found it in my locker," Tommy said, voice tight. "Like it wanted to come with me."

Mark took the whistle gently. The metal was cold. Ordinary. Human.

He set it into the hole with the ash.

Alyssa slipped a folded scrap of paper in too—one page torn from her grandfather's journal, the line that had started all of this for her: The council kept the land's hunger at bay… but what happens when the council is no more?

Mark looked at her.

Alyssa's eyes were wet, but steady. "If we leave it buried," she said, "it stays a warning. Not a secret."

Mark nodded.

He covered the hole with soil and pressed his palm down, firm, sealing it.

For a moment, all three of them stayed crouched there, breathing cold air and listening for something that didn't come.

No hum. No cadence. No pull behind the eyes.

Just wind moving through branches the way wind was supposed to.

Tommy exhaled shakily. "Is it really done?" he asked.

Alyssa didn't answer right away. She stared at the rows of stones, at the dim purple that still clung to some graves like bruises that hadn't faded all the way.

"It's done like a fire is done," she said. "The blaze is out. But you don't stop checking for embers."

Mark stood.

He looked across the cemetery toward the stadium, visible beyond the fence. The bleachers sat empty, a skeleton of devotion. The field was just a field in daylight. Green and quiet. No roar. No worship.

For the first time, Mark could look at it and feel nothing like hunger looking back.

Tommy followed his gaze. "Coach sent me a message," Tommy said. "About spring training. About 'getting the program back on track.'"

Mark's mouth twisted. "Of course he did."

Tommy shook his head slowly. "I didn't answer," he said. He held up his ring, then slipped it off and tucked it into his pocket. "I don't know who I am without this," he admitted, voice raw. "But I don't want to find out inside Lowridge's story."

Alyssa's eyes softened. "You will," she said. "You're stubborn. You'll survive it."

Tommy gave a weak, offended snort. "That's the nicest insult anyone's ever given me."

Mark looked at the marker again. Pecos's name sat in stone, sharp against gray morning.

"Thank you," Mark said under his breath. Not to the land. Not to the town. To the absence that had saved them.

A breeze moved through the cemetery. Light, clean. It carried no sweetness.

For a heartbeat, Mark thought he heard footsteps behind him—cleats on gravel, the old rhythm, one-two—

He turned.

Nothing.

Just Alyssa brushing dirt from her knees. Tommy staring at the ground like he was daring it to speak.

Mark's chest loosened.

Maybe some echoes would always live here. Memory had weight. But echoes weren't the same as chains.

They left the cemetery together and walked back toward town, toward cars parked along the road. Lowridge looked almost normal in morning light—houses, streets, the diner sign flickering like it always had. A few people stood on porches and watched them pass. Some looked away. Some nodded. Some held their gaze like they wanted to ask questions and didn't know how to live with the answers.

At the edge of town, the new growth corridor rose like a different promise—glass buildings, fresh pavement, banners advertising expansion. A billboard showed a smiling family in front of a modern school with the words BUILD YOUR FUTURE HERE.

Mark stared at it and felt the old bitterness rise.

Lowridge had always built its future on someone else's body.

But the billboard didn't pull at him. It didn't feel like an altar. It was just marketing. Just optimism.

Old rot didn't vanish because someone printed a new sign.

It vanished because people stopped feeding it.

Alyssa climbed into her car. She'd decided to stay—for now. Not out of loyalty to the town, but out of responsibility to the truth. She'd talked about archives, about recording names properly, about making sure no one could rebrand the flowers into something pretty again.

Tommy climbed into his truck and sat for a moment with his hands on the steering wheel like he was learning how to hold on without gripping.

Mark loaded his bag into the trunk of his mother's car.

His mother stood at the curb, coat pulled tight, eyes fixed on him like she was trying to memorize the version of him that was leaving.

"You call me when you get there," she said.

Mark nodded. "I will."

She glanced toward the town, then back at him. "If it comes back," she whispered, voice small. "If you feel it—"

"I'll tell you," Mark said. "And I'll come back if you need me."

His mother's mouth trembled. "I don't want you to," she admitted. "But I might."

Mark stepped forward and hugged her hard, the kind of hug you gave when you didn't trust the world to keep what you loved safe.

When he pulled away, her eyes were wet again.

"Go," she said.

Mark got in the car.

The engine turned over with a familiar sound. The radio crackled on, then off. He didn't want music. He wanted quiet.

He drove.

Lowridge fell behind him in small pieces—Main Street, the diner, the school, the stadium's lights like dead stars. The cemetery fence slid past, known and distant.

For a moment, as the road curved, the town lined up in the rearview mirror.

It looked ordinary. Almost peaceful. A small place under a pale sky.

No fog rolling thick. No purple glow announcing hunger. Just streets and roofs and trees.

Mark stared until the road shifted and the town disappeared from the mirror.

His hands didn't twitch into cadence. His chest didn't tighten. His eyes didn't burn with pressure.

He was still himself.

He didn't know if Lowridge would heal, or if it would simply learn to hide differently. He didn't know if the land forgave anything at all.

But he knew this:

For the first time in his life, the town wasn't calling the play.

Mark pressed the gas and drove toward the horizon, toward a future that wasn't built on a bargain.

And behind him, in the damp soil where ash and metal and truth were buried under a simple stone, the land stayed quiet.

Not sleeping.

Listening.

But no longer fed.